CW00555441

THE
BILLION
POUND LIE

'A funny, touching
novel about friendship,
love and lottery
tickets.'

Erin Kelly

BILL DARE

Press for Bill Dare's writing

'...cleverly manages to provoke both laughter and thought.'
Ian Hislop (*Brian Gulliver's Travels*)

'A truly Swiftian satire on modern life and full of surprises. And very funny. It is marvellous.' The Daily Telegraph (*Brian Gulliver's Travels*)

'It's terrific!' Producer John Lloyd (*Brian Gulliver's Travels*)

'Dare's play is neatly written and deftly performed... just when you think it's going to be a thriller it blossoms into a touching love story.'
Lyn Gardner, The Guardian (*Touch*)

'The comedy is tinged with mystery and even poignancy... the play's emotional texture is palpable.' The Independent (*Touch*)

'The dialogue crackles and fizzes in compelling fashion.'
Metro (*Touch*)

'Dare's writing is rattling and quick. Laced with wit and humour... Dark, poignant... heart-warming.' The Scotsman (*Touch*)

'Good new writing that manages pretty much simultaneously to be a Hitchcockian psychological drama, a romcom and a short thesis on logic and philosophy.' British Theatre Guide (*Touch*)

'Superb black comedy. Very funny...'
Evening Standard (*You're Breaking Up*, BBC 2)

'Quite brilliant.' The Times (*You're Breaking Up*, BBC 2)

'This is hilarious from start to finish. If you're not laughing by the end of chapter one, you must be an *EastEnders* script writer.'
OK Magazine (*Natural Selection*)

'Witty, well-acted and at times moving, this is a sharp script.'
What's On Stage (*Misconception)*

'Has more twists than a curly-wurly... a funny, clever baked Alaska of a play – warm and sweet on the outside, ice cold at its heart.' The Scotsman (*Misconception*)

'*Misconception* is a smartly scripted comedy of modern manners that proves that in the battle of the sexes everyone suffers a few flesh wounds ...it strikes a pleasing balance between quiet introspection and belly laughs.' London Metro (*Misconception*)

'Laugh-out-loud stuff.' Heat Magazine (*Natural Selection)*

'Funny and sad. I recommend this book.'
John O'Farrell (*Natural Selection)*

'Dare's comedy credentials are impeccable. This is classic romantic comedy in which the gags come thick and fast...'
The Daily Mirror (*Natural Selection*)

'It was a pleasure to lend both ears entirely.'
Daily Telegraph (*Barker, Belgrave and Bigweed*)

'Gripping drama.'
The Times (*Barker, Belgrave and Bigweed*)

Bill Dare is also a comedy producer for TV and radio.

For Lucy, who said, 'that's a great idea,
you should write it.'

PROLOGUE

A few texts, a dozen missed calls. Nothing from Helen. Leo places his phone on the table beside a saucepan into which he's emptied a tin of Prince's Irish stew. A fork sticks out. If cutlery had feelings, then this high-class piece would be horrified. The whole kitchen is made for the connoisseur, or connoisseur manqué. There's an Aga that Leo has barely touched, food processing contraptions he's never used, cupboards he hasn't opened, and probably a larder he doesn't even know about. Still, none of this has cost him a penny.

Low morning sunlight streams from the conservatory and bounces off steel, chrome and marble. He looks around, a valedictory survey. His eyes pause at a pile of newspaper cuttings; headlines about the 'Billionaire Barista'.

His phone buzzes on the table. Having dodged so many calls from Frank, he must answer this time.

'Frank.'

'At last we speak. Are you all set for your thank you gala?' asks the Chairman of Byford Council and Leo's father-in-law. He talks more loudly than necessary, the vocal equivalent of man-spreading.

'I didn't know it was a *thank you* gala.'

'For all you're doing for the town.'

'I'm touched,' says Leo, reflexively. Perhaps he should have sounded surprised.

'That is, if you're not too busy meeting Prime Ministers,' Frank says, with a laugh that is more to do with occupying conversational space than humour.

'Not today.' Leo tries to sound just a little jovial. 'I don't want a big fuss, Frank.'

'Why not? You've done so much for us all to fuss about.'

Soon everyone will be fussing like demented chickens. He pushes the pan of stew away – it's developed a porcine smell.

The doorbell rings. It's probably Driver Dave wanting to know when the limo would be required.

'You're the most famous man in Byford,' says Frank.

In truth, that isn't saying much. Byford, a post-industrial town 70 miles north of London, has few claims to fame: Sting's dad had once lived there, it has a historically significant bridge, and it's home to the second ever Poundland.

'But seriously, you are someone *very* special.'

Leo has grown used to praise: people thanking him, telling him he's a great guy. Funny how the things you've always wanted can turn irksome so soon.

'Now, I've heard a rumour—'

Leo's heart sinks.

'That you've been helping people on the quiet.'

As you were, heart.

The doorbell rings again, for longer this time, and it sounds angry. And angry voices too, calling his name. Perhaps a small crowd has gathered, concerned citizens having had the wool pulled from their eyes.

'Imagine,' Frank continues, 'we all thought you were… well, you know…'

'A waste of space?'

'I wouldn't go that far, ha. But a lot of young men would be knee deep in cocaine and pussy by now.'

Leo feels himself redden. Is Frank talking like that because that's how he thinks Leo talks?

More shouting, and hammering on the door. He imagines a mob wielding brooms and Magic Mops, little girls with hate-filled eyes. If they smash down the door, he could call the police. Unless they *are* the police. He fights down the fear – a multitude of fears – of arrest, of prison, of sharing a cell with a dead-eyed psychopath with a scar and an ironic nickname like Big Baby. But it wouldn't be easy making anything stick.

'There'll be quite a crowd,' says Frank, 'press, a few snappers – national press, not just local.'

Leo does not respond because his mind is racing ahead to the gala. If he could just keep the lid on things for a few more hours, then this could be a controlled explosion. Frank laughs again at nothing in particular and they say goodbye.

Afraid he might be spotted from windows, he crouches below the centre island. He runs his hand along the marble floor.

Then, quite suddenly, everything stops. Maybe Driver Dave told the mob that the 'bad man' had fled over yonder wall.

He strokes the marble floor again. Wouldn't it be nice to sink into sleep, a nest of unconsciousness, just for a few minutes – seconds, even? Sleep does not come easily these days. For a moment, he's under the kitchen table with bits of Lego while his mother reads *Take A Break* magazine, and the smell of Welsh rarebit wafts from the grill.

He feels something soft in his hand: a square of sticky brown stodge. Vince has been at the waffle-maker. When this is all over, he must buy Vince one of his own. But with what? Leo has no money – he even had his card rejected at Waitrose.

His phone again. The breathing is both strange and familiar.

'Helen?'

More breaths – a blocked nose. Crying?

Why doesn't she speak?

'Helen? What's the matter? Talk to me.'

'They've got me, Leo.'

He freezes.

'What? Who? Tell me.'

Silence. Not even breathing. *Why doesn't she speak?*

'*Helen?*'

Her voice bleeds through a wall of fear.

'You need to transfer a million pounds to an offshore account. Take down these details. You have fifteen minutes.'

PART ONE

11 Days Earlier

1

MAZDA MAN

This was the third time Leo had seen the red Mazda MX5 outside Helen's house, the terraced cottage they used to share. The car was out of place in a road peopled by families too busy searching for lost mittens or cobbling together costumes because it was Come As Something Or Other Day to bother with sports cars, even ones with stabilising traction control.

Helen must be seeing a man, and not just any man, but a man of means, prospects, a career, and one with no need to sellotape over the gaps in his windows to keep out the draught.

And it had to happen. Sooner or later she would start seeing someone else. She was beautiful and funny and hardly anyone had a bad word to say about her. Apart, that is, from her mother, whose main gripe was her daughter's poor choice of men. Men like Leo Morphetus, the one who sells coffee from that tricycle thing – is that a prober job? Can you support a family on that? Has he ever read a book? Nice enough fellow, but surely not husband material, not for my lovely, bright, radiologist daughter.

At this moment, the nice-enough-fellow-but-surely-not-husband-material was stationary, frozen by indecision, a gangly leg resting on a pedal. He'd found a spot for his Trike ('that tricycle thing'), right next to the Mazda. He ran his fingers through his thick, almost-black hair that made him look younger than his twenty-eight years. Should he go forward or retreat out of sight?

He hadn't phoned ahead like he usually did, so Helen wasn't expecting him. And that was another clue – for the first time since their separation, she had started asking him to call first so she could 'plan things with Amy'.

Having decided to face the music, he walked up the path past the four climbing roses that he'd planted six years ago, expecting them to clamber up as far as the bedroom window at least. He didn't want to open the door with his key for fear of walking in on a vision he'd never be able to erase. (A man with a Mazda probably does it in the hall). But as he waited, he let calmer thoughts prevail: this man, if he existed at all, was merely an unsuccessful suitor. The door opened.

'Amy here?' he asked, relieved that Helen was fully dressed and not dishevelled. She wore her usual blue jeans, and a T-shirt with a planet-saving slogan that he had never bothered to read. Her chestnut hair was bunched up with wisps falling down here and there. She held the butt of a salad sandwich.

'No, she's at Mum and Dad's – it's in the diary. Anyway, you really ought to call ahead, you know.' Leo immediately felt the unique pang of hurt that only came when she seemed irritated by him.

'Mind if I come in?' he asked.

'It's not massively convenient,' she said, looking genuinely sorry.

'I need to count out your cash.'

Counting cash had become a bi-weekly ritual. Although Leo could take card payments, the last year or two had seen a resurgence of paper money, which was generally thought to be caused by an epidemic of online fraud for which the banks were ducking responsibility.

'Oh, right.' She looked at her watch. 'Can you count it another time?'

Perhaps she's getting financial support elsewhere, Leo couldn't help thinking. It was time to try a different lure.

'Would you like a choca caramel latte?'

A fancy coffee almost always worked.

'Well…' She supressed a grin by pursing her lips. *A smile wants to come out*, thought Leo, so he decided to liberate it with a smile of his own.

'Resistance to my caramel-choc-late is futile.'

Success. Helen had the sweetest of mouths. Slightly lopsided. If she smiled broadly enough a 'fang' tooth would emerge, which she hated, but Leo loved. He would say almost anything to see that smile, even after all these years.

Having earned a tentative 'okay', he retraced his steps along the path and fired up the espresso maker. The Trike had two wheels at the front that supported a counter, one metre square, which had all the apparatus necessary to grind beans, heat water and milk, and make delicious coffee. A roof gave hardly any protection from the rain, and was a constant source of frustration in windy conditions, but it provided some old-fashioned charm. As vital as the smell of fresh beans was the aura of an imagined past, which Leo cultivated by wearing a full length striped apron and sometimes a straw boater. When in the mood, he would adopt a cheery olde-worlde patter with a 'Thank you kindly, sir', and 'Mind how you go, madam'.

Customers had two different beans to choose from and three flavours of tea. Home-made cookies and flapjacks were on display to tempt the sweet-toothed.

Leo had leased the Trike four years ago from a Dutch franchise operation that was supposedly expanding all over Europe.

Take the step into independence! All you need is to share our passion for coffee, your own motivation, good communication skills and the commitment to deliver an excellent service. We will provide the rest: your own Trike, professional Barista training and equipment, all the know-how of a proven concept as well as ongoing support. This should be a promising start to a long-term relationship.

Well, it wasn't. There was no training, no support, and four months later the firm went bust. On the plus side, Leo got to keep the Trike with no further payments.

With his back to the parked Mazda, he prepared Helen's choca caramel latte. He added a touch of froth on the top and a sprinkling of cocoa dust in the shape of a heart – well, he wasn't going to stop doing that just because she might be seeing someone.

Just as he was finishing, he noticed he'd foolishly forgotten to put away the Pounds for Poppy collection tin. Poppy was a girl with a rare blood disorder and there'd been a small local campaign to raise funds for treatment abroad. Leo had promised Poppy's father that a tin on his Trike would provide at least thirty pounds a day. In fact, Leo himself usually had to put in at least fifteen in order to honour the promise. He stowed the tin in the locked cabinet below.

Helen tasted the coffee and gave it the thumbs-up. Then, barefoot, she picked up a toy with her free hand and padded to the kitchen with the gangly gate of a teenager. She was two years older than him but looked younger, probably because she never stopped moving – in contrast to Leo, whose default state was one of stillness. She once joked that he moved so little he could be one of those human statues.

'That's not a bad idea.'

'It's a *very* bad idea.'

'Extra income and I wouldn't have to do anything for it.'

'Ha. Don't even think about it.'

Leo detected no physical signs of a usurper. No MX5 car keys, no size tens in the hall, no lingering smell of aftershave or male sweat. And the handle on the patio door still looked wobbly. He had promised to fix it, so a functioning handle would have been a bad omen indeed.

But there was something about Helen. She had the springy energy of the just-shagged, a freshness to her skin, and here's the clincher: she hardly looked at him. Perhaps she knew that he knew. She wouldn't want to see him hurt. That's why she wasn't meeting his gaze – well, that and her constant cleaning and re-arranging. But sooner or later she would have to tear the plaster off.

Having removed his apron, he reached into his pockets and pulled out paper bags containing neat bundles of cash – mostly fives and tens – bound by elastic bands. There were also bags of coins. He began counting.

Helen placed something in front of him: a watercolour of a blue man standing in front of a red house.

'Amy painted it.'

'Yes, I guessed that, Helen.'

'Well?'

He was required to say something positive.

'It's great.'

Helen was now busy washing a breadboard, but even with the noise of rushing water, he heard a tut. The praise had been inadequate.

'It's *very* good.'

Too little, too late. He resumed his reckoning. Wanting to say something upbeat to break the tension, he said, 'I stopped buying lottery tickets,' more loudly than he'd intended.

'Great timing, Leo.' She laughed. 'Just as they've announced there's a billion pound winner. Why did you stop?'

'The Globomillions thing. It's a crazy amount of money, and the chances of winning big have gone from ludicrous to… whatever's more ludicrous than ludicrous. So I put it all behind me a while back.'

With EuroMillions flagging, Camelot had joined forces with lotteries around the world and came up with something exciting and new. A new game, Globomillions, was instigated, and its eye-watering prizes had been hitting the headlines but most people thought that they couldn't last.

'Anyway, it's not a billion. It's about ten million less than a billion, but the press are *calling* it a billion. Typical disregard for facts.'

'You sound rather grumpy about it,' said Helen, playfully, and Leo was pleased that he was still tease-worthy. She would never mock someone she pitied.

'You know the winner is from around here, don't you? It's been on the news.'

'It doesn't mean I would have won it,' said Leo, trying not to sound too defensive.

'Well, I'm pleased you've moved on.'

But he knew she didn't entirely believe him. He was a man of habit.

There was a time when his interest verged on obsessive. He calculated odds, imagined patterns where there were none, told Helen about new 'systems', and researched every minute detail of how the winners were informed, exactly how the winnings were paid and when. He was probably one of few lottery players who had bothered to read the terms and conditions. He knew the whole thing bored Helen to death, and so he'd stopped talking about it. Perhaps her theory was right: his lottery habit was a sign of some kind of emotional deficit. Something to do with not having a dad.

'Yes, it's quite easy to change a routine when you try,' he said, and immediately felt embarrassed. She could surely see through his pitiful attempt to transform himself into the kind of man she might want. He felt naked, like in the recurring dream in which he lost all his clothes in a petting zoo.

He continued counting in silence. He could have totalled it all before coming of course, but that would have meant less time with Helen. Once he'd finished, he'd hand it all over. He loved this moment, delivering the hard-earned cash to his wife and child.

He chose this moment of serenity to ask a question to which a large part of him did not want to know the answer.

'Are you seeing someone?'

There was no verbal response but there was immediate cessation of kitchen sounds. *Here it comes, brace yourself mate, and she's even sitting down.* She's sitting down and she's stopped doing stuff. Helen pursed her lips for a moment before speaking.

'I have *met* someone,' she said, gently, cupping her hands round her coffee.

'Drives a red Mazda?'

He was impressed by how quick and calm he sounded, like someone giving the correct answer on a daytime quiz.

'Yes. Don't worry, he's not here. And before you ask, he's only met Amy once, and that's how it will stay for a while.'

Leo would save the gibbering and wailing for the privacy of his own home.

'Leo? Wake up.'

'What? I wasn't asleep, I just shut my eyes.'

'You're the only one I know who goes to sleep when something stressful happens.'

'I'm not stressed, I just… have I counted this pile?'

He wanted to count it all again, it might calm him.

'Have you done due diligence?' he said, feeling this question was perfectly reasonable.

She smiled benignly. 'Leo, this isn't a hostile takeover or management buyout.'

'But still, have you checked him out online?'

'Durr.'

'What's he do for a living?'

'Well…'

She waved back her hair. 'He's a gem trader,' she said, with an unspoken *since you ask.*

'A *gem trader*? I don't even know what that is. I mean, someone who *trades gems*?'

Helen shrugged: you-guessed-it. Again, Leo felt the need to say something positive.

'I don't mind you meeting people as long as it's just… well… not serious. You know, while you and I try to… sort stuff out.'

'*Sort stuff out?*'

Why the incredulous questioning? Surely this is just a long blip, their year-long separation thing. As soon as he was making a decent profit, and he had support from the bank, and addressed some of his other failings, things would get back to normal between them.

'Yes, sort stuff out. I'm getting a business loan. I'm going to the bank today, in fact.' He omitted to mention that he didn't have an appointment.

'But you've been to lots of banks.' She put her hand on his forearm and squeezed, while leaning towards him. 'They don't want to lend you any money.'

Leo took his arm away because her touch felt too like one of sympathy.

'I've got a new strategy. I've thought of another great name for a coffee shop: Bean Roasting. As in, I've *been* roasting.'

As the words dropped from his mouth, he wished he could suck them back. It was a terrible name.

'That's not why we aren't together any more,' she said, firmly, looking him steadily in the eyes. He responded by putting down the money and returning the gaze.

'What?'

'Bank loans and coffee bikes. Or names for coffee shops!'

Why was she shouting? She hardly ever shouted.

'That's not why we aren't a couple, it's not why we split up,' she said, now standing up and wringing her hands. Leo had heard the phrase 'wringing hands' but had never seen someone actually do it before.

'Our marriage is ending for all the reasons we talked about.'

The truth was, Leo didn't really know why the marriage was ending, and anyway he didn't think of it in those terms. During the many talks they'd had he'd got the feeling that Helen was holding something back, not quite getting to the crux of the problem for fear of hurting him. He could find solutions, but a lot of the things Helen spoke about didn't seem to have solutions, and as soon as he thought he understood her, she would talk about some other problem. He knew that she wasn't happy, but the reasons never seemed to sit still.

Helen had tears in her eyes. Was she sad or angry? She shouldn't be either of those. If anyone was going to cry, it should be him. But instead he felt an urge to impress, to show that he was no loser, but someone on the up-and-up.

'This could be the kick up the arse I need. This could *galvanise* me.'

Helen shook her head.

'Please just go. Go and see Amy. And take the money, take all of it.' She began gathering up the wads of notes, stuffing them in his pockets and the pouch of his apron.

'What about the moneybags?'

'It doesn't matter about the bags!'

The moneybags that had neatly held all the cash were now in the bin and soggy with food debris. Helen wiped away some tears and sniffed. The best thing Leo could do now was to gather the cash and go.

Standing by the front door, Helen said something strange.

'Why aren't you angry?'

Leo was not angry as a rule. Customers were sometimes rude or dismissive but he rarely behaved in kind. Drivers sometimes raged at him for obstructing their way, but he would try to defuse the situation by offering a cookie. Admittedly, this sometimes enraged them further.

'Well, funny you should say that, Helen, but...' He monitored his mood for a moment, like someone checking wind direction, 'Actually, I *am* quite angry.'

'Good.' She nodded, as if something had been achieved, but he didn't know what.

'But I was trying not to be,' he said.

They exchanged glances for an instant, then the door closed and Leo stood staring at it as if it held an answer. Then he turned and shuffled towards his Trike.

Anger. Yes, that's what must be slowly building up inside. But what to do about it? Shake his fist at something? Maybe he could shake his fist at the red car. Almost in a dream, he reached for his house keys, took a step towards the offending vehicle, and half thinking it was someone else doing it, he pressed a key in hard before drawing it towards him, leaving a silver track in its wake. It felt good, *very* good in fact, so he gave the car a kick for good measure. That also felt good – until the alarm screeched, hazard lights flashed, and the window of the room that he used to call his bedroom opened and out popped a man's head.

'So you were there after all,' muttered Leo.

The usurper began shouting but Leo didn't wait to decipher the garbled words. He folded the Trike's support legs, not bothering to pick up a couple of fivers that fell from his pocket. The front door to the house opened and the man – bare feet, jeans, vest – began running towards him with the momentum of an angry hippo. Helen was now at the door shouting something. Leo chased away his impending sleepiness (Helen was right about that) and began to pedal.

A coffee trike is not like a getaway car. It's probably the worst kind of vehicle one could use for escape. Luckily, the road was on a hill (ten per cent gradient) and the trike was pointing down. Standing up on the pedals, he gave them everything he could. He got off to a strong start, but Mazda Man loomed large in the rear-view mirror. In the midst of imminent peril, Leo sized up his rival. He looked a good five years older than him, about the same height but broader, and had a fair amount of dark hair, but Leo noticed with pleasure that the top was wispy and could quite possibly be a comb-over. Suddenly a gust of wind lifted the lid on a spam-coloured scalp, and an unruly clump flapped around like the sail of a toy yacht.

It was only Leo's quick thinking that prevented an altercation. A handful of coffee beans jettisoned onto the road was enough to slow down the barefooted assailant. (A bare foot on a coffee bean can be painful, as he knew only too well.) Having built up some speed, he made good his getaway, leaving his adversary cursing the tarmac and stroking down his unruly tuft.

2

MONEY, MONEY, EVERYWHERE

He drew up at Hamir News. The owner, a second generation Bangladeshi Hindu, was outside, having just dragged the umbrella stand to a more prominent position, as clouds began to gather. Thickset with a protruding belly, Hamir's cheeks were chubby and puffed, as if they were hiding a couple of the gobstoppers that he sold to wide-eyed children.

'There's money coming out of your pockets, Leo. Money, money, everywhere!'

Flustered and breathless, Leo began stamping his foot on the notes before they blew away, but there were more notes than he had feet. Hamir rushed over to lend a hand – and a foot.

Once inside the shop and order restored, Leo checked his phone to confirm the inevitable: several missed calls and one text:

For fuck's sake

There was no point in dealing with it now. He would wait for Helen's fury to die down a bit and then… apologise? Offer to pay for a respray? Tell her he would take an anger management course? He'd think of something.

He placed his usual packet of chocolate buttons for Amy on the counter.

'Lottery ticket?' Hamir asked, wiping sweat from his face. It was a reasonable question; this was where Leo had been buying lottery tickets for ten years, always on a Wednesday.

'I've given up. Didn't your missus tell you?'

'You are joking. Pulling my plonker, man?' said the shopkeeper, opening his mouth wide. 'After all these years?'

'Yup. And I've just told Helen now, so you know… better make sure I stick with it.' He felt self-conscious about the wads poking out of his pockets.

'Or maybe you don't *need* the lottery.' Hamir tapped his nose and winked. 'Maybe you already won? Huh?'

He nodded towards the newspapers on the shelf, and chuckled. News of the third ever billion pound jackpot was on the front page of half of them. It was described variously as enough to pay for the NHS for days, buy forty Challenger tanks, build 16,000 new social homes, buy a tablet computer for everyone in Wales, or a pen for everyone on the planet. Many of the columnists thought it obscene and over the top, and muttered about 'values' and 'unfairness' and the like.

'The winner bought the ticket from around here,' said Hamir, nodding and smiling, as if he had done something of which he was quietly proud.

'So they say,' said Leo, not paying much attention.

'But no one has claimed it yet,' said Hamir, with another wink.

'Well, it ain't me.' Leo returned the wink without knowing quite why.

And then he had a thought. This new man of Helen's would soon be throwing his money around. He'd spoil Amy, and she could be corrupted by this blatantly materialistic, Mazda-owning show-off, this strutting alpha male, trying to curry favour in the only way he knows how. Amy won't be impressed by her dad's paltry packet of buttons for much longer.

'On second thoughts, I'll have a bar of that Swiss Milka stuff. And a box of those Ferrero Rocher.'

'Celebrating something?' Hamir wiggled his hips, belly-dancer style.

'No, not at all,' said Leo.

'Amy's birthday?' And he began singing Happy Birthday – the words at least, to a random series of notes.

'No, no, not at all,' repeated Leo. Embarrassed about the real reasons for his extravagance, he mumbled something about only living once.

'That's going to be six pounds forty-nine,' said Hamir, then he added with a note of paternal concern, '*Sure that's okay?*'

'Yes. Actually, I'll have a load *more*,' said Leo, feeling that this was no time for half measures. Leo, a man of routine, prudence and decorum, grabbed handfuls of sweets and chocolate while Hamir observed, arms folded, head cocked, and eyes narrowing. After thirty-odd items had accumulated, Leo noticed his curious expression, and felt more explanation was needed.

'Amy is um… having some friends over.'

The shopkeeper nodded in a way that said he *knew* the coffee guy was hiding something. When he had run up the total cost, he let out a long whistle.

'It's going to be twenty-one pounds sixty.' He shook his head sombrely.

Leo tried to get hold of three tens, but a large wad fell on the floor then another dropped from his top pocket as he bent to pick up the first.

'I've got some tens here somewhere,' he said, as more money fell.

'Must have had a *very* good day on the Trike?'

'Not especially. And I won't be needing that thing any more,' said Leo, remembering a slogan from his many business books: *tell people your intentions, and you're more likely to stick to them.*

'Yeah?' said Hamir, clearly wanting to know more.

'My life is taking a turn for the better.'

'A turn for the better?' Hamir nodded towards the newspapers again. 'A billion pounds better?'

By now Leo felt relaxed enough to laugh.

'Yeah, right.'

'But would you admit it if it was you?'

'Er, no.'

'There you are then, isn't it?'

Leo isolated three tens and handed them over.

'Keep the change.'

'S*ure?*'

'Of course.' After all, it was probably what Mazda Man did all the time. *To be successful, behave as if you already are. Dress for the job you _want_.*

He left the shop, stowed his purchases on his trike, and then hopped on. All the while he could see Hamir leaning against the doorway, watching curiously, as spots of rain began to appear on the pavement.

3

PILLARS OF THE COMMUNITY

West Byford was where senior managers and lawyers lived, where estate agents aspired to live, and where duster-sellers wrongly believed there must be rich pickings. Leo parked his Trike in front of the four-bedroom semi. Mock-Tudor timbers tried to evoke a bygone era but failed because the front garden was now the concrete home of a Land Rover Discovery.

Leo had managed to avoid getting really soaked, but even on dry days Helen's parents required the removal of shoes upon entering because the carpets were made of a special wool, the name of which he hadn't registered. But that said, he did notice how soft the living room carpet felt under his stockinged feet. Fair play to the Sterlings, their carpets were good.

The photographs on the mantelpiece above the coal-effect fire were mostly of Frank Sterling shaking hands with local luminaries: business folk, charity organisers and community leaders, all happy to be seen with the chairman of the local council. There were two pictures of Frank in hospital wards semi-circled by children in wheelchairs, and one of him in wellington boots standing beside a sad looking equine, above it a sign: Byford Donkey Sanctuary. There were also some photographs of his wife Harriet at local agricultural competitions and fund-raisers. Baked goods featured heavily. Any visitor to this household would be in no doubt that the Sterlings were pillars of the community.

Leo always noticed the picture of himself, Helen and their daughter. Amy when she was just a few days old.

They had only been dating for a few months when Helen missed her period, and together they bought a pregnancy testing kit, which she used in a Wetherspoon's toilet opposite Boots. Leo tried to keep a cool head in front of Helen, but never had delight and horror exploded inside him with such equal force. It was time to get serious. At just twenty-one, he had no experience of business but knew that gardening wasn't ever going to provide for a family, partly because he didn't have the enthusiasm to get much further than labouring.

He'd heard about a retail lease going cheap. This was something he felt he could do, although he had no hard evidence for that. For reasons that wouldn't become apparent until a year later, his mother offered him most of the money he needed. After some misgivings about taking money from a retired dental nurse, Leo accepted. He worked all day and every weekend to convert an old video rental shack. He did some of the building himself, and begged favours from family and friends. He got together with an experienced barista, taught himself book keeping, made friends with local suppliers, liaised with planners and the council, and managed to make a small profit after only two weeks of trading. He went on to make a decent if exhausting living for three years, after which trade began to slacken off. Leo believed there were two reasons: one, a Costa opened up a few doors down, and two, the ever-diminishing footfall in the area due to the rise of online shopping. Revenue dropped to unsustainable levels. His in-laws, having provided a derisory contribution in the first place, declined to throw more good money after bad. Leo accepted that the cafe couldn't recover, but didn't accept that it was because of his own lack of acumen, which is what the in-laws seemed to believe.

These days, Leo was compelled to spend more time at their place than any of them wanted. This was because his tiny flat, with its smell of damp and its dodgy electrics, was not deemed suitable for little Amy to endure for very long. 'Daddy time' tended to be either at Helen's, or at this citadel of respectability.

Once he had hidden his huge bag of treats, and given Amy one of his 'ginormous hugs' he sat down on the living room carpet, surrounded by dressing-up clothes, while Harriet perched on one end of the sofa trying to look invisible. She was apparently deeply absorbed in last week's *Daily Mail*.

Amy was seven years old with serious eyes, permanently messy brown hair and a high forehead, which made her look wise. She declared that she wanted to play princesses.

'Okay. What are the rules?' asked Leo.

'Rules?'

'Yes. What do we do to win?'

Amy scrunched up her face.

'Are you being silly, Daddy?'

Leo noticed that Harriet also scrunched up her face, doubtless for the same reason. She had always thought he was silly – stupid, even. That's the impression she gave. A sigh, a tut, a raised eyebrow, a shrug, sometimes all four. The woman was a Swiss Army knife of mild disapproval. She had apparently once told Helen that Leo was 'not worthwhile'. *Not worthwhile*? That hurt. It hurt, because it was an opinion so low that Leo had never held it about anyone at all.

In the early days, Leo wanted the respect of the Sterlings. After generally failing to engage them in his interests, he tried engaging in theirs – wine, antiques, golf, local politics, Brexit – but they seemed to know exactly what he was doing and, deliberately or not, made him feel stupid. So he stopped trying.

'Can I be a king, then?' Leo asked.

'Yes, you can be king and I will be the princess.'

'Or how about *you* be the king and *I* be the princess?'

Amy stamped her foot.

'No!'

Harriet tutted, which was just fine. She could sit in judgement – in fact, she could hold up cards with numbers rating his parenting from one to ten for all he cared. Amy started to don the orange feather boa, which would transform her into royalty.

'Shall I be a good king or a bad king?' asked Leo. Amy stopped to consider this gravely, and when she'd arrived at a decision she beamed. 'I think my Daddy would be a *kind* king who gives money to the poor.'

'All of it?'

'*Most* of it.'

'Does the king have a name?'

Amy frowned and stroked her chin. Her eyes studied the ceiling.

'Arbuthnot,' she said, nodding decisively.

'*Arbuthnot?* Where did that name come from?'

'Inside my head, of course.'

And so the game of princesses commenced and the king did his best to say and do the sort of things the princess wanted him to say and do, but without any rules to follow, he found it hard to focus.

'Can we play doctors now?' said Amy.

Rather than start another confusing game without rules, Leo presented the bag he'd hidden behind a sofa. Amy's eyes widened.

'You won't eat that all *today*, I hope,' Harriet cautioned.

'Your grandmother's no fun.'

'There's a childhood obesity crisis, you know,' retorted the grandmother.

Amy broke off a piece of the Swiss stuff.

'Why don't you show Daddy the bracelet?' asked Harriet, without looking up.

'Bracelet?' said Leo. Amy went all shy, smiling and looking down at the carpet.

'Cat got your tongue?' asked Harriet.

'It's gold,' mumbled Amy, holding up her wrist, not especially proud of the acquisition.

'*Solid* gold,' added Harriet, lest there be a shadow of doubt about the value.

'Mum's friend gave it me.'

He didn't want to look, but Leo's eyes were drawn to the trinket. Helen had said that the Mazda-driving imposter had only met Amy the once, and yet he had given her a bracelet of *solid gold*? This is what he was up against, and it was just as he'd thought: Mazda Man was a materialistic corrupter of young souls. Mazda, Midas, the clue was right there. He needed to get out.

'Right, I'm off.'

'Where are you going, Daddy?'

He lifted his daughter up in his arms and felt the gentle tug of her little arms around him. She kissed his cheek and it felt like warm breath on his heart.

'Off to the bank. Next time you see me, I'll be rich!'

In the corner of his eye, he saw a look to the heavens from Harriet, but he didn't care because the adrenaline was really kicking in now. It's amazing what the intrusion of a rival male can do to a man.

'Is that *Trike* going to make you rich?' she asked, but it wasn't a genuine inquiry. She and Frank had never accepted the Trike as a business, more a very public display of penury. He'd once overheard Harriet say, 'He might as well go round with a sandwich board telling everyone how poor our daughter is.'

'I'm ditching the Trike. It's all change for me.' Take *that*, mother-in-law.

He tried to give Amy a last kiss, but she denied him as punishment for his sudden departure.

'I want you to stay.'

'I'll see you very soon and we'll play any game you like.'

Leo tried to bat painful thoughts from his mind: of Amy finding Helen's new man more fun, more generous, and more able to play princesses without asking silly questions.

Anger was not something he had had much experience of, but right now he found it not at all unpleasant, and discovered that it could be put to useful purpose. It could light up the areas in his brain that had been running on low voltage for years.

This was a turning point. Seeing that Mazda *was* going to galvanize him. Leo Morphetus *was* worthwhile, dammit, and no one was going to tell him he wasn't.

4

YOU'RE TEN-A-PENNY

Barclays was one of only three bank branches now left in Byford. It looked dated next to the estate agent with its exposed brick, concealed lighting and fridge full of mineral waters. Leo had opened an account there a year ago because he'd heard that the branch was part of a pilot scheme whereby the old-fashioned 'bank manager' position was revived in answer to a customer backlash against online questionnaires and loans-by-algorithm. The bank manager, one Donald Hughes, had authorised a loan to refurbish Leo's friend's pizza restaurant. Unfortunately, Hughes had not been as generous to Leo. He had not been impressed by his plan to open a juice and smoothie bar. 'Byford isn't a smoothie kind of place.' Leo took the knockback with good grace, and after a few weeks, he came up with a more modest vision: a free-standing coffee kiosk in the town centre car park, licence permitting. It would be a step down from when he ran a bricks-and-mortar café, but a step up from the Trike.

The bank had positions for four tellers, but today there was just one pudding-faced girl with a facial piercing that failed in its sole purpose: to make her look interesting. Leo sat on one of two blue plastic chairs as he waited for the assistant business manager to finish with a client. He had time to think things through. He believed the key to success would be hiring the right staff so the kiosk could be open from dawn till dusk, seven days a week. He would manage well. And how do you manage well? By being a good boss and inspiring confidence. And it was vital to encourage initiative. He had lots of mottos.

A good boss hires talented people and then gets out of their way.

You can change only what people know, not what they do.

The key to success: start by doing the opposite of what everyone else is doing.

Accountants are in the past, managers are in the present, and leaders are in the future.

Anything plus management amounts to success.

Leo had sent a detailed business plan to Mr Hughes two months ago and he hadn't even received an acknowledgement, despite follow-up emails. Well, that wasn't good enough, not any more. Life was passing him by.

'Can I help?'

Startled by a voice from behind, he jumped before turning and glancing at the lapel badge: Ms L Banach, assistant business manager. The woman had the pallor of an East European who had spent most of her life wrapped in animal skins.

'I want to see the boss, Ms Banach.'

'Is it urgent?'

'Yes, my Trike's double parked.'

She shook her head decisively.

A voice from somewhere said, 'The coffee guy?'

Leo turned to see that it was Mr Hughes himself, all five foot four of him. He wore an impeccably ironed shirt, which sported proper cuffs and shiny silver cufflinks. He beckoned Leo to follow him to temporary partition.

'Mr…'

His fingers made a silent click.

'Morphetus. Did you get my emails?'

'Yes, thanks. Now, Mr Morphetus—'

'Leo.'

'Let me tell you something, man to man,' said Hughes, lowering his voice, as if he was about to say something of such importance that it must not be shared with the hoi polloi. 'The money we lend – do you know where it comes from?'

Leo knew the answer, but Hughes didn't give him a chance.

'Your *neighbours*.'

It was an over-simplification, but Leo didn't want to argue.

'If I lend you money, I am taking it out of your neighbours' pockets.' He mimed a deft, Fagin-like snatch of a wallet. 'What am I going to tell them if you blow it?'

Leo wanted the banker to know that he'd learnt a thing or two about finance, so he decided to show off a little.

'But there are investors and bond holders who know there is risk involved, so they should expect that some ventures won't perform as well as others and besides, I don't think the risk—'

Hughes held up his hand to halt the impertinent rambling. 'What am I going to tell my boss? That I've chucked some money at a man with a bike who thinks he's Mr Starbuck?'

'But did you read my new plan? Let me—'

'You don't have a plan, you have a *dream*.'

'A free-standing coffee kiosk?'

Leo had the feeling that Hughes hadn't even read the proposal.

'You're ten-a-penny,' said the banker.

Leo felt a falling sensation, like when a lift starts its decent. Mr Hughes strode towards a security door.

'But, Mr Hughes…'

Hughes turned to give this chancer just one more moment of his precious time.

'Yes?'

'I've been learning a lot. I've read just about every business book going. I can read balance sheets, I download shareholder reports, financial statements. What I'm saying is, that I don't think I'm just a dreamer. And…'

He stopped because he realised Mr Hughes wasn't listening, he was attending to his phone.

Leo had heard the line about being 'ten-a-penny' and it had gone virtually unfelt. But, as with a snake bite, it can take time for poison to reach the heart. He said firmly, 'I'm not ten-a-penny.'

Hughes blinked, then gave an exaggerated frown, as if the comment was a baffling non sequitur.

'Try NatWest,' he said, and swivelled round, punched a code into the lock, and pushed open the door. Leo felt as if the man was walking away with his future.

'Cunt,' he whispered, and immediately willed Hughes not to have heard him, because if he turned back round, he'd see his watery eyes.

Car horns blared in discordant unison like an angry brass band. He ran out and pushed the Trike onto the pavement to make way for the traffic.

'Calm down everyone. Chill! I was only two minutes. Who wants a treat?' He attempted to calm angry drivers by offering them chocolate chip cookies.

5

ROCK BOTTOM

By the time he turned the corner onto his road the rain clouds had dispersed, leaving a blotchy sky and a listless sun sitting on a rooftop. He had stopped to sell a few coffees to tired office workers, but his heart wasn't in it. He pedalled home and made good time. Anger is great for getting around.

The last thing he expected to see was a trio of burly, besuited men in the front garden. As he parked up, he saw what appeared to be all his possessions thrown into disorderly piles. Suitcases, bags, clothes, a few tools, all his business books, an ancient ghetto-blaster. It was the underwear that shocked him most. Pants don't belong in a front garden.

'You're locked out, mate,' said a man who looked exactly as you'd expect a bailiff to look: thickset, and with a face that radiated a 'no' before any question had been asked.

'What's going on?'

'It can't come as a shock.'

'Of course it's a shock.'

'You were sent a notice to quit. Several. Mrs Klyne wants to sell.'

He proffered some official-looking papers. 'It's all there.'

Leo couldn't answer this, so he fell silent. The bailiff nodded, barely perceptibly, as if that is exactly what he'd expected.

'What am I supposed to do?'

'I can't help you, Mr Morphetus.'

Leo watched the bailiffs climb into their van and drive off to their nice, warm, secure homes, having levied their distress.

He shuffled towards a kitchen stool – one of the few pieces of furniture he owned these days. It had steel legs and a soft round seat. He felt as if today a dam of bad luck had burst. But it wasn't just bad *luck*. He'd been stupid. At the bank he'd been boasting about his financial expertise, and yet he hadn't bothered opening the letters with the red warnings on them.

It felt right to sit and think things through while he gazed at the spectacle around him: an old anglepoise lamp, a box of trainers, another box of papers into which he'd thrown the letters and notices.

Although most of his books were still at his old house, he had brought the ones on economics and business: various tomes about the causes of the dotcom boom and bust, the events leading to the 2008 recession, an account of the collapse of Enron, and unauthorised biographies of Robert Maxwell, Bernie Madoff and Donald Trump, everything ever written by Malcolm Gladwell, Daniel Khaneman and Nasim Taleb. They were piled up between a stack of pots and pans, and a dozen ten-kilogram bags of coffee beans.

Next to the books... what was that? A bottle of Jack Daniels? He went over and pulled it from under a packet of Cheerios. It had been a gift from his best mate, Vince, and it was half full. Leo wasn't much of a drinker, but what the hell, he poured a large measure into a teacup, took it down in one, coughed, and refilled the cup before returning to the stool.

This, he thought to himself as he looked around, is what they call 'net worth'. This stuff, strewn on some crazy paving, was the material manifestation of his value as a human being. What was he worth? If he were to sell all the objects? Probably three hundred quid, minus what he would have to pay for someone to take it all away.

He shivered and wrapped his arms about his shoulders. A pregnant woman and her boyfriend walked past. Lampposts were just blinking into life. He messaged Vince – *help, I need somewhere to stay*. While waiting for a reply, he decided to marinate his pain in more alcohol.

Twenty minutes later, a red car pulled up on the other side of the road and at first it only *looked* very much like the

Mazda that had been parked outside Helen's. But when the driver turned his head, reality dawned.

The man looked smooth and confident, and had tamed his hair. He strode across the road, his eyes directly on Leo.

'Morning,' he said.

'Morning.' Leo immediately regretted joining in with the little joke; it showed weakness. He would have to regain some authority.

'I mean, I suppose it's morning *somewhere,*' he said.

'Oh, you're a geographer, are you?'

Christ, thought Leo, *this is sounding like a crappy TV drama.*

'You owe me an apology,' said the man, folding his arms.

Leo answered with an all-purpose shrug. He realised that they were both doing the same thing: asking themselves which of them would come off best if it came to a fight. That is the bottom line with all disagreements amongst men, and it goes back to the dawn of unintelligent life.

'I'm Tony, by the way. What have you come as?'

Leo was wearing his striped apron, but luckily the straw boater was not in evidence.

'Oh very good, I've not heard that one before.'

Tony nodded, as if giving a score of one-all. He glanced at the sad pile of belongings. 'So what's all this?'

There was no point in trying to put any kind of spin on this. When it came to a status war, there was a strange kind of honesty in losing so completely. Leo smiled as he shrugged, then stretched out his arms.

'Been evicted. Yup. It's everything I have.'

Tony seemed taken-aback by the comprehensiveness of his victory. Something caught his eye.

'Those your *pants?*'

'Yup.'

Tony smirked; half amused, half bewildered.

Leo needed to find some weakness in his opponent, then realised it was staring him in the face.

'I can't believe Helen's dating a forty-year-old.'

Leo chalked this up as a direct hit. He was ready with another shot.

'I guess all the decent men her own age have been taken.'

'Like ones who can't afford a home for their underwear?'

Tony laughed, but without humour. Leo laughed too.

'Oh, by the way, do come and visit us in the Costa del Sol sometime. Got a villa there. I think Helen and Amy will enjoy Spain. Great schools, nice lifestyle, big demand for English medical workers.'

After a second of confusion, a sentence formed in Leo's head and made its way to his drying mouth.

'Helen wouldn't take Amy away from me.'

His voice was weak, like a sleepy child's.

'Not yet. But soon, maybe? There's not a lot for Helen in Byford, is there?'

The thought of this wanker taking his family abroad had some strange effects. Leo's internal monologue was replaced by a series of pictures, a photo-story. One photo was of him punching Tony on the nose. Then an emergency switch seemed to flip inside him. His blood felt like rocket fuel. He was powerful enough to pick this arsehole up and throw him ten foot into the air. Engage: all systems go.

He punched him right on the nose, just like in the photo. As he withdrew his hand Tony caught it, bent it back, right back, and held it there. Pain shot through Leo's arm like hellfire. He considered a knee to the groin but some vestige of fair play stopped him. Suddenly air whooshed from his lungs and he couldn't suck it back. Despite the pain, he wanted more fighting. He wanted to hit and be hit, he wanted to settle this with blood and guts. He was still on the ground when he saw Tony slip into his Mazda, give the engine a victorious rev, and zoom away.

It was almost dark now and the road was quiet. Windows of houses lit up, families preparing meals.

Now he had physical pain, which needed numbing, along with his emotional hurt. He held his nose and got as much Jack inside him as he could take. The burning in his throat seemed to help somehow. He assessed his situation.

He'd been evicted, he'd been refused a bank loan *forever*, the woman he loved and his daughter were in the hands of a bastard – who they probably thought was wonderful because evil men must make like saints in order to conceal their malignant souls. Those were the facts on the ground.

With the clarity of thought that only comes with being drunk, he now began an appraisal of his prospects. These days he found that he could interpret almost any human situation in terms of business. He knew well that the most common mistake of the new entrepreneur is clinging on to an enterprise that isn't working. He could see it every day: a shop, cafe or hair salon that couldn't possibly be making money, but the owners keep telling themselves *business will pick up. Give it time.* This mindset is called *commitment bias* or *the sunk costs fallacy.* He had nearly fallen for it himself once. And he could see it in relationships too: *this will get better, he or she will change – I've put so much into this I can't throw in the towel now.* The books say that in these circumstances it's best to stomach the loss, dust yourself off, and start again with a new venture or a new lover.

He went to pour more bourbon into his cup but the bottle was now empty. He held it vertically and waited for any last drops to fall. It was time to face facts. *Leo, if you were a business, you'd be Woolworths, circa November 2008.*

Plans drifted in and out of his mind. The most extreme was suicide. Six months ago, after a near miss on his Trike, he took out an insurance policy and it would pay Helen a hundred grand upon his death. It wouldn't be hard to make it look like an accident: pelt down Green Hill at 40mph and run headlong into the oak near the bottom. Wife and daughter would be looked after. No sooner had this wonderful idea formulated, than Leo pictured Amy at his funeral, one hand in Tony's.

Plan B: injure himself. There'd be a smaller payout but Amy would still have a Dad. He could use the money to invest in a brilliant new business idea. Somewhere deep in Leo's brain there was a muffled voice telling him that this was the second stupidest idea he'd ever had, but the great thing about being drunk, muddled and emotional, is that all the regions of the brain come together like the crowd flattering the emperor with no clothes.

He felt a surge of optimism. Somehow or other, with details still to be arranged, he was going fix this, just as he'd done when he found out he was going to be a father. He'd managed to up his game then, and he would again. Somehow, Old Failure Leo would be put into receivership, and in his place there'd be bright new start-up: Successful Leo. Maybe a juice kiosk was the way to go.

What to do right now? With pockets full of cash and nowhere to go, there seemed to be one not-unpleasant option. When Vince made contact, Leo would tell him to head for The Swan. They would drunkenly laugh in the face of adversity. Perhaps, since his life was about to change, he could celebrate by buying everyone there a drink or two. That would shock them.

But there was something he wanted to do first. He gathered up a couple of framed photographs of his mother, Helen and Amy, his passport, and a few items of clothing. He changed out of his stripes round the back of the house, then made a pile of everything Old Leo possessed, poured on some lighter fuel, and lit a match.

PART TWO

6

IT COULD BE HIM

Gira, Hamir's Punjabi wife and co-owner of the shop, came downstairs to help close up. Hamir was quick to tell her about Leo 'the coffee guy' giving up on the lottery, buying expensive chocolate and selling his Trike.

'And his pockets were full of fifty pound notes!' Well, a little exaggeration is harmless. 'They were dropping everywhere – he barely bothered to pick them up. The billion pound winner? What do you say?'

'Maybe.' Gira shrugged, wanting to dampen her husband's enthusiasm.

She was tiny compared to her husband, and it was her waif-like frame that first attracted him when he spotted her at a cousin's wedding. He pursued her with relentless vigour, and his ardour paid off. They fell in love, their families conceded that this was unstoppable, and Hamir won his bride. It wasn't long before he discovered that although she came in a handy size, she was not easy to move.

She began emptying the cash register. 'It could be him. But it could be lots of people,' she said, trying not to sound too much of a killjoy.

Hamir expected this kind of reaction from his cautious wife. He began drawing down the metal blinds.

'But the papers are saying it is someone from round here. Round *here*, Gira.'

He had been giving it some thought, and the more thought he gave it, the more convinced he became.

'It would be good for us,' he said.

'How?'

'Remember the world's *first* billion pound winner? The waiter in Cleveland, Ohio? The store that sold the ticket is practically a shrine. People flock from miles.'

'But all Americans are mad, you know that,' said Gira. 'And you haven't put these twenties in the right compartment,' she scolded, gently. 'And, Hamir, isn't this the *third* billion pound win? Or fourth? Surely there's not much interest now.'

'Nonsense, my dearest.'

He bent down behind the counter and switched the fan heater to maximum. Gira would appreciate the warmth, and she might even warm to his dream.

'And get this, the billionaire in Ohio gave his retailer *one million dollars* as a 'thank you'.'

'Don't believe everything on Google.'

But Hamir wasn't listening.

'We could expand. Imagine opening another store. Imagine that.'

'I don't think Leo's bought a ticket for quite a long time, not while I've been on duty anyway.'

'The guy more or less *told* me he won. I winked at him, he winked back. Nudge, nudge, wink, wink. He is the guy, Gira,' he said, standing as close to his wife as he could without getting in her way.

'*I've* been doing the afternoon shift on Wednesdays,' said Gira.

Hamir was confused. Why was his wife questioning him?

'Maybe you should check with Camelot if we sold the ticket.'

'No, Gira.' He sighed heavily to indicate that he was trying to be extra patient. 'Camelot only say the *area* where the ticket was bought, never the shop, otherwise people might be able guess the winner. *Hamir knows.*'

He liked the way he sounded so authoritative. Now, why couldn't she just enjoy the good news? Especially when it came from him, the man she should trust.

'Why is my wife the *only* one not to believe me?'

Gira stopped what she was doing.

'You mean you've been telling people?'

'Just one or two,' said Hamir, with cheeky smile. In fact, he had told anyone who'd listen. And the general verdict was: *he's the guy.*

It was high time for Gira to comply with her husband, even if she didn't agree. Would a rendition of *Always Look on the Bright Side of Life* do the trick? It certainly did when they were young, especially if he did a little dance. And so he clicked his fingers, swivelled his hips and began to emit noises of varying pitch. Gira responded with surprising alacrity – before he'd finished one bar.

'Can we take the children to Florida?' she said.

He laughed. It was always Florida.

'And you can have a corner bath. Now, who should I call? A radio phone-in? I love those shows.'

Hamir willed his wife to look up from the cash register and see how happy he was.

'Call if you really want, but look through the CCTV footage first,' she said, closing the drawer.

'Very well, my little balushahi.'

He knew his wife was right. She usually was.

7

DEFINITELY *NOT* A COMB-OVER

Helen had put Amy to bed an hour ago and was preparing for a couple of miles on the exercise bike. This entailed donning a tracksuit, training shoes and hair band, lining up exactly the right tracks on her phone, and then deciding not to bother – at least until she'd done every conceivable displacement activity.

When she couldn't put off the tedium any longer, she climbed onto the dreaded contraption, and – hooray – her phone rang.

Tony.

She felt a thrill, but it was not unalloyed. Instead of being simply a pleasure, Tony felt like a *guilty* pleasure. Why? She put some of this down to loyalty to Leo, but that couldn't be the whole story. Perhaps it was also because some puritanical voice told her that a newly single mother of a seven-year-old shouldn't be enjoying such fantastic sex. Puritans have a lot to answer for.

'Hi honey, is Amy asleep?'

'Yes,' she said, loving the *honey.*

'I'm two minutes away. Can I pop in?'

Amy rarely woke up in the night these days, but it still felt like a risk. She had met Tony once (introduced to her as a friend) and that was enough for the time being. Helen wasn't even nearly ready to explain that there might be a new man in their lives.

'Sure... but only for a few minutes and we can't... you know.'

'I will do my best to resist.'

Helen had met Tony through an online introduction agency and he was her second ever date. (The first was Keith, a man twice as fat as his profile picture, who proudly revealed that he was a world-renowned collector of *Star Wars* toys.)

She'd warmed to Tony's manner on the phone, his mild cockney accent, and the way he seemed so at ease with himself: 'life was good, but a soulmate would make it even better,' he'd said. There was no getting away from the fact that the real clincher was his profile picture. He was sitting at a bar – somewhere stylish – a wine glass in front of him. Light from the bottles behind the bar played on his face. He wore a crisp white shirt, a hint of a smile with a slightly open mouth, and the most penetrating eyes. He could be mid-conversation about a favourite book with a friend – no, not a friend, a lover – someone he desired, anyway. If Helen were a man, this is what she'd want to look like, and this is the kind of profile picture she'd want.

As she prepared to meet him, she convinced herself that in person he was bound to disappoint.

The shocker was that in the flesh Tony was only fractionally less appealing than in his photograph. His hair was a little thinner and, although it was definitely *not* a comb-over, it was strategically styled. He more than made up for that bagatelle by being taller and broader than she'd expected. His smile was nice enough, but less compelling than his face in repose: mean and moody was his forté.

As the wine flowed, he asked questions and listened to her talk as if her life was a fascinating adventure; he was intrigued by stories about her gap year in Indonesia. His conversation about himself was modest, sparse, enigmatic. He mentioned, with an apologetic shrug, that he'd had to spend a lot of time offshore. 'Gem traders don't tend to go round in Fiat Unos. Yachts are pretty boring, actually.'

She was engrossed by the intrigue and danger of it all. Gem trading was rife with fraud, smuggling, money laundering, false bank accounts, midnight assignations, and straightforward theft. 'When I started, the hardest part was keeping out of the sewer,' he said. 'But there are some straight people too; I stick with them. We're the good guys, doing our bit to clean it up, but we have to watch our backs.'

An hour into the date, they were holding hands and occasionally kissing. After a rare moment of silence between them, Tony sighed heavily, looked at this hands, and said, 'I have a confession to make.'

Helen felt surge of disappointment.

'Go on.' Married with ten children?

'You see… I've never read Jane Austen. Well, not a whole one. Just half of Emma.'

It took Helen a moment to remember she'd mentioned Jane Austen on her profile page. She joined in the game by remaining straight-faced.

'Not sure I can live with that, Tony.'

'In my defence, I'm a keen Forster enthusiast, and they say he's twentieth century's Austen, although I couldn't vouch for that.'

'Nor me,' she said, with pursed lips, showing mock guilt.

'Does that make us even?'

'Not quite, but you're forgiven.'

Helen was now sure that they would fuck at some point, but had no idea just how soon. Tony excused himself, and she wondered how she would respond if he suggested following her into a cubicle. She'd probably have declined, but only probably. She'd never felt quite like this before, and was gutted to hear that he was temporarily staying at his sister's because they had to look after their sick mother. Helen had hired a babysitter and needed to get back by midnight. They shared their frustration at not having homes to go to, and went on to detail what they'd like to do when they eventually had each other alone.

Helen said it would be almost sinful to let their feelings go to waste.

There was only one thing for it.

After half an hour walking around in fine drizzle, they decided on a car park behind an insurance building. For Helen, this was a first. Unfortunately, the act was marred, not only by the chafing of a wall on her buttocks, but by the sad vision of Leo, and the thought of how upset he'd be if he knew. No matter how firmly she told herself it wasn't, it still felt like a betrayal. But at least she had done it: she had tangibly moved on.

***

She opened the door to see Tony holding a little gift bag. Inside was a plain blue silk scarf.

'You said your neck was cold, remember?'

She had indeed complained of a 'chronically freezing neck' the other night after a meal at the local Italian.

'It's lovely.' This was the third or fourth little present he had bought her, always inspired by something she'd said or done.

'Not exactly warm, but better than nothing,' said Tony, wrapping his arms around her.

'No, it's actually very much my style,' she said, feeling small inside his embrace. He leaned down for a kiss.

'You look gorgeous in a tracksuit.'

He slid his hands under the elastic and squeezed her bottom.

'They say sex is the best exercise,' he whispered, so close that it tickled her ears.

'Ha, not with Amy here,' – fuck, she really wanted him – 'but come inside before my neck gets cold again.'

'So we will make up for it when we get to London,' said Tony, as they walked through to the kitchen.

'London?'

'On Saturday week. Thought we could stay over, maybe see a play. Isn't Amy with her grandparents that weekend?'

'Yes, she is.' Helen was impressed by the absorption and retention of this information. She didn't want to make comparisons, she *really* didn't, but it was hard not to. Tony actually *listened* to times, dates, comments about a cold neck, whereas Leo had been in a world of his own.

'I've got a few options.'

He brought out a couple of show leaflets and placed them on the table. Again, Helen tried to dismiss a contrast with Leo, who rarely made arrangements in advance. She looked through the leaflets – about some rather interesting plays – while Tony uncorked the wine.

'I've got something to tell you,' he said, sitting down with two glasses and the bottle. 'I drove past Leo's place.'

'How do you know where he lives?'

'I'm very resourceful,' he said, with a wink.

Helen had already gained the impression that he was someone who knew how to get things done.

'I wanted to have a word, clear the air.'

Helen closed her eyes. 'Oh God, I wish you hadn't.'

They had discussed the car-scratching débacle right after the incident. They'd agreed to let her deal with it, and Leo would have to pay for the damage.

'He should know he can't go round damaging property. Anyway, he's sitting there in the garden amongst all his junk and I—'

'Wait, what?'

'Didn't you know he'd been evicted?' asked Tony, surprised.

Helen slapped the table in frustration.

'Oh for God's sake. He's an idiot. A total fucking idiot. I always said that Mrs Klyne was a bitch. I'll phone him, he's probably desperate.'

She was standing, phone in hand, pressing Leo's number.

'Can I finish this story, first?'

'Oh God, yes, go on.' She sat down and took a breath.

'I try to reason with him, build bridges, but suddenly, you'll never guess… he punches me on the nose.'

'*What?*' Helen's mouth opened wide. She could barely register the news. 'I can't believe he would do that. He hardly ever even gets angry.'

'I beg to differ.'

She felt pity mixed with contempt, like one might feel for an addict who relapses after months of being clean, bringing everyone's hopes crashing around them.

'I restrained him using minimum but decisive force.'

Minimum but decisive force was probably a phrase he'd had to use professionally a few times, thought Helen. Tony seemed like a man who was used to dealing with difficult people in a way that left no grey areas or ambiguity.

When he went to kiss her goodbye, she told herself to *put sex out of your mind*.

'Tony, we can't.'

But her tracksuit bottoms were already around her knees and she began unzipping him as fast as she could, while keeping an ear out for movement upstairs.

Once he'd gone, she knocked back the last drops of wine and left a voice message for Leo, but rather than upbraiding him, she offered help and measured sympathy. She pictured him in Mrs Klyne's crumby garden surrounded by his pathetic possessions, having completely humiliated himself with Tony. He must feel utterly lost and ashamed. Then she phoned Vince, telling him to get his arse over there.

The marriage had been expedited by her surprise pregnancy, and if it hadn't been for that, Helen wondered if she would have said yes to Leo. Like Vince, Helen loved Leo's honesty, integrity – which verged on innocence – his slowness to anger and the way he gave everyone the benefit of the doubt. She also found him funny, both accidentally and on purpose, probably more the former.

But like a small boy, he was a serial obsessive, going from one interest to another, one scheme, one dream that would consume him to the exclusion of human relationships and occasionally to the exclusion of reality. Sometimes the obsession could be something they could share, such as his short-lived interested in cooking and his brief flirtation with politics, but his fascination for corporate scandals and business ethics seemed just a little pathetic for someone who sold coffee from a tricycle.

She could quite see how the only child of a mother for whom English was a second language, and who'd learnt most of it from soaps, might lag behind on the sophistication front. Leo knew a lot about a small number of topics and didn't mind a bit that he knew nothing about vast areas: literature and art especially. It amused Vince, but it often embarrassed Helen. When belittled by her friend Suzie for thinking Frankenstein was the name of the monster, not the doctor, he asked Suzie what the bubbles in boiling water contained. She made some guesses (oxygen, hydrogen, air), which were all wrong. 'You know about a book written ages ago, but you don't ask yourself what's in the bubbles you see every day?' he'd said, not angrily, but with bemusement. He then talked enthusiastically – without realising that no one seemed interested – about Galvani, whose experiments with corpses had apparently inspired the novel.

Leo's points were reasonable, but Helen wanted someone with a more artistic intellectual hinterland, rather than a man who at times even *she* thought might have Asperger's or ADHD. 'Differently intelligent' is a term she privately used for him. She also dubbed him the 'man who isn't there' because increasingly he seemed so seldom to be mentally present: quite cheerful, but ultimately unreachable. When they did talk, it was often simply about money and the Trike, 'I got a reduction on the next consignment of beans.'

She'd persuaded him to move out 'for a while' and only then did he seem to realise their marriage was in serious trouble. Helen had to admit that she'd been cowardly by not explicitly and unequivocally stating that it was irretrievably over – she just hoped he would get the message. Leo tried to change, expressed remorse, but most of Helen's friends (and certainly her mother) told her that this was the typical male response. If she let him back in, he would surely revert to type.

After ruminating on Leo, she checked her phone for messages, filled the kettle, and then went on to consider a related matter.

Tony. Was he a keeper?

In the six weeks they'd been dating, she'd put a lot of ticks in a lot of boxes, although she would never admit to doing that. There were the thoughtful little presents, the palpable affection, references to books he'd read, an interest in 'seeing more theatre', a passing comment about wanting to be a father one day, the ease with himself and with money. And the sex. Several of her friends had said that this man seemed to have it all.

Except... for one thing.

She tried to tell herself it wasn't important right now. Besides, this one thing would surely evolve between them once they knew each other better. And maybe it wasn't even something he lacked, but something she was failing to appreciate – the fault could be with her. But whenever they met, she noticed its absence. And she noticed it a little more each time.

That one thing was humour.

She had hardly ever been tickled by anything he'd said or done, and his rare attempts to raise a laugh (usually with a bad pun) left her struggling to fake a chuckle. Nor had she found anything silly about him, anything daft, sweetly ridiculous, unintentionally funny, endearingly anomalous. There was a confidence and competence about the man that left little room for mirth.

8

THE MORNING AFTER,
PART ONE

A balloon inside Leo's head was expanding. He had only felt this bad and this peculiar once before: the day after his stag do.

Before moving or daring to open even one eye, he orientated himself using the sense data coming from his body that told him he was in a bed, and fully clothed. By rubbing his feet together, he registered the absence of shoes. He moved his hands around him, and everything felt smooth and silky, so he concluded that he wasn't in his own bed. With trepidation, he reached further afield. And then a little further…

He was alone. Thank Christ.

He opened an eye, just a tiny bit. Lying on his side, he had a narrow, oblique view of a bedside table, an orange patterned carpet, a door. He opened the other eye and moved his eyeballs. A few feet beyond the bottom of the bed was a desk, the drawers of which appeared to be made of black glass. Above it hung a painting: red circles of purple, pink and blue overlapping each other – someone's idea of art, but it was so nauseating that his eyes shut involuntarily.

Next step: lift neck.

After raising his head, he forced his eyes open, wider this time. Thick curtains, half drawn, a notebook and pen carefully placed on a coffee table next to a bowl laden with fruit and crowned with a pineapple. Conclusion: he was in a hotel, a *posh* hotel.

He heaved himself to a sitting position. From this angle, he spotted something on the carpet: vomit. His? It must be, but Leo had never been so drunk he had actually puked. He had a definite limit when it came to alcohol: when the world started spinning, he stopped drinking. He knew from bitter experience that getting drunk messed up his brain.

His phone vibrated in his pocket. It would have to wait. He looked to his left. The hotel phone flashed red. Closing his eyes, he tried to picture last night. It was as if fifty blurred photographs had been thrown up in inside his head. Champagne glasses, shots, people slapping him on the back, laughing, cheering. A celebration? Suddenly a new picture formed: a red Mazda. This image was quickly followed by another: all his belongings thrown in a heap. Then another: an actual *fight*? *Really*?

Let's deal with one thing at a time, he thought, trying to make his internal monologue sound sensible. He must look out of the window – that might tell him where he was, because he had the feeling he wasn't in Byford any more. Before he could lurch to the curtains there were three quick taps on the door.

'Get up. Life is calling.'

Unmistakably Vince. He felt a warm sense of gratitude to whatever kind force had delivered his best friend.

'Gimme a minute.' His voice sounded like an old man's. Keeping his eyes half closed, he fumbled for the lock and opened the door.

Vince, beaming ear-to-ear, wearing a jacket that was green like a copper roof.

'Good morrow, for fortune has smiled upon you,' he said, with a freshness and sparkle that made Leo want to slam the door in his face. Instead, he just scowled. Vince, undaunted, lifted his arms out wide.

'We never hug,' grunted Leo.

'It's what rich people do.'

'Huh?' Something about the word *rich*…

After the hug, probably their first, and somewhat asymmetrical, Vince sauntered past Leo, his thick, sandy hair even bouncier than usual.

Leo followed. Then, feeling dizzy, flopped down on the bed, while Vince drew back the curtains. Vince's face had masculine angles but full lips most women would happily settle for. It was a contradiction that earned second glances from both women and men. He looked around with a contemptuous huff.

'Is this really the best they could do? And it stinks.'

'Why are we in a fuck-off hotel?' moaned Leo.

'Why not?'

Vince and Leo had been firm friends ever since they skipped games together in favour of hanging round the shopping centre, smoking, trying to talk to girls, and occasionally managing to look cool. In his early teens, Vince was a social reject because of his camp flamboyance and unashamed enthusiasm for books (the 'book-fucker'). He had a kind of unschooled sophistication, like the cockney taxi drivers who sometimes win Mastermind. Leo wasn't so much rejected as ignored. As they got older, Vince's brand of extrovertism became steadily more popular. He possessed a fearless optimism that Leo tried to emulate, with some success, but never quite to the same level. Vince said that, if he only had twenty pounds left in the world, he would spend it all on champagne, and then added, 'but only if no cocaine was available'. He excelled at English (the head of English said he was 'gifted') but no other subject had any meaning for him. He left school at sixteen and took various mentally undemanding jobs because he wanted to leave his mind free to pursue grander goals, or wait for 'something to happen, the Universe will provide.' But his temporary jobs linked together to form a permanent chain of drudgery.

'Hey, they do kedgeree,' he said, flapping the menu in the air. 'Want some?' Typical of him to make refreshment the priority.

'I don't even want you to *say* kedgeree again,' said Leo. 'What are we doing here?'

'Who *cares*?' said Vince, with a shrug as if nothing mattered any more. 'You know someone offered you some mandy? And you took it?'

'Mandy? And what does that do?'

'Fucks with the memory. Actually, it fucks with everything.'

'Fuck.'

Vince got up, stepped over the vomit, helped himself to a bunch of grapes, honed in on the minibar, and grabbed a bottle of orange juice. Leo noticed, in a bleary way, how comfortable his old mate seemed in these opulent surroundings. For someone who went to work at midnight to supervise a small team of bakers for thirteen pounds an hour, he had an incongruous sense of entitlement.

'Tell me where we are,' said Leo.

Vince threw a grape into his mouth.

'The Carlton.'

'Twenty miles away?'

'Away from what?'

'Byford.'

'Byford is no longer relevant,' said Vince, with utter conviction. His mouth was beginning to drip grape juice. 'If we ever go back to that arsehole town, we will arrive in style, preferably in a horse-drawn carriage. Or how about a giraffe? I've always wanted to ride into town on a giraffe, flanked on either side by big-bosomed Azande tribeswomen.'

There was no point in trying to stop Vince when he was like this.

'Think of your existence in Byford as an unpleasant dream from which you are now awakening.'

'Then tell me the good news,' said Leo. Vince replied with his palm out flat, like a traffic policeman. Then he rose to assess himself in a full-length mirror.

'I've made our shopping list.'

Shopping list, echoed Leo to himself.

'Old friend, we have been plucked from boring arseholedom, and dropped into a world of dazzling possibilities. I believe the Universe provided all this, as I always knew it would.'

Words and images came into focus in Leo's befuddled brain. Congratulations/you lucky bastard/don't forget your friends/lend us a tenner/don't let it change you/couldn't happen to a nicer fellow. These splintered memories coalesced, like a smashing glass played in reverse. One single, immovable fact linked everything together.

'People think I've won the billion jackpot, don't they?' he said.

'I'm afraid so,' Vince said, gravely.

The embarrassment of it all. The whole town will hear about this. Tony, the Mazda guy, will laugh through his sleeve, Helen will be furious, her parents will get the final confirmation that their daughter married a fool.

Vince turned to look at himself sideways on.

'Would I suit a velvet jacket?'

'Just tell me what happened.'

Vince straightened his collar, then decided it looked better askew. He flopped onto the armchair, sideways on, with his legs dangling over the antimacassar, pulled some more grapes from the bunch, munched them, and shot the pips in the general direction of the bin. When he'd finished he gave his fingers a lick.

'Okay, listen up.'

Leo braced himself for more cringe-making news. He hugged a pillow.

'I'm at home and I have finished my book-reading for the evening – Richard Forde's The Sportswriter, since you ask – and I turn on my phone and get your message. You're clearly wankered, and you mention something about Helen and a new man.'

That much Leo remembered, and it felt like a finger prodding his heart.

'I think, fair enough, Helen's got a new squeeze, so Leo's having a crisis, and what better way of dealing with an important emotional watershed than going doolally in a pub? I wonder if I will be too late to mitigate the always-disastrous personality change that happens when you've had a skinful. By the time I get there, you are spark out.'

He paused for more grapes.

'Carry on.'

'So I make sure you aren't actually dead. I do this by giving you a little slap, and you mumble something about having been very silly. From what I could garner, you'd thrown your cash around, and told the entire pub that *Old Loser Leo* was no more, you're the *New Winner Leo*.'

'Oh, Jesus fucking Christ,' shouted Leo into another pillow, torn between needing to hear more, and wanting it all to stop.

'Then there's some rumour about a newsagent called Haziz or something saying he sold you the billion pound lottery ticket.'

Leo could see it all: Hamir's conspiratorial wink, cash falling onto the floor; things were beginning to make a sickening kind of sense.

'And someone says you burnt all your stuff, or tried to. Someone else saw you throwing money around in the street.'

Leo replayed these events from last night, but viewed them in this entirely new perspective.

'So: burnt stuff, the newsagent blathering, throwing your cash around, but what convinced *me* that you were the much-vaunted Byford billionaire is that you'd actually bought champagne for everyone in the whole pub. I mean, *stop right there*, I said, if Leo has bought even *one* round of drinks, then he's definitely won the lottery.'

Leo laughed at this, but the laughter soon turned into a kind of cry.

'I didn't win,' said Leo, propping himself up on his elbows.

'Listen, mate, if you didn't want people to know, why go to the boozer and throw your money around like a bellend?'

Leo closed his eyes and asked himself, just to be sure: *could* he have won the billion? *Could* he have found the winning ticket, maybe bought weeks ago, checked online last night, and somehow forgotten all that? Could booze and whatever drug he took have wiped all that away? No. Impossible. He'd stopped playing the lottery, and even when he used to buy tickets, he checked every draw.

Vince grabbed a banana, took one bite and tossed it binwards. 'So I call a limo – why not?' he said, with a wave of his hand.

'Limo – as in *limousine*?'

'It's not easy getting one at that time of night, but the driver is a one-man-band, and when I mention the billion pound jackpot, he's all, 'What time do you want it, sir?'

Christ, thought Leo, *he could be in debt for years.*

'I stuff you in the back of this long white monstrosity – I had to pull Kirsten off you by the way, she knows a meal ticket when she sees one – and I haul you in here. I tug your shoes off – leaving your socks on because I don't carry an angle-grinder. You're welcome, by the way. Right, time for a Brad Pitt.'

Vince gyrated his way into the bathroom, taking a pointlessly circuitous route, while singing an inevitable medley: *Who Wants to be a Millionaire, Money, Money, Money.*

Leo's phone vibrated, and this time he reached for it. Holding his breath, he scrolled through messages from people offering congratulations and, worryingly, their thanks.

He stopped at a message from Alan Lethco, the father of Poppy, the girl with a rare blood disorder who needed to go abroad for life-saving treatment. The NHS had deemed the treatment not-cost-effective.

God bless you, Leo. The words 'thank you' are not enough.

Leo felt a cold dagger of dread slip cleanly under his ribcage. This could be so very much worse than an embarrassing episode of drunken excess.

9

A GOOD PRANK

Donna White hated motorway driving. Not a minute went by when she didn't imagine carnage: her blue Nissan Micra spinning on its roof, bursting into flames, and her, trapped inside, the door jammed. Every other driver on the road was a potential cause of slaughter, all of them just pretending to be sane, until one (that smoothy in the Audi?) would go berserk and kill everyone.

As much as Donna hated driving, the train wasn't a good option this morning, because Derek wanted her to take her camera and kit, and this Carlton Hotel was a good few miles from a station. Derek was the editor of TrueNewz.com, the UK's fasted-growing news outlet with a subscription element. It had been given a seven-figure cash injection by Google as part of their answer to fake news and the accusations from the publishing industry that it 'drains money from quality journalism'. Now Google could say that it was 'helping journalism thrive in the digital age'. TrueNewz was getting a reputation for accuracy – 'more trustworthy than the BBC and much more fun,' as one ex-BBC reporter had put it.

Derek was a highly respected old dinosaur parachuted in from a waning print title to ensure that traditional newsgathering standards were upheld. 'We aren't here to regurgitate press releases, or do puff pieces or make stuff up.' He had been sent on a course so he could use terms like AddThis, Filter Bubble and Geotargeting with confidence.

He wanted to go big on this billionaire story. Camelot had released the news that the winning ticket had been bought in Byford. The rumour was that the lucky man was one Leo Morphetus, who sold coffee from a tricycle. Of course, both Derek and Donna knew this could be baloney, or a deliberate hoax, but it had gained enough traction locally that, even if it was a prank, it was probably worth covering. A good prank could be fun, provided they were on the right side of it.

Donna tuned in to the local radio station. A man with the gentlest of Edinburgh accents was asking listeners to call with answers: was the prize excessive? Had it gone too far? And what about this Coffee Guy? Do you think he's the winner? He was soliciting for the usual mix of guesswork and ill-informed opinion that these phone-ins devoured.

'And now, I'm hearing that we have a very special caller on the line, someone who claims to have actually sold the winning ticket! Hello, Mr Hamir?'

'It's just Hamir. Of Hamir News, on Fleet Road, opposite the BP garage.'

Donna turned up the volume.

'Are you the one who phoned our news desk last night?'

'Ha, I might have been. Leo Morphetus buys his tickets from us without fail. My wife served him, or maybe it was me. I'm sure he's the winner. Money was falling from his pockets, I've never seen anything like it. I'm telling you, man, he was buying up the whole shop!'

This guy seemed genuine enough, thought Donna.

'Did Morphetus tell you he'd won the jackpot?' asked the host.

'More or less. He said he would keep it secret.'

'Ha, ha, that didn't work out too well, did it? Judging from the locals at The Swan.'

Donna laughed along with the host.

'No,' said Hamir, his voice getting higher. 'Leo mate, if you're listening, don't forget who sold you the winner!'

'Do you have CCTV of him buying the ticket?' asked the host, and it was just the question Donna wanted him to ask.

The newsagent hesitated.

'I leave that to my wife. She's head of security.'

And it was time for the news: flood-damaged Byford Bridge still has no date for works to begin, a sex shop has been denied permission to open in the high street. Nothing about a coffee guy.

Good, thought Donna. Prank or not, it wasn't 'news' yet, so she had some time in hand. But she was in a metal box moving at seventy miles an hour, while most of her rivals would now be gathering digital information at the speed of light. Maybe Derek should have asked her to work from home. Then she forgot about all that because, at any moment, she could be lying face down in her own blood.

10

THE MORNING AFTER, PART TWO

The text from Poppy's father had cleared some of Leo's alcohol-induced fog. He called to Vince, who was still in the bathroom, having showered – singing 'Big Spender' all the while.

'Vince, listen, remember my stag do? I drank all those vodka shots? And told everyone that I was going to pay for you all to go to Las Vegas for the wedding?'

'Yes,' said Vince. 'Classic. No one believed it. You can't put this genie back in the bottle, matey. I believe *this* because of the newsagent guy. And you actually burnt all your stuff. The genie is out of the bottle, stark naked, swinging his todger on Byford High Street.'

He emerged with his trousers on but with his chest bare, reeking of hotel cologne.

'And Ken saw you outside your old house,' he said, 'dropping tenners on the road, not bothering to pick them up – and I've seen you pounce on pennies.'

'I want to tell you something fucking serious.' Leo's voice was grave enough to stop Vince talking. He put on his shirt and sat down as he buttoned it up. Leo waited for him to sit still.

'All ears,' said Vince, resting his arms on the chair.

No point in mincing words.

'I didn't win the billion.'

Vince frowned, and his eyes narrowed for a moment before shrugging.

'How much *did* you win?'

Leo closed his eyes. Why wasn't Vince joining the dots? Or rather, why was he joining the dots in the wrong way? The answer was, of course, that there was only one pattern Vince wanted to see. Leo got up and stood in front of his friend, then bent down to hold his shoulders firmly with each hand, and spoke as earnestly as he could.

'I didn't win *anything*. Not even the bonus ten quid. I have no money. Actually, I have *minus* money because I have to stump up for a hotel and a limo!'

Leo waited for him to laugh like a drain or go nuts or both, and he didn't care which. Instead of either, he looked remarkably relaxed.

'Keep calm, Leo,' he said, as if talking to a child. 'You go a bit strange when you're plastered, we all know that – plus the mandy. So, don't you think it is quite *possible*, given the news purveyor's alleged testimony, that you have completely forgotten that you are now *a fucking billionaire.* Rejoice and let the angels sing.'

He got up and began strutting around and gesticulating like an actor trying to fill a huge stage. 'Our futures will be resplendent with primary colours. Each day will taste of lobster, and sound like trumpets, and feel like silk, and smell of French perfume.'

Leo decided to do something he hardly ever did: shout.

'Vince. I stopped doing the lottery weeks ago! I have no lottery tickets, I didn't fucking win anything... *I swear on Amy's life.*'

Like an electric toy whose batteries are slowly draining, Vince's strides became smaller, his gestures slower – until his arms flopped down by his side and finally came to a complete stop.

'Okay,' he said, gently. He lowered himself slowly and carefully onto the armchair, as if nonchalance was a luxury he could no longer afford. It was sad to see this force of nature completely void of gusto.

'Too good to be true, wasn't it, mate?' he said, staring at the floor.

The men maintained a respectful silence, like sailors in a lifeboat watching their beloved vessel sink beneath the waves. Vince's dream had died unexpectedly at a tragically young an age. Leo was tempted to say 'I'm sorry for your loss.'

A full minute passed, with only the sound of the air conditioner and a distant rumble of traffic.

'It was the local yokels who began saying you were the winner,' said Vince, calmly, as if recounting a distant memory. 'You spent half the night denying it.'

'*Good*,' said Leo. It was a crumb of comfort to know that some other people might at least be partly to blame for all this.

'Then you just seemed to… admit it.'

Leo had vague memories of believing that he had won, or half believing it.

'Last night, I called my boss,' said Vince, with a wistful smile. 'I told him where he could stick his coconut macaroons.' A hollow chuckle.

'I'm sorry, mate.'

As they sat in another silence, Leo felt grateful to Vince just for being there.

'Total fucking disasters are great bonding experiences, don't you think?' he said.

The remark hung in the air. Vince pulled a piece of paper from his pocket.

'Our shopping list,' he announced. 'First stop was going to be Bond Street. Then Liberty's. Then South Molton Street – there are some *great* little boutiques there. Pablo would have sorted us out – lovely boy. I left a message telling him to expect us.'

Leo wondered how this nocturnal baker could be on personal terms with a purveyor of high fashion, but this was not the time to ask. He lay back on the bed and closed his eyes.

'Now, shoes,' said Vince, 'I had my heart set on Jimmy Choo Argyles. What say you?' He sounded almost as excited as he'd been three minutes ago.

'I'll buy you a pair of Jimmy Choo Argyles,' said Leo. He knew that for Vince, shopping would have meant much more than material gain. This was to have been a deliverance, the Universe finally coming good.

'I suppose I should tell Dave to stand down,' said Vince, absently.

'Dave?'

'Driver Dave. Limo man. Obsessed with Neil Diamond. It's the only thing he plays on the music system. Weird guy.'

'So… the limo's been waiting for us *all night*?'

'As I requested. Because, you see, what with you being a *billionaire*—'

'Yes, all right,' interrupted Leo. There was another long silence, with both men too absorbed in their own thoughts even to fidget.

'And I've never told you this, Leo, but I've always wanted an alpaca.'

'A what?'

'A little camel. I've been looking at pictures online. Big eyes, funny little ears. Very *very*, cute. Yes, I had lots of ideas…'

Leo decided to let his friend witter on, which he did with muted relish. Depictions of restaurants, shops, and a world that Leo 'could only dream of'. He would also replace his digital collection of novels with real books. The poor guy must have spent half the night excitedly planning, imagining, seeing himself transformed. He had surely come to believe that his external circumstances were now, at long last, in equilibrium with his character. Isn't that what everyone wants? Our inside at ease with our outside.

The least Leo could do was fix him one of his favourite drinks – a gin and tonic – hang the expense. He cracked open an OJ for himself, and they toasted the life that was never to be. After more languid pauses, punctuated by the sound of clinking ice cubes, Leo felt it was time to coax his friend into addressing the present predicament.

'Last night, I think I made a lot of promises. Do you know what I promised and to who?'

'To *whom*,' corrected Vince. He scratched an eyebrow with his thumbnail and looked rueful. Leo realised that Vince, who generally had to be nudged into thinking about anyone but himself, had suddenly remembered something.

'Umm… while waiting for Driver Dave to arrive last night, I did chat to a few people, yes.'

'Go on,' said Leo, dreading the next sentence.

'From what I can *gather*, you promised… that you'd pay for Poppy Lethco to fly to America for treatment. It slipped my mind, sorry.'

Leo rubbed his eyes, trying to obscure the vision of Alan Lethco at The Swan. He wanted to punch himself in the face and then disappear.

He didn't know Poppy well, but recalled letting her make a cappuccino on the trike, keeping a watchful eye on the steam. Her curiosity was delightful: she demanded to know the purpose of every button and lever. Only a few weeks later he learned of the condition, and the real possibility that in a matter of months this beautiful child, not much older than Amy, might no longer exist.

'And it's probably all on YouTube,' said Vince, his head turned towards the window.

'What else?' asked Leo, as memories came back like a series of muted gifs.

Vince began scrolling on his phone.

'Some of the folk seemed keen for me to make a note.'

He looked at his phone and ran through three or four struggling businesses Leo had promised to rescue. Dan at Snappy Snaps was behind on his business rates, so Leo promised a year's back payment, Dave and Rob were promised a new driving instructor's car, and Sally was pledged enough to move her sex toy business from her attic to an industrial park.

Leo knew all about the trials and tribulations of these struggling traders, so it was hardly surprising, if he had got it into his head that he was a billionaire, that he would try to help his friends. He would need to contact them before they started spending.

'But relax, Leo. I doubt the promises add up to more than loose change for you – fifty grand? A fart in a hurricane for someone who's just bagged a billion quid.'

11

HARRIET GETS A CALL

Donna pulled into a Welcome Break to make the calls that might put her ahead of the pack. After slotting into the parking bay, she enjoyed a moment's peace from the stress of imagined carnage. *No one looks their best at a service station,* thought Donna. Sitting in a car draws fat to the buttocks and colour from the skin.

She had asked one of the girls from the small muddle of researchers at the office to send her the stats on Morphetus: marriages, births, parents, criminal records, social media profile, the usual tiresome trawl. The girl emailed a load of documents and a link to the Coffee Guy's website. That's what researchers do now – send links, often to Wikipedia. No wonder they're a dying breed.

She scrolled through the files and found a contact that looked fruitful. After a little mental rehearsal, she was ready.

'Harriet Sterling?'

'Yes.'

'Donna White,' said Donna White. 'Calling from the *Daily Mail*,' she added, because to get the truth you don't have to be truthful, and a Tory wife would almost certainly read the Mail.

'Oh? Did you want to speak to my husband?'

'Or I could speak to *you*,' said Donna, knowing she'd be taking the woman off guard.

'Oh um… The Mail, you said?' Harriet Sterling sounded a little wary, but also a little flattered. 'I um… I… what's it about?'

'I know Frank of old, by the way. He's my go-to man on local politics. Great guy.'

'Oh, that's nice.' Mrs Sterling sounded more relaxed.

'Got a local election coming up, right?' said Donna.

'Yes, yes, all very busy. Er – why don't you give him a call on his mobile?'

'Yes, I would love to talk to him about the way he's trying to save the bridge and all that.'

'Oh, I'm sure he would be *very* interested, yes.' Harriet was taking the bait faster than Donna could lay it.

'But actually, Mrs Sterling, I wanted to talk to you about something else. Leo Morphetus.'

A second's hesitation.

'*Really*? Leo? Gosh. What's he… er…' *She was going to say 'what's he done?'* thought Donna.

'How can I… er, help?'

'So you don't know?'

'Know what?'

The voice was concerned – alarmed even. Donna watched a man holding two cardboard cups hurry to his car before they burnt his hands.

'Are you sitting down?'

'Um, well…'

'Mrs Sterling, you've heard that the billion pound lottery ticket was bought in the Byford area?'

Donna let this fizz like the taper on a firework. A good few seconds passed before it went off.

'No. Are… no, really? *Leo*? Oh my God. Oh my God.'

A lot of shock but no delight. 'You don't know about this?'

'Not at all. Oh, I knew he bought those silly tickets. The whole thing is out of hand. Nearly a billion pounds – it's ridiculous.'

'Before we get carried away, it's just a rumour. That's why I was calling, I wanted to ask if you knew anything, given he's your son-in-law.'

'*Former*, really. They're separated.'

Whoa, she wants to make that *very* clear.

'Have you seen him recently?'

'Yes, but I really don't know anything about this.'

'He's separated, perhaps he doesn't want your daughter to know.'

A man walked past Donna's car loaded with bags of food, his tracksuit bottoms slipping half way down his underpants.

'I really can't comment.' The woman was back on the defensive. 'You need to speak to Leo himself. Or my daughter.'

There was caution in the voice now. Donna had to get her back on track. She transferred her phone to her other ear.

'I shouldn't say this, but I am under a lot of pressure, you know? My boss is breathing down my neck, I've been given the third degree because a few of my leads have gone down the pan and… I really *need* this.'

A motherly sigh.

'Well… oh, it's all making sense, now…'

'Great.'

'He had this big pile of nice chocolate for my granddaughter, and normally he only brings buttons. A trivial thing really,'

You're telling me it's trivial, thought Donna. *And yet…*

'Mrs Sterling, I don't have to attribute any of this. So is there anything else? Anything at all?'

'Oh, my Lord. He told Amy he was off to the bank, and *next time you see me, I'll be rich,* but I am sure he was joking.'

'Maybe the joke's on you?'

'Well, it's hard to tell with Leo. Oh, he said was going to get rid of his trike thing.'

The woman is getting into it now, thought Donna. An SUV stuffed with children and a dog parked up beside her. Little pieces of evidence, like strokes of a painter's brush, created a picture in Donna's mind.

'And he was definitely in a good mood,' said Harriet, 'Had quite the swagger. He's normally a little withdrawn. But he was very much a show-off. Don't quote me on that.'

'No problem.'

The family exited the car leaving behind their dog, who started barking.

'I haven't said anything bad, have I?'

'No, not at all. I really appreciate this. It's so hard to get people to talk to journalists these days – people think we're out to stitch them up. Mrs Sterling, do you get on with Leo?'

'We… he's a perfectly nice man.'

Faint praise indeed.

'I really need to go now.'

'You've been great, Mrs Sterling. Tell Frank I said hello.'

'Yes, okay. What's your—'

'Bye now.'

Donna hung up before Mrs Sterling could ask for her name – because she'll have certainly forgotten it.

The dog in the car chose a different window to do his lonely barking, as if that would make a difference. Time to hit the road again. Donna stifled her nerves by congratulating herself out loud on having landed the kind of gen no amount of google time will get you.

12

THE MORNING AFTER, PART THREE

Leo was just finishing the most terrifying 'to do' list he had ever written. Who would he call, when, and what would he say? The hotel phone rang. Vince picked up.

'Vincent Campbell speaking.' He had his posh voice on. 'No, he's busy. I'm his publicist.' Leo couldn't begrudge him this little roleplay. 'By the way, thank you for being so understanding last night. My client is not used to strong drink.'

Vince was standing up straight, his strong chin jutting upwards.

'That would be most welcome, thank you,' he said, before replacing the receiver. 'The manager's outside.'

'Why?' said Leo, assuming they must have done something wrong.

'*Why?*' echoed Vince. 'I imagine it has something to do with you being a *billionaire*. Let's shift the bed over that.' They looked down at the vomit, which was shaped like a map of Greece complete with an archipelago of solids.

'Oh, and by the by,' added Vince, 'What I said just then was true. Last night in the limo, between incomprehensible babble, you hired me as your publicist – hence me kissing the bakery goodbye.'

The two men managed to cover the offending sick before they heard a tentative tap on the door. Vince answered it and a moment later a rotund, middle-aged man appeared: short, mostly bald, wearing a suit meant for someone considerably thinner. He was followed by two smart waiters pushing a tray of Danish pastries, yoghurt, fruit salad, smoked salmon, baked goods, orange juice, a coffee pot, a tea pot, and a silver bucket containing a magnum of champagne.

'I am Mr Karaloka. I thought the famous winner might like a little champagne brunch,' he said, rubbing the tips of his fingers together. He had an accent but his English was good.

Vince and Leo exchanged a glance. This was surely not the moment to let the cat out of the bag. This had to be an *organised* train wreck. After this unspoken decision, Vince viewed the offerings.

'No kedgeree?'

'I will order some immediately,' said Karaloka, bowing his head.

'Actually, neither of us are hungry,' said Leo, thinking of the cost. He was about to ask them to take everything away when Vince bit into a bagel, simultaneously imbedding a fork into a kiwi fruit.

'Compliments of the house,' said Mr Karaloka.

Free champagne for a billionaire? Of course. *That's how the world works right there*, thought Leo, but at least there was one less bill to worry about. One of the waiters began opening the bottle.

'It's a great honour that you picked our hotel,' said Mr Karaloka.

'Yes, we could have crashed at the Royal,' said Vince, to underline the point, but his mouth was so full of bagel Mr Karaloka probably didn't hear.

'I want to let you know that there are a number of press representatives gathering in the lobby,' said the manager. Leo felt a surge of terror.

'Would you consider having an impromptu press conference, Mr Morpheus?'

Leo hardly had time to digest this information before Vince answered.

'We would consider that, yes,' he said, with his food on one side of his mouth. 'I feel it is in my client's interest to say a few words.' He took a moment to swallow.

'I'm not talking to the press,' said Leo. 'And why are they even *here*?'

'Not so fast, friend,' said Vince. 'First rule of PR, if you don't speak to the press, then they make stuff up.'

'I can't face anyone right now. Besides, they'll soon realise it was all a drunken mistake and go home.'

The implications of the last statement were lost on Mr Karaloka who had adopted a posture of neutrality.

'If you *do* decide to speak to the press, may we place our hotel banner behind you?'

'No press conference,' said Leo, folding his arms, as if the gesture would decide the matter.

'Obviously,' said Mr Karaloka, 'there will be no question of you being billed for your stay.'

It took Leo about half a second to realise this was a game-changer.

'Just a moment,' he said.

While Vince chomped on the brunch, Leo began calculating. The hotel bill would be waived. It might be worth doing the conference just for that. And how traumatic would it have to be? He could give a very brief statement, get the truth out to everyone in one go, be *utterly* sorry, and then start trying to put things right. Somehow.

'Mr Karaloka?' he said. 'I'll say a few words in front of your banner, if you're *sure* about waiving the fee.'

'Of course,' said the manager, who seemed pleased but also a little confused.

'He'll be nicking the towels next,' said Vince.

'We will start getting things ready.' Mr Karaloka bowed and took a few steps backwards towards the door, as if he were the servant of a great emperor. The waiters followed him out.

'That twonk actually thinks winning the lottery is *clever,*' declared Vince, as the door closed. He wiped his mouth with a crisp linen napkin, and stabbed his fork into a brioche.

13

HAS HE PHONED YET?

Helen had had several calls, texts and voice messages from friends – *What's going on? Is it true? WTF?* But nothing from Leo since ten past seven last night. She poured her fourth cup of coffee of the morning. Lots of coffee and no food: stress mode.

Helen's brain worked best when she was physically active. She wanted something to wipe or dust, but as she looked round her cottagey kitchen, everything was spick and span. She had a rule never to clean something she'd just cleaned, because that's what crazy people do. Instead, she made herself sit still at the kitchen table, and think things through.

The scratched car, Leo homeless, an actual fight between grown men, and now... a *billion pounds*. It was too much to take in. She still couldn't believe it, not really. And yet everyone was telling her it was true. Without even realising it, she had opened the table drawer and was straightening her store of tea lights.

For Leo not to phone with good news, especially if it involved money, was unprecedented. He must be furious with her. But at least he felt *something*. During so much of their time together he'd seemed to be asleep, inside an impenetrable bubble.

Had he known he'd won while he was sitting just here, counting the cash? Had he tried to keep it a secret, even from her, but then a boozy night at The Swan had loosened his tongue? She'd asked herself this ten times already, so why ask it again? The answer was the same: if he had won a billion, or even a thousand, it would be impossible for him not to tell her all about it. Leo doesn't scheme or plot or lie, it's just not in his nature. It was one of the things she'd loved about him: he was transparent, like the walls of his bubble. What you saw was what you got. It's something her silly mother never appreciated – his lack of guile.

As usual, when Helen disparaged her mother, the phone rang.

'Yes, Mum?' she said irritably, because this was the third call of the morning.

'Has he phoned yet?'

The inevitable question.

'No.'

'Well, he obviously doesn't want you to know, then.'

She had a blasé certainty that made Helen want to scream. Instead, she got up and concentrated on folding a tea towel.

'*If it's true,*' said Helen, 'then he's completely overwhelmed and doesn't know if he's coming or going.'

'It's been on the radio again,' said Harriet, ignoring her daughter's hypothesis, 'They're still saying it's just a rumour. It's Amy I worry about. All that attention. And he'll spoil her – he's already started, with all those sweets and chocolate.'

If anyone could be entirely negative about someone winning a fortune, it would be my mother, thought Helen, unfolding the tea towel just so she could fold it again.

'Mum, you didn't like him because he was poor, now you don't like him because he's rich.'

'I didn't dislike him because he was poor. I just never thought he was a very…' Helen waited for her mother to choose her weapon, '*substantial* person.'

What Helen had learnt from Leo was that stupidity and intelligence are not mutually exclusive character traits. They can perfectly well reside in the same brain, and Leo was a perfect example of that. Sadly her parents only saw – or wanted to see – Leo's dumb side.

'What is a *substantial* person?'

'Your father,' said Harriet, without hesitation.

'Just because he's chairman of the local council?' And just as she said it, she realised it did sound quite substantial.

'Actually, Mum, let's not get into this.' She straightened one of Amy's paintings on the fridge.

'Are you going to get back with him? He's very keen, I'm sure.'

'I'm not even going to answer that, Mum.'

She was relieved to hear a distinctive tap on the front door.

'I better go. Bye Mum, bye.'

She opened the door to Tony, who was holding a huge bouquet of flowers, mostly pink carnations.

'For the prettiest girl in Byford, and soon to be the richest,' he said, but it was a statement of fact rather than a joyous exclamation.

'Thank you, they're lovely,' she said, taking the bouquet, 'but it's just a rumour.'

Tony really is a man for the gestures, thought Helen, as she carried the flowers into the kitchen and found a couple of vases. But there was something odd. They should be talking over each other and laughing excitedly about all this. Instead there was tongue-tied silence. Perhaps it was understandable, given that he and Leo had just had a fight.

'Isn't it all just too weird?' she said, as she trimmed the stems, 'Not that I'm totally convinced. I'll believe it when I see it. Oh, how's your poor car?'

'I'm going to have to jack it in,' said Tony, leaning against the counter.

'Jack it in?'

'Send it back to the rental people. There'll be a penalty of course, but there you go. Leo can afford to pay for all that now.'

'I thought you owned the car.'

'Long lease. Buying is for mugs.'

'You told me you owned it.'

'No sweetie, I said I *leased* it.'

She was sure he'd said that he'd bought it, but it seemed too trivial a thing to argue about now.

'Heard from the billionaire barista?' asked Tony, flatly.

'Not yet.' She didn't want another conversation about why Leo hadn't called.

'He obviously doesn't want you to know.' He sat down at the kitchen table and ran his hands along the top, feeling the roughness of the oak.

'I'd be the first person he called if it were true,' she said, arranging the flowers in vases.

Tony shrugged.

'I know how men's minds work. With me here, he won't want to give you a penny.'

Helen had considered that this could be the reason Leo hadn't called. It made sense. Why would he want to give her a load of money so she could live a life of luxury with the man who, in his mind, had stolen her away?

'I should never have told him about us. It was too soon. I should have lied or something,' she said, sweeping up some fallen petals with her hand, 'But Leo's not vindictive and he doesn't really get really angry.'

'Ha,' Tony tapped the tip of his nose where he'd been punched. 'Maybe you don't know him as well as you think.'

Helen didn't care for this suggestion. And why was he acting so coldly? He seemed quietly resentful. She gathered up the pieces of stem and dropped them in the bin.

'Things will be different from now on,' said Tony, with a sigh, as if an elderly relative had just died.

'To pay off the mortgage, that's all I want,' said Helen, looking at Tony. 'Hey, and a handyman,' she added, referring to the broken patio door handle. Her levity only seemed to deepen Tony's gloom. His eyes were fixed on the table, as if that's where his future was mapped out.

'You're going to be a very, very rich woman,' he said.

'Could be worse, couldn't it?' she said, trying to get a smile. Tony grabbed Helen's wrist as she walked past and pulled her towards him. What followed was a different kind of sex, in which Helen had the feeling she was being punished for something.

14

THE MORNING AFTER, PART FOUR

He gazed into the mountains of foam. He'd told Vince he needed a few minutes alone to think things through. The brightness of the bathroom helped him stay sharp.

What must the Lethcos be feeling? By now, the church-going family had probably lit a candle, joined hands and given thanks. Leo thought of Amy, and how he would feel if she was dying, but was then suddenly thrown a lifeline. The despair, then the exhilaration of hope, followed by despair again… but this was too gut-wrenching to think about. He took a deep breath and sank under the water – a little benign self-harm. After twenty seconds his head was clear of those morbid thoughts.

As he listened to the death of a million tiny bubbles, it occurred to him that he might find strength in numbers. Use the press conference to begin a crowd-funded rescue for Poppy? Once he'd explained to everyone that it had all been a terrible mistake, he could appeal to people's hearts. Lines started coming: 'I have been a fool. I expect no sympathy. But I want to put things right, and everyone can help. Let me tell you about a little girl called Poppy…'

As he visualised this, he realised that the press would simply scoff at a hoaxer trying to distract attention from his selfish antics – they might even think it was another hoax or even a scam. And it certainly wouldn't solve the problem of Dan, Rob and Dave, and Sally. He couldn't very well ask the British public to stump up for a new driving instructor's car and the expansion of a sex toy enterprise. Rob and Dave might at this moment be buying a new vehicle, expecting him to settle the bill. All the possible solutions in his head were pathetic, and he said the word out loud.

'Pathetic!'

As if the exclamation had unclogged a pipeline to a font of wisdom, a solution suddenly burst into being. But just as it was about to crystallise, it vanished like the cake-filled dream of a waking child.

A rap on the door.

'How long are you going to be, Stinkbomb? The press are waiting.'

'Let them wait,' said Leo, and tried to recall his idea, but it had disappeared, leaving only the feeling of brilliance and nothing more.

He left the bathroom wearing the hotel's gown and bath slippers.

'What are those for?' asked Vince, indicating the little bottles in Leo's hand.

'They're for Amy.'

He slipped the shampoo and shower gel into his jacket. Vince tutted in dismay.

'Can't you at least make like a billionaire until after your confession? And on that note, they just rang to say the press are dug in, the cameras are rolling.'

'*Cameras*? Fuck,' said Leo, looking around for his shirt.

'Just local TV, I should think, but news is spreading. The world's third ever billion pound winner? You'll be bigger than Mohamed.'

Leo felt ripples of fear as if his abdomen were a pool and a pebble had dropped into it.

'Get a move on,' said Vince, handing him his shirt. Leo put it aside and picked up his boxer shorts.

'You see, matey, the press...' Vince stopped mid-sentence. 'How long have you had those?'

The boxers were grey and threadbare, and the elastic was no longer elastic. 'Since Helen and I split, undergarments have been a low priority.'

'If anyone needs to win the jackpot, it's you,' said Vince, shaking his head.

Three minutes later, the two men were walking along the corridor to the lifts, planning opening gambits, preparing answers.

One bang on a button and the lift doors parted. Once inside, Vince studied his reflection in a mirror and tried to make a tuft of hair stand at exactly seventy degrees.

They say that in the moments near death your life flashes before you, and although Leo didn't think he was dying, several images came unbidden: Amy in her cot, Helen on their wedding day, his childhood bed with its Spiderman duvet.

'When this is all over, we will look back and throw up,' said Vince, perhaps sensing that Leo was far away. 'Meanwhile… let's *slay this*,' he said, reprising a confidence-boosting mantra from their teenage years. The two men high-fived, chivvying some serotonin into their blood.

A second later, the doors parted to reveal Mr Karaloka waiting with a smile, a bow, and a guiding arm.

'This way, gentlemen.'

Leo was the first to step onto the marble floor of the lobby. He turned and saw something that made him recoil: Alan Lethco, his wife Dawn, and their daughter, Poppy, were standing in a little semi-circle, holding hands and smiling.

'Gave you a fright?' said Alan Lethco, and everyone laughed.

Poppy, who wore a red baseball cap, was sat in a wheelchair, holding up a card the size of a breakfast tray with a message that she had clearly written herself. 'Thank you, Leo. Your (sic) my hero!' and three little kisses. Hearts and stars of every colour adorned the card. Leo simply froze, ashen-faced. Poppy might as well have been aiming a gun.

'She's missing lessons, but the nurses were fine about it, weren't they, Poppy?' said Alan Lethco.

She nodded vigorously. To Leo, Poppy was a truck pulling out of a blind turning. No time to think.

'Thank you, Poppy, that's lovely,' he said, but then realised he hadn't said it, Vince had.

'Yes, it's lovely,' Leo heard himself say.

'You wanted to give Leo a great big hug,' said Dawn to her daughter.

Poppy held out her arms. Leo leaned down, and as he inhaled the hospital smell that wafted from her skin, he ordered himself to find a solution by the time he rose up.

'Poppy, Alan, Dawn,' he said, trying to sound jovial, despite a dry mouth and almost debilitating panic, 'let's talk about the problems and possibilities very soon. I'll chat to the press, then we'll all have a chinwag, okay?'

'Everything all right?' asked Alan Lethco, the skin round his jaw tightening. Leo noticed some flecks of paint on his hair – the marks of his trade.

'Everything's fine.'

Lethco took a step forward and lowered his voice.

'You were quite um… tanked up last night, but we're all still good, aren't we?'

Alan and Dawn's smiles, which had until now been unequivocal, flickered uneasily.

'Yes, definitely,' said Leo. 'Whatever happens, whatever you hear, it's going to work out. *Promise.*' The attempt to reassure only increased the unease.

'Is something the matter?' asked Dawn, her smile now quite forced.

'Of course nothing's the matter,' said Alan, not wanting his wife to bother their benefactor any further.

Vince, say something.

'It's all going to be cool and groovy and wicked.'

Vince had said something. Then he struck a rock star pose with one hand on his hip, the other pointing skywards.

'Rock 'n' roll, baby.'

Poppy laughed at the funny man.

Leo wanted time to stop but it moved relentlessly on as Mr Karaloka, who had been standing off to the side, took a step forward.

'Are you gentlemen ready to proceed to the press conference?'

Leo nodded, and the two gentlemen began what they would later call the longest walk of their lives.

15

HE'S DEFINITELY THE GUY

Donna White had found a quiet corner of the hotel to make her calls. It was at the end of a short corridor leading to a garden where blue hydrangeas where already in bloom.

While waiting for her editor to pick up, she used her free hand to flip open a makeup mirror. She didn't look her best, but there wouldn't be much competition. In the hour since she'd arrived in Byford, she'd guessed that quite a few residents had married their cousins or maybe even their siblings.

She'd seen a few journo types lurking around the hotel. They'd probably arrived days ago because, regardless of Leo Morphetus, Byford was the town fate had chosen. Donna imagined the vox pops: do you think the winner will stay in Byford, madam? Sir, what would *you* do with all that money? Yawn, yawn.

She began checking her kit. These days, hacks have to multitask, and Donna's arm muscles were proof of that. A Canon EOS 5D with spare battery, charger, tripod, and separate boom mic, were all packed into two canvas cases.

She'd been holding on the phone for a full minute before Daisy, Derek's assistant, came back on.

'He wants to talk to you, but he's on another line,' she said, sounding like a child pretending to be grown-up.

'I'll hold.'

During the wait Donna went through her thesis yet again. She was *sure* that this Morphetus guy was the real deal. Her best guess was that this guy had seriously messed up. He'd tried to keep his win a secret, and why wouldn't he? Most big winners do. And he had the added motive of a possibly resentful and greedy ex-wife. But during a boozy celebration with his mates, the young chump just couldn't keep it to himself. On YouTube it looked like the guy was drunk, stoned, and wired to another planet.

A couple more press came dribbling through the main entrance, some with cameras, some trailing flight bags. No big names or familiar faces, which was good news. This story was still a tiddler.

'Putting you through.'

Click.

'Donna?' He sounded as if he'd just yawned.

'Derek.'

'Well?'

'So I can't say he's definitely the guy, but he's *definitely* the guy. I quizzed the mother-in-law. She said he was making this big deposit at the bank, throwing his money around... plus the newsagent says he basically admitted it was him, pockets overflowing with notes, buying everyone champagne at the pub... I mean, he chucked everything he owns in his garden and *set it alight*. And—'

'—Woah. Donna,' interrupted Derek, 'remember Worcester Woman?'

She had an answer prepared.

'Worcester Woman was mad as a sack of cats. We're talking about a responsible dad. I've checked out Facebook, he's sane, his Coffee Guy site screams "normal" – why would he mess around?'

'His fifteen minutes?'

'If he wanted fame he would be shouting from the rooftops, not sleeping till noon. Besides, I'm guessing that this guy wouldn't have the smarts to pull off a con.'

'Is he a retard?'

'People don't use that word any more, Derek.'

'Is he a retard?'

'From his website, I'd say he's a little brighter than you.'

'A smart cookie, then. Is he on a spectrum? People love a spectrum.'

'I'll get a feel of that when I clock him. Oh, I didn't mention the limo. There's dirty great *white* limo outside with a driver who's slept there all night. If this is a hoax, then who's paying the bills?'

She was sounding too breathless, too excited – Derek would think she was carried away. She took a deep breath and leaned against the wall.

'Nothing from Camelot?' asked Derek.

'They never confirm or deny, you know that,' she said, trying her best to sound relaxed.

She could almost hear the cogs in Derek's cautious mind cranking round. While Donna's brain ran on superfast electricity – synapses flashing and snapping into action – you had to wind up Derek's brain with a key. That said, his slow thinking often made him infuriatingly right.

'This is not rolling until we know it's true.'

'You are so last century, Derek, no one cares about the truth anymore.'

'We need more than a crappy town calling it.'

'*Proof,* I know.' She was sounding irritable, dammit. Take it down a notch. 'Oh, it's a shame you didn't send a snapper with me, Derek. The guy is cute. Of course I'll get what I can with the Canon.'

'If he's cute, then don't be afraid to… you know…'

'What?'

'You're single, aren't you? I mean, if he *is* a billionaire, then he's very eligible I should think.'

Donna prided herself at absolutely *never* taking offence. Not showing it, not feeling it. Unlike some of her female colleagues, she knew the difference between being teased, being patronised, and being insulted, and she could handle all three.

'If I pull a billionaire you won't see me for dust, Derek. I'll start a rival network and TrueNewz will be history.'

Derek stifled a laugh. They didn't often laugh at each other's quips, they were too competitive.

As more hacks trundled past reception, Donna wanted to get back to business.

'Derek, my mind is still open – just. But by the end of this little press shindig, I will *know* if this has legs.'

'I have *complete* confidence in you.'

'I don't know if you're just being sarcastic, but the great thing is, I don't care.'

Derek stifled another laugh. She sensed something happening in the foyer – faces were turning in one direction. She followed the line of sight and saw two young men flanked by a hotel employee marching across the foyer.

'Gotta go.'

She picked up her bags and strode toward the conference room as fast as her high heeled ankle boots, two bags of kit, and a strong sense of poise would allow.

16

ARE YOU INCLUDING THE SHOP SIGN?

Hamir and his wife stood side by side. The sun had come out for them, and Hamir was puffed up with pride. Two photographers, shoulder bags and lenses round their necks, snapped away. The couple who sold news were now news.

A young Asian journalist, the only one who'd made any attempt to look smart, talked in low tones into her phone, 'I'm running to the hotel after this – it's all kicking off.'

'Are you including the shop sign?' asked Hamir to one of the photographers.

'Yeah, we're getting that,' said an older snapper wearing a green army jacket with more pockets and flaps than actual jacket. He looked like he'd photographed the last interesting thing on the planet many moons ago.

The newsagent couple had discussed the situation earlier, and although Hamir loved to joke, and loved the limelight even more (or imagined that he might if he ever got any), Gira had very gently persuaded him not to say much to the press. She was afraid that under pressure he might elaborate and embroider, which was very entertaining around the dinner table, but fibbing to the media could be dangerous.

'Thank you very much for coming,' she said to the photographers. 'Now we must go back to work. Thank you again.'

But the smart young Asian, now off the phone, was not going to let the couple go just yet. She followed them into the shop along with two others. The questions began. What made them so sure he'd sold Morphetus the ticket? Do they know the date it was bought? Is there CCTV footage? Did they know anything about a fire outside his house?

Gira's caution had been wise, but her action insufficient. It wasn't long before Hamir was holding forth. His wife would later chide that his nose grew longer with every reply.

17

SHALL WE RUN AWAY?

Leo, Vince, and Mr Karaloka strode along the marble floors towards the conference room.

Having to face a group of strangers to confess an embarrassing secret is the stuff of nightmares, and Leo wondered if that was exactly what this was. If at any point he lost his trousers or spotted his old art teacher, Miss Duggins, he'd know for sure.

The trio stopped by a door.

'There is a problem with the PA. My staff are changing the mics.'

Vince and Leo had a moment together. Leo whispered, 'Shall we run away?'

Vince nodded – it was tempting. Leo pictured himself under a bridge. He would get a woolly hat and grow a big beard and ask the homeless guys if he could doss down with them. People would think he'd gone a little mad, feel sorry for him, their anger would subside, wounds would heal, and then he could quietly creep back into the world.

He peeked through the glass window in the door and saw the gathering of press. About twenty five in all – some smart, some casual, of varying ages. A dapper woman of about thirty, struggling with bags of camera equipment, entered through a rear door, looking flustered. She wore a tailored jacket, skirt and high-heeled ankle boots. *The only women in Byford who dress like that are estate agents*, thought Leo.

Vince leaned in and whispered, 'Your flies are undone,'

Leo glanced down.

'Made you look.' It was a little 'hello' from two young schoolboys, a comforting memento from the past.

'Ready, gentlemen,' said Mr Karaloka, his face perspiring.

Cameras flashed as they went through the door. *Leo, Leo, Leo, over here Leo, congratulations Leo*, and the occasional, *Mr Morphetus*.

The alleged billionaire and his publicist walked as coolly as they could from the side to the rostrum where a podium had been set up in front of a large banner displaying 'Carlton Hotel'.

The two friends hadn't planned exactly what they were going to say but had agreed that there was no point in defending Leo's actions. Vince would soften them up with something jokey, then Leo would do some abject grovelling. Both men knew that whatever they did would soon be digitally available to millions, and would stay with them for the rest of their lives.

Leo stayed to the side of the rostrum and watched as his old mate Vince Campbell, a man of twenty eight, who had been a baker half his working life, walked up the two steps, rubbed his hands together and looked out at his audience. He had always been someone of whom people said, 'He should be famous'. He was *a bit of a legend.* Now was his moment to prove his mettle. Leo willed him to grow into the part.

He tapped the mic a couple of times to gain the attention of one or two press who were still fiddling with bits of kit. The room fell silent. But now it looked like he was having trouble breathing. When he opened his mouth, it emitted something between a rasp and a squeak. Leo had to look down at his shoes. After an agonising few seconds, he heard Vince's words as they found their way through the PA.

'I represent my client, Leo Morphetus,' he said, straightening up as he spoke. 'I'm his publicist.' He sounded clear and true, but Leo's knees weakened. This didn't make sense. If Leo was *not* the billion pound winner, why would he need a publicist? Could things be going wrong so soon?

'Thank you for your patience,' continued Vince. 'Sorry we're late. As I was saying, my name is Vince Campbell, or did I tell you already? Can't remember, who cares? Anyway, sorry to keep you all waiting.'

The repetitions were clumsy. There was uncomfortable fidgeting and a few coughs.

'Leo is not only my client, but also my best chum. A mate going back twenty years. He used to steal Smarties from me. You bastard.'

A few people smiled. He was gaining confidence, but Leo silently urged him to get to the point.

'Now then, we've had a natter and... well, to be honest, he has a confession to make. Now, we've all done it, haven't we? Gone down the boozer, had a few too many, and things have got out of hand. You're all journalists, that's what you do every night, right?'

A few people laughed.

Just then, on the left of the room, bi-folding doors slid across to reveal something Leo found utterly terrifying: Poppy in her wheelchair, and her proud Mum and Dad. Leo knew one thing for sure: they *must not* find out the truth like this. They'd think they'd been the victims of a sick joke, it would be cruel beyond belief.

***

'Yeah, we've all gone to the pub,' said Vince, beginning to look and sound like a seasoned comic, 'got ourselves shit-faced, and started shooting our mouths off, only to wake up the next morning thinking, *what the hell did I say*? It was a pack... of, er...'

Vince stopped because Leo had coughed into his hand and at the same time nodded towards Poppy. After clocking her, Vince let out a little noise that sounded like a laugh, but Leo knew it was just air escaping from lungs that had momentarily lost coordination. Vince cleared his throat.

'Anyone here a fan of alpacas?'

This is a runaway truck, thought Leo.

'I love alpacas. Seriously though, old Leo, um... he really didn't mean to say those things last night.'

While the press seemed willing to laugh along, Leo's eyes darted to Alan Lethco, who shifted his weight from one leg to another.

'I mean, he meant *some* of what he said. But not some of the other stuff. A load of rubbish.'

Poppy looked up at her father – what does he mean? Did he mean those promises or not? Lethco, lips tightening, placed a hand on his daughter's shoulder and then looked at his wife, who had closed her eyes. The woman who'd come as an estate agent raised her hand.

'Donna White, from TrueNewz.'

'Hello, Donna White from TrueNewz,' said Vince, who looked grateful to have been relieved of his death-spiral.

'Two questions,' she said, tapping a notepad with a pen, 'may we speak to Mr Morphetus? And did he win the Globomillions jackpot?'

She looked around the room for support: don't we all want the answers?

Leo was going to have to mobilise the sleepiest of his brain cells. The sleepy coffee guy, the dreamy dude, was wide awake, and in the most profound way.

It was time to climb the rostrum.

'I give you the man himself,' said Vince, with an arm stretched out.

When he arrived at the double mic stand, Leo opened his mouth, not quite knowing what would come out, but knowing that he had to convince twenty-five professional interrogators that he had a billion pounds in the offing.

'My advisor is right. I did have a few too many lagers last night.'

'So you *did* win it?' asked Donna.

'Hold on,' said Leo, quick as a flash. 'Okay, we hired a posh limo and it's waiting outside, you've probably all seen it, and yes, this is a pretty classy hotel, but it's nice to treat oneself now and again, isn't it, Vince?'

'It is indeed, Leo,' said Vince. Leo sensed that an immediate crisis had been averted, or at least delayed. With the exception of Donna, the press seemed to be enjoying the game they had begun. He looked at Poppy and her parents. They were all smiling again now, with relief. Had he stumbled upon a way through this? Could they get by on nudges and winks?

But Donna wasn't going to make it easy for them. She had the look of a woman who knew she was smarter than her peers.

'Are you saying you *didn't* win the jackpot?' asked Donna.

'I'm not saying I didn't,' said Leo.

'And he's not saying he did,' said Vince.

'And it's goodnight from him,' added Leo.

A few of the older journalists chuckled at this. Donna acknowledged the laughter with a smile and a slight nod, and flicked back her biscuit-coloured hair. As she sat down another hand shot up. It belonged to an elderly man who might have stepped out of a 1950s edition of *Philologists' Quarterly*. His trousers came up to his navel.

'Martin Savers from *The Byford Gazette*. The newsagent, Mr Hamir, says he remembers selling you the ticket. Do you recall buying it?'

Vince responded. 'Blimey, you guys *have* been busy. Are there no wars to report on?'

No big laughs this time – perhaps they'd heard that one before.

'But do you recall buying the ticket?' said another voice.

'No.'

True enough, thought Leo; he didn't recall it because he didn't buy it. Maybe he could get right through this without actually lying. The man from the gazette looked like he had been saving something up.

'Mr Morphetus, it's customary for Camelot to release the news when a big prize has been claimed. As yet, they haven't. Can you proffer an explanation?'

Leo coughed into his hand to buy a few seconds.

'You see,' he said, 'the winner has twenty-five days in which to claim.'

'So are you saying you have the winning numbers but haven't yet approached Camelot?'

Vince came back with an answer.

'I don't think he did say, that, no. Next question?'

Donna White, not content with merely putting her hand up, rose to stand.

'Leo, did you ask for no publicity?'

'No,' said Leo, surprised at how easy it was to tell the truth and conceal it at the same time.

'*No*, you didn't ask for no publicity, or *no*, you *did* want no publicity.'

'Does anyone understand what she just said?' asked Vince. This got a big laugh and Donna bowed slightly, as if to take credit for supplying the great feed line, but her dignity had been compromised.

'Gentlemen and ladies,' said Vince, emboldened by the laughter, 'I have advised my client not to make any comment *vis à vis* the billion pound jackpot or the identity of that lucky man or woman who's won it.'

Donna White tapped her tablet and nodded impatiently.

'So, have you called a press conference only to say what amounts to *no comment*?'

'*We* didn't call the conference,' said Leo. 'We were told you guys wanted to speak to us. So, you know…'

'We thought it only polite to say a few words,' said Vince, taking up the slack, 'If you wish to ask about any other topic, such as the twentieth century American novel, then please feel free.' He was enjoying himself. There were smiles all round. Even Donna managed a grin.

'Next question?' said Leo.

'Sarah Harper, Byford News—'

'Since when has there been any *news* in Byford?' said Leo, to a few chuckles, but Ms Harper was not amused.

'Regarding the stretch limo waiting outside,' the journalist continued, 'do you plan to adopt an ostentatious lifestyle?'

Leo threw the question to Vince. '*You* ordered that white monstrosity.'

'My client needed somewhere to crash, being worse for wear and not much good at pulling.'

More laughs. A middle-aged man wearing a dark suit so shiny it looked like it had been waxed, nervously fingered some notes.

'We understand you've already left your old flat,' he said. 'Have you found a new house yet?'

'How about a mansion somewhere?' interjected Sarah Harper.

'That would certainly be nice,' agreed Leo. 'I would want an indoor pool and carpets made from responsibly sourced angora wool.'

Donna White was back on the warpath.

'I spoke to your in-laws. Had you been deliberately keeping it from them and your estranged wife?'

This question gained everyone's attention. All hands went down.

'Keeping *what* from them?' said Leo, feeling that a part of his brain that he'd hardly ever used before was really kicking in now. 'And my wife is not estranged,' he added.

'Wouldn't you have preferred to tell your family rather than have them find out through the media?' asked Donna, standing her ground.

'Have you been stalking his family?' asked Vince.

Donna chuckled, but it sounded forced. 'Your mother-in-law offers her congratulations, by the way.'

'I'm always happy to be congratulated for *anything*,' said Leo, surprising himself with his quick thinking.

'Okay,' said Donna, 'let's just *suppose*, for a moment, that you *have* recently come into a lot of money.' She looked around the room, allowing time for the hypothesis to resonate.

'What would you, *hypothetically*, do with it all?'

'Supposing I were a billionaire?' asked Leo, searching for something that would interest the expectant faces, all of whom must be hoping for a quote. Time conveniently slowed.

I think my Daddy would be a kind king and give his money to the poor.

'Well, *if* I had an enormous fortune…' he said, now feeling more at ease, 'I would try to be a *kind* king. I'd give most of my money to the poor.' A few journalists frowned, some raised their eyebrows, the redhead folded his arms. 'Mind you, that's an easy thing to *say*.'

Suddenly, Alan Lethco took a step forward, and, with a confidence that comes from knowing God is on his side, began to speak.

'He's being too modest. In fact, he's paying for Poppy to go to the states for treatment – travel, accommodation, everything.'

He started clapping, and his wife joined in. Poppy lifted her 'thank you' card and one or two of the journalists decided it would be churlish not to applaud. Leo stole a glance at Vince, who whispered, 'Quit while we're ahead?'

But Leo hadn't finished. 'I would want to give people hope, to help them overcome the doubters, all those people who tell them it can't be done, get back in your box, *you're ten-a-penny*, sod off to the Nat West.'

Vince cleared his throat, but Leo was on a roll.

'And I'd start a foundation so that others could contribute, and make sure the money was spent in the best way possible, not because I know the best way, but I would find the people who do. I would carefully check their worthiness and competence. I know a bit about business and I certainly understand value for money. It's all about due diligence, making sure the—'

A jab in his back confirmed that Vince thought it was time high time to wrap things up.

'Making sure,' repeated Leo, 'that the money works hardest for those in greatest need. And how well…' he lost his thread and Vince seized his chance.

'That's all from us, thanks for coming.' He was about to step down when Donna piped up again.

'Do you expect people to believe you have won all this money without giving us any proof?'

Leo put his hand on one of the microphones.

'Ms White, I don't mean to be rude, but I don't care very much what you believe. In fact, I can say with hand on heart that I would much prefer it if no one had ever thought I'd won anything.' Leo felt a surge of relief as the truth poured out of him. 'I'm only standing here because last night I said some things I shouldn't have, and you all wanted a word. Has everyone *got* that?'

There were no nods, but an acquiescent silence. 'Now, I will pose for photographs, but only because you'll take sneaky ones if I don't.'

'He gets *very* grumpy when he's hung-over,' Vince said, before they stepped down.

After Vince had flattened his hair with the help of water from an Evian bottle, they posed in front of the hotel banner, with Mr Karaloka looking on approvingly. Leo refused to hold aloft the wad of prop bank notes proffered by one of the snappers. Once the press had had enough of this young man standing stiffly with a rigid grin, they began packing up.

The two celebrities made their way to the limousine, itching to speak but afraid to. They approached the car to find Donna White leaning against the rear door, putting the finishing touches to her lipstick.

'Hello, boys,' she said, with a much more casual demeanour than before. Perhaps she was even a little flirtatious, thought Leo.

'No more questions,' said Vince.

She waved away the instruction, and maintained her position between the men and the car door. She presented a business card.

'Leo, if you come to London, I can recommend some fabulous restaurants. I'm a food writer on the side.'

'Yes, well, thanks,' he said, taking the card.

'We could have a lot of fun.' She left a pause long enough for interpretations to reverberate before dropping her lipstick in her bag and turning to walk back to the lobby.

'Get in,' said Vince, opening the door.

Closing the door brought sighs and guffaws of relief. The smoked glass windows made them invisible to the world outside, and there was also a dark screen between them and the driver. They lay back on the purple, faux leather seats, breathing fast and deeply, like when they ran from a cafe without paying, something they'd done once or twice in their teens.

'Do you think she meant—' began Leo, looking at the card.

'You'll never know,' said Vince, taking the card and throwing it on back seat. 'What the fuck,' he said. 'That was *one hell* of an adventure.'

Leo closed his eyes, feeling giddy. 'They *really* think I'm a billionaire.'

'And it's going all around the world, mate. You'll be almost as famous as the guy in Idaho.'

'Ohio.' Leo corrected. 'Cleveland, Ohio. A waiter called Joseph Hernandez, twenty-eight years old, just like us.'

'Yeah, the only difference being, he actually won,' said Vince.

Through the darkened glass, Leo saw that the snappers had not yet finished. The limo was a star in its own right. He waved at them regally, knowing they couldn't see.

Vince opened the minibar, which Driver Dave had restocked. He reached for a small bottle of Moët and unwrapped the top. He handed Leo an OJ.

'Nice speech about the poor,' said Vince. 'Where did that come from?'

Leo didn't reply because he didn't really know. He put his hand on his chest, in an attempt to comfort his heart because it was beating so fast. At this moment he didn't much care about the mayhem that was about to be unleashed, his only concern was the Lethcos. No plan had crystallised, but nascent connections were forming.

The driver's screen came down with a futuristic hum, and Driver Dave turned to face his passengers. Half his hair had been removed with a razor, the other half by nature, and between them they had made his skull look like a ball of wax sprinkled unevenly with pepper. His jowly face implied a voluminous, lorry driver's belly and his white shirt contrasted with the veiny ruddiness of his cheeks.

'Media circus over. Where to nah, gents?' he asked, in broad cockney. He revealed teeth so crooked they looked like they'd been thrown in.

'Anywhere but here,' said Vince.

'Righto.'

The screen went up, and the limo's engine purred into life. Leo turned to face Vince, who was pouring his champagne in and around a plastic flute.

'At least we never actually lied,' he said. Maybe somewhere along the line that fact might be helpful.

'Except by omission,' said Vince. 'One planet-sized omission.'

The car rolled out of the driveway and more champagne landed on Vince's lap. Neil Diamond's version of 'Yesterday' wafted from invisible speakers.

18

REEL THE FUCKER IN

Donald Hughes, sitting behind his desk in the only private office in the bank, brought his computer out of sleep mode. Like everyone else, he had heard that someone in Byford had won nearly a billion pounds, more than all his other clients' wealth put together.

Hughes had given it some thought. He would offer the lucky fool personalised banking, financial advice, investment options, a range of financial products; all the bells and whistles. A nice business lunch would certainly be in order. He imagined a sweet old lady. No, a couple. Naïve, wide-eyed, getting out of the first cab they'd hired in years. They'd be wearing clothes that had last been seen at a sibling's funeral. A whiff of mothballs. They would shake his hand, awed by meeting an actual bank manager, and they would hang on his every word.

Whatever happens, Hughes couldn't let a billion pounds walk out the door – he'd never live it down. *You did what?* But handle this right, and there'd be a bonus at the very least.

Sure, the winner may have requested anonymity. But if a billion quid drops into the account of some piss-poor old bint, it won't take an Einstein to find a way of getting stuck into her.

He banged on the keyboard.

Where is the news when you need it?

He entered: billion, lottery, Byford. Something might have leaked. A few seconds. Some results. *Coffee Guy.* Fuck off, Coffee Guy, I'm not interested in you. Scroll down. *Coffee Guy* scroll, scroll, *Billionaire Barista.* What? Scroll, scroll. *Leo Morphetus...* but he was in here just yesterday!

It is just a rumour, says *The Byford Observer. Not confirmed,* says some other news outlet.

Hughes laughed out loud. The guy wanted a *loan.* Had he won by then? He probably hadn't even checked his ticket, the prat.

He leaned back, resting his head against his clasped hands, taking a deep sigh and swivelling on his chair. He had Byford's first and probably last billionaire in his grasp. *The Coffee Guy.* Bloody hilarious. So random.

He texted Piers: *Hey, I've just bagged the billionaire!*

His heart boomed. 'Let's hope he doesn't bear a grudge,' he said out loud.

19

THE BUCKING BRONCO
OF FAME

Sarah Plank was one of the three women who worked in Camelot's PR department at the Watford headquarters. Her desk was by the window looking over the high street. It was one of those days that made idle threats to rain. Sarah might have found this depressing, but the excitement of the morning had lifted her mood. The press release about a record-breaking winning ticket had done its job: it had nudged all the players in Byford to check their tickets, and the winner was now aware of his good fortune.

Or at least, everyone in the office *assumed* that Leo Morphetus was the winner, although he hadn't yet made an official claim. That's often the case. For whatever reason, winners can wait days or weeks before contacting the office, and it's not as if anyone else had come forward.

'Press office, Sarah Plank speaking,' she said into her cheek receiver.

'This is Philip Pearson, from BBC News.'

Sarah had come to know many journalists, but this name was new to her. Talking to the BBC made her feel important.

'How may I help?'

'You must be very busy,' said Philip Pearson.

'We sure are very busy,' echoed Sarah.

'I'm just doing a piece on the winner. Leo Morphetus. I mean… at least, the guy who people *say* is the winner…'

Sarah was disappointed, because this caller was almost certainly not from BBC news, because he'd know that fishing for the identity of an anonymous winner is utterly futile. Sarah decided not to respond.

'Hello?' said the man.

'Yes?'

'Well… er… *did* he win?'

Sarah found this funny but didn't want the caller to detect amusement in her voice.

'I can't comment on the winner's identity, even if I knew.'

'Er… *don't* you know?'

'No more than you do.'

'*Really*?' said the man.

Sarah could hear music in the background. Was it Neil Diamond?

'I mean, you must have *some* idea,' said the man. 'I mean, you know he's from Byford, right?'

'No. We know the ticket was *bought* in the Byford area, but the winner may just have been visiting.'

'No one visits Byford.'

It was time for Sarah Plank to reel off the usual speech, which she could do using about five breaths.

'Winners' identities are known by only two people in the company or at the *very most* three. Namely, the Regional Winners' Advisor and sometimes the Senior Winners' Adviser, plus the person who takes the first call. Protecting the privacy of winners is of the highest priority. To date, we have never revealed, accidentally or otherwise, the identity of *any* winner who expressed a wish to remain anonymous. And, for obvious reasons, we never comment on *alleged* winners, or rule out anyone as *not* having won.'

Sarah waited for a response but only heard muffled chatting, then a different song by Neil Diamond.

'But you must have *some* clue,' said the caller when he returned.

Sarah would give this clown another thirty seconds of her time.

'Do you have any questions about the wonderful causes the lottery supports in the arts, sport, recreation and heritage?'

There was a pause long enough for Sarah to confirm that the song she could hear was 'Sweet Caroline', and she would no doubt be humming it for the rest of the day.

'Okay. Thanks for your time,' said the man.

'Thank you for calling Camelot, Mr um…?'

'Potter.'

'Actually, it was *Pearson*,' said Sarah, feeling rather pleased with herself.

'We are all as one to the gods.'

***

Vince put his phone down. Leo, who had been listening on speaker, gave him a told-you-so look, and took a swig from a bottle of juice.

'Forgot your own name?'

Vince shrugged.

'Who cares? Winnie the Pooh could say he'd won and they wouldn't comment either way.'

The call confirmed to them both what Leo already knew: as along as no one else proved they'd won, then no one could prove that *he* hadn't. He'd also calculated that the odds on a claim within the next twenty-four hours were slim, and the chances that the winner would want to go public were even slimmer. He had time to plan his next move.

A few wafts of smoke seeped through the inch of an opening on the driver's window; Driver Dave was on a fag break. They had asked him to drive around till he found a quiet residential turning, away from prying eyes.

The limo's interior was like a weird futuristic submarine. Dave had cleaned it since last night, and Leo was relieved that there was no trace of vomit or wee anywhere. Half the light was coming from six small TV screens – showing a cookery programme with the sound muted. The rest of the available light shone from invisible sources under seats and behind the three drinks cabinets, and half the ceiling appeared to be luminous. Having no notion of where light or sound was coming from gave Leo the feeling that the car was smarter than him. The colours were garish, with pink and purple in abundance, and it occurred to him that he'd rarely seen a limo that wasn't full of screaming girls. He could almost smell the perfume.

'How do you feel now, Moonface?' asked Vince, spreading himself across the long seats.

'A bit less panicked,' Leo said, and stretched his arms on the tops of the seats. 'I think we have some time in hand. This isn't going to blow up in our faces in the next few hours.'

'And maybe you feel calm because last night you hit rock bottom, yes?'

'Pretty much.'

'Being in the eye of a storm is better than being at the bottom of the sea. *Anything's* better than the bottom of the sea.'

Vince put his flute into the one of the glass-holders positioned around the limo and Leo took another swig of juice. His phone rang – Helen. He couldn't lie to her – she'd see right through him. He'd have to let the phone ring out. He felt prickly stabs of guilt until the rings finally stopped.

'Sooo,' said Vince, with as much volume and significance as that short word can accommodate, 'The shit has hit the fan. But luckily, the fan was switched off.' He put his brown, calf-length boots up on the drinks table. 'What do we do when some arsehole switches it back on?'

Leo took a moment before answering.

'I don't have a plan,' he said. 'But, you know what? I think there *is* a plan. Any minute I'm going to see what it is.'

Vince snorted at this. The car rocked as Driver Dave heaved his frame back into his seat. The dividing screen came down and he twisted his body to face his passengers.

'All change for you, then, Leo?'

'I suppose so.'

'New house? Villa somewhere?'

'It's not impossible,' he said, and noticed that Vince was absenting himself from the conversation by scrolling through his phone.

Balancing the books was as instinctive to Leo as breathing, so he wanted to broach the subject of what the limo was costing.

'Dave, what about payment for this… are you okay if we settle in a few days?'

Dave was amused.

'Normally it's half up front, but somefin' tells me you're good for it.'

From somewhere in the distance, a phrase came to Leo: *To him that hath, shall be given.*

'Are you getting into Neil Diamond yet?' asked Dave, changing the subject.

'Definitely not,' said Vince, suddenly joining the conversation, but without looking up.

'What about you, Leo?' said Dave, ignoring the intrusion.

Leo listened to a few bars of what was now playing: 'Song Sung Blue'.

'He's growing on me a bit,' he said, to be polite.

His attention was drawn to something outside. A couple of girls were standing there, waving, blowing kisses. One wore faux sportswear, the other was in shiny bright jeggings and an oversized denim shirt.

'Want me to let them in, boys?' said Dave.

Leo and Vince exchanged a look.

Dave said, 'I'd have to check their IDs. If they're eighteen, do what you like. But no drugs. Don't forget, I got free eyes at the back of me 'ead.'

'Three?' said Leo.

'Free invisible eyes.'

Dave pointed to three spots on his bald bonce.

One of the girls lifted her top to reveal a pink bra. The other followed suit to giggles and screams. Then a bra came off and the brunette pressed her breasts against the window. The other girl, a redhead, took pictures.

'What do they want?' asked Leo.

'To fuck the rich and famous, I should think,' said Vince.

'Want to?' He couldn't begrudge his friend that pleasure. 'While I go for a coffee?' he added, quickly.

The brunette now pressed her lips to the window. They looked like the underside of a slug.

'We'll pass,' said Vince to Dave.

The girls began rocking the car and that was enough for Dave. He opened his door and was barely on his feet before the duo ran away, screaming and laughing, phones in hand, ready to post to the web. Leo was reminded of a maxim: a lie can be half way round the world before the truth has got its boots on.

Vince began reading out tweets.

now I wish I'd given Coffee Guy a massive tip #BillionaireBarista.

those two guys are like The Beatles. #ByfordBillionaire,
why doesn't he just admit he won? #BillionaireBarista.

While Vince was getting giddy on the attention, Leo's brain focused on more serious matters. He asked Vince to put down his phone.

'I think there's a way of raising the money.'

Vince took his feet off the table.

'For Poppy? Go on.'

'Remember Mr Cope?'

'History teacher?'

'He said, *if the lie is big enough, everyone will believe it.*'

'He was talking about Joseph Goebbels – not a good role model.'

'Look at Trump. He told people he was a billionaire long before he became one, and he used the lie to borrow and invest.'

Leo leaned closer to Vince and lowered his voice.

'What if... what if... we play this thing?'

'Play?'

'If Enron can do it, and Madoff and Trump and the whole fucking banking system, then why can't we?'

Vince stroked his chin in mock contemplation.

'Because... we're not them. And especially you. You're...'

'A failed entrepreneur, and a drunken idiot.'

'Rather harsh, but I wouldn't argue.'

'I need to stand by my promises of last night – all of them,' said Leo. 'But it will entail keeping up this pretence.'

'For how long?'

'A day, two, maybe three. However long I need.'

Vince's eyes narrowed.

'Leo, do you expect me to believe you'll be doing this just out of the kindness of your heart, to help poor Poppy and those duped souls at The Swan?'

Leo knew there were other reasons but he couldn't articulate them at that moment and didn't want to probe too deeply; there was a decision to be made.

'Maybe there's another reason and, when this is all over, I'll hire a plane and write it in the sky. Well?'

Vince scratched the back of his neck. Then cocked his head this way and that, rubbed his nose, looked out the window, then back. Leo was surprised by his friend's caution, even if it was partly for show. Vince had always swum in the present, seldom concerned by whirlpools ahead. 'Don't be a future-botherer' he would say. Leo needed to dangle a carrot.

'You're an unemployed baker with fuck all to lose. Don't you want to be famous?'

'Oh, don't think I haven't been weighing that in my mind. Better to be known as a rogue then not to be known at all. And so much cleaner than shooting people in a shopping centre.'

Vince exhaled through his nose and tapped his knee. This was uncharacteristic concentration. Leo felt they were both on the crest of something.

'What's the plan?' said Vince.

Neither of them had noticed that a news bulletin had appeared on the screens around them. It was only when they saw two ungainly young men who looked a bit like them – no wait, *it was actually them* – that they asked Dave to turn up the sound. They watched and listened with hearts in their mouths, as if at any moment those fools on TV would say something irrevocably stupid. When it was all over, they looked at each other. Somehow, they'd got away with it.

Dave's screen came down.

'Have you two VIPs decided where you're going next?'

20

A ONE-ARMED BARBER?

Donna White, perched on a soft stool at the Carlton Hotel bar, ordered an espresso – the variety of coffee least likely to be abused by the acne-ridden barman. A few hacks were milling around between Romanesque pillars and verdant palms, making calls and typing on tablets with an enthusiasm factor of six out of ten on Donna's hack-watch scale. There was a nascent rumour going round that the *real* winner was a one-armed barber from West Byford, but there was very little about him on the net, and anyway, a one-armed barber? Still, the more rumours the better, they could distract her rivals.

She watched the footage of the press conference via a local news website. Then she viewed what she'd shot herself, which would soon be available on TrueNewz. All this stuff was going round the world: two young men giving cryptic or silly answers to earnest questions. The way they radiated camaraderie, jostled each other, laughed at each other's quips, their demeanour was irreverent without being cocky.

So far none of the serious news outlets were claiming that Morphetus was the billion pound winner. They were all hedging their bets. The BBC had finally come round to covering the story but very much from a 'the people of Byford believe they know who the winner is' angle. Sky News coverage was tongue-in-cheek, 'it's all a bit of a local mystery'. Not even the tabloids were calling it, all too worried about being hoaxed and looking like fools.

Donna put her tablet down on the bar, asked the barman for a glass of ice water, and gathered her resolve.

It was time to break the story. *Come on, Derek,* she imagined herself saying, *look at the evidence: the mother-in-law, the promise to the sick girl (these guys are not monsters), the limo, the posh hotel, the newsagent guy, the fact that they didn't want publicity, even the fact that they aren't claiming to have won – hoaxers are never coy, you know that. Morphetus is just a naive guy who can't take his drink. Come on, this could be great for us.*

The glass of ice water arrived and Donna was surprised to see a slice of cucumber floating on the surface – someone had no doubt told the barman that 'that's how they do it in London'. She punched in the office number, grumpily reminding herself not to get too excited because the chances of swaying Derek without documentary evidence were small.

21

LET THE GREAT UNWASHED DO OUR LYING FOR US

In the industrial outskirts of Byford, the shiny white limousine was stuck in a bottleneck, standing out like a bride in a post office queue. Warehouse stores selling sofas and fridges loomed like giant pieces of Lego. One, Dreamland Beds, was where Leo had first met his bride-to-be. He had been nineteen, and had never bought anything bigger than a kettle, but he needed a mattress for his first flat-share. Awed by the choice of bedding available, and wondering how he could afford even the cheapest, he felt a tap on his shoulder, and he turned to see a young woman, maybe twenty one or two, with a shy smile that looked a little put-on, as if she wasn't nearly as bashful as she made out.

'Can you help me, kind sir?'

'I don't work here.'

'I didn't *think* you worked here,' said the girl, 'but I need someone to lie on a mattress with me.'

Leo ignored the obvious lewd response that popped into his mind.

'Okay.'

'I'll lie here, would you lie on that side?' said the girl, without the slightest doubt that her request would be granted.

They lay down, staring at the high warehouse ceiling.

'Thank you,' said the girl, demurely, but she wasn't finished with him yet.

'Could you turn over onto your side, like my boyfriend would?'

Leo, disappointed to have the existence of a boyfriend confirmed, did as he was asked. Besides, her unkempt hair and uncool trainers gave her a studenty look, so maybe she was out of his league.

'And could you now turn back again?' she said. 'Only could you do it more roughly? I want to see if I'd wake up.'

Leo was then instructed to twiddle his feet, fidget, and act like he was tossing and turning during a fretful night. When she was satisfied that the mattress was robust enough to absorb all such nocturnal shocks, she went off to find a sales assistant. Leo, intrigued by the spirited young woman, lingered around long enough to say, 'I hope you and your boyfriend enjoy the mattress.'

'Oh, I don't have a boyfriend,' said the girl, waving a wisp of hair from her face. Without glancing back, she walked through the automatic doors and into the car park.

A week later he spied her on the other side of the street. (In truth, he had been keeping an eye out for her). Heart racing, he crossed the road.

'Remember me?'

'Ah. The mattress boy?'

'How's it working out?'

'It's very… stout.'

He had prepared a question days ago.

'If you don't have a boyfriend, why did you make me do all that?' He really wanted to know.

'I wanted you to act as my boyfriend would, *if I had one.*'

He had just seconds to decide whether to let the girl slip away forever, or try to start something.

'Do you *want* a boyfriend?'

'I wouldn't mind.'

It was do or die.

'Would I do?'

She looked him up and down with the same sort of scrutiny she'd given the mattress.

'Do you come with a guarantee?'

And so something started.

He was a garden labourer, she was training to be a radiologist. They did their best to narrow the status gap: he presented himself as a man with Great Expectations, and she wanted to believe it.

After enduring the bottleneck, and rolling through the suburbs with its terraces of Edwardian two-up-two-downs, the limo turned into the high street two hundred metres from Barclays. Leo's plan, which he'd explained at considerable length to Vince, was to pull off a kind of daylight robbery.

As the bank came into view he felt as if something was being syringed into his stomach, and he imagined his adrenal gland was a little imp wielding a needle.

'Stage fright?' said Vince. Leo had been very fidgety, his knees oscillating, his hands tapping.

'Yep.'

Vince smacked Leo on the thigh, as he often did in order to snap him out of whatever world he was in.

'We're Bonnie and Clyde,' he said, cheerily. He'd spent the journey on Twitter and YouTube, and as Leo had predicted, was finding fame a heady drug.

As the limo came to a stop, some shoppers dropped their bags to gawp. Leo recognised a few of them. He tried to interpret the expressions. Respect? Admiration? Curiosity? Perhaps they wanted to stick around in the hope that good fortune was contagious. So many of the theories on behavioural economics that he'd read about were being played out here, chiefly the one about facts being believed according to how appealing they are. The young billionaires were two very attractive facts.

Cars behind started to beep.

'Can't stop here,' said Dave.

'Can you just give it another minute?' asked Leo, noticing that some of the beeping seemed to be celebratory rather than punitive.

'There's cars backing up,' said Dave.

'Come on, let's do this,' said Vince, ruffling his hair in a mirror.

'Let's wait just a second,' said Leo. 'I want everyone in the bank to know that there's a bloody great Lincoln outside.'

And just as he said that, a couple of bank staff, including Ms Banach, appeared at the glass door to see what the fuss was about.

Success.

'Would you open the door for us, Dave?' asked Leo.

'And can you put your jacket and cap on?' added Vince, straightening his collar.

Driver Dave fumbled around for bits of his chauffeur's uniform. He even took time to don his leather gloves. He got out to open a passenger door and the two men exited to applause and cheers. They waved at their audience – it just seemed like the right thing to do. *It's a strange world*, thought Leo, *where great wealth, however randomly acquired, is assumed to be deserved.*

'Drive round the block until we come out, would you, Dave?' said Leo, and Dave saluted.

Less than twelve hours since he'd been told by Ms Banach to (in so many words) 'get lost', she was now inviting him to take a seat, and would he and his friend like a hot drink? The condescending smile of yesterday was now nervously fixed. It was a sign that the enemy had been softened up. The limo had done its job.

'Yes, I'd like a coffee, Ms Banach,' said Vince, after glancing at the name badge.

'And a cookie?' Creature comforts were always important to him.

The two men sat down and Leo went through his instructions once more, at times hardly believing that he'd have the balls to follow this through.

'Now, remember, you're the loose cannon, the nasty cop.'

Vince nodded, but not in a way that meant he understood, just that he would do as he was told. It felt strange to Leo, and perhaps to Vince too, that Leo was the mastermind here.

A minute later a sickly waft of cologne coincided with the arrival of Mr Hughes.

'Leo Morphetus, as I live and breathe! What an unexpected pleasure. May I offer my congrats?'

So the bank manager had seen the news, and probably clocked the Lincoln. Leo played it cool, not smiling, just nodding.

'And are you being looked after?' asked Hughes, rubbing his hands together like a brothel owner welcoming a big-spending client.

'Looked after?'

'Teas, coffees? Not up to the standard you make yourself, of course.'

'You've never tried my coffee,' said Leo, with the attitude of a teenager opening a present that he actually wants, but who is buggered if he's going to look grateful.

'And this is…?' said Hughes, holding out his hand to Vince.

'Vince. Leo's financial advisor,' said Vince, shaking hands, and doing his best to adopt the fearless swagger of Johnny Rotten circa 1977.

'We want a joint account,' added Leo.

'Er… *okay*,' said Mr Hughes, his cheek twitching. 'Do step into my office, we are in the middle of moving things around, so please bear with us.'

Once in the room, Hughes hastily found a chair for Vince. 'First off, here are the forms that Vince needs to fill in so you can both have access to the account, if that's… what you really want.'

The men sat down and Vince took the pen he was offered.

'Strictly speaking,' said Hughes, 'I will need to see your passport and proof of address, Vince. Oh, is that a passport I see before me? Tick!'

Hughes laughed and Leo joined in with minimal enthusiasm. Vince remained sullen, as per his brief.

'Gentlemen, I want to help you in whatever humble way I can,' said Hughes, showing a row of whitened teeth. 'We do have a special banking service for private clients, if you so desireth.'

He slid a leaflet across the desk with his index finger. Leo pretended to read it while he tried to work out what it was about this man that so repelled him. He oozed something. Something cowardly. Leo pictured him in the famous scene from *Spartacus*. There was Hughes, waiting until the moment when the number of men who'd stood up just outnumbered the ones who hadn't, before leaping up with his 'I'm Spartacus'. Hughes was a man who watched the human tide, and never got wet.

'Well… Mr Hughes. To be honest, I'm not very happy about how I've been treated here these last few months,' said Leo. This marked the beginning of serious play. Hughes's teeth retreated behind oddly feminine lips, and his head moved an inch further away.

'I only wish I had been *able* to provide a loan, Leo. It's just that these days we banks have to make sure we're lending responsibly.'

'He is responsible,' said Vince.

Hughes looked as if he was trying to be keep down a burp.

'You see, Mr Hughes—' said Leo.

'—Donald.'

'You see, Donald, my life has… *changed quite a bit…*'

Hughes looked both ways conspiratorially.

'Yes indeed,' he said, 'and I *totally* get that you wanted to keep things hush-hush. You didn't want people to know your little secret, but then…' he sighed, 'well, these things happen. Perfectly understandable, with all the excitement and a drink or five.'

He chuckled. So, thought Leo, there was no doubt at all in this man's mind that Leo had won the lottery. If this was a conventional heist, they were past the bulletproof glass without having fired a shot.

'So, I mean… a loan to tide me over would be handy,' he said.

Hughes's eyeballs flicked back and forth between the two men.

'You see,' Leo said, 'I need time to sort things out.'

'Ah, yes,' said Hughes, 'you haven't met the lottery people?'

'No. In order to get the payment, the big winners have to have a face-to-face meeting.'

No word of a lie.

'Yes, I've done a little research myself on the QT,' said Hughes, proudly. 'No problem whatsoever, I will arrange a loan to bridge the gap.'

This was like stealing candy from a—

'Obviously all loans need approval,' he added.

A setback, but Leo was prepared. He gave Vince the signal for him to pipe up again.

'But we want a loan *now*,' said Vince. 'We want millions and millions. Well a million. Maybe two million.'

Their victim smiled weakly. 'Ha. I don't know if you're joking or not,' he said, now beginning to perspire.

'Come on, lend us a hundred million, you big banker!' said Vince.

Before Hughes could bluster an answer, Leo came to his rescue.

'Obviously we are not *really* asking for a *million*.'

'I should hope not. A million would be... that's simply unthinkable.' He loosened his tie.

'In terms of a loan I was thinking of something less than that.'

'Phew,' said Hughes, with a mock wipe of his brow.

'Can you lend us...' Leo paused for just a few seconds, 'a couple of hundred thousand?'

Hughes's relief was palpable. Having anchored a million in his mind, they had made two hundred thousand seem very reasonable.

'Two hundred thousand? But, um... I would still have to clear it with head office.'

'Nah, mate,' said Vince, 'We need to shake on this right now, Banker-man.'

Nicely played, thought Leo.

'But I would need authorisation. It would only take a day or two,' said Hughes, almost pleading.

Vince was on his feet.

'Come on, mate, he's disrespecting you. We're off to the Nat West.'

Leo stood up.

'I can understand you're in a hurry but—' said Hughes, half rising.

'You see,' said Leo, 'We've got the limo to pay for, and the hotel bill.'

'Plus the Starbursts and Haribos. Let's not waste our time,' said Vince, and he opened the door.

'Please give me a moment,' said Hughes, sitting back down. He picked up a pen and clicked it a couple of times. A bead of sweat began growing on his temple. Just as it began to slide, he caught it with a knuckle.

'Technically, Leo, it is possible for me to transfer the money. It *shouldn't* be, but it is…'

'We don't want any paperwork,' said Vince, as he re-entered.

'No paperwork? I'm not sure about that. You see, I'll need—'

Hughes stopped as Vince swivelled and took a step back towards the door.

'Guys, guys,' said Hughes, waving Vince back, 'Listen. This is completely against protocol, and I could get hauled over the coals for this… but I can help you… if we keep it just between us.'

'Much appreciated, Donald,' said Leo.

'Absolutely,' said Vince. 'We won't forget the dudes who help us.'

But Hughes had something on his mind. Everything stopped as he squeezed his chin with his hand. He looked into Leo's eyes.

'You're not trying to shaft me, are you?'

Leo didn't have time to consider what had prompted this very unbankerly question before Vince answered,

'Of course not, Banker-man.'

Hughes looked like someone at the edge of a deep chasm, wondering if he could jump to the other side.

'Okay. You're great guys, I like you, so let's just shake on this. The money will be in your account in minutes.'

He jumped.

'Can we take half in cash?' asked Vince.

'What?' spluttered Hughes.

'Okay, ten grand?' said Leo.

The banker leaned forward. 'It could draw a lot of attention,' he said, softly. 'Can you be discreet?'

They assured him they could.

Six minutes later, the limo pulled up by the bank. The two wealthy young men paused for some selfies, and a moment later they were reclining on the shiny seats. The victory was not fist-pumping or high-fiving, but contemplative.

Leo looked out onto the high street as it went by. He'd often told himself that if he was ever a major employer, he would throw his staff in at the deep end and expect them to swim. And that's exactly what he had just done himself. Necessity, as well as being the mother of invention, is the best teacher. He had acquired a two hundred thousand pounds unsecured load without actually lying. There was absolutely nothing to indicate that the money had been fraudulently obtained. Had they even committed a fraud? That would be a fascinating legal issue. It had been a long time since he'd felt that he was good at anything besides frothing cappuccinos.

Suddenly, Vince sprang out of his reclining position and leaned toward the front of the car. He'd just received a text.

'That chap I know in South Molten street has offered us a free personal shopping service. What do you think?'

Leo shook his head.

'I need to see the people I made promises to. Starting with Poppy. Once I've done that, I make a confession and then... I don't know, we disappear.'

'Leo, you owe me a little fun.' Vince was flicking through the wads of cash. 'Come on, man! I've stuck by you. We could go to London and spend some of this stuff. Ride the bucking bronco of fame. Do your virtuous thing, then let's have our cakes and ale. Please, Leo?'

Leo took a moment to think this through. He did owe Vince. A few hours ago Vince thought he was best friends with a billionaire, now he's unemployed, with an uncertain future.

Besides, maybe being seen arsing about in London would do them good when things go tits up: they'd be harmless pranksters, lads up for a good time, rather than cloak-and-dagger villains. Leo could settle his debts, have a night of fun, and then make a statement to the press in the morning.

'Can I use your laptop, Vince?'

They took a detour to Vince's home where they gathered up what they needed for a mobile office, some overnight essentials, and some books. Ten minutes later they were on the road again, passing a sign: London, 67 miles.

22

LOOKING UP TO MONEY

To: Leo@coffeeguybyford.co.uk
From: Helen1sterling22@yahoo.co.uk
Re: Congrats!

My Dear Leo,
First off, con-bloody-gratu-bloody-lations on your win!
WOW! Mr Famous, too! (You look cool on TV btw, and you
played the press brilliantly – very much the organ grinder
to those monkeys).

Of course, I am eating a massive slice of humble pie.
The number of times I asked you to stop wasting your
money on those tickets. I am very, happy. And I'm even
happier that Mum and Dad will simply *have* to respect you
now, however much they don't want to – they can't help
looking up to money.

You will now be able to start whatever business you
like and be the wonderful, benign, caring boss you have
always wanted to be. Or maybe you will lead some charity?
(*Good kind king?* Where did *that* come from???)

I know you're angry. For you to damage a car, then
start a fight... that is so unlike the Leo I know.

They say a relationship isn't over till one person starts
seeing someone else. I know that is hard.

I am upset that you didn't tell me the good news.
Sorry, can't help that. I don't want to make a big deal of it,
and I guess that is a sign that I too, have not 'moved on'.
Mind you, if you'd told me I would have probably fainted...
(or maybe I would have thought it was a big joke? Another
'wedding in Vegas' moment?)

I think my last words to you were 'I don't need your money' or something and, Leo, that's still true.

Radiology pays perfectly well, and as you know my dear parents paid off a chunk of the mortgage when we split.

I don't need to ask you to provide for Amy because I know you'll do that. Maybe we could discuss when and how – maybe some sort of trust fund (whatever that is) so she can access it when she's twenty-one. Anyway, I'm sure you'll do the right thing. (Perhaps she and we could have a trip to Disneyland?)

You deserve every bit of happiness that comes your way.

Love always,
Helenx

To: Helensterling22@yahoo.co.uk
From: Leo@coffeeguybyford.co.uk
Re: Congrats!

Dear Helen,
Thanks for your email. I was touched. Yes, things do seem to be on the up for the coffee guy. Not before time. Sorry I haven't been in contact. I don't know, things are very weird at the moment.

Of course I will always do my best for Amy, as I think I've always tried to do.

But I don't want kids at school teasing her, and this media circus is bad enough without bringing on more change. So, at least for the moment, can it just be business as usual for as long as possible?

Look, I'm worried, Helen.

Please hear me out. I did start the fight with Tony (well, it ended up not really being a fight, more a flattening) but he threatened to take you and Amy to live in Spain, and I'm afraid I lost it. I know you will just dismiss this as jealousy, but... I think I know an industrial grade wanker when I see one. And giving Amy a solid gold bracelet? What next, a pony and trap?

And what about the comb-over? WTF, I thought you had more style.

All love,

Leo x

To: Leo@coffeeguybyford.co.uk
From: Helensterling22@yahoo.co.uk

Dear Leo,

Mm... well, I'm obviously not going to accept your description of Tony (and IMHO it's not a comb-over). He has been extremely kind and thoughtful. A gold bracelet isn't a big deal for him, since it's his stock-in-trade. I have spoken to him about 'the fight' and he doesn't remember any mention of Spain, and he hasn't talked to me about it, other than to say we could visit his villa. So put your mind at ease.

Amy. Of course, that's fine. Business as usual. Luckily, she's not very materialistic, the sweetheart. (Although she has dropped subtle hints about a scooter.)

Love Helen xx

23

A WEIGHT OFF

While Leo set up his mobile office on the back seats, Vince began fielding enquires, which were forwarded from the hotel, or came via The Coffee Guy website. Leo's instructions were clear: he would do no interviews or make any comments, and he would not post anything at all on social media – in fact, Leo had decided to keep his feet on the ground by not engaging with any media at all. Zero communication would feed the notion that he had ticked the lottery's 'no publicity' box.

As soon as he'd established an internet connection, he logged on to his account.

'Checking account now,' he said, like an astronaut flicking a vital switch. Vince stopped to watch. Leo pressed the mousepad and his details appeared. His eyes danced nervously around the screen until they landed on a string of zeros which gave him a throb of anxiety: point of no return. He increasingly found that, instead of words, his mind filled up with images. He saw himself jumping out of an airplane.

'Well?' said Vince.

A nod. The money was there. Vince went back to his phone.

Leo had serious business to attend to. He selected Lethco in his contacts. Even though he was about to give rather than take, he still felt like a crook, stepping into the home of a good-hearted, God-fearing family.

'Leo?'

'Hi, Alan.'

'Leo!' said Lethco, with his West Country twang. 'Wait till you hear this. I checked the winning numbers, and the first four are just *one day* from being Poppy's birthday.'

Leo had to proffer a 'Wow', but he felt phony.

'What are the odds? A zillion to one?' Lethco was convinced that nothing *just happens*, everything is for a purpose. Leo wanted to ask why the numbers weren't *exactly* the same as Poppy's birthday – had God made a mistake? But instead he found himself gently agreeing with everything.

After taking down Lethco's bank details, he broached the subject of the amount.

'I seem to remember, Alan, that you needed to raise a hundred thousand on top of what you have already, am I right?'

There was a pause, which told Leo what he most feared: that it wasn't enough.

'That is so, so generous, Leo. You are a great man!'

'It's *not* generous and I'm not great.' Leo couldn't bear the idea of being adulated for this.

'Leo, if anything's left over, we'll donate it to the other families in our support group. They are all great people, it would be wonderful to help them too.'

Even though the deceit was benign, Leo couldn't stand it any longer. He quickly said goodbye and hung up. Vince seemed about to say something, but whatever it was he decided to leave it in his head.

'All sorted, Vince.'

'Fabulous. Saving a life has surely earned us a little fun. A *lot* of fun. Where do you fancy staying tonight?'

'A cheap hotel?' said Leo.

'That's going to look fucking weird.'

'An expensive one, then. Or we could sleep in here.'

'So much money, and so little style,' said Vince, and huffed contemptuously. 'We're going to have the night of our lives.'

Leo had always envied Vince's ability to enjoy himself even when things seemed to be going badly wrong. Invincible Vince.

He looked at his to-do list of people who needed paying. After some calculations, he determined that he'd need forty thousand to make good his promises. His speech about giving money to the poor would work in his favour – he would say he was being careful, with so many good causes to consider. Whatever was left over, he would give to a few local charities, and top of the list was the hospice that had looked after his mother so well in her last months. He would keep the calls brief, as he had done with Lethco. The less time, the less chance of being found out.

He caught his reflection on the lid of the chrome ice bucket. Looking at his face, he wondered what had changed. He certainly felt different. He reckoned his heart was beating a good fifteen per cent faster and he hadn't felt tired since he woke up at the Carlton Hotel.

Was he a criminal, a hero, or just a chancer?

From time to time, Leo had set up his trike at the visiting funfair (for a price) and he sometimes wondered why even grown-ups chose the teacup ride when they could go on the dodgems. He'd never considered that he was on the teacup ride himself. Well, not any more.

24

MY SPIRITUAL HOME

After an hour at Liberty's, Vince dragged Leo to South Molton Street and the surrounding turnings, eschewing the main thoroughfares of Regent and Oxford Streets which, according to Vince, only existed 'to keep the riff raff away from the good stuff'. Leo grew weary of the expedition even sooner than he'd imagined. Traipsing around with armfuls of clothes was tedious, but worse was the constant decision-making. Would this go with that?

'It's like asking a vegan how he likes his steak,' he said after being asked a tricky question about stripes. And he was constantly appalled by the price tags; 'We're being shafted'. He kept a careful tally on the outgoings, but even with the agreed budget of nine thousand pounds, at the rate Vince was spending, they'd be through it in no time. One Marc Jacobs jacket alone cost £549, and it didn't even have a warm lining.

News of the Byford Billionaire had gone national and the boys reckoned that at least one in ten people recognised them. Selfies were posed for, and the occasional peck on the cheek was bestowed by a girl or woman, and sometimes more than that: a gentle hand would find its way onto Leo's buttock, and a breast would press up against his side. Vince warned him that, when posing, both his hands should be clearly visible, 'especially if the girl or boy is sub-legal. Invisible fingers could be up holes or in cracks. Don't leave yourself exposed to the imagination of scoundrels.' So in every shot he displayed both fists giving the thumbs-up. He felt like a wanker, but as Vince said, 'not one who's visibly abusing.'

Some of the youngsters wanted autographs, their eyes wide with admiration. Leo frequently explained, 'You think I've won a billion pounds, but the lottery is just luck, I'm not a role model. Invent a thing and change the world,' at which point Vince would yank him over to the next boutique. (Sadly for Vince, his friend Pablo, who was going to be their personal shopper, had had a last minute booking from a High Net Worth Individual, and couldn't turn him down).

What they both began to find irksome was the constant joshing: the women of all ages joked about being available for sex or marriage, and the men tended to offer services – if you ever need a plumber/window-cleaner/interior designer/ drainage engineer. Jokes rarely improve with repetition. All the while, the two pretenders kept up the game of never explicitly claiming they had won anything. As Leo said, the world would do their lying for them.

After two hours, he concluded that his job of making coffee was easy compared to shopping. Even so, he couldn't return to Byford without a scooter for Amy (Hamleys, Regent Street) and a scent for Helen (Chanel, Bond Street). Back in the limo, he dumped his purchases, found a place that wasn't piled with bags, and closed his eyes.

Exhausted as he was, he couldn't sleep straight away. Questions circulated in his head. How was he managing to pull off a hoax of this scale when only yesterday he'd thought himself a fool? Why can't families get life-saving treatment for their children? When the deeper questions weren't circulating, he would rehearse his confession. There were so many ways he could go: remorseful, humorous, cocky, defensive... what was the right combination? And who was the most important audience? Helen? Amy? The in-laws? Even Tony?

He felt Vince shaking him awake. It was ten o'clock. By eleven, after a friendly hotel had let them shower and change, they were cruising the streets.

Leo had been to London before – a wedding, a trip to see *Guys and Dolls* with his mother, a visit to the zoo when Amy turned five, and one adolescent excursion to a strip joint with Vince, where they managed to spend every penny they had without seeing so much as a nipple. (They were told that the girls don't usually turn up until after lunch).

He looked out through the tinted windows as cool young urbanites mingled with tourists. The limo didn't attract many second looks: anyone who stared was probably from Byford.

He rested his feet on the coffee table, and turned to admire his brand new shiny black Chelsea boots, hoping they would be comfier than they looked. His baggy trousers had a pattern on them, little blue and grey squares. Trousers should not have patterns, but Vince had insisted this pair had the 'look-twice factor'.

'I ought to have been born in Soho,' said Vince, who had come to sit next to him, plonking his fancy Jimmy Choo Argyles next to Leo's boots. 'It's my spiritual home. My Mecca. Sin, money, booze, sleaze, lunatics, criminals, the *demi-monde*. Some people are born in the wrong body, I was born in the wrong town.'

'Everyone in Byford was born in the wrong town,' said Leo, turning his attention back to the city outside.

'It's a tragedy that we must experience this wondrous melting pot to the soundtrack of an aging easy-listening Yankee.' The tune now playing was Neil Diamond's 'The Art of Love'. Vince had raised his voice to make this remark, but the screen was up so Driver Dave's hairless scalp did not respond.

A homeless man began shouting – something inaudible. Leo sympathised, the car was indeed a crude display of excess.

Dave's screen came down.

"Ere we are, boys. I fink. We are definitely in Mayfair and it's the right street.'

'There's no sign,' said Leo.

'Exclusive clubs don't need *signs*,' said Vince. 'Their mission is to deter as well as attract.'

On the pavement, Vince adjusted his clothes and then spent a little while fiddling with Leo's, who felt like a child being groomed by an over-anxious mother.

He instructed Dave to wait in the car or drive around, whichever he preferred. He added that he should listen to Neil Diamond at full volume to help get it out of his system. Dave responded with his middle finger.

And so the two young dandies descended some steps and Vince easily talked them in to the ironically named Cloud Club. It was unlike any nightspot Leo had been to before and yet it was like every one he'd been too before. The bar was stocked with more spirits than he'd had seen in his life. And instead of reeking of stale beer and BO, it smelled of delicate perfume and flowers, with a cool breeze from unseen air conditioners. To process the surroundings, he needed to find words he hardly every used: opulent, salubrious. The lighting was subdued, concealed. The walls were mostly black and looked soft to the touch. Hardly anyone was drinking out of bottles – it was all proper glasses, and mostly cocktail, ones containing colourful liquids, straws, and pieces of precariously balanced fruit.

Despite these differences, the main ingredients were in Mayfair as in Byford: music, sex and alcohol.

After a tour of the place, he found a corner snug in the VIP lounge that Vince had appropriated, and nursed his vodka-martini-cocktail-straight-up-with-a-twist. Vince had assured him it was *the* choice of the elite. Leo decided to make it last the whole evening. He wasn't going to give up drink altogether, but he would definitely never get drunk again.

He sat back on the leather bench and absorbed his surroundings. He would leave Vince to do all the chatting, the laughing, the patting people on backs. He had always been the showman, even when they were teens and managed to blag their way into proper clubs. Leo had tried to be silent and mysterious, but really he was just shy and didn't like having to repeat his less-than-witty remarks three times. Now he watched his friend work the room as if he were hosting a party in his kitchen. From time to time, Vince would stroll over with a stylish looking man or inordinately glamorous woman. The women offered Leo both cheeks for a kiss and the men wanted hugging, frequently planting a kiss at the same time. The feel of a man's stubbly chin on his face was new to Leo and he wondered how anyone could like it. Even here, the selfies didn't stop: instant proof of happiness. They only had to check their phones to see that they were enjoying themselves.

In the moments when he was left alone, his thoughts turned to Helen. As the music boomed and the lights illuminated girls in figure-hugging dresses and miniskirts, he imagined himself in his old kitchen, a beer in hand, Helen in her jeans and T-shirt. He tried to picture her face as he told her that the whole thing was a lie. He couldn't expect her to join in this crazy game – she was too tidy, too neat, and had too much sense. She would say 'You have to stop this *now*'. She'd be thinking of Amy, and how this might affect her. She would ask him to make a public apology. His fifteen minutes of fame would be like an embarrassing tattoo he could never wash off. He poked the twist of lemon in his martini with his finger, enjoying the way it twirled round and made patterns with the light.

A pleasanter subject of contemplation was Tony. The guy who'd laughed at Leo's pathetic pile of belongings in the garden. A man who clearly set so much store by status, with his golden bracelet and red Masda, how would his alpha veins be processing all this? Very badly, hoped Leo.

A girl with a shiny silver dress made of what appeared to be fish scales loomed from nowhere and began swaying to the music. He could have reached out and stroked the shimmering material. The silver scales made her look like a mermaid, and Leo guessed that that was no accident. They locked eyes as she slowly gyrated. Her hair was platinum blonde and ultra-straight – a wig?

The girl began pouting and licking her lips suggestively and Leo felt an intense urge to look away, but where? The floor? The ceiling? The only option seemed to be her body.

How long was it appropriate to stare at which bits? Without warning, the young woman sat on his lap, causing a buckle in his penis, a discomfort that soon turned to mild pain as she writhed around and tousled his hair. He introduced himself by shouting his name, but he couldn't catch hers – something Russian. It seemed the girl had virtually no English. After she had played with his hair and attempted to kiss him, he persuaded her to leave by gently removing her arm from round his neck and pressing her back. The beautiful sea creature shimmered away with all the poise she could muster.

Leo's thoughts turned back to his situation. For the umpteenth time, he went through the possibility of being charged with fraud. He had read enough about such cases to know that after a successful prosecution he could get eight years inside. He was relying on the fact that banks hate drawing attention to fraud: it exposes their vulnerability, and they are even more reluctant to press charges if the crime involves one of their own. Mr Hughes had lent them money without authority, which was tantamount to embezzlement. And they had not lied about their circumstances, and there was nothing to prove that he did, no documents, no signatures. At some point, motivation would be raised. He had taken the money mainly to save a life. He needed to be careful about how much he blew on Vince's hedonistic excesses.

At this moment the excessive hedonist was downing shorts with a group of young people who looked like they'd stepped out of an enhanced reality soap. Throwing their heads back with laughter, punching each other playfully, it all looked too much like a competition. Leo would rather be cuddled up on a sofa, with Amy playing on the floor and Helen…

He was deep in reverie when he felt the presence of a young woman sidling up along the bench. They had been introduced about half an hour ago, but by that time he'd stopped trying to remember names.

'You've forgotten my name, haven't you, Leo?' shouted the girl, so close that he felt a warm lip on his earlobe.

'Monique?' he shouted, his memory having delivered in the nick of time.

'It's *Moon*ique.'

'*Moon*ique?'

'It's Unique.'

Even through the medium of shouted-words-in-earholes, he got the little joke, which he showed with a nod and smile.

'You um… French?'

'Dutch. How-do-you-do again.'

They shook hands with mock formality, and Vince loomed into his eye-line. He proffered some visual advice about an activity he could try later with Moonique.

After a few pleasantries, Moonique shouted, 'Do you have a girlfriend?'

The way she looked at him left no doubt that this wasn't an idle inquiry, but he didn't want to answer. Instead, he inclined his head in a way he hoped would say, 'it's complicated'.

Her eyes were green, but she had swarthy, Italianate skin. The effect was not just attractive, but fascinating, beguiling, even a little scary. He couldn't imagine ever wanting to look away from them.

And then, without knowing why, he said, 'I have separated with someone… my wife, the mother of my child.'

Why on earth had he said this? What relevance did it have?

'Are you heartbroken?'

He shrugged and reached for his glass.

'I suppose I am.'

'Your heart is broken. And I'm broke. What do you say? Want to come back with me?'

At first he was confused, and asked her to repeat what she'd said, but she didn't seem to hear him above the music.

Heartbroken, broke. Was this to be some kind of transaction?

'Come on,' said Moonique, standing up.

'I need to have a word with my friend,' shouted Leo.

'I'll be in a car outside.'

He found Vince in a corridor talking to a couple of wispy girls. Here, conversation at normal volume was possible.

'Moonique has asked me back,' he said, once he'd managed to pull Vince to one side.

'Text me her address and I'll pick you up tomorrow.' Vince wanted to get back to his new acquaintances.

'But listen, I think she wants money.'

'So?'

'But… it's crossing a line.'

Vince responded with a dumb face from his considerable repertoire. Then: 'Leo, but for the Universe granting you this brief sojourn in the sunny uplands of milk-and-honeyville, you would be riding your little tricycle around rainy Byford until arthritis addled your knees or you died of boredom – and you *can* die of boredom – it's the most dangerous condition known to young men.'

'This from the bloke who worked in an all-night bakery.'

'I was logging the oven temperatures but I was looking at the stars. Go on, enjoy.'

Like many a man who tells himself he was seeking advice when what he really wanted was absolution, Leo did what he would have done anyway. He strolled out of the nightclub, up the steps, and into the back of a shiny black Mercedes.

25

IT'S GOING TO BE AWKWARD

Harriet opened the oven to check the fish pie. It was bubbling but hadn't started to brown. Like their daughter, the Sterlings had a spotless kitchen, but theirs was cleaned by a Latvian called Biruta who came twice a week and made everything smell of Alpine disinfectant.

Frank, balding, mid-sixties, a too-small shirt stretched over a pregnant belly exposing the odd chink of blubber between buttons, poured two glasses of white wine.

'It's buyer's choice at the new Waitrose.'

Harriet took the glass.

'Fruity,' she said, after a tentative sip.

'But not sweet,' added Frank.

He took his usual place at the table, and looked over some newspapers.

'We'll have to invite him round for dinner.'

'That's going to be awkward, isn't it?' said Harriet.

'Oh, I don't know. I don't think he realises I never rated him.'

'He knows *I* didn't. Besides, I'm sure he has bigger fish to fry than the likes of you and me.'

Frank pondered this information. The young lad from East Byford would soon have a full diary, and lots of voices in his ears. He'd be harried by do-gooders, concerned liberals, all trying to lure the kind-hearted naïf to their cause. When he wasn't being pursued by the worthy, he'd be up to his eyes in totty. If he and Harriet were going to have any influence at all, they would have to move quickly.

'How shall I play him?' he asked his wife's back. 'I can't exactly say, 'Leo, now that you're a *billionaire* we've decided you can come to dinner to discuss how you can help me get re-elected.'

As Harriet began laying the table, he lifted the newspapers out of her way.

'So make it all about the people of Byford,' she said. 'You know; the organisations, the charities, what people need, you have the contacts. Together, you can channel his bounty to the right people.'

'And make sure I'm there to be photographed when he hands over the cheques?'

'That seems only fair,' said Harriet, smiling.

He had the story in his head: *Frank Sterling, the Chairman of Byford Council, father-in-law of the billionaire barista, is helping the East Byford boy put his home town first, working night and day to make sure that the money will benefit the families and pensioners of Byford.* Frank had a quip ready: *I'm an opportunist. Any opportunity to help Byford, I take.*

'Should we invite Helen, too?' he asked. His wife was good at these awkward calls.

'I think that would be very odd. She's dating a new chap now. She hasn't told me much, but it's looking quite hopeful.'

Frank held his wine glass up to the light. He gained no insight from doing this, it was just a habit.

'If she had any sense, she'd ditch the new chap and go back to Leo.' He was careful to add a chuckle so that if his wife demurred, he could say he was only joking. But Harriet did not demur. After wiping her hands she sat down at the table.

'So what do I say to him?' he asked, placing a hand on her knee.

'Oh, you know,' she said, 'something friendly but casual: "Congratulations, let's see how we can help make this work for Byford." Something like that?'

Frank gave her knee a double pat of gratitude – she always knew the right approach.

'This could make a difference. A billionaire on our side, spending on good works. Hey, what's better than a billionaire coming to dinner?'

'What?'

'A *dumb* billionaire coming to dinner.' He laughed at his own joke. Things were taking a turn for the better. The timer on the oven pinged and Harriet got up to remove the pie.

26

WANT TO HAVE A BATH TOGETHER?

The black Mercedes arrived at its destination a few minutes after passing Fenchurch Street Station. Moonique's apartment was on the sixth floor of a 70s-built block with an expensively dressed concierge. Leo checked him for signs of I-know-what-you're-here-for, but found none.

Moonique showed him into the kitchen-sitting room and he was reminded of the Carlton Hotel. Nothing about the pictures, furniture or ornaments (all thoroughly modern) told him anything about the owner other than... no, he couldn't think of anything. While Moonique opened a bottle of champagne, he sat down on one of the two cream sofas, and glanced at the magazines on the coffee table: *Vanity Fair*, *The Economist*, *Esquire*. He surmised these were for clients to read or simply to be flattered by.

In the car he had learnt that Moonique was twenty-six, an aspiring model and TV presenter. She had a biology degree and her dream job would be presenting a wildlife show, but it was so hard to get in through the door. And maybe her past would follow her – 'It only takes one guy'. The conversation had been easy and, as far as Leo could tell, she wasn't putting on an act.

'What do you think of the apartment?' she asked, holding two full flutes.

'It's all very modern.'

'I don't even live here. We girls rent it.'

That explained the impersonal feel of the room. This was a business, not a home. Moonique produced a photo on her phone of a fairly drab block of flats.

'That's where I live. Miles away. Want to have a bath together?' she said, without leaving a beat. She took Leo's hand, led him to a pink and white bedroom, and began running a bath in the en suite.

Leo sat down on a four-poster bed, which was adorned with satin sheets and heart-shaped pillows. She had warned him it was tacky. As he pulled off a sock, he considered bailing. It had seemed like an exciting idea in the club, to go on a little adventure with this beautiful young woman, but now the reality of what was about to happen became sticky and difficult. Moonique still felt like a stranger to him, one who controlled events, making him feel more like a patient than a lover. But leaving now would not be a case of hurt feelings, but of lost income. She had the apartment to pay for, plus the champagne, not to mention lost opportunity costs. She'd be out-of-pocket, and a fellow sole trader, he could feel the pain of her financial loss.

A few minutes later he was resting his chin on his knees, surrounded by bubbles, and candles that smelt of ice cream. Emile Sande came from a bluetooth speaker – a pleasing change from Neil Diamond.

Moonique appeared wearing a short, kimono-style dressing gown and leant against the doorframe.

'You are a very *serious* man.'

'Yeah, well, I'm… I've got a lot on my mind.'

She let the dressing gown fall to the floor and stepped into the bath. Leo faced the familiar problem of not knowing where to look and for how long.

'I suppose this has been a rollercoaster ride for you?' she said, after wetting her face.

'No, a rollercoaster has tracks, so you know where you're going.'

The rest of the communication was almost entirely non-verbal: flicking bubbles, playing footsie, squirting water out of mouths and creating little waterfalls. In the laughter that ensued there were moments when Leo forgot about the transaction. At one point, he grabbed her hand and held on to it, and they looked into each other's eyes for all the world like real, non-fee-paying lovers. Moonique chose that moment to reveal her real name.

'It's actually Monica. Moonique is a moniker,' said Monica.

'Very good,' said Leo, relieved that he just about knew what a moniker was.

***

He lay on the four-poster while Monica touched his nipples with her fingertips, examining them as if she hadn't seen a man's chest before. A ripple went through Leo's whole torso and it made him giggle. It was apparent that whatever happened between them was going to be slow rather than feverish. *You can't expect a paid service provider to be overwhelmed by lust*, thought Leo, and for his part, he still felt business and sexual pleasure to be an awkward combination.

'I don't know about this,' he said, finally wanting to get his feelings out in the open.

'What?' Monica's hand, which had been gliding over his chest, abruptly halted.

'I've not done this before. I mean obviously sex, yes, but…'

He hoped Monica's experience would mean she'd have a ready-made response, but before she could answer he realised something.

'Oh, that sounds like a line, doesn't it? Well, I assure you it's true in my case.'

'I believe you. Apart from anything, you haven't been able to afford it. Well, not a classy broad like me at least.'

Leo felt a playful nudge, then Monica turned so that both of them were looking at the ceiling.

'Don't you want to?'

'No, I do. I mean, don't worry, I will pay you.'

'Normally I ask for money up front, but I thought you would probably be good for it.'

Leo smiled to himself – it was almost the exact phrase Driver Dave had used.

'Why did you come back with me?'

'I'm not sure exactly. I mean… I couldn't hear a word you were saying in the club, for a start.'

'So you just wanted to hear me speak?'

'I don't know.'

And that was true.

'Well? Why *do* people go to bed together?'

'You're the expert,' said Leo.

Monica laughed. 'Let's make a list.'

Leo kicked things off with the obvious.

'They have sex because they're horny. That's *my* reason, by the way.'

'No, Leo. It's to help you forget your ex. You're heartbroken.'

He felt like a piece of paper that had just been read, processed and spiked.

'Well… maybe some of that,' he said. He certainly had felt quite alone in the club and had been missing Helen.

Monica raised one hand in the air, performing a little ballet with her fingers as they both watched. 'I once went to bed with an Azande tribal chief just because I really wanted to know what he'd be like. In fact, curiosity is one of the reasons I went into this business. I'm fascinated by what I discover. Other reasons people have sex, Leo?'

'Okay. Because… they're a long way from home and can't afford a taxi. A girl once admitted she used me as a place to doss, and a shag was basically my tip.'

'I have another one. Because they want a good anecdote.'

'Really?'

'Oh, sure. I mean, if you've slept with George Clooney that's every dinner party conversation sorted for life.'

'Or Rolf Harris.'

'Ha! A different kind of conversation.'

Leo thought of asking if he would be an anecdote one day but felt it might come across as needy.

'How about this, Monica, you *have* to have sex because you've got a condom that's nearing its sell-by date.'

This produced a throaty laugh. 'Yes, you phone a really environmentally aware girlfriend, and say, help me out.'

'We must have sex by midnight!'

She shifted to her side and rested her head on her hand.

'How about… because… they want intimacy, they want affection. Maybe even love, or an imitation of it?'

Leo wondered about that. Not many of his encounters before Helen had had much to do with intimacy, love or affection.

'Dear Leo, do you know the pleasure of sex without the burden of love?'

He took a moment to digest this. He understood that the love he felt for Helen had sometimes been a burden, even a passion-killer, because he cared too much. For the same reason, he had previously enjoyed sex with girls he hadn't much liked more than with those he did.

'Yes, I have.'

'But not for a while?'

'I suppose not.'

Did the prospect of paying Monica absolve him of responsibility to give her pleasure, so he could concentrate on his own?

She slid her leg onto his, and the sheet began to fall away to reveal her coffee-coloured body in small, enticing increments. The music had stopped, and now all he could hear was breath, and the slide of skin on skin. Her lips gently touched his cheek, and her hand inched its way slowly down from his chest.

27

THE PLUCK OF A DOUBLE BASS

Helen was bumped out of sleep by Tony tossing and turning. This was only the third time he had stayed the night. (Amy was on a sleepover). The mattress, though the most stable Helen could afford, did not fulfil the manufacturer's promise to absorb the bumps and knocks of the restive.

A thin beam of moonlight found its way through a gap in the curtains. All was still for a moment. Then a heavy sigh.

'What's up?'

'Nothing,' mumbled Tony, his mouth sounding dry and his tongue thick. 'But I've been thinking about you and me.'

Conversations in bed have a rhythm all their own, a pause can last five minutes. Helen waited, knowing that what followed would be a continuation of the talks they'd had before they'd turned in.

'Now that this billion quid has entered our lives...'

'I know. Look, Tony, I don't think it's going to change things all that much.'

'Ha.'

'Sorry. It's bound to – but in a good way?'

Tony had seemed more negative about all this than even her mother. Could it simply be male rivalry? Leo was now the beast with the biggest antlers? Surely not. Tony had always seemed confident of his status; he was a man at ease with who he was, what he'd achieved.

Whatever the problem, their conversations last night had become circular, always arriving only inches from where they'd started. Even the sex hadn't interrupted the thread of conversation for long.

'You'll be rich,' he said. He'd said this so many times that Helen was running out of responses.

'I think you're running away with this. Leo's a nice man, and I'm sure he's going to want to look after me, but I meant what I said last night, I'm just going to take things as they come. I don't want money to get between anyone – not me and Leo, or…' she hesitated, 'me and you, or Leo and Amy or…'

She felt his hand hold hers.

'I love you, Helen,' he said, and she wished he hadn't. This acceleration didn't feel right.

The slow rhythm of nocturnal conversation meant she could let the words hang in the air for as long as she liked. She liberated her hand by stealth, pretending it was just to change her position in the bed. Now, instead of a moonbeam, a car's headlamps shone through the window and swept over the walls like a prison searchlight.

'That's a nice thing to say,' she said, realising it would be a disappointing answer.

'I want to be with you… I want this to last,' he said, and she willed him to stop. It was too much. 'But saying it *now*…' he continued, '*now* that you could be a millionaire in a week… It sounds…'

'I'm not going to think you're after my money.' She wanted to lighten the mood. 'But if I see you digging up the patio I'll think again.' She laughed at her joke, and then remembered that Tony didn't laugh much, not really.

'If only I'd told you how I feel *yesterday*.'

'That's okay, don't worry about it,' said Helen, trying to sound casual. 'I believe you're sincere.'

There was another long pause, which she hoped would be the precursor to sleep. A solitary bird, perhaps three houses away, began to tweet tunelessly.

'There's something I wanted to say.'

'Well there's no rush.' She immediately realised that sounded far too casual.

'Last week, I bought a ring,' he said.

A vibration like the single pluck of a double bass went down her body.

'Being a trader, I spent a while looking out for the right one. I have the receipt with the date on, just to show I bought it before all this.'

'Well, that is quite a shock, Tony. Um… most unexpected. I don't really know…'

'You sound concerned.'

'I'm not *concerned*.' But she was. 'I just think… I just think it's really too soon to… I mean, my priority is Amy and what's right for her, and she has only met you once.'

'Is she the one in charge? I have to get approval from Amy?'

This sounded a little aggressive, but it was surely only his hurt feelings talking, and that was understandable – he had made a big statement and was being knocked back.

'Amy is only seven, and she's just been through her parents' separation. Plus all this lottery stuff. It's bound to affect things at school. Children need stability.'

'She'll be loving it.'

'And she doesn't even know you're my *boyfriend*.'

'She must have guessed.'

'Yes, she probably has.'

Tony turned on his side away from Helen. The conversation appeared to be over and she didn't want to prolong it. She had spent the last few weeks believing this thing with Tony was exciting, but she had not made up her mind as to its longevity, and she wasn't going to be rushed. There was *sexual* chemistry, but not much of any other kind. It was still a long way from being love.

She listened to Tony's breathing. He was not a man asleep, but a man deep in thought.

28

ARE YOU SURE?

Some men have to think of boring things to delay climax. Leo had the opposite problem: his brain often filled up with extraneous concerns and anxieties making pleasure difficult. Questions about the transactional nature of this relationship refused to go away, and even if they quietened for a moment, they were replaced by visions of Helen. Whatever Monica was, first and foremost, she was *not* Helen. Her not-Helenness was unmistakable.

Leo managed to fulfil the minimum requirement of a male sexual contributor but it lasted all of a minute. The more Monica had tried to please him, the more he felt obliged to put on an act, and the phonier he felt. He was a firework that had fizzed weakly, and then gone out.

Monica sat up with her head resting on her knees. If she was in any way disappointed, she didn't show it – but then she's paid not to, isn't she? Leo lay on his side, head resting on his arm. A question listed in his brain until it finally reached tipping point.

'How much do I owe you?'

Monica seemed shocked – even embarrassed – by the abruptness of the question. She swept hair out of her eyes and recovered herself.

'You're a billionaire, what do you care?'

And therein lay the problem. If he were a billionaire, he would want to pay her… what the hell, a hundred grand? She began drawing on his stomach with her finger.

'I'd like to get this out of the way,' he said.

'*Now*?'

'Why not?'

She shrugged, got up, reached into a chest and brought out a card machine while Leo fumbled for his wallet.

'Why the rush?'

He didn't know why he was rushing, but then again, he did. He'd been a flop in bed, and this was quickest way to compensate for it, or at least distract from it. He'd decided on a figure of two thousand pounds: that would surely help obliterate the memory of his pitiful performance and compensate her for her time. He took the card machine in his hand, pushed in his card, and punched in a two followed by three zeros. And then, as he glanced at Monica's sweet green eyes, and her embarrassed, slightly vulnerable expression, he felt an overwhelming need to do with his index finger what he'd failed to do with his penis: impress the hell out of the girl. He pushed down on the zero one more time, and then he punched in his PIN. He handed back the machine, and Monica glanced at the figure. She frowned, as if he was teasing her.

'Um…?'

'What?'

'Er… are you sure?'

Leo wasn't sure. It was a crazy, crazy thing to do, and Vince would do his nut. But he couldn't change his mind now.

'I suppose I'd better be going,' he mumbled, just for something to say. But like a lot of times when he'd said something just to fill the air, he found that the words did much more than he'd wanted them to. Monica turned her back. There was a pendulous silence, a tacit stubbornness on both sides, and neither of them moved. After a minute, she opened the drawer where the card machine had been and closed it with unnecessary force.

'You've paid for a whole night,' she said tetchily, still not looking at Leo.

'Don't you have other…?'

She turned abruptly.

'*What?* Other clients? No, I don't.'

It seemed to have been an infuriating question. She turned away again and put her head in her hands. After another silence, in which Leo tried to fathom what had gone wrong, because *something* had, he decided to gently touch her arm.

'Just so you know… I like you. Really. I mean…'

She lay back down, still facing the ceiling. Having got both the sex and the money out of the way, and knowing that they had the whole night ahead of them, Leo began to feel more relaxed. He put money out of his mind.

'Do you have any brothers or sisters?' he asked.

And so began a conversation about families, childhood, relationships, dreams, phobias, favourite films, music and food, that went on until long after dawn.

29

HOW LONG IS YOUR SARI?

West Byford Junior was a school of about 300 pupils, and it stood next to a white, seventeenth century windmill. It was housed in a high-windowed Victorian building, surrounded by several acres of grass. Physically attractive, and with a decent reputation, demand for places was always high.

It was lunchtime, and Amy filed out of class, holding hands with her very best friend, Samira. Mrs Allam asked her to stay behind for a moment.

'You haven't done anything wrong,' she said, with a warm smile.

Amy let go of Samira's hand, and felt butterflies in her stomach. Already that morning she had had more attention from her classmates than ever before, and now, her favourite teacher wanted to speak to her. Mrs Allam pulled up a chair for her, right up at the front, near teacher's desk.

'Just sit there for a moment while everyone files out,' she said softy, so that the other children wouldn't hear.

That morning, Amy had been asked more questions than she knew how to answer, but she delivered her parents' line as consistently as she could – *My dad wants me to be normal, no, I'm not going to be spoilt, I'm not going to get lots of presents, no, I'm not going to go to a private school, or boarding school, or live in America, or Switzerland, or get a swimming pool, or move to London, or get expensive clothes, or even designer trainers.*

'I just want to ask if you're okay,' said Mrs Allam, as she sat down, not at her desk but on one of the children's chairs, so she was almost eye-level with Amy. She smelled of pine bubble bath.

'This is quite a change for you, and sometimes children can be mean about other children who are a little bit different.'

She has a face that seems to be sorry about something, thought Amy.

'Do you understand?'

'Yes, Miss.'

'Has anyone teased you?'

'No, Miss.' Amy wanted to fiddle with her hair, but Mrs Allam was bound to tell her not to because she always did.

'I heard Janet and Samira talking about your bracelet. It's pretty.'

Amy hadn't expected the bracelet to make everyone so excited. *Solid gold. It must be worth thousands. Why don't you sell it and buy sweets for the whole school?*

'Did your father give it to you?'

That's what everyone thought, and Amy wasn't going to tell them otherwise. It was embarrassing enough that her parents were not together, without having to explain that a man who wasn't her father had given her such a big present. She had a feeling that made her want to go to the toilet, but even so, she didn't want to tell Mrs Allam the truth.

'Yes.'

The teacher nodded, as if she already knew that.

'Did you know we Indians love gold?'

Amy shook her head.

'We do. India imports more gold than any other country. It's important for weddings, but we also like it because we don't trust the banks. It's very wise.'

Mrs Allam must have thought what she said was funny, because she laughed. Amy began to wonder what Samira was doing now, and whether she would be eating her sandwich or saving it so they could eat together like they always did.

'I'm sure your father means very well, but you aren't meant to wear expensive things at school. It could get lost, or a bad person might take it from you on your way home.'

Amy wasn't really listening. She was thinking about the eyeliner on Mrs Allam's face. The way it went on further than her eyes made her look like a beautiful Egyptian pharaoh. Then she looked at her sari and wondered if now might be the time to ask the question she'd been wanting to ask for ages.

'How long is your sari?'

Mrs Allam laughed even more than before.

'This one is about six metres,' she said, and then indicated the distance from her desk to the door. Amy wondered how long it took to put on, but thought it might rude to ask.

'Are there any pockets?'

Mrs Allam smiled.

'No, there aren't any pockets. Maybe there *should* be. And do you remember what this is?' she asked, touching her scarf.

'It's a hijab.'

'That's right.'

'Why do you always wear the same colours?' asked Amy. It was always grey or dark blue.

'Because in my religion we tend not to wear bright colours. The colourful saris you have seen are probably worn by Hindus, which is another religion in India. Now then, I think I should look after the bracelet for today.'

Amy nodded. She was pleased to hand it over because she didn't like lying about who gave it to her. Mrs Allam helped her unclasp it. She took the chain in her hand and seemed to weigh it, and then she frowned just a little. Holding it up to the window, she looked at it very closely. She then opened a big drawer full of all kinds of sciencey things like beakers and weights and batteries, and she brought out a magnet and held it to the bracelet, and then held it up using the magnet's power. She seemed puzzled.

'That means it has iron in it, Miss,' said Amy, hoping that her teacher would be impressed that she had remembered the lesson with iron filings.

Mrs Allam, still looking confused, dropped the magnet in the drawer and handed back the bracelet.

'Let me help you put it on,' she said, reaching for Amy's wrist.

'But you said I couldn't, Miss.'

'It's not quite what I thought it was. It's still very pretty, though.'

Mrs Allam seemed to be thinking hard about something, then she smiled.

'Okay, you can go now.'

Amy thanked the teacher, but wasn't sure why. She fetched her lunch box and ran off to find Samira and tell her all about her talk with Mrs Allam – and to tell her the news: *six* metres!

30

YEOVIL FEELING

Donna was in her flat, a one-bedroom conversion in East Ham. It was simply the nearest place to Chalk Farm – her dream location – that she could afford, even though it was ten miles further east, seventeen stops on the Central Line. Donna felt that, at age thirty-three, owning her own place was a priority. The biggest downside was that there was nowhere within a mile that she could sit and have a beer or a glass of wine.

The flat itself was pleasant enough, despite having had every original feature removed, and the sash windows had been replaced with uPVC years ago. The kitchen was too small for a dishwasher, but at least she had a washing machine.

If Donna was at home in the afternoon, she made tea in a pot. Disappointingly, there were no biscuits in the cupboard so, by way of compensation, she poured a spoonful of sugar into her mug.

Sitting at the tiny breakfast bar, she scrolled through Twitter: *#billionairebarista*. Most of the tweets assumed the coffee guy was the real winner. He was popular, and the consensus was that he'd got drunk and blabbered, which was unfortunate for him but it was good for everyone else, because it provided free entertainment. There were several pictures of Leo and Vince around Oxford Street, having a ball.

Scrolling through the news outlets, she was relieved to see that *alleged, supposed, assumed, apparent,* were still the words of the day. None were claiming that Morphetus was definitely the winner. There was time for TrueNewz to be the first to make an unequivocal call.

Her mobile rang – not a number she recognised.

'Donna White.'

'Hello, my dear Donna.'

Foreign accent.

'My name is Monica.'

Dutch?

'Derek said I should call you.'

'Hey, Monica, how can I help?'

'It's about Leo Morphetus. Derek said you're the one following the story?'

'Yup, that's me.'

Derek wouldn't have passed on a number if this wasn't a decent lead.

'There's something I'd like to talk about.'

The girl sounded confident. Donna composed herself. Her 'serious journalist' voice must be deployed.

'If you're based in Byford, we could meet up tomorrow.'

'Byford?'

'Umm… Where Leo lives? I thought you might be calling from there.'

'I live in London.'

Donna stirred her tea and waited a few seconds before speaking.

'And…?'

'Obviously, I would need some sort of deal.'

'I'd have to get approval from my boss first. Journalists don't hand out cash the way they used to, it's all got very abstemious these days.'

It was the usual spiel: dampen expectations. And it also happened to be true.

'Yes. Well, it's not just about the deal. I'm a model and aspiring TV presenter…'

'Okay.'

'I know how that sounds, crap, right?'

'Not at all.' It did sound crap, but she was impressed by the girl's self-awareness. Donna knew this was going to be a sex story, and that was fine. TrueNewz wasn't above that.

'I really want my pictures to get out there, you know? I'm trying to make a splash in your country.'

Donna took her first sip of tea. 'Okay, let's just… if I could just rewind and get a rough idea of the situation.'

'Okay, well… I met him for the first time last night.'

'And I take it something happened between you?'

'Ha, well, yes.'

'How old are you, Monica?'

'Twenty seven.'

She sounded younger.

'Okay. I'd be very keen to know more about it.'

'Yes. He's lovely. The perfect gentleman.'

This is the kind of informer who wants to get into the sewer but come up smelling of roses, thought Donna.

'That's very nice to hear, but we might need something more than that.'

To her surprise, Monica laughed – a proper guffaw.

'I know you need something salacious. Do you want to see his boxer shorts?'

This time it was Donna who laughed. 'Um… *should* I want to see his boxer shorts?'

'He left them behind. You see, he went shopping yesterday but forgot to buy new underwear. Holes everywhere.'

'*Okay…*'

'They're funny. I could take a picture of them.'

The Billionaire's Boxers. Donna could see it. A picture of the 'before' item, next to an expensive designer pair he might be wearing now. For a moment she saw herself from on high, and remembered that while studying English at University she'd wanted to write serious plays for the National Theatre.

'Send a picture, and we'll talk some more.'

And then she decided that she wouldn't wait any longer to ask the obvious question. She reckoned the girl was savvy enough to take it in her stride.

'Monica? Um… I don't know you at all, so please don't be offended. But did… did money change hands?'

There was a pause: so money changed hands. No surprise. It wouldn't be hard for a high-class hooker to reel in a young man like Leo.

'You see, Monica, from where I'm standing, unless money changed hands there isn't much of a story. Okay, there's a *bit* of a story, just because he's the famous billionaire, but if you can prove that he paid you then—'

'No comment. I don't want to put a stain on Leo.'

'Off the record?'

'Off the record?'

'Yes. If it's off the record then it will *never* be published.'

And she meant it.

'Ri-ight,' said Monica, doubtfully.

'Hey, my reputation as a journalist would depend on it.'

Donna listened to the girl's breath hitting the phone receiver, and figured she needed a little more convincing.

'You see, I'd just like to know if he paid you a lot of money, not because I want to make that the story. It's actually part of my investigation as to whether he is the billionaire or not.'

'You mean you're not sure if he's a billionaire?'

'There's no actual proof. What do *you* think?'

Monica laughed – in fact, she seemed to be laughing *at* Donna.

'He's a billionaire,' she said, emphatically. 'He is definitely a billionaire.'

'Why are you so sure?'

'Ummm… let's just say I have never met anyone so generous, and I have met billionaires before.'

Donna needed to know exactly *how* generous.

'Okay… was it cash?'

A pause.

'No, debit card.'

Donna's heart began to bump harder.

'Can you tell me how much? Off the record.'

'Off the record.'

'Off the record.'

'Twenty…'

Woah.

'Twenty…'

'Thousand.'

'Are you still there?' asked Monica.

'Just stunned into silence.'

They both laughed. Donna was within an inch of what she needed to break the story. She also thought this girl might be someone she could have fun with.

'I'm just pleased I didn't have a mouth full of tea or I would have spat it out.'

They laughed again. 'I know, crazy, huh?'

'Totally crazy.'

'But then if you have a billion in the bank, what's twenty grand, you know?'

That is absolutely true, thought Donna.

'Or perhaps you just gave him a particularly good time.'

She reddened as she thought it was something that a dumb bloke might say. 'Monica, listen, here's an idea. Send me a copy of your bank statement – just the relevant page with that figure on it. I can then meet you and we can talk about how to play this.'

'But the money – it's off the record.'

'Of course. Once that's sorted we can talk about your story and your deal.'

Donna waited. It doesn't do to push people, they back away.

'Okay. I'll email it along with the boxer shorts jpeg, and my portfolio in a zip file.'

'Great, please do that now.'

This was getting *so* close.

***

Donna spent the next few minutes talking to her laptop, begging it to receive the email. After six minutes it obliged. Such things can be forged, but and unless Monica just happened to be a superfast whiz with graphics *and* a paid-up member of the hoaxing community, the billionaire story was now standing up, solid as a rock. No ordinary barista boy from Byford could pay that kind of money. Donna forwarded the document to Derek with the message: *only a billionaire pays 20 grand for a fuck*. A minute later her phone rang.

'Well done, mate. Write some copy and send it over.'

'Remember, it's off the record.'

'Yeah, I got that. We'll say we have seen definitive evidence, but won't say what it is. And Donna, you can punch the air now.'

After she'd hung up she punched the air. And she also said 'Yeah!' quite loudly but then felt a little ridiculous. She dashed off some copy, which took all of ten minutes because Derek and his team would write most of it themselves. Then she considered phoning a few friends, but they rarely reacted to her good news in precisely the way she wanted them to, and it made her furious.

After knocking back a glass of wine, she told herself that at times like this, a girl deserves a reward. Jeremy, the married guy, was out of the question because he needed booking well in advance. Geoff was fun and sexy but was also unreliable – if he said he'd come at eight, he'd come at ten – plus he was also getting too druggy. Good old Winston? He was okay, but wanted to talk for hours and in the end he was just too draining. Tonight, it would have to be the internet.

Twenty minutes later, she lowered herself into a steaming bath. Her head touched the water and she closed her eyes. She smiled at the thought of the two inoffensive young men trying to cope with their sudden fame and fortune. She admired them for having had no contact with the press or social media since they'd left the Carlton Hotel. Images of the press conference came to mind. She re-ran it like an old film. Suddenly her eyes opened wide.

Yeovil.

Dammit and fuck.

Yeovil was a very specific feeling. Donna had named it *Yeovil* because that's where she'd first felt it, or first recognised its meaning. She had been a student, hitching with her friend Julia on their way back from a Devon holiday.

After half an hour of thumbing, a green Ford Mondeo hatchback stopped and a friendly guy asked them to hop in. Donna point blank refused. Julie couldn't understand why, and it was all quite embarrassing. She could never explain it to Julia, or even to herself. It wasn't that the man had an evil eye or a role of duct tape in the back seat, but she felt sure she had seen *something*. The message to her brain had been so quick that it activated the fear response, by-passing her conscious mind. There might well have been a knife – or part of one – somewhere in her peripheral vision. Even to this day, Donna watched *Crimewatch* expecting to see the driver's mugshot.

With her towel wrapped round her, and a pool of water gathering on the floor, she called Derek.

'I'm sorry, but I'm getting my Yeovil feeling about this.'

'Oh, for fuck's sake.'

She had told him about her Yeovil feelings and he'd even begun to adopt the term himself.

'We were about to go live with this,' he said.

'I'm sorry. I could have kept it to myself, but you tell me to speak up about any doubts.'

She stepped out of her puddle and began a new one.

'What's changed your mind?'

'I don't know, that's the *point* of a Yeovil feeling.'

'Ha, yeah.'

She could feel his frustration. All she wanted at this moment was for him to make a decision.

'Don't you have *any* clue?'

'I was just thinking back to their press conference. Something about it. Dunno. I need to look at it again. What are you going to do?'

'Any suggestions?'

'Your call.'

There was a beat.

'You know what? I bet that Yeovil driver was perfectly innocent.'

'I'm *ninety-nine per cent* sure he was, too.'

'Fuck, I'm going with the story.' And he hung up.

Donna felt relief as she exhaled, but when she inhaled she felt a swell of guilt. The evaporating water tickled her skin.

Once she had dried and dressed, she opened her laptop on the kitchen counter. She clicked on the zip file of Monica's photographs.

Wow. You are one extremely hot girl, she thought. *Twenty thousand pounds doesn't seem so crazy at all.*

31

THERE WAS A
CONNECTION

The Lincoln cruised along the A1, Byford bound, driving into wind and rain. The grey of the clouds matched the grey of the motorway, making a continuum of gloom. Vince had been dragging Leo round clothes shops for two hours. Bags were now piled on top of each other along with shoeboxes and tissue paper, and on the coffee-table stood a family of designer toiletries that Vince had selected from Liberty's. The car, which had previously been cavernous, was now cramped, and there was barely a place to sit, let alone lie down. The men were shoved up at the back, huddled opposite each other, unable to get comfortable. Vince had his nose in *The Great Gatsby,* which he was reading for the third time, 'but not the last'.

Leo had called Byford Sound, to ask if he could come on the air at drive time. He had a few things he wanted to explain. Vince and Leo liked the idea of doing the big confession on a struggling radio station in their arsehole of a home town.

There was no music on in the limo because, while Leo had been 'entertaining his lady-friend' (Vince's words), Dave and Vince had nearly come to blows. Vince told Dave that Neil Diamond sounded like a drowning moose so Dave started chucking everything out of the car onto the pavement. It was only Vince's highly convincing display of contrition that meant they still had a driver – albeit one who would now only communicate in staccato grunts.

And it wasn't just Dave who was sulking.

Vince had not said a word since the row that had followed Leo's revelation of exactly how much he had paid, a bombshell Leo had decided to leave till after the shopping. He had half expected Vince to laugh and then congratulate him, but the worm had turned: the come-what-may libertine was bloody furious. The whispered shouting match that followed had made their throats sore.

'Twenty thousand pounds,' said Vince, after a silence of about twenty minutes. Leo knew he'd say it again in a few seconds, and he did. Then he repeated the phrase in a variety of styles: a question, an exclamation, an incredulous shout, a quizmaster announcing the bumper prize, Oliver asking for more porridge (*Please Sir, twenty thousand pounds*), various *South Park* characters, Joe Pesci in *Goodfellas*, Forrest Gump, Sheldon from *Big Bang Theory*, and many other voices that Leo assumed were literary icons. He'd leave it just long enough for Leo to think he'd finished before reiterating, in an ever more bizarre manner. Leo stubbornly refused to appear provoked. Instead, he stared at the traffic and green fields going by. Maybe he *had* been 'a wanker's idiot' (Vince's words) but he wasn't going to admit it. Besides, all the business books warn against beating yourself up about one bad decision. *Assess yourself from your long-term record, never from yesterday's failure.* Taken as a whole, his life of decision-making had been cautious, frugal, and, apart from a harmless lottery habit, his choices had been based on sound judgement. Twenty grand to impress a woman was a small dent in the box that he had spent most of his life thinking inside.

He adjusted his position on the seat, so that he could either sleep or pretend to.

'How much do we have left?' asked Vince.

'About four hundred quid cash. That's all the fun money left.'

'There goes my alpaca.'

Leo felt his encounter with Monica needed rescuing.

'There was a connection.'

'Her job is to make you *think* there was a connection.'

'I'm *allowing* for that. Taking *all that* into consideration, I think there was a connection.' Vince began shoving some detritus off the seat so he could lie down.

'She's played you like a violin. Your foreskin has been sliced off, tied to a stick, and used as a bow. She's cut off your arsehole, put chimes on it, and called it a tambourine. Besides, you're still in love with Helen.'

'Helen has a new man. I'm trying to move on – is that wrong?'

He noticed a smear of saliva on the window left by the girl who had french-kissed it. The drops of rain were avoiding it.

The experience with Monica had failed in what had been its main purpose, conscious or otherwise: to take his mind off things for a moment, and prove that there was intimacy, sex, after Helen.

'Did she do a Sally Albright?' asked Vince. 'Because for twenty grand…'

Leo refused to ask who Sally Albright was. He leaned his head on the window and watched droplets race each other.

'You know she's probably had a chaotic life?' said Vince. 'Chances are she's a head case.'

'Says the publicist of a man pretending to have won a billion pounds.'

'Best job I ever had.'

It wasn't the funniest line but it was lightning quick and the fact that it was probably true made them laugh despite themselves. Vince was the first to regain a straight face.

'You just *had* to impress the lady with the size of your chequebook, and do you know what? You've been doing that all your life. You did it with Helen – always trying to be the great provider.'

Leo looked around for something suitable to throw at Vince but not finding anything, he tried a different tack.

'All right, it was a stupid thing to do. I'm a fool.' This admission worked like a judo move, harnessing the opponent's momentum to neutralise the assault. Vince let out a huff and fell silent. For Leo, the worst fallout from the

Monica thing would be if it ever became public. It would put a very different slant on his motivation and character.

He distracted himself from all the messiness in his brain by picking up one of the newspapers Vince had bought.

'It'll do your head in,' said Vince.

Page two of *The Sun*: the Barista Billionaire's wish-list, based on the testimony of 'close friends'. The list included an underground gym and a private helicopter, neither of which had ever occurred to Leo. Number seven was a wine cellar – sure proof that they were no 'close friends', just the imagination of some sloppy old hack. Number eight was a long-distance drone. This had not occurred to him either, but he liked the idea, and decided he wanted one. In that instant, fake news became fact.

While Vince dozed, Leo pulled *The Mirror* from the pile, and read some quotes from 'the people of Byford'. One that struck a chord was from his former teacher, Mr Haskins. 'He was not the most academic of pupils. He always had a far-away look.'

At junior school most teachers thought Leo was *uneducable*. That was the term they used at the parents' evenings his mother, Eva, never missed. The evidence they gave for the condition was that he couldn't spell, was behind with reading, was physically uncoordinated, and every so often had brief flapping fits that no one could explain.

One day in the run-up to Easter, Leo was asked to stop drawing his map of Canada and go and see a 'special doctor'. He was taken to a room he had never been to before and it smelt of Germolene ointment. He sat down in front of a woman who had lots of toys: bricks and funny plastic shapes. She seemed kind, and had shiny skin, like Action Man. All he had to do was arrange the bricks to make various simple patterns, like placing them in order of height, or grouping similar shapes together. Then he had to answer questions on a form. Once he was all finished, the lady gave him a boiled sweet with its own wrapper and Leo showed it to his classmates before eating it.

When he got home, his mother explained that the school had wanted to 'make sure nothing was wrong' and the next day they rang to say that he was 'normal'. However, the teachers weren't happy with the psychiatrist's conclusion, and a month later Leo did similar tests with a different 'special doctor' who didn't give him a sweet, which made him sad. But the result was the same, and the school conceded that there was nothing *clinically* wrong with Eva's son.

Much later, at big school, the careers advisor, who was also his English teacher, asked him what he'd like to do after leaving school. Leo said he was interested in discovering something that would change the world, like Penicillin or X Rays. The man listened patiently, and when Leo finished, he handed Leo an index card with the details of a local hairdressing salon, Hair Today, which had a vacancy for a trainee. 'You'll be shampooing, working with your hands – seems right up your street.' Leo spent the next few days wondering how the conversation could have so quickly turned from discovering penicillin to shampooing hair. Vince, meanwhile, had a different experience. The English teacher urged him to stay on to the sixth form and even apply to University – Oxbridge had been mentioned.

Leo left school after failing most of his GSCE's, except maths and physics, and got a job as a garden labourer. He sometimes passed Hair Today, and once went in to be shampooed by the trainee he could have been.

The limo had been stationary for five minutes, stuck in a thicket of bollards and signage. Driver Dave asked if he could smoke if he kept the screen between them down. The smell still managed to find its way up Leo's nostrils.

He began picking up the boxes that had fallen and creating a semblance of order.

'By the way,' said Vince, 'some people want to donate money.'

'What? Why?' asked Leo, confused.

'At the hotel you mentioned a foundation, remember? You painted yourself as the next Bill and Melinda Gates. A few kind-hearts want to know how they can contribute, so I posted up your bank details.'

'You did *what*?'

'Why's it matter?'

'It could look extremely shabby, that's why.'

'We won't touch it. We'll open a donor's account.'

'We'd better.'

'You can keep tabs on the figures – you're good at that.'

It wasn't meant as a compliment, but Leo privately took it as one. He leaned back in his seat and watched the world go by. The truck in front was producing so much spray it seemed to be still raining.

His phone rang. It was Alan, probably with an update on Poppy.

'Hi Alan, how's it going?'

Alan explained that they were in the early stages of making plans and they were very hopeful. Just when Leo thought the conversation was coming to an end, Alan's voice changed.

'Leo, look. I've called for a reason.'

Leo stiffened. The money hadn't been enough?

'You see, we're part of a very small support group. And um… when we started it, we all promised we'd help each other. That's what a support group is, after all. And…'

Leo knew where this was heading and could feel panic rising.

'It's just four families, Leo. It's a pretty rare condition.'

'Why the fuck can't they get help on the National Health?'

A few seconds passed.

'I'm sorry, Alan.'

'I didn't mean to make you angry, Leo.'

'I'm not angry with *you*. I'm angry with whoever… you know, the system.'

'You mean the drug companies?'

'What?'

'Oh, I hear you. They're profiteering. That's what this is all about. You've hit the nail on the head. They are selling drugs of no-choice at prices the NHS can't afford.'

'That's shit, that's really shit.'

Lethco talked at some length about the injustice of it all, and the powerlessness they all felt. At any other time, Leo would have been fascinated – corporate impropriety being one of his interests – but he could only think about the bind he was in. Of the two hundred grand he'd got from Hughes, a hundred had gone to Lethco, he'd spent most of the ten grand cash, the forty for the folk at The Swan, and then there was the twenty he'd given...

'Alan, I'm afraid... I can't help them,' he said, interrupting Lethco's flow.

A pause.

'Okay. I understand.'

'You see... I have so many other causes to consider.'

Well, he *was* considering some other good causes.

'Of course, of course. So many people in need.'

Alan's voice sounded weak. How could he possibly understand?

'Please give them all my best wishes, Alan.'

'I sure will. Thanks again for what you've done.'

Leo felt Alan's disappointment with a hollow thud. He imagined a row of families sitting in church hall, holding hands and praying for the billionaire to have mercy on them. As soon as he heard a goodbye and the inevitable 'god bless' he hung up.

He began to explain the situation to Vince, but he'd already gathered the gist.

Nothing was said for a while. Leo's mind turned to the drug companies. Surely they were just as much to blame for this mess? He opened Vince's laptop, and perhaps only to find some target for his anger, he googled pharmaceutical scandals.

Becoming absorbed in a subject, particularly something involving money, numbers and corporate impropriety, was very much in Leo's comfort zone, the equivalent of a good book or box set for most people. He read about Martin Shkreli, the C.E.O. of Turing Pharmaceuticals, who hiked the price of a sixty-two-year-old lifesaving drug from $13.50 to $750 a pill overnight. Shkreli was called "the most hated man in America." Yet the true scandal was that it was all entirely legal. What surprised Leo is the way the pharmaceutical companies could game the system. Even when a drug went off patent, the big pharmas could maintain their monopoly, especially if the drug was never going to make a lot of money because too few patients would ever need it. The NHS has a threshold of up to £30,000 for a drug that gives a patient a year of good-quality life. But many experts argue that the threshold should be dropped to £13,000. Above that level, other patients will pay the price in inferior treatment.

After reading a handful of articles, Leo's thoughts churned around in a big shitty muddle. He needed to get out.

Service stations aren't great for long treks, but Leo wanted blood in his legs, air in his lungs, and clarity in his head. He would go round the car park, walking at a brisk pace. He wanted to ask Lethco a lot of questions. Why was the treatment not funded by the NHS? Was it entirely because the four drugs needed were too expensive? Or because it was deemed ineffective? Or even unsafe? Were these families deluded, or even being manipulated by someone who stood to profit from a new operation? How long would the treatment last – were they going to be involved in a never-ending cycle of treatments? He would need to get independent advice from a specialist. Then he'd need to gather documents, diagnoses, prognoses. It would take time. And if was going to help, he would need more money.

After two laps, Leo tried to think through his own motives – altruism or egotism? He came to the conclusion, as he had done before, that the two things are not so different. Then plausibility. Could he raise the money, and what would be the consequences? The best, worst and medium scenarios. He deployed his business brain to go through it all systematically, knowing that his books would tell him to be wary of motivated reasoning.

After four laps, he was ready to get back on the road. He found Vince and Dave at two separate coffee tables at Costa Coffee, both wearing headphones, but presumably listening to very different entertainment. Leo stopped off at a shop to buy them both treats before the three of them walked back to the limo.

As soon as Dave started up the engine, Leo said, 'I don't want to go to Byford Sound. I'm not ready to spill the beans.'

'Really?'

'Let's be billionaires for a little longer.'

'The sick kids?'

Leo nodded. He didn't expect Vince to empathise with a group of children he'd never met, however sick, so he'd need some other inducements. More fame, more notoriety, more clothes, more adventures. Before Leo could muster his persuasive powers Vince came to sit closer.

'I never told you this, but I once nearly died.'

'What? When was this?'

'It was after you announced that you were going to self-replicate, I thought… My best mate will soon be absorbed by absorbent nappies and baby wipes. Time for me to do something I've always fancied – mixing with the lowlife of London.'

Leo remembered that Vince had disappeared for a while.

'I thought I might write a book or something, you know, a *mémoire scandaleux*, and you can't pen one of those unless you're prepared to get down and dirty.'

Leo nodded as if he understood perfectly.

'One day, someone helped me to an overdose, Leo. I was rushed to hospital. I didn't bother you with it, responsible dad that you were.'

'You should have told me.'

'When I recovered, I thought, I nearly died having done fuck all with my life.'

'And so you decided to become a Christian missionary?'

Vince laughed.

'No. I've *still* done fuck all. Absolutely fuck all.'

Leo couldn't remember when Vince had admitted a fundamental failing.

'But this… we could do something.'

This was so unlike the man for whom personal gratification was sacrosanct, never to be questioned, and worthy causes were for lesser mortals. Leo couldn't quite believe it.

'Are you sure?'

'Leo, when it all goes tits up, which it most certainly will, then think of this: searing regret is the proof that you grabbed life by the cock. Richard Forde said that, or something like it.'

'Let's grab life by the cock.'

Leo had nothing more to say for a moment, and perhaps wouldn't for a while. He began slowly tearing a piece of tissue paper into shreds. He thought about the twenty grand he'd squandered on Monica. Perhaps he should confess all and ask for half of it back.

'Fuck.' Vince had just seen something on his phone.

'What's up?' The range of possible bad news was so vast Leo didn't even bother to guess what it might be.

'Shit, fuck, shit,' continued Vince.

'What is it?'

'A text from a Mr Sender Unknown.'

'Read it.'

'Leo didn't win the lottery.'

'Fuck.'

They sat in silence for a moment, listening to the spray on the roof and the deep purr of the engine. Leo was not completely unprepared for this, but even so, his leg began to oscillate.

'Chances are, it's some jealous random,' said Vince, but without conviction.

They agreed to ignore the text, because that's what a real billionaire would do. Vince put down his phone and laptop and picked up his novel, but after turning a page he dropped it on the table. He then resumed his ursine scratching and fidgeting.

'You're edgy as hell,' said Leo, but he realised he was probably just as restless.

Vince's phone bleeped again. He checked the message and smiled wryly. He held it up so Leo could read the text:

I know Morphetus didn't win. Because I did.

32

BAD MEN

Helen sat with her laptop at the kitchen table answering work emails, but her mind wasn't on it. She stopped to gaze out of the glass patio door and noticed the handle that Leo had promised to fix. It made her smile.

She had made a decision – although it would be truer to say that a decision had grown inside her like a plum and was now ready to fall. She would finish with Tony. The times between sex required more and more effort, the lack of shared laughter was more noticeable, and this whole Leo-billionaire thing had made him even more sombre. And... although she tried to push this from her mind, was there something fake about him? Some of the stories about business deals on yachts were a little far-fetched. The actual *fact* was that he was pushing forty and living with his sister – sure, it was a mercy mission for his mother's sake, but if he was half as wealthy as he appeared you'd think he'd be staying at the Carlton.

Quite when and how she would end it was still up in the air. The moment would present itself. Very disappointingly, she would, at some point have to give up the best sex she'd ever had. As the saying goes, she would be good, but not yet.

After giving up on the emails, she took a call from her mother, who wanted to talk about the upcoming election – not a subject in which Helen was in the least interested. In spite of her doubts, she was pleased to hear Tony's tap on the door.

He presented a fancy box of chocolates. She wondered for a split second if he was going to formally propose – but then reminded herself that she had dropped enough adverse hints and been sufficiently distant to kybosh that idea. She took the chocolates and wondered how many miles on the exercise bike would be needed as penance.

'Would you like some fishcake and salad?' she asked, when he'd sat down at the table.

'No thanks, I grabbed a sandwich.' Having just sat down, he stood up again and touched her arm. 'Look, Helen, I really need to talk to you. It's quite serious.'

'Okay,' she said, her heart beating faster. She pulled up a chair, put her hands together, fingers intertwined, to indicate that she was not going to do any fiddling or tidying. He had her full attention. Perhaps she had overdone the coldness and *he* was going to do the dumping?

'Things are a bit tricky for me, darling,' he said as he sat down again. 'That's an understatement. You see… my trade, the gems trade, well, it can be a nasty old business.'

This wasn't the topic Helen was expecting. She had a bad feeling about it.

'Is something… what? Tell me,' she said, impatient to have the bad news out where she could see it.

'Conflict diamonds. You know what they are?'

'Of course.' She felt herself edging into unknown territory 'They're illegal. And wrong. You haven't…?'

'No, no. Nothing like that. But a couple of years ago I turned in a band. A *band* is like a firm, a group of traders. I squealed. A couple of band members got done. Sent down. And… well, some of the ones who got away aren't very happy about it, and they lost money.'

He looked down at his hands. *Poor man*, thought Helen: *doing the right thing, then having to suffer for it*. She felt warmer towards him that she had done for a while.

'They say I owe them half a million.'

It took Helen just a couple of seconds to connect the half a million with Leo and his billion. What the…?

'It's okay, no one is actually threatening me yet because they don't think I have the money, which is true, I don't.'

She tried not to let her imagination run wild. Just concentrate on what Tony is saying, one phrase at a time, and keep still.

'But as I've told you… sometimes things can get nasty. I tried to do what was right. Sometimes that has a cost.'

She wondered if this was why he seemed so serious. He'd spent months living under threat from violent men.

'They know my car, they know where to find me.'

Helen pictured the red Mazda parked outside her house. This problem was getting closer to home. She felt herself grip the fabric of her dress.

'You see, what if they find out that you and I…?'

He gestured, inviting her to fill in the blanks.

'If they find out about us… and about Leo, you mean?' she asked.

He adjusted his watch strap. 'It's hardly a secret.'

Helen didn't know where to put her panic, so she slapped her forehead with the palm of her hand and let out a stifled scream.

'Jesus Christ,' she said, and then got up and walked to the sink, which she leaned against, head bowed, eyes closed.

'It would have been much easier,' said Tony, 'if, like a sensible fellow, Leo had kept his gob shut. But no, he mouthed off at the pub, then went on telly like a fucking—'

'Don't blame him, he's not the one with gangster mates.'

'Sorry. It's just that—'

'So what happens now? Should I call the police? Get 24/7 security? Is Amy in danger right now? Should I pull her out of school?'

He got up from the table and took her hands in his. Then he lifted her chin and wiped away a tear that had travelled half way down her cheek.

'Right now you're not in danger and nor is Amy. No one's to know there's a connection between me and a billionaire. I've sent the car back so we don't need to worry about that any more. I just needed you to know about this, so that we would be discreet. As few people as possible should know about us, that's all. It's a precaution, that's all it is. I will keep you safe.'

The corners of Tony's mouth went up, a rare sight.

'Are you *sure*? Don't you think security would be—'

'I'm sure.'

Having been frightened out of her wits, Helen began to feel tearily relieved, and grateful to Tony for making her feel that way.

He pulled her closer to towards him, lifted her chin and began kissing her, starting with her mouth then moving down to her neck.

Okay, thought Helen, but perhaps this would be the last time.

33

ARBUTHNOT

The Lincoln was still heading north, in the slow lane. Adrenaline and confined spaces don't mix, and its two passengers revealed their anxiety by repeatedly shifting positions between the bags and boxes and accusing each other of hogging space.

Vince clambered over to the minibar and fixed himself an Absolut and Red Bull. He then poured crisps into a white plastic bowl he'd unearthed.

'Why put your crisps into a bowl?' asked Leo, just because he wanted an argument.

Vince blinked in slow motion before answering.

'Snacks taste better from a solid receptacle. I'm surprised it doesn't say that in your psycho-economic tomes.'

When not engaged in low-level bickering, Leo focused his mind on the supposed real lottery winner, and the risks this had for his plan to play billionaire a little longer while he obtained money for four desperate families. Vince thought the real winner might reveal his or her identity at any minute. When they reached Byford, a mob of hacks would surround them, and they'd look like criminals, rather brilliant philanthropic young hoaxers who played the media at their own game. Leo, calling on his lottery expertise, explained a few things to Vince. For a start, it was likely the real winner did not yet know they'd won, because Camelot only identify the winner's location if there hasn't been a claim, in order to nudge the winner into checking their ticket. So far, the winner had not responded to the nudge, or there would have been another press release saying that the prize had been claimed. Even if the winner had come forward in the last twelve hours, there was a very strong chance he or she would want to remain anonymous – most big winners do. And if the winner ever tried to prove Leo was a fraud, they would risk revealing their identity. As for the text, Leo wondered about the odds of the real billionaire happening to have Vince's mobile number, and why would they bother sending a stupid anonymous message? 'He'd be too busy shopping and fucking.' Leo's best guess was that it was some druggy associate of Vince's who either bore a grudge, or just liked a bit of mischief.

'Yeah,' said Vince, 'but telling a *real* billionaire they're not a billionaire isn't much fun is it? Pointless, actually. It's only mischief if they're *not*.'

Leo didn't have an answer for that one, and so they both remained on edge.

Vince selected the largest crisp in the bowl and bit into it.

'What do you suppose he's like, the real winner?'

'You think he's a bloke?' asked Leo.

'I can feel it in my new Louis Vuitton underpants.'

Leo remembered that he had missed out on the underwear-buying, probably because he was busy choosing a scooter. His boxers were so embarrassingly threadbare he'd thrown them in a bin at Monica's.

'I reckon the real billionaire is a fat, bald pensioner with no friends,' said Vince. 'His two kids are ungrateful brats who have gone to live in Australia, and he doesn't want them to know about his fortune. Right now he's sitting in an armchair, Guinness in one hand, fag in the other, watching us on catch-up, chortling to himself.'

'Let's give the guy a name,' said Leo, reaching for a crisp, but Vince deftly moved the bowl out of reach. 'He's leading a double life, so let's call him Walter White. Or Tom Canty. Or Algernon, or Tom Ripley,' said Vince.

He pushed some shopping bags aside so he could put his feet on the seat. His trousers rose up to reveal his new orange and white socks. Leo looked at the garish colours and tutted disdainfully. He tried again for a crisp but was again denied.

'How about Arbuthnot? As a name?' he said.

'Mr Arbuthnot?'

'Just Arbuthnot.'

Vince shrugged. 'It doesn't resonate. Apart from Pope. *Letter to Arbuthnot* or something.'

He placed the crisps beyond Leo's reach, secured his glass of vodka and Red Bull, and began opening a giant Toblerone. He threw over a chunk of chocolate.

***

After a mile further on, the limo began slowing till it reached a pace no faster than a dawdle. Dave lowered the screen and shouted grumpily something about road works, or traffic, Leo wasn't really listening.

'We better check on our very good friend Arbuthnot,' said Vince, picking up his phone to check on the news. He tutted.

'It seems that he has come out from the shadows.'

'Fuck,' said Leo.

Vince read the news bulletin.

'Camelot has announced that the winner or winners of the record breaking Globomillions jackpot has claimed the prize. They have asked to remain anonymous.'

He looked at Leo. 'Are we in the clear, Mr Expert? Or are we about to come crashing to the ground?'

Leo leaned back and exhaled with relief. This could be good news. At the hotel press conference neither of them had said anything about contacting Camelot. They may have simply had the winning ticket, and not yet made a claim. For all anyone knew, this new press announcement was all about Leo.

'No one's going to know it's not me they're talking about.'

Vince narrowed his eyes, trying to work it all out.

'Unless Arbuthnot changes his mind about being anonymous.'

Leo shook his head. 'No, I reckon he'll keep shtum. He wouldn't want to ruin our fun.'

'You're right, he loves us.'

'And we love him.'

'Isn't blind faith wonderful?' said Vince.

34

CARIM CAN FIX THIS

Hamir was sweating. He always carried a hanky to mop his face, but he was too late to stop a drop plinking onto his computer keyboard.

He and his wife were in what they called their 'office', but it was a deliberate misnomer; it was simply one half of the kitchen table they used for book-keeping, stock tracking, VAT returns and banking. Hamir liked working right in the centre of things, and he didn't mind being interrupted by one of his three children or occasionally getting chutney on a delivery document. Gira, who was in charge of VAT and corporation tax, did most of her work once the children were in bed. She would have much preferred a dedicated office, and its corollary: a dedicated kitchen.

Hamir had spent an hour going through the CCTV footage, which was stored on a hard drive. Old footage was kept until there was no more memory, then it was wiped in favour of new data. Since there had been an intermittent fault on the camera, he found he could access random footage going back a couple of months.

'*The Express* rang again,' he said. 'I think they will pay good money for video of him buying a ticket, just one ticket. *Is this the billion pound moment?*'

Gira peered over her glasses.

'I think you just want to be famous.' It was an affectionate rebuke.

'I wouldn't mind,' he said, feeling cheered by his wife's playful tone.

'I don't understand it, though,' he said. 'There's nothing of him buying a ticket on any Wednesdays.'

'Like I said, maybe he stopped—'

'He did *not* stop doing the lottery weeks ago!'

He hadn't meant to raise his voice, but he couldn't help it sometimes, and it was the third or fourth time she had made the same point. Gira busied herself with her accounts.

The basic *fact* was that Leo Morphetus had bought a billion pound ticket from his shop. That's what he had told all his customers, and that's what he'd told the radio guy. Already business was on the up – okay, hardly at all really, but still, lottery tickets were definitely more popular. But the main thing was this: the more Hamir could establish himself as the seller of the ticket, the more likely it was that the nice coffee guy would remember him, and come good with a thank you.

'He must have bought it when the camera wasn't working,' he said.

'Or perhaps he went somewhere else?' Gira looked up with the slightest of smiles.

'Why would he go somewhere else? He always comes to us. For years.'

Hamir was definitely winning this argument. 'Carim can fix this.'

'Fix this, *how*?' said Gira, less affectionately now.

'We get footage from an earlier date. He can just change the indicator thing, the date stamp, which is probably faulty anyway.' He looked down at his keyboard because he didn't want to see his wife's expression, which was bound to be disapproving. 'Carim is good at that sort of thing, he knows all about computers, our boy. He can do that.'

'I don't think that's a good idea,' said Gira, sounding anxious now.

'It's a perfectly good idea and who is it going to hurt?'

'Maybe *you*, Hamir?'

'It's just a bit of fun.'

'Hamir—'

'We will never agree on this,' he said, still avoiding her eyes. 'We sold him a ticket, and that's that. I just have to make sure the video agrees with me.'

He called for Carim to come into the kitchen. Then he sang *Who Wants To Be a Millionaire*, but only in his head.

35

HARAM

Mrs Nina Allam had very little time to herself. As well as her teaching job, she had two teenage daughters to look after, plus a large and demanding extended family. She would use her twenty-minute walk home from school to mull things over.

The rain that had pelted down earlier had subsided, and there was now just the occasional drop, enough to provoke only the most hydrophobic pedestrians to open their umbrellas. In the sky above the windmill a few clouds parted and she glanced up to see a promising hint of blue.

Three years ago Nina Allam admitted to herself, but to no one else, that there was a problem in her marriage. Her husband, Zakir, was becoming angry and intolerant, and while he used to turn a blind eye to some of their daughters' wayward behaviour, he was now vigilant. Small transgressions would make him rage. He had come under the influence of new faces at the mosque and expected stricter adherence to the tenets of Islam than he had as a young man.

Nina believed that the root cause of this change was his failure in business. He had sunk the family's money into a storage facility that had never made a profit, but he refused to accept that it had flopped. He threw good money after bad until he was left with nothing but debts, which even with the help of family members, he was unable to settle. Nina believed that he mitigated his feelings of inadequacy by leading a more spiritual and observant life. Without the business, Zakir's sphere of influence was so diminished that he sought more control over what little remained, namely, his wife and daughters.

She supported her husband's devotion and tried to respect his views, but there was one issue over which they could not agree. More than anything, Nina wanted her daughters to go to University, just as she had done. Zakir, in a complete reversal of the beliefs they'd shared as young parents, refused to contemplate financially supporting them through further education, even if he could raise the money. He would not listen to talk about student loans, stating that even so-called 'Sharia loans' were un-Islamic. This was now the main source of conflict in the family. Nina could not stand by and let her daughters be denied the opportunity that she had had herself. She read hadith, and she prayed every day that Zakir would change his mind. But each day he seemed more entrenched, and almost every week a new edict would find its way from the mosque to the home.

Although the conflict with Zakir was forever in the background, Nina's present preoccupation, as she walked past the sports centre towards the high street, was that she had committed a great sin, haram, and Allah in his wisdom might be punishing her for it.

A cold gust blew between some unused office buildings, and she buttoned up the puffa-jacket that she wore over her sari. Byford's Asian community was enough in number for the sari and hijab not to draw a second glance, but she dreaded bumping into neighbours, who she felt might somehow guess her secret. Her heart missed a beat when she heard her name being called, but was relieved to see that it was only little Amy and her mother on the other side of the street.

Nina smiled and waved. Mrs Morphetus was wearing a scarf and sunglasses, and Nina wondered if she was afraid of being harassed by the press. What a very strange business it was. Amy's father seemed such a decent man, with kind eyes. He always came to the school fête with his coffee contraption, helping to raise funds for the new gym. He was the first to arrive and last to leave. How could he fool so many people? And why?

Lost in thought, Nina failed to see a puddle and she felt a cold rush of water on her feet. Before musing on Mr Morphetus any longer, she reminded herself that this was not the time to be thinking of others, she must plan for herself, and plan carefully.

Tomorrow she would leave school early, saying she had a migraine, but make sure Judy, one of the supply teachers, could take over the class. She would take the rear exit by the kitchens. If she met someone, a neighbour, they might ask questions – Where was she going? Who was she seeing? Nina would have to think of a story. She would be vague.

At times of stress she thought of her departed mother; a determined woman with bright round eyes, who had high hopes for her daughter. 'Your generation will not be slaves to men,' she said. 'And your daughters will be free to follow their dreams, God willing. But always teach them to be observant, and protect their husbands' honour.'

Right now, Nina would ask her mother this: What if doing what is right *and* being observant seem impossible? How can I not bring shame on my husband after what I have done? The two of them would sit down and talk through this dilemma with tea, and with tranquillity and love. Her mother would admonish her for her offence, even scold her and say she had been very foolish, but she would add that no one is free from sin. She would look for a way for her daughter to make amends. And that is what Nina Allam must do.

As she walked past Hamir's store, she shivered. Why hadn't she crossed the street? Had the lady behind the counter glimpsed her? She bowed her head and turned away, but still felt touched by cold rays of shame.

36

COWS HAVE MUCH HARDER SKIN

The limo had been crawling at a snail's pace for twenty minutes so Driver Dave suggested taking another stop at a Welcome Break. Rather than park in the car park where there would be selfie-hunters, he found a place in the truck bay. He sandwiched the Lincoln between a Sainsbury's lorry and a tanker containing something toxic, corrosive, radio-active, flammable and, lest there be any doubt, hazardous. The tanker's driver, sipping tea in his cabin, eyed the stretch limo like a pigeon might eye a pink flamingo landing in Trafalgar Square.

Vince and Dave had decided to take a nap – Dave in his cabin, Vince under a patch of the floor he'd cleared at the back. He lay under his brand new duffle coat, curled up like a prawn.

Leo's phone rang. It was the in-laws' landline: probably Harriet calling to simultaneously congratulate him and make him feel bad.

'Hello?'

'Am I talking to the richest man in Byford?' came Frank Sterling's bombastic tones.

'It's possible,' said Leo, because it *was possible*. Without knowing it, he sat up straight and patted down his hair.

'Been celebrating, I hear. Let the cat out of the bag, did you? Bit too much of the sauce? We've all been there!'

Leo waited for Frank's humourless chuckle to subside. Laughing should be reserved for things that are funny, not just to make noise.

'Hello? Still there?'

'Yes, still here, Frank.'

'Righto,' said Frank, with another meaningless chuckle.

'Can I help you?' Leo knew this was right on the edge of being rude.

'Um, no, well, yes,' came the reply. 'Um, that is, you could certainly help Byford, the people of Byford. I was *so* impressed by your fine words at the press conference thing, you know, on telly, and I thought, you and I should get together, and see how we can join forces.'

For a seasoned politician, he wasn't a very smooth talker – at least not at this moment.

'Hello?'

'I'm still here, Frank.'

'As you know, I am hoping to be Byford's council leader for a second term – for my sins, ha. There's so much I want to *do* for the people round here, and I think you feel the same. I know all the local organisations, the charities, the groups, you know, the hospitals and let's not forget the hospice. I don't know if you've ever been to these places?'

'I've been to the hospice, my mother died there.'

'Absolutely, absolutely. I, er... she was a wonderful woman.'

Frank had only met Eva Morphetus half a dozen times: at the wedding; Amy's christening, which Harriet had instigated; the house warming party. Frank blustered some more kind words, while Leo gazed at the huge wheels of the lorry next to him, impressed by the number of nuts and bolts. He realised that he had been asked a question.

'Still there, Leo?'

'Yes, Frank.'

'So what do you think?'

He didn't know what the question was.

'I think... whatever, you know?'

'Great.' Frank seemed satisfied. He made various throaty noises that didn't amount to anything but they were preferable to the chuckle.

'Look, Leo, rather than listen to me witter on – I'm sure you have lots to do – how about coming for dinner? I know Harriet would love to see you.'

Would she fuck.

'How are you fixed?'

'Well, I *am* pretty busy.'

'I am sure you're fighting off the totty.'

Leo blushed – this was his father-in-law.

'Hello?'

'Still here, Frank.'

'It's just that a lot of people in Byford are in real need and…'

He gabbled on. It occurred to Leo that maybe this mover and shaker might be able to help Poppy's support group. Perhaps Frank could pull strings. And even if he couldn't, a dinner with the Sterlings, now that he was a 'billionaire' would surely prove entertaining. Wasn't this partly what it was all about? Turning the tables on the people who'd despised him?

'Would it be okay if my mate came to dinner, too?' he asked. It just felt right for Vince to be there.

'Of course, that would be wonderful. Harriet will weave her culinary magic. That reminds me, is there anything you don't eat?'

Without thinking Leo said, 'walnuts' even though he had no issues with them. Perhaps it was the nuts on the truck's wheel that had brought them to mind.

'And anything else that's brain-shaped,' he added.

'Walnuts? And, er… brain-shaped things, ha. Okay, I'll tell Harriet.'

And then Leo sensed in himself what he could only describe as a kind of bloodlust.

'And peas.'

'Okay, no peas. Not keen myself, the little—'

'And anything with egg in it. *Chicken's* egg. Other eggs are okay.'

'No chicken's egg… actually, my pen's run out. Just a sec, because I need to write these down.'

'And anything with claws.'

'Er… right, so no chicken? No birds, essentially?'

'I eat birds with webbed feet.'

'Er, so ducks are okay, then… are there any, er—'

'No vinegar, or anything with a hard skin.' He couldn't seem to stop himself.

'A hard skin? You mean like… oranges? Coconuts?'

'And cows. Bulls are okay, but cows have much harder skin.'

'That's a new one on me. Ha!'

'Have you ever stroked one?'

'Er, maybe once.'

'Much tougher skin than bulls.'

Frank chuckled, but less assuredly than before.

'Do you like fish? Harriet's great with salmon.'

How far could he push it?

'I only like salmon on Thursdays.'

'Er, Thursdays, okay, got that.'

Quite far, it would seem. Frank's chuckles began to sound like high pitched coughs.

'How does tomorrow evening sound? Too short notice?'

'No, we're free. See you tomorrow, Frank.'

They said their goodbyes.

The tanker's engine powered into life and reversed out of the bay. The smell of exhaust seeped in. The fact that Frank had no trouble believing that he only liked salmon on Thursdays gave Leo pause. For all these years, had he really thought he was *that* much of a fool? Or had the prospect of having dinner with a malleable billionaire dazzled him – and deafened him? He thought about Bernard Madoff, whose clients made no effort to find out how the money magically arrived – provided it kept coming: wilful blindness.

***

The bellow of an ostentatious yawn came from the rear. The tanker had roused Vince from his slumber. His head popped up and he looked around, his hair standing like a church steeple. He frowned as he blinked. Then his head flopped down again and he closed his eyes. It was as if his brain cells wanted to retreat and regroup.

Leo's phone rang.

'Yes?'

'Ah, Leo. Clive Entwhistle here.'

Leo took a moment to recall who this was. It was the estate agent that Mrs Klyne had hired to expedite his eviction.

'Yes?'

'Congrats, mate. I trust all's good with you? *Very* good, I shouldn't wonder.'

'Yes, fine. Homeless, though.'

There wasn't so much as a beat before Entwhistle continued.

'Don't worry about the fire damage. We're going to sort all that out gratis, Leo.'

It hadn't occurred to Leo that the little fire he started might have damaged anything.

'Thanks.'

'I have great news, Leo.'

Leo wanted to get off the phone.

'I have a wonderful property for you. A fabulous six-bedroom detached house on the top of Greenfields Hill. I mean, I assume you are looking for somewhere?'

The man seemed oblivious to the possibility that Leo just might hold a grudge against him.

'A six-bedroom house?'

'Yes. And the owner has just left for the Middle East. He says you can rent or buy. To be honest, mate, he's hoping you'll rent *then* buy. He's very flexible. I think you'll love it. But if you don't fancy it, I have other options.'

Leo thought quickly. This could be a very useful break.

'Can I move in tonight?'

Well it was worth a try. Staying in Vince's flat would surely arouse suspicion – why isn't the billionaire in luxury accommodation?

'Ha! Well, it is *very* unusual and ultra-short notice, but… the owner left it all ready to be let out, and I have the keys, *so that's a green light.*'

Entwhistle sounded as if he'd just found the cure for cancer. He described the property in more detail and said the owner was hoping that Leo would fall in love with the place and then make an offer to buy with cash.

As Leo hung up, Driver Dave, having finished his nap, heaved himself out of the car, unzipped, and relieved himself onto the wheel of the Sainsbury's lorry. He pulled a packet from his pocket, extracted a cigarette, put it in his mouth, and then lit it, all with one hand. *Everyone has hidden talents,* thought Leo.

37

I'M BLOODY TERRIFED

Donald and Piers lived in a hamlet four miles west of Byford. It had been their dream to move to the country. From the bedroom window of the eighteenth century cottage, the couple had a view of a pond shaded by a willow tree. A pair of resident swans completed the picture of a country idyll. Donald and Piers likened themselves to Mr and Mrs Swan. They imagined that, like them, the handsome birds paid dearly to live in this desirable location and they had a mortgage, a garden to keep tidy, and a nest to maintain.

The couple, who were both born in East Byford, embraced the bucolic life. They'd signed up to as many local clubs and groups as they could, including some for antique collecting, wine making, bird watching, and pheasant shooting. They'd had a friendly dispute with each other about the fact that on Saturday they would watch birds through binoculars, and marvel at their beauty, then on Sunday try to blow them out of the sky with a twelve-bore shotgun. Donald insisted that the two activities presented the warp and weft of country living.

Donald, unable to sleep, had come downstairs to sit in front of the fire, which still radiated a faint glow. A bottle of Irish whiskey was on the coffee table next to a tumbler, half full. He looked around, trying to find comfort in the oak beams and picturesque little windows: everything about the place suggested peace and old-fashioned simplicity. But nothing could take his mind off The Problem. The Problem loitered in the dark corners of his skull like a stranger who would neither leave, nor come into the light.

When he'd hefted himself out of bed, he had accidentally-on-purpose kicked Piers because he hoped his spouse would wake up and, after a few minutes, follow him.

The ploy worked. Piers blearily padded his way down the treacherously steep staircase.

'You found it,' he said.

'Yup.'

The bottle of Jameson's had been hidden in the bottom of a chest reserved for spare throws and cushions.

'Why are you drinking?'

'Because the drugs don't work,' said Donald, quickly and flatly.

'You asked me not to let you—'

'Not now, Piers,' snapped Donald. Piers sat down and rubbed his face, trying to wipe away sleep.

'This about the billionaire man?'

Donald had told him the basic facts: he'd put £200,000 into the man's account, flouting the proper procedures, and had approved a joint account for the two men without seeing the required ID.

'I'm bloody terrified, Piers.'

He could hear the desperation in his voice and hoped Piers could, too.

'In a day or two it will all be fine,' said Piers. 'Besides, you couldn't let them walk away.'

This is exactly the sort of comfort that Donald needed, but it wasn't enough. He pressed his left fist into the palm of his right hand and twisted hard. He wanted to scare Piers, and he knew how.

'But Piers, listen. *Listen*. I don't know what the *fucking hell* I was thinking!'

He shouted the words *fucking hell* so loudly that Piers flinched.

'The fact is, I didn't even *lend* him the money, I *gave* it to him. There is no paperwork, no schedule for repayment, we didn't discuss interest, nothing. The jackpot money should have come in to the account today. And they've started spending – there are pictures of them arsing about in Liberty's – those guys are laughing at me.'

He could hear Piers trying to control his breathing, a sure sign he was rattled.

'But Donald, the guy – Morphetus – is going to have nearly a billion in a day or two, surely? You said so last night.'

'Yeah. I *said* so. But what if he doesn't? If he doesn't, I am finished, completely fucked and so are you.'

'You don't think he won the money?'

'No, no, he *won* the money. He won the money!'

'You're shouting.'

Donald would try, but not very hard, to be quieter. He took a sip of the warming liquid, and then a large gulp. If Piers was judging him, then so be it.

'What if he's trying to punish me?'

'Why would—'

'The guy hates me.'

'How could *anyone* hate you?' Piers smiled cheekily.

'Yeah, yeah,' said Donald, refusing to be cheered by the joke. Instead, he was just irritated by Piers's failure to feel the enormity of The Problem.

'I told you, I refused him a loan. What if he goes to Nat West with the money? It's what *I'd* do. I would want to *stick it* to the man who refused me a loan.'

'Yeah, but not everyone is as vindictive as you, Don.'

Donald knew this was affectionate mockery, but he deliberately took it the wrong way. He picked up the silver wine-holder from the coffee table – the first thing the couple had ever bought together – and examined it with contempt before flinging it back, where it skated along and fell off on the other side.

Piers said, 'The guy seems pretty cool. He wants to give money to charity and help the people of Byford. He's a nice boy and I'm—'

'I haven't told you the full story.' Donald wanted put a stop to this gushing. 'You remember what he said to the press? *All those people who tell you it can't be done, you're ten-a-penny, sod off to the Nat West.* Almost my exact words. The man is fucking with me.'

Go on, Piers, tell me I'm getting things out of proportion. That was his job: to lift him out of these black moods. And it was Donald's job to make it as hard as possible.

He knocked back his drink and poured himself another. As he put the bottle down he glanced at his husband, who remained fixed in his abject posture. After a moment, Piers took a breath and dared to speak.

'He might not be as angry as you think.'

Donald wasted no time in crushing this thought.

'He called me a cunt.' Piers flinched. 'When I refused the loan. He hadn't meant me to hear, but I did.'

Why wasn't Piers smothering him with positive thoughts? There could only be one reason: there was nothing to be positive about. This was Armageddon. All the years Donald had put into working his way out of the grim suburbs of East Byford, the efforts he and Piers had put into making themselves acceptable to the rural, old-rich society they were now hovering on the fringes of, all this was—

'Do you know what you could do?' said Piers, slapping his thigh like a principal boy. 'Tell your boss. Come clean. She'll understand. You were trying your best for the bank. It's a great idea.'

This was not a great idea.

'Piers… do you mind if I make a suggestion? *Be less fucking dumb.*'

Piers bowed his head and found a pyjama button to fiddle with. The sides of his mouth drooped like a schoolgirl who'd just been picked on by the class bitch.

'Be less fucking dumb.' Donald repeated. He knew that he was hurting Piers because of what he, Donald, had done, but *someone* had to be punished.

'I took money from the bank,' he said, 'without permission, and gave it to a customer.' He stood up, hovering over Piers, who shrank into his chair. 'If I told my boss, I'd be dismissed and charged with embezzlement. You want to put me in jail? Because if you do, keep making suggestions like that.'

Piers raised his eyebrows and kept them raised, an act of micro-defiance. 'You gave the guys some money, so what?' he said, shakily. 'If they're billionaires you'll get it back. Even if you have to beg them. You can tell they're nice guys from their TV thing, they're like Ant and Dec.'

Donald sat down. Was this morsel of hope worth grabbing?

'You can tell that from the TV?' he asked.

'Absolutely, Don. They don't have a nasty bone in their bodies.'

Donald willed himself to turn his juggernaut of despair around. After all, Piers was better at reading people than he was.

'You're sure?'

Piers almost bounced on his chair.

'Positive. They will *definitely* deposit the money soon, you don't need to worry, Don.'

This was nectar for the soul.

'So you think it's going to be okay?'

'I do. You've played a blinder.'

This was *so* right. Donald had been worrying about nothing. Tomorrow or the next day, a payment would show on the account and he would wonder why he'd ever doubted it.

'Besides,' said Piers, now on a roll, 'you said last night that banks never call the cops.'

That was true. The very worst, *worst* that could happen is that he'd be fired with a decent reference. He lay back in the armchair, closed his eyes, and allowed himself a deep, deep sigh.

But the relief didn't last. The air left his lungs like the sea leaving a beach only to be drawn into a tidal wave. He was going to drown and there was nothing anyone could do to save him.

Piers picked himself up and stood behind the armchair to run his hands through his husband's thinning hair. After all these years, he knew, he just knew. It wasn't so much what Donald said or did, it was a change to his face, the shape his eyes. The bottom rims sagged: the first sign of Bad Times. Donald even *smelt* different. And he was right – the drugs don't work.

'I don't want you to get ill again,' said Piers.

38

CAN YOU EXPLAIN IT?

Although Donna was more productive when she worked from home, visiting the office gave her the feeling she was part of the nine-to-five world of Prêt salads, kitten videos, 'hilarious' double-entendres and gossip.

The headquarters of TrueNewz was on the second and third floors of a red brick Victorian warehouse in Mile End, East London. Until the 80s the building had been a sweatshop for the rag trade, and there were holes in the floor where sewing machines had been screwed down. It was a mix of glass, chrome and industrial shabby-chic. The only item that was shabby without being chic was Derek. He was a fish out of water, or as he once described himself, 'a dodo at a disco', but even the metaphor dated him.

Donna acknowledged a few 'well dones' as she walked past the desks. She had landed the hard evidence that Leo Morphetus was the billionaire. Fair play to her, she was good.

But this morning she kept her chatting to a minimum because there was something on her mind. A little scoop was in the offing. She'd spent an hour checking news outlets and came across a video that warranted closer examination. One of the tech guys would help her. She fired up her tablet and showed it to Paul, the oldest and smartest IT guy, who had an official title that she had never saved to memory. He was forty, but he was jowly and looked more like fifty. She stood over him, his dandruff a little too close for comfort, but this wouldn't take long.

Paul viewed the footage on *The Daily Express* website, and read the accompanying copy with a frown.

'Anything odd?' she asked.

'Yes, there's something *very* odd. *The Express* got hold of it *first*, and they never get hold of *anything* first. How come *you* didn't scoop this?'

Another reason why Donna liked coming in to work: office banter.

'Well Paul, I was just a *little* busy sourcing documentary evidence that Morphetus is the actual winner, meaning TrueNewz broke the story.'

'Rumour has it you backed down from that.'

He clucked like a chicken, which Donna found amusingly puerile.

'Well Paul, I supplied all the facts, but the decision to publish was Derek's, so not really a case of cowardice, but circumspection, which I think is rather *wise*. Can you make like an owl?'

He made a desultory hoot.

'Good. Now, the footage?'

He leaned back and tapped his hands on the arms of his chair a few times before bestowing his considered view.

'It's a guy buying a ticket.'

'Excellent. A *billion pound* ticket?'

'I suppose so. What's your point?'

'*The Express* are saying it *could* be the winning ticket. Only Camelot know the time and place a ticket was bought but of course they never reveal those facts.'

'Okay, so it *could* be the winning ticket. So what?'

He's being the ideal stooge, thought Donna.

'Let's watch it on your desktop.'

Paul sourced the footage on his own computer.

'What am I looking for?'

'Start with the date.'

He peered at the pink date stamp on the bottom left of the screen.

'April 2nd.'

'The day of the draw, a Wednesday.'

'Ah, Wednesdays, the dullest day of the week. They should scrap Wednesdays.'

'Now can you enlarge the image?'

'Like in *Blow-Up*?' Donna didn't respond. 'Antonioni's minor masterpiece?'

Typical IT guy, she thought, *referencing something he knew she wouldn't get*. She shrugged.

'Young people today have no cinema,' he huffed.

'I read. But thanks for the *young*.'

A moment later they were watching the newsagent's footage, enlarged.

'You need to tell me what to focus on,' said Paul.

'The newspapers on the shelf. Try to freeze and enlarge one of those headlines.'

A headline became large enough to read quite clearly.

'I thought so… but I wasn't sure,' said Donna, out loud, but to herself. 'I could only read *rail* something.'

'You've lost me… Hello? I'm over here.'

Donna remembered where she was.

'The rail strike?'

'What?

She pulled up a chair and sat down.

'The headline doesn't match the date. The headlines are about the national rail strike. I've gone back four weeks. This footage is *27 days* old, so before the winning ticket could have been bought.'

Paul sat back and smiled quizzically.

'This really *is* like *Blow-Up*.'

'Can you explain it?'

He stroked his chin. Men like Paul rarely admit to not having an answer, he'll bluff something.

'Sure. The date stamp could have been set incorrectly. Unlikely, but possible. But the user would know – if they have any sense.'

'So someone's pulling a fast one?'

'Conspiracy or cock up. You choose.'

'But whatever, that is definitely *not* a guy buying a billion pound ticket, correct?'

'Correct,' said Paul. 'But that doesn't mean he didn't buy it on another day, or from somewhere else.'

'Thanks for the mansplanation,' said Donna, getting up.

'Hey. You ask me for advice and now I'm *mansplaining*?' he harrumphed. Donna picked up her bag and swung it over her shoulder.

'It's a tough old world,' she said with a smile, and made to leave.

'You know, Donna…' She stopped and turned round. 'You're more than just a – oops, mustn't say things like that anymore.'

She gave him a friendly punch and strode towards Derek's office. He was just about to take his second bite out of a breakfast Subway.

'Want to hang *The Express* out to dry?'

39

I KNOW WHERE THE HOLY GRAIL IS

The house that Clive Entwhistle had found for Leo was, according to Vince, so tastelessly appointed that it would make Liberace wince. He asked Entwhistle if some of the tat could be removed. He was especially keen on expelling the dozen or so life-size porcelain figures of dogs with drooping faces and sad eyes. The estate agent said he would consult with the owner about having them rehoused. 'We'll pay extra if we can smash them to bits with a hammer,' said Vince.

While Vince was critiquing the decor and furniture, Leo's role had been to keep Entwhistle sweet, by pretending to consider whether the property, a detached Edwardian, double-fronted home with a hundred-foot garden, was something he might buy. This resulted in Entwhistle becoming so excited that when he got in his car, and thinking he couldn't be seen, he pumped his fist and shouted something with such vigour his face went crimson.

The house, having been occupied by the owner only weeks before he went abroad, had everything they needed, from bed sheets to towels, and even a well-stocked larder.

Once Entwhistle had gone, the men gave Driver Dave the night off, eschewed the larder and ordered a ludicrous amount of food and booze from local eateries and online grocers.

They spent the evening in front of a fire with flames that seemed to emanate from stones. As Leo pointed out, their conversation was an unconscious game of pessimist/ optimist. Each took an opposing 'ist', thereby creating a balance, which Leo thought might be a semblance of 'reality'.

In the morning, Vince donned a striped apron and made breakfast. He did this while singing money-based songs, of which he had a growing repertoire. Leo joined in a chorus or two while manning the espresso machine. He was grateful for Vince's buoyant mood, because he'd spent the night fretting, and at one point nearly knocked on Vince's door to tell him he was going to call up Helen and tell her everything and then do whatever she told him. But that's what Old Leo would do. Instead, Leo focused on a plan.

Breakfast was bacon and eggs with homemade waffles, fresh orange juice, and a selection of berries and cream.

'I could get used to this,' Leo said, wiping his mouth on a linen napkin with a bulldog's face on it.

Once breakfast was over, it was time to summon Driver Dave and ask him to take them to the bank. Leo felt reasonably confident that a new loan was on the cards. Hughes had taken a big step into the dark side by giving them the first loan, 'commitment bias' would make the next one easier. Worst case would be an apologetic refusal from Hughes, and if that happened it was no disaster. There would be no shortage of people willing to lend money to those who apparently had an excess of it.

***

'I am so glad to see you boys, so glad you would not *believe*,' said Donald Hughes, as he filled three tumblers with a couple of fingers of Jameson's. It did not appear to be his first of the day. His cheeks were red and shone with a moist glow.

'Strictly speaking this is forbidden, but hey, we're celebrating, aren't we?' He winked as he sprayed his mouth with a pocket freshener.

His clients, sitting side by side in front of his desk, exchanged furtive glances. There was something very odd about their prey this morning. His hands were trembling.

'I'll be honest, I haven't slept. I did a crazy thing, transferring that money. Okay, I can now heave a sigh of relief, but I took a big risk. I put my job on the line, maybe more than my job.' Hughes winked again – conspiratorially this time.

'We appreciate it, man,' said Vince, flippantly.

Hughes sat down and Leo noticed that this neat and tidy man had forgotten his left cufflink.

'Love your style, guys. Shop till you drop. Splash the cash. Spend, spend, spend!'

As he gabbled on about shops and clothes, Leo felt increasingly ill-at-ease. The rhythms were all wrong. Gesture, expression, words, nothing fitted together. It was like watching a singer suddenly getting ahead of the beat. It was worryingly strange, and Leo felt a drop of sweat slide down from his armpit.

'So, you spent some time in London? I saw all the selfies online. Let's have a look at it... The cheque? Did you ask for an old-fashioned banker's draft?' He mimed signing something.

Leo would have to give him some very bad news, and the guy seemed to be teetering on the edge as it was.

'Mr Hughes, Donald, let me explain. Before handing over a big win, the lottery people need to see the ticket.'

Leo conveyed a 'but' with a gesture.

'But...?'

Leo took a ticket from his pocket, which Vince had purchased on the way there and scuffed up a little to make it look older. Leo had bet on Hughes not checking that the ticket had the winning numbers.

'As you can see, there is a tiny tear just here.'

The tear was all of half a centimetre.

'So it's invalid? Is that what you're telling me?'

Hughes's face paled, and his skin seemed to drop as if drawn by a sudden gravitational surge.

'Hughes, listen to the man,' said Vince.

'If a ticket is even very slightly damaged, they wait a while before transferring the money,' said Leo. 'If you don't believe me, look it up online, or better still, phone them.'

'Phone them now,' added Vince.

'It's because technically, and I emphasise, *technically*, a damaged ticket could conceivably be a fake, so they wait ten days to make sure no one else comes forward with a 'real' ticket.'

This was all true.

'You know, I *thought* maybe you were going to fuck me over,' said Hughes, trying but failing to sound calm. 'Because I heard you, I heard what you called me, *I heard you.*'

Leo looked towards the door, and although Hughes hadn't shouted loudly, he still expected staff to come rushing in.

'Calm down, man,' said Vince.

'Don't tell me to fucking calm down! You're fucking messing with me,' he whispered-shouted.

'We're not, this is the truth,' said Leo. Technically he still hadn't lied, not so much for moral reasons, but because he knew he was a bad liar.

The banker's hands went to his keyboard and typed and clicked, clicked and typed with total concentration. Something wasn't working. He shook his head and reddened. He seemed to be trying again. Then:

'Bingo. I can only do half a million without authorisation. It's in your account, do what you like with it.'

Leo and Vince had nothing to say. This had been shockingly swift and more than they were going to ask for.

'You didn't just…?' said Vince.

Hughes slammed his fist to his mouth and seemed about to explode. When he took it out again he spluttered through tears.

'Please, don't destroy me.' A balloon of saliva appeared from his mouth, then burst.

Leo, now feeling that things were reeling out of control, tried to find words to calm the man.

'I'm not trying to shaft you.'

Hughes put his hand up to silence his tormentors. He breathed deeply for a moment, and then spoke more calmly.

'Okay, now listen to me, listen to me please,' he said.

'We're listening,' said the men, in near-unison.

Hughes's eyes became focused, as if he could see clearly for the first time.

'I don't know if you're punishing me or not. I guess I'll know in ten days. But we're quits. Just get out of here. Go.'

Leo wondered if they should thank him, but it didn't seem appropriate somehow. Just before they left the office, Hughes said, 'I do have one trump card.'

'Yes?' said Leo.

'I know where the holy grail is.'

Leo took a second to wonder what this could possibly mean, but there was no doubt it was some kind of threat. He didn't want to extend the meeting a moment longer so he nodded and they both left.

***

As the limo purred past the UK's second ever Poundland, Leo felt sorry for Hughes. This adventure was never meant to harm anyone. Vince was more concerned about his own fate.

'This is fucking serious now.'

'We're grabbing life by the cock.' It was Leo's turn to play the optimist.

'So we have ten days?'

'It's going to take that long to sort out who gets what anyway. The Lethco families.'

'What do you mean? Just give them the money.'

'I need to check everything.'

Vince rolled his eyes. There was no point in Leo going through all the details of how and why he wanted to make sure each family got the money they needed, that it was a realistic treatment, all the bona fides.

Neil Diamond came through the speakers.

Leo's phone bleeped with several texts from Helen, asking him to call asap. Like any urgent message from parent to parent, it caused his heart to quicken. He couldn't not phone.

'What's up?'

'Leo…' she sighed. He sensed a reprimand was coming.

'Have you considered what all this means for Amy and me?'

He *had* thought about how all this might affect them but in this instant he realised that he probably hadn't thought about it enough.

'Is there a problem?'

Helen answered with another sigh, giving him time to anxiously conjure some possibilities.

'Is Amy being bullied?'

'No, but don't you think that this might be putting us in danger?'

'What's happened?'

'Nothing's *happened*, Leo.' This was emphatic. 'But… Amy is now the daughter of a billionaire, and don't you think that in the long term both she and I could be some sort of… target?'

The rippling anxiety froze into a lump in Leo's chest.

'What the fuck is that music?'

He tapped on the dividing window and pointed to his phone. Neil Diamond was duly muted.

'Something must have happened, Helen – just tell me.'

'Nothing's happened. I don't want you to do *anything*, okay? Or discuss this with anyone, not even Vince.'

He didn't want to believe he'd put his family in harm's way, and so he searched his memory for reassuring facts.

'Helen, lots of people win the lottery and they're fine.'

'Most of them don't shout about it on TV.'

'Even the ones who go public – I mean apart from Abraham Shakespeare, of course.'

'Who the hell is Abraham fucking Shakespeare?'

Leo allowed himself a little smile.

'From Florida. He was killed for his money.'

'Fuck. Who by?'

'His wife. She buried him under the patio, and then for several months she pretended he was still alive.'

A little chuckle from Helen. So things can't be *that* bad.

'Yeah, well, I wouldn't want to ruin my nice patio. But Leo, every day some arsehole rings the doorbell. One long-lost sister and your long-lost dad, plus a couple of press people. I've stopped answering the door. But it's not like we live in a fortress. Anyone could nip round the back.'

'You didn't tell me this.'

'We don't talk much, these days. We *need* to talk, Leo. Sooner or later, we will have to make arrangements, perhaps send Amy to boarding school, maybe move to a house with gates or a big wall and security guards, all that.'

Helen almost managed to get to the end of the sentence before her voice faltered. Something must have triggered this. Maybe just a TV show or a news report. She was often alarmed by crime stories or the latest cancer scare.

'Believe me, Helen, people have big wins all over the world and they don't go into hiding. Winning the lottery is not considered a high-risk activity.'

'Good old Leo.'

'What do you mean?'

'Nothing.'

But Leo kind-of knew what she meant. She meant he was bringing statistics into a personal context. He did that a lot. They said their goodbyes as the limo rolled into the double driveway of what they would call The Manor.

As soon as he could, he checked his bank account. The money was there, as Hughes had said. He was surprised to see a half a dozen deposits – all under a hundred pounds. He surmised that they were the well-wishers that Vince had mentioned. He transferred the deposits into a separate account. Next, he called Alan Lethco. He would need to arrange to meet the other desperate families, check them out carefully. It wouldn't be easy – he would have to ask questions, seek professional verification and examine documents.

40

REMEMBER WHAT I TOLD YOU ABOUT SANTA?

'Now!' said Leo.

Amy opened her eyes and looked around at the enormous room, and in the corner was her first ever scooter.

'O... M... G. Wow.' She rushed over to it. 'It's amazing, Dad.'

'You like it?'

'It's so cool.'

'Your mother might not approve of the colour.'

She shook her head, 'Pink things aren't going to make me more girly, Dad,' she said, as if talking to a much younger child.

She asked if she could ride it but Leo insisted that since it was now nearly dark, she could only use it inside. Given the size of The Manor, that wasn't an especially onerous request.

He watched her whiz around the kitchen island. Sometimes he ran after her, and sometimes he slowed down enough to be chased. After an exhausting number of laps, they stopped to have a fruit juice at the breakfast bar.

She was going to be tall and gangly like him, he thought. Her serious forehead and wise eyes were Helen's, and there were times, like when she raised one eyebrow in a way that combined suspicion with curiosity, that she reminded him of his mother. If he were a religious man, or even if he just believed the universe distributed luck in some meaningful way (like he used to when he did the lottery), he would thank it for letting his mother live long enough to hold Amy in her arms. Their convergence on Earth lasted five months.

Once she had gone off to explore every room in The Manor, including a snooker room, father and daughter settled down on a huge yellow sofa in one of the two 'receptions'.

'That is the biggest screen ever. Can we watch it?'

The TV was the width of a small car.

'If you can find out how it works, you can,' said Leo, and he meant it.

'Can I bring my friends here one day?'

'Well, maybe. But this house doesn't belong to me.'

Her eyes narrowed, then one eyebrow ascended.

'Didn't you buy it?'

'I'm borrowing it.'

Satisfied that he hadn't stolen the house, she snuggled into his shoulder, and Leo pushed a button. Their backs went down and their legs went up.

'It's moving.'

'Cool, huh?'

'How it is happening?'

'It's a secret.'

'Dad.'

'Mind control.'

'*Dad!*' She punched her dad on the arm.

'I pressed this button.'

When they were almost horizontal, staring at a chandelier that wouldn't have been out of place in the lobby of a five star hotel, Leo patted her leg.

'I want to tell you something about life.'

'You're always telling me about life.'

'Don't you like it?'

'As long as it's short.'

He promised to keep it brief.

'Okay, well, when someone has a lot of money, or people *think* they have a lot of money, then the funny thing is, people want to give them even more.'

She frowned. 'Why?'

'Because they feel sure that the rich person will pay them back, often with a little extra, called 'interest', as a thank you. And another thing, the rich person can blag all kinds of favours and free stuff, because people hope he will return the favour in the future.'

'Why don't they give money and favours to poor people?'

'Oh, that wouldn't work. How would the poor person ever be able to give the money back or return the favour?'

She gently slapped her father's arm.

'It's not fair.'

'No, but that's life. And that's why someone lent me this house. For free.'

'A rich person?'

'Someone who owns a massive car clamping business. They hope I'll buy the house. And the man who deals in property hopes I'm going to buy this property or some other one he has on his books. These men are really, *really* nice to me. Because they think I'm really, really, *really* rich.'

'Aren't you rich now?'

He paused for a moment.

'Remember what I told you about Santa?'

'You said, umm… that you think he's real?'

'No, I didn't say that.'

'Oh, no. You said that a lot of people *say* he's real.'

'Yes. And a lot of people *say* I'm a billionaire.'

Leo wondered if she would ever give him even the slightest credit for never actually lying to her. Probably not. In the end, if her mother was in tears, he was in prison, and her world was turned upside down, she wasn't going to give him credit for anything much.

'But Dad, is Santa real or not?'

'People say he is.'

Amy folded her arms and knitted her forehead, a sign that the questions wouldn't stop until she was satisfied.

'But I want to know what *you* think.'

'What do *you* think?'

'You're a grown-up, so you know more than me.'

'Lots of grown-ups say he's real.'

'But even if lots of grown-ups say he's real… he could still not be real, couldn't he?'

Not for the first time, he momentarily wished his daughter wasn't quite as sharp as she was.

'That's an interesting question. I'll have to ponder that one.'

It was time for a cheap trick.

'Now, do you want to see something special, because Vince has been on a shopping trip, and if I know Vince, he'll have bought a ginormous amount of things your grandmother would not want you to eat.'

'Yay!'

'And do you know *where* we're going to eat it?'

'Where?'

'In the back of the limousine, or here, or in the garden, or… how about the hot tub?'

'Hot tub! Hot tub!'

'No, you wouldn't really want to get in the hot tub like a big Hollywood movie star, would you?'

'I would, I would.'

'No, I don't think you would.'

Amy hit her father hard on the arm.

'I would, I would!'

'Come on, let's make like movie stars.'

In the kitchen, Vince, as predicted, was unpacking a heap of goodies high in salt, sugar, and fat. He'd also bought a tin of Prince's Irish stew, which he threw for Leo to catch.

'For a trip down memory lane,' he said. Leo had eaten a lot of Irish stew in his salad days.

41

I CALL IT HUMPTY DUMPTY

Leo and Driver Dave had their arms full of flowers. Realising he hadn't bought a gift, Leo had asked Dave to pull into a service station. Since there was nothing that a billionaire would choose to buy, he considered the cheap bouquets in plastic buckets and made a decision: buy the lot, all 14 bunches. It was exactly the sort of idiocy his in-laws would expect. To be fair, when the flowers were piled into their arms, Leo barely detected a flicker of condescension.

Vince had decided not to come – why spend an evening with a couple of wrinklies who had always treated Leo like a bad smell? 'Tell them I'm too busy whoring.'

After an aperitif in the living room, Frank showed the young man into the dining room, and it was just that: a room exclusively for dining. Two dark wood display cabinets contained fine looking glasses and plates that were reserved for occasions so special that they'd probably never happened. Leo had only been inside this dedicated room once before, for an Easter lunch. (In fact, had *anyone* been in the dining room apart from at Christmas and Easter?) He'd felt uncomfortable and clumsy so he drank a lot of wine, which had made him more comfortable but clumsier. There was an endless succession of serving plates, jugs, bottles, jars, gravy-boats, with vegetables, sauces, salt, pepper, wine, water, condiments going backwards and forwards, with family members offering, asking, thanking, holding, passing, scooping, pouring and ladling. At every attempt to take a bite of something, someone would politely ask him to pass the buttered carrots. By the time he'd swallowed his first mouthful, people were starting to clear the plates.

Once they'd all sat down, Harriet declared that the meal was free from all items to which he had expressed an aversion. This provided the alleged billionaire with the opportunity to talk nonsense about food ('clawed animals have a high manganese content') and stay off the topic of the jackpot, because lying is hard.

Once conversation about dietary anathemas had been exhausted, other topics chugged along easily, pulled by the engine of sycophancy. At Harriet's instigation, the subject moved on to all the wonderful things her husband had achieved during his tenure as chairman of the council. After the pudding (chocolate brownies made with goose egg instead of chickens') she mentioned the Carlton Hotel press conference.

'I was so pleased that you wanted to do your bit for the local area, Leo.'

'And the sick kiddie,' added Frank, into his wine glass.

'Yes,' said, Leo, 'actually there are some other families I'd like to help out. And I wondered if you knew why the NHS can't provide the treatment. From what I can gather—'

'Not my area, but let me show you all the brilliant organisations I work with.' Frank wiped his mouth with a napkin and stood up.

'Sure,' said Leo, deciding to let himself be shut down. He could bring the subject up again later.

'And I'll clear the table so you have somewhere to work,' said Harriet, gathering the dessert bowls.

A few minutes later, Frank pushed the dining room door open with his back, and reversed in carrying a box full of pamphlets and papers. He set it down on the table, and panted as if he'd achieved something athletic.

'Don't worry,' he said, 'we won't go through *all* this.' He handed a leaflet to Leo. On the front was a picture of three obviously blind children smiling.

'BlindAid. It's all about giving the blind kiddies days out, the equipment they need, helping the kiddies.'

The word *kiddies* annoyed Leo.

'What happens when they're not young anymore?' he asked.

'When they turn eighteen? Um…'

'I mean,' said Leo, not really knowing where he was going, 'it would be rubbish if they were just abandoned on their eighteenth birthday. *Get out of here, you're not cute anymore.*'

Frank forced a smile and moved the subject on.

'Have a look at these. Photographs of the bridge.'

Byford's historic bridge had been damaged in a storm two years ago.

'Yes. I ride the trike over it. I call it Humpty Dumpty.'

Frank's eyes darted around the room as if some explanation for the comment would be written on a wall.

'Because it's a humpback bridge,' said Leo. 'Humpty Dumpty sat on a bridge, not a wall, as is often claimed.'

Leo didn't know why he'd said this, and if Vince were there he wouldn't have been able to keep a straight face. Perhaps, somewhere in the back of his mind, he sensed that Frank wanted a useful idiot, so he became that idiot – but to a punitive degree, giving Frank too much of what he'd wished for.

'I love Humpty Dumpty,' he said, thinking that was as far as he could go. Frank's fingers tapped nervously.

'So, Leo, would you like to contribute to repairing the bridge?' He sounded as if he was asking a child if he'd like more pudding.

'Could I see the budget?'

'Oh, don't worry about that,' Frank laughed. 'It was tendered by three different companies, and has been approved by the Scrutiny Committee.'

Having despatched that enquiry, he began shuffling papers, but Leo wasn't finished.

'I'd still like to see all the costs myself, the insurance, and penalties for late completion and so on.'

Frank stopped shuffling and looked over the reading glasses he'd donned earlier.

'The actual *figures*?'

'Yes. And I'd also like the BlindAid accounts.'

Frank chuckled.

'You've heard of the Charity Commission?'

Leo didn't like this patronising question, but he was on home turf now because he'd read quite a bit about charity scandals and impropriety.

'The Charity Commission scrutinised Kids Company, but it went tits up because the board put too much trust in the executive. Not to mention the sex scandals involving Oxfam and Save the Children. I can give you more examples if you like.'

Frank looked at him as if he were an idiot who had just said something clever by accident. He removed his glasses and wiped his hands over his head. Leo guessed what he must be thinking: 'Just give me the money, then pose with me by the bridge so I can get all the glory. Do the same for all these other worthy causes, and then fuck off.'

'The most important thing is *due diligence*,' said Leo.

'I agree, but—'

'You see, you'll want to be photographed with me with some of those massive blown-up cheques. Very high profile. I need to know everything is on the level.'

'But—'

'All I need is the *detailed* accounts from all these organisations…' Frank's cheeks sagged. 'I mean, look at what happens when people don't do due diligence. The collapse of the subprime mortgage market. I mean, the banks had the regulators in their pockets.'

Frank sighed heavily, unable to hide his frustration. One minute he was talking to a halfwit about Humpty Dumpty, now the same man seemed to be an expert on financial impropriety. He reached for the water jug, but it wobbled so much that Leo had to help take the weight.

'I understand all that about due diligence,' he explained, like a wise man whose patience was being sorely tested, 'But election day looms. Would you be willing to work quickly on this, and in the meantime maybe… *pledge* the cash?'

'Pledge?'

'Make a promise.'

Leo made him wait a moment.

'Sure. Anything for you, Frank.'

Frank's relief was palpable. The two men spent the next hour going through a list of projects, organisations and charities. Leo was careful not to promise money, but agreed that certain amounts 'seemed suitable'. By the time they'd finished, several million pounds had been earmarked for the deserving citizens of Byford. All the while Leo almost pinched himself. Only a year or two ago he had wanted to impress this pompous fool. Perhaps he'd been the bigger fool for wanting to.

Later, in the limo, Leo told himself he had just been digging a grave, and it was up to Frank if he jumped into it. While going over some of the conversations in his head, he remembered that he hadn't followed up on the issue of over-priced drugs. He dialled the Sterlings' landline.

'Hello?'

'One thing. Would there be any chance, any chance at all, of meeting your leader?'

There was a pause and a supressed chuckle.

'Leo, the boss of my party just happens to be our Prime Minister.'

'Cool. Yes, I'd like to talk to the PM about the drug companies and how much they're screwing out of our health service… Hello? I think there are ways round it, you see. I've read about a way the companies could make a fair profit without—'

'Leo, Leo, Leo. The PM is very, very busy, and I'm just a local politician, near the bottom the food chain.'

'But you're chairman of Byford Council. Doesn't that count for something?'

'In my dreams.'

'Seems a bit much to expect me to start pledging if I can't meet the boss and get my ideas heard.'

Leo could almost see Frank gripping his thinning hair, wanting to pull it out.

'Look, it's not *impossible*. I'd need to make a lot of calls.'

'See what you can do, and give big thanks to Harriet for the dinner. Have a great evening, Frank.'

42

SORRY FOR ALL THE CONFUSION

With the streets empty, Hamir could keep this humiliation to himself. Even before the newspaper delivery, he began unscrewing the sign that said, 'The shop wot won the billion'. It had failed to attract new customers, although that's not what he told his wife or his brother-in-law. 'I'm seeing quite a few new faces,' he'd lied. The sign had been made on the cheap by his regular sign writer, but still, at £90, it had taken a hefty chunk out of profits.

The sign wasn't the worst of it. The low point had been having to admit to a radio journalist that the date on the footage had been a 'technical error' and that no, he didn't have any video of Morphetus buying a lottery ticket during the period that he could have bought the winning one. Gira had urged Hamir to come completely clean and say that Leo may have stopped buying lottery tickets from his shop for the relevant days, and the confusion had arisen because she, not he, had been on duty most Wednesday afternoons.

The couple had argued about whether the line should be 'my wife doesn't remember him buying tickets' or 'my wife remembers that he didn't buy tickets'. Hamir insisted the two statements meant the same thing, even though he knew full well there was a world of difference. 'Sorry for all the confusion, it was an understandable mistake,' he muttered to anyone who asked. The fact was that, for whatever reason, Leo must have bought his billion pound ticket elsewhere.

The Express ran a *mea culpa* piece and offered a thousand pounds for anyone who could provide a video of Leo buying any lottery ticket during the relevant period; a shopkeeper, supermarket or service station somewhere in Byford, must have CCTV footage of the possibly life-changing moment.

Hamir broke the sign into four pieces, which he then hid behind some pallets in the back of the shop. As soon as he heard the bin men, he would chuck them in the dustcart himself. He would cling to the fact that the famous billionaire had been a very loyal customer over many years. Hamir's successful brother-in-law couldn't begrudge him that.

43

YOU ARE AN HONEST MAN

During the last couple of days, Leo visited two of the families in Alan Lethco's support group, and he'd had Skype and email conversations with the others. He explained that it wasn't that he was suspicious, he was just being careful. They seemed to understand and went to great lengths to provide all the information he required, and Leo followed up by contacting a specialist who agreed to look into each case for him. It would take a week at least to come back with figures.

He also honoured the other promises he'd made that fateful night at The Swan: six months' rent to a retail park for sex-toy trader Sally, a new (used) car for instructors Rob and Dave, and a year's business rates for Snappy Snapper Dan, who was being stymied by franchise fees. But he had a few other people he wanted to help out: first and foremost, the staff at St Mary's Hospice. Vince had persuaded him to make these donations in person – and with an old-fashioned chequebook, because people were bound to take photos and post them on social. 'All good for the image.' The amounts were relatively small – which Leo explained by saying that he was taking a long view, with many good causes to think about around the world. The real reason was of course that the money needed to go a long way.

His largest donation was to a gym in a converted telephone exchange. His gift would go towards building a boxing ring, something that would benefit the kids on the estate on which he'd spent much of his youth. As he stood in front of a dozen burly would-be boxers for some photographs, he considered donating an industrial supply of deodorant.

He saw Amy as much as he could. On Thursday, he made a point of going to pick her up from school on foot, dodging fellow parents by arriving early and waiting inside the second gate, no doubt contravening regulations. While Amy was by the water fountains deep in conversation with her friends, he saw one of her teachers walking towards him. He knew Mrs Allam from parents' evenings, and had chatted to her at fêtes. To Leo, a sari and hijab signified devout status, and he felt the same kind of involuntary reverence to Mrs Allam as he had towards nuns, vicars and priests.

'Mr Morphetus – Leo,' she said, offering her gloved hand.

'Mrs Allam,' he said, unable to address a teacher by her first name. She seemed to have something on her mind, and he feared she had come to tell him that Amy's new status as a billionaire's daughter was having negative repercussions.

'I am keeping an eye on Amy, with all this change. And she's doing fine.' She'd read his mind.

'I'm very glad to hear that, and thank you,' he said, relieved. 'I advised her not to talk about it if she can help it.'

Mrs Allam nodded and smiled as if she already knew that. She had an air of someone who already knew a hell of a lot.

An alarming series of screams filled the air and Leo was about to run towards Amy and her friends. He was still not used to the fact that when little girls scream it doesn't mean there's an emergency.

'Leo,' said Mrs Allam, 'you said on television that *if* you won a large amount, you would give most of it to charities, after carefully checking their worthiness and competence, deploying the wisdom of experts and your own sense of value-for-money.'

'Yes, I did say that,' said Leo, surprised and flattered at being quoted so accurately. Then a thought crashed into his mind: he had not made a donation to his own daughter's school. What must Mrs Allam think of him? He was about to suggest how he might make a contribution, when she asked another question.

'Was all of that *true*?'

'The stuff about good causes? Yes, it was true,' he said.

'Good,' she said, but again, only seeming to confirm something she already knew. 'I noticed you were at great pains not to lie.'

'I did try not to,' said Leo and suddenly realised something very strange had just happened: the real winner would not have to *try not to lie*. Why had she said that? And why hadn't he immediately challenged her about the question? While his mind raced, Mrs Allam looked at him in a way he found strange. How to describe it? He decided she had an air of *serene amusement*.

'Being at pains not to lie as you are,' she said, 'I have been wondering why Amy thought her new bracelet was solid gold.'

The memory of the gold bracelet tumbled chaotically into his mind.

'Um, Mrs Allam, that bracelet has nothing to do with me. It was given to her by… well, by someone else.'

She nodded, reassured by the answer.

'But *isn't* it gold?' he asked. 'I thought it was.'

Mrs Allam's smile almost turned into a chuckle. It was as if the two of them had done something silly as children, and they could laugh about it now.

'Amy and I did a little experiment. Gold is not magnetic.'

He nodded. So *that's* why she's suspicious – why would a billionaire buy a bracelet of gold *plate*? That must have got her mind working.

A little boy came up to her and asked a question but Leo was too preoccupied to listen.

'I hoped you had not misled Amy about that,' she said, once the boy had gone, 'Because you are an honest man.'

Leo had lost the reigns of this conversation – no, he had never had them in the first place. Had the fact that he was not the one who had bought the bracelet now cleared up the matter? Could she now believe he was a billionaire? He felt compelled to add a convincer.

'Look… I would like to donate some money to the school. For the um… new, er – gym,' he stuttered.

The teacher looked gently reproachful.

'Can you afford to?'

Dammit, thought Leo, as loudly as his brain could think. *She knows!* Those dark brown eyes… perhaps they could see into men's souls. He had nothing to say, nothing at all. He just shrugged like an idiot, then to make matters worse, he began to laugh. It was a *you-got-me-bang-to-rights* laugh, but he couldn't help it. Mrs Allam laughed a little too.

Without saying anything more, she began walking back to the school entrance lobby. After a few paces, she turned, bowed her head and smiled sagely, before continuing.

Could they have been talking at cross-purposes? Or maybe Mrs Allam didn't really understand lotteries – it's hardly a subject she'd be interested in. But that parting glance: what did it mean?

As Amy's friends began drifting off with their parents, he tried to talk himself to a place of safety. He made a mental list of what he knew, starting with the observation that Mrs Allam seemed to *like* him, in some mystical way. Secondly, she had said quite emphatically that he was an *honest man*. Thirdly, she could not *know* he was faking all this – that was impossible. And lastly, even if she suspected something at the back of her mind, this gentle, softly-spoken Muslim woman was not going to run to the press or go round gossiping in pubs or wine bars or hairdressers. If some doubts were floating in her head, he felt sure she would keep them to herself. He had arrived at his place of safety in just four facts.

He took Amy's hand for the walk home. Although the other parents stole glances at him with a new curiosity, he was touched by the way they had unconsciously decided as a group that at this moment he was just a dad doing the school run.

Father and daughter spent most of the homeward journey talking about food groups, which had been a topic of one of her lessons. Somewhere along the way, Leo remembered what Mrs Allam had said about the 'gold' bracelet.

So. Tony, Mazda Man, you're a liar.

He would choose the right moment to share this intelligence with Helen.

44

GET YOUR NOSE IN THE TROUGH

Donna had been waiting in Groucho's members' bar for ten minutes, and was half way through her white wine spritzer. The girl was late, but then young girls often are, especially pretty ones, perhaps because they think their beauty will compensate.

A waiter took away the empty bowl of crisps and replaced it with a full one, and then he reminded her that computer tablets were not allowed in the club after six. It was now well past nine. She stowed it away and took out her phone. Just as she did so, she sensed someone approaching.

'Donna?'

Donna stood to shake hands. This young woman starkly contrasted with her glamour portfolio. She was makeup free, wore skinny jeans and a plain grey hoodie: *I'm not just a glamour-puss.* Message received and understood.

'Thanks for coming,' said Donna. 'You look great,' she added, suspecting that it wasn't what the girl wanted to hear, but it was true; Monica was almost annoyingly petite and pretty, and had an intelligent demeanour to boot. Some girls…

'Thanks,' Monica said casually, and chose to sit on a small stool rather than the armchair. She fussed with her rucksack distractedly.

'What can I get you?' asked Donna.

'Oh um… um… vodka and diet coke, please.'

Of course. The beverage of the stick-thin.

'No, actually, just water. I can't stay long.'

Oh, so this wasn't going to go the way Donna had planned. Her assumption had been that they would spend an hour talking about her night with Morphetus. This chat would form the basis of an article – the sex part would only be implied, and the money not mentioned at all. Once Morphetus had passed through Monica's front door he had, in legal parlance, *a reasonable expectation of privacy*. But what they said and did in the club, canoodling in the car, the *fact* that he had gone to her flat, all that was fair game. It could be adorned with a few standout details, a quote, something readers would want to talk about… and the boxer shorts. Monica continued to fidget – with her nails, rucksack and phone, while Donna made a few remarks about the club and its usefulness for meetings. The waiter arrived with a glass of ice water. Once he'd left, Monica drew a long breath.

'I don't want to do this story. Sorry.'

Donna shored up her disappointment. Disappointment, but not total surprise. Punters often get cold feet – it's par for the course.

'What's the problem?'

Monica gripped her glass of water as if it was about to slide off the table.

'I don't know… I just… I don't know.'

'A rival offer? Because we can do a very good deal for you. I had a word with—'

'Nothing like that. I guess I just don't want to be *that girl*.'

Donna nodded. A moral compass was getting in the way. Or was it moral vanity? Monica started pulling at her hair like a little girl. Perhaps she subconsciously wanted to assume the unaccountability of a young child.

'This would all be very tastefully done,' said Donna. 'Well, *fairly* tastefully, given—'

'I don't want to upset him.'

'Why should he mind being associated with such a… a charming and intelligent young woman?'

But it seemed that Monica was hardly listening. She was looking around the room as if expecting the arrival of a friend.

'I've thought about it,' she said, looking back at Donna, 'and it's just not really me. Leo is a really nice person.'

Donna listened carefully, impressed by the girl's command of English, even though, being Dutch, that should come as no surprise.

'I see.'

'See what?'

'You've started dating? Or want to start?'

It was a shot in the dark but could be revealing, and Donna took the girl's hesitation as a 'yes'. This was potentially more interesting long term, than a story about a date.

'You're going to date a billionaire,' said Donna. 'Get your nose in the trough, why not?'

From Monica's sudden change in colour, Donna knew that she'd messed up. Sometimes her mouth had a mind of its own, dammit. She'd spent too much time bantering with rhino-skinned hacks like Derek who were impossible to offend.

'Obviously I'm just kidding around. I take it back.'

She realised immediately this wouldn't do; Monica's face was starting to boil. Donna was too busy trying to think of a way out of this to notice a hand spring from under the table, and a second later her lap turned ice cold, forcing a sharp intake of breath.

Monica reached for her rucksack and stood up.

'Arsehole.' She headed for the door and there was no point in trying to stop her.

Waiters and customers turned to look, so Donna threw her arms up in the air: *yup, I'm the arsehole, everyone.* There was an amused pause before everyone went back to their boasting and flattering.

Donna had been soaked before, so she knew what to do. And at least it was a *white* wine spritzer. She would retreat to the ladies using her coat as cover, then rub like mad with tissues. In five minutes her skirt would be all but dry.

45

HE WANTS TO MAKE THE WORLD A BETTER PLACE

When it came to open-plan workspaces, Derek knew all about the benefits: creative cross-pollination, breaking down barriers, flattening hierarchies. He could admire these modern innovations while sitting behind his own desk and looking through the glass walls of an office that was his, and his alone.

Derek, Donna White and Tamar, the TrueNewz legal eagle, were seated in the 'soft' part of his transparent domain. A sofa, a couple of small armchairs and a biscuit-laden coffee table provided the ersatz comfort of a living room. Tamar, a British-educated Sri Lankan, tall, slim, thirty two, and the snazziest man in the office, made an agreeable contrast to Derek, a crumpled fifty three, needing a haircut, and a stranger to exercise, sunlight, and vegetables. But Derek had been hired for being wise and experienced, not for being down-with-the-kids.

Donna had called the meeting so they could all take stock of the Morphetus story, and get the legal handle on it. Since Derek had decided to run with the barista as the genuine billionaire winner despite Donna's misgivings, the two had been a little awkward together.

'Okay, give us the lowdown,' said Derek.

Donna had jotted her salient points in her notebook, a technology which she often found more user-friendly than her tablet, and her ballpoint pen a more intuitive interface than a keyboard.

'Okay, here's the big picture,' she began, while Tamar put his phone away. 'Morphetus is a record-breaking lottery winner and he says he wants to make the world a better place.' Donna didn't put quotes round *the world a better place*, although she guessed that Derek and Tamar mentally had. 'He's getting lots of love on social and his refusal to speak to the press has made him more intriguing. He's not interested in fame.'

'Except,' interjected Tamar, 'that he's been snapped handing out cheques. Virtue-signalling for all he's worth.' There was just a trace of a Sri Lankan accent tripping between the consonants.

'True,' acknowledged Donna. 'But they're just selfies, taken by the public.'

'Smart phones have made paparazzi of us all,' declared Derek, who leant back in his chair, rather pleased with his *bon mot*.

'How profound,' said Donna, dismissively, and Derek stuck his tongue out. 'But you're right, he seems to want to project an image of philanthropy.'

'Or maybe he just *is* philanthropic,' said Derek, holding his hands up in a but-what-do-I-know expression. 'I mean, not *everything* people do is about projecting an image.'

Donna wanted to get to the meat.

'Now, as you know, we were contacted by a young woman, Monica, a part time escort. Morphetus paid her the phenomenal sum of twenty grand. We have some very sexy pictures of her topless and—'

'Can we see those?' said Derek.

'They're just the usual sort of—' but Donna stopped when she realised she'd missed the joke. A rare lapse. Tamar snorted.

'I'll send them to you with a box of tissues, okay?'

'Done,' said Derek.

'And you've both had the J-peg of the boxer shorts?'

'Jeez. Yes. Hard to forget,' said Tamar, who was one of the few staff who not only wore smart suits, but ironed shirts, and quite possibly ironed underpants.

'But the girl has withdrawn co-operation, hasn't she?' said Derek.

'Exactly. I think she wants to start dating him,' said Donna.

'Who can blame her?' said Tamar.

'Or *him*,' added Donna, 'but I think it means we'd have to cobble something together, maybe by talking to some other drinkers at the club where they met, but I'd like to know the legal position.'

Donna and Derek looked to Tamar, who cocked his head a few times before answering.

'Okay. At the news conference at the hotel, Morphetus never said he was going to spend *all* his money on charity. Oh, and of course, he's separated from his wife. There's nothing hypocritical here. He hasn't presented himself as a pillar of traditional values, so even if we could persuade Monica to let us use the payment story, it would be tricky.'

'Reasonable expectation of privacy,' added Derek, reaching for a shortbread biscuit. Everything Tamar and Derek had just said were things Donna already knew, but she didn't feel patronised – *don't take offence, they would have said the same things to anyone.*

'So forget about the money thing,' Donna said. 'It was off-the-record and I don't think she'll shift. I was talking about a basic shagging story. We could publish her pictures. And let's not forget the boxer shorts.' Neither Tamar nor Derek cracked a smile. 'Come on guys, this is fun.'

Donna was surprised she wasn't getting more enthusiasm. TrueNewz had a reputation for reliable reporting, but it was not po-faced. Derek was not above silly or even tacky stories if they could be proved.

Tamar shook his head. 'We would be obliged to notify Morphetus, and it could be super injunction time.'

'But does *he* know that?' asked Donna.

Derek agreed. 'He doesn't look like he'd know a super injunction if he shat one out.'

'But it's a risk,' said Tamar.

'You always say that,' said Donna, closing her notebook noisily.

'Because there's *always* a risk,' retorted Tamar, with a don't-shoot-the-messenger shrug. 'Plus the portfolio will be copyright Monica or her photographer, and the photo of the boxers will be copyright Monica.'

Again, Donna knew all this. She cleared her throat before putting forward her idea.

'So listen. We publish, we tell the story of boy meets girl, we use the photos, and if Monica complains, we apologise profusely and pay her off – what, a thousand quid? It's worth it. Come on, guys, let's roll with this.'

Derek put his hands on each knee, as if they represented both sides of the argument. 'Could Mr Billionaire sue over the boxer shorts, Tamar?'

The lawyer shook his head. 'Going to court over some old pants would make him look fucking ridiculous.'

'And, guys,' said Donna, 'it would be hard to argue substantial reputational damage. It would just be boy-fucks-girl. No one gets hurt.'

Tamar adjusted his position in his seat — it was time to give his full professional résumé.

'Okay, first off, we can't touch the story about money changing hands because it was off-the-record, and anyway we'd have to inform the guy and risk a super injunction. Now, a mere shagging story wouldn't be damaging reputationally *but...* nor is it in the public interest, because he's basically single, she's not underage, or an employee, or a spy, there was no harassment, it wasn't rape, no hypocrisy. The risk is that it could be an invasion of privacy – not a big deal, but if the guy takes offence and wants a fight? He might feel hurt by this girl going to the press, we don't know. He might want to get back with his missus and this might scupper that, we don't know. And if someone else breaks the news that she's a call girl, it could look bad for him – he might resent people knowing that. If he's pissed off, he can afford to take us to the cleaners and back. The guy is a *billionaire* so can afford to sue about anything he likes – even with only a gnat's chance of winning.'

'But he probably doesn't know his rights,' said Donna with a glance to Derek. Tamar straightened his back. 'Look, I know I've said this before, but we can stick it to soap stars, we can stick it to millionaires, but billionaires? No. Not post Mosely. Richard Branson could fuck a goat in a children's playground and I'd say don't touch it.'

'What if the goat made a written complaint?' asked Derek.

'So we spike the whole thing?' shrugged Donna. She dropped her notebook noisily on the table.

'I love you, Donna,' said Derek, swallowing some biscuit, 'and you've done some great work, but to be honest, a cobbled-together kiss-and-tell and some old pants?' All three of them had to smile. 'You're better than that. Try to get an exclusive. Here's an idea: use the fact that you know about Monica as bait.'

'Yeah, I had thought of doing that.'

'No you didn't, *I* did,' said Derek.

'Of course I thought of it. It's obvious,' said Donna, her voice rising.

What might have been a faux spat ended when a young woman from the news desk waved on the other side of the glass wall. Derek beckoned her in.

'Sorry to butt in, you guys, but you're meeting about the billionaire barista, right?'

They all nodded. The girl – jeans, plain blue T-shirt and flame-red shoulder-length hair – was excited and breathless. She took a moment before continuing with her upward inflections.

'So… apparently, Leo Morphetus and the other one, Vince, don't have any money? So the whole thing is one big joke and they're actually broke? That's what this caller said?'

Everyone looked at everyone else for a moment. Donna shook her head, this 'caller' was almost certainly a nutjob, so let's not get too excited.

'Evidence, Jessica?' asked Derek. The girl nodded vigorously.

'So, the caller said he has definite proof?'

'Stop saying *so*, all the time!' said Derek. He had become inured to the upward inflection, but drew the line at the superfluous *so*.

'What kind of proof?' asked Donna.

'He wouldn't say,' said Jessica. 'So he just said that if someone were to meet him, he has *conclusive proof*, like a document, that would blow the whole thing apart.'

Derek steepled his index fingers and tapped his chin with them.

'What do you think, Donna? Any Yeovil sensations? Are your hormones giving you a signal?'

'Not right now, Derek. What's your penis telling you?'

'I never listen to it.'

'Guys, guys,' said Tamar, 'we're not seriously doubting that Morphetus won the jackpot, are we? *Are we?*'

'I hope not, because we broke the story,' said Derek, running his hand through his hair. 'But that said... the newsagent's footage? That was false.'

'But he could have bought the ticket anywhere,' said Donna, wanting to put the brakes on this. Derek scratched his eyebrow with his thumbnail.

'Come on Donna, this is your story. What's your take?'

Donna shrugged, 'Nutjob.'

'Exactly,' said Tamar. 'Morphetus is going round giving his dosh away. The twenty grand for a fuck. The stretch limo. He lives in a *mansion* doesn't he? Seriously, guys, get real.'

Donna waited for Derek to speak. If this was going to be a mess, he needed to own it. His hand came down hard on the arm of his chair.

'Bollocks.'

'Gimme the caller's details,' said Donna, holding her hand out to the young woman. 'I'll phone the guy, see what he's got.'

Jessica flushed crimson and looked down at the little scrap of paper she'd brought with her. Derek shot an incredulous glance around the room.

'*Well?*' he said.

'So – sorry – I *did* ask him his name,' said the girl, 'But he didn't want to give me any details. And I forgot to make a note of the incoming number on the system.'

Derek bolted back on his chair. '*That's* why you get the name and write down the number at the *start* of the call,' he said, '*before* anything else, you understand? Clear your desk.'

Jessica flinched.

'Wait there, Jessica,' said Donna. Derek's ire should have been directed at himself for prematurely breaking the story, not this hapless employee. 'Come on, Derek, don't be mean,' she said. Tamar nodded in support.

'The girl has to learn moral hazard,' said Derek, and looked as if he wouldn't be moved.

'Shall I go?' said Jessica, her voice now fighting to stay steady.

Derek looked at her for a moment, and then suddenly slapped his thigh.

'*Always* get the name and number – *first* thing you do. And *never ever* start a statement with *so* again, okay?'

'Okay, thank you very much,' and the young redhead left, heading for the restrooms.

There was a calming pause in which Derek bit into another biscuit, this time a chocolate digestive. Donna said, 'So…'

Tamar snorted. 'You asked for that,' and Derek conceded the point with a huff. Donna continued, 'We just cross our fingers and hope this informant calls back?'

'I'm crossing all the hairs on my hairy arse that he's a crank and *doesn't* call back,' said Derek. 'Meanwhile, let's keep an open mind and keep digging. And try to get an exclusive with the billionaire boy. We're counting on you, Donna.'

They all knew if Donna White could go eyeball to eyeball with Leo Morphetus, then the truth would out.

46

COPS MEAN NOTHING TO THESE GUYS

Helen opened the door to see Tony wearing a white shirt, which put her in mind of his profile picture. They hadn't seen each other for a few days, and had only communicated with some 'how are you?' texts. There had been no more news about 'bad men' and Helen had begun to relax. Perhaps Tony had just been ultra-cautious about everything.

Despite her reservations, and the near certainty that this thing would not last for much longer, she'd been looking forward to seeing Tony. She'd thought about what they would do together many times, in some detail, with a number of variations. Sure, she worried just a little that he had a sexual hold over her, but what the hell, sexual holds don't last, and for Helen this kind of attraction was as rare as gold dust, so make the most of it. Besides, Amy was with Leo, and child-free nights should not be wasted on box sets and too much wine.

The immediate question was, should she tease herself with deferred fulfilment or get down to it straight away? She decided on the former because it was more exciting when Tony made the first moves.

But he was in a strange mood. He had a foreboding expression and only kissed her perfunctorily.

'Something wrong?' she asked, as they entered the kitchen.

He began opening the wine he'd brought. 'Are you going to stay calm and sensible?' he said, not looking up from the bottle.

'Oh for Christ's sake,' said Helen, more with disappointment than fear. 'What's happened?'

He tilted his head from side to side, as if he was struggling to find the right words.

'*They know*,' he said, sitting down and beginning to pour.

'Right.' She felt a brick in her stomach. 'Your gangster friends know you're seeing me, and my connection to Leo? They know both those things?'

He stroked his cheek with his free hand, but she was in no mood for enigmatic pauses.

'*Yes, or no*?'

'Promise me you won't do anything rash.'

'Oh for fuck's sake.'

'Keep your voice down.'

'No,' she said.

'Do you think I wanted any of this?' Tony said, raising his voice now. 'If Coffee Cunt hadn't blathered to the whole world then we wouldn't be in this position, would we?'

'All right,' said Helen, with a consolatory sigh, no point in stoking the flames here. 'But I am calling the police.'

'The cops mean nothing to these guys.' He spoke softly but urgently now. 'They have cops in their pockets. We are talking rich, powerful, greedy, violent men.'

Helen reached for her phone.

'We must call them!'

She punched a nine before he grabbed it from her.

'Give it back right now!'

'First, I will tell you about an associate of mine who went to the cops. Listen, because you need to know this.'

Helen sat still, but it would not be for long. She was coiled for action. Tony composed himself. His hands clasped together, his eyes closed, he took three deep breaths. Helen was sick of waiting.

'What the fuck? Just tell me.'

'I am *going* to tell you,' he said, with a self-possession she found infuriating. He opened his eyes, and ran his hands along the table, wiping away some drops of wine that had spilled.

'Look… Helen, if you promise not to call the police or tell anyone—'

'I need to tell Mum and Dad.' Even in her alarmed state, she realised how childish that sounded.

'You can't tell *anyone*. It would put us all at risk. Now I'll tell you what happened to Clara.'

'Clara? Who the fuck?'

She didn't want to know who Clara was.

'A trader. Worked in the business for ten years. Specialised in diamonds and rubies, mostly from Africa, a little in the Middle East. She came from Oxford originally, had a degree in music.'

And then she was thrown in a canal. Helen could see the body.

'She got into the trade via someone at Uni, an Arab I think.'

'But she's dead now, right?'

Tony ignored the interruption as if she were a tiresome child.

'She got on the wrong side of… some people. They thought she'd ripped them off, but she hadn't. Anyway, she felt threatened so she went to the police. Weeks later, she arranged to meet a contact in Delhi. And they asked her to wait on a corner for a car to pick her up.'

Helen pushed her two fists together in her lap. She wanted to tell him to stop, it was obvious how this would end.

'When it arrived, Clara walked to the car and the driver threw acid in her face.'

She pushed her fists tighter together.

'They operated, did skin grafts but… most of her face was gone.'

Helen covered her own face with her hands, unconsciously protecting it. Tony brought out his phone.

'Want to see a picture?'

'Fuck off.'

Still stroking the table, he resumed, as calmly as before.

'After three weeks of agony, she died of her injuries. These people could do that again. Here, right here, in Byford. To me, to you, or—'

She didn't wait for *Amy*.

'This can't be happening, it can't be happening. Please tell me it can't happen!'

'I did think it would be better if I disappeared. Just left you alone.'

'Yes, yes it would.'

Problem solved. It would be easier if he disappeared in a puff of smoke.

'But it's too late for that.'

Helen tried to steady her breathing, but it was hard. She didn't want to be the woman who cries, she wanted to be the one who thinks of a solution. Even so, tears ran down her cheeks. She would be the woman who cries *and* thinks of a solution. She could only do that if she controlled her fear.

'I'll call Leo. We'll work out a plan together. And we'll get security. We don't need to tell anyone why.' She had to stop speaking as a ripple of dread shot up from her ribs. 'We could have a man parked outside 24/7. And they could take Amy to school – with me, of course – I'll get leave from work.'

'Security will only provoke them,' said Tony, with the confidence of one who had intimate knowledge of his subject. 'They see a guy sitting outside they'll think I've been talking. Or that I've decided not to pay up. They want their money.'

Helen looked at the ceiling. She didn't want him to see the tears but she would not put her head in her hands again, like a victim. She looked down when she heard him take a tissue from the box on the table. He pressed it into his eyes.

'Perhaps I should have kept shtum,' he said, 'just walked into the sunset, without any fuss.' His voice sounded high and constrained. 'Just vanished and left you and Amy in peace. I let my heart rule my head.' He dug the tissue harder into his sockets. 'I feel terrible.'

Even with her mind filling with a million thoughts, Helen had space to wonder why, just after telling her that she and Amy's lives were in danger, he was talking about himself. And why this sudden outpouring of emotion when up till now he had been cold as winter earth?

When he finished his wine she asked him to leave because she needed to think things over. He reassured her that, if there was a threat, it was not imminent. This could all be resolved with time and negotiation, but at some point Leo might have to 'dig into his pockets'. Helen promised that she would tell no one about the situation.

He stood up, but instead of making towards the door, he took a step towards her, and before she really knew what was happening, he'd lifted up the dress she'd chosen for just such a purpose.

'Tony...'

A hand between her legs. Part of her wanted it, but she pushed him away, saying that she needed space to think and he needed to leave.

Later that night, as she was preparing for bed, she had a text from Leo. *That bracelet Tony gave Amy? Not gold!! Did he say it was? What a twonk.*

47

DISMANTLE THE SHITHOUSE

Leo holed himself up in what he called 'the study'. It had bookshelves, but no books. The room had a floor-to-ceiling window that had once had wooden frames and shutters, but was now an oblong slab of double-glazing. On the floor there were an intimidating number of reports and accounts that Frank had biked over. Leo knew he wouldn't have the time – even if he had the necessary knowledge – to do an audit of each organisation but he would do his best, in between sorting out the Lethco families. He now had the advice of a medical expert and a medical practice lawyer, both of whom agreed to work *pro bono,* and he'd told them that time was of the essence.

'I have bad news,' said Vince, appearing from the hall in the yellow silk pyjamas he'd bought at Lillywhites. The bottoms had a thick white drawstring. He looked like an Indian prince.

'Go on,' said Leo, shooing away some doomsday scenarios.

'You've been had.' Vince casually threw his phone in the air. It did a couple of summersaults before he caught it. 'That Monica bird? She's pulled off all your skin, stretched it over a giant bongo drum, and handed it to a calypso band.'

Leo stopped listening after he heard the name Monica. It sent a pulse from his knees to his stomach. He knew what was coming.

'Fuck.'

'It would appear she has been in contact with our old friend Donna White.'

Leo kicked whatever was under the desk.

'I just got off the phone to White,' said Vince. 'She's digging. Maybe she suspects...' He made a circle with his arms, which Leo took to mean *everything*.

'The whole caboodle?'

'White has also been phoning round our nearest and dearest – not that it'll do her much good.'

Leo tried to get his new concerns to form an orderly queue. At the front was Monica's betrayal. Sure, they weren't close friends, but he had felt there was a connection, ships-passing-in-the-night kind of thing, mutual respect, and also a shared sense of humour. Next in the queue came the thought that Helen and her parents would know that he'd paid for sex. Then another concern queue-jumped to the front: Amy. She would be informed of the tawdry facts via Channel Playground. It would surely change her view of him forever. He saw a nineteen-year-old saying, 'the thousands you spent on one shag could have paid my Uni fees, you fucktard,' and slamming the door.

Guilt, rage, shame, joined in an emotional scrum.

'So what exactly did Donna White say?' he asked, not wanting to reveal quite how upset he was.

Vince sat down on a soft round object Leo had thought was a footstool but had recently learned was called an *ottoman*.

'She said she'd like an exclusive, to discuss Monica and other things. She dropped the *Monica* in casually, but obviously thinks it will reel you in. I said I knew nothing about a Monica but I would check with you about her request, and call back.'

Leo tried to fight off a feeling that he'd been ransacked by the kind of burglar who shits on the bed.

'Don't worry too much, mate. Deals can always be done.'

'Really?'

'Sure.'

'How do you know this?'

'I *read*. I will tell White that if she intends to publish, we will slap on a super injunction, and threaten to sue. IPSO, the press watchdog, won't help us because TrueNewz is only online, but I happen to know that they work by the same guidelines.'

Vince looked like he was enjoying himself. 'Remember,' he said, 'they *think* you're a billionaire.' He surveyed the boxes of papers and files. 'A labour of love?'

Leo moaned something.

'When do you think you'll be finished? Before this whole thing responds to the second law of thermodynamics?'

Neither of them had addressed this question of The End for a while.

'Why? Are you bored?'

'A bit. But… It would be good to dismantle the shithouse ourselves rather than have it fall around our ears, don't you think?'

The last thing Leo needed was a disgruntled Vince.

'I thought you were having a ball.'

Vince rested his arms on his knees, his mood thoughtful.

'It's as if the Universe has provided some sort of key, but I don't know what to open with it.'

He got up to leave and moments later Leo made out the words 'Ello, Donna?' before a door closed.

48

I TRY TO BE A GOOD MUSLIM

Nina Allam chose to meet Mrs Farheem at the community centre because she heard they provided meeting rooms for women in need of a safe place. The assistant who took her call didn't ask questions. Nina was offered a portacabin, which was being deployed while parts of the centre were being refurbished. There was nothing in the portacabin except half a dozen plastic chairs, a stack of tables in one corner and a gas heater, which emitted a smell of burning dust. Fluorescent strip lighting gave the cabin a bygone feel, like a 1970s post office. There were several posters blu-tacked to the walls, with the usual themes: smoking, drinking, domestic abuse, and how to claim winter fuel allowance.

Nina had considered waiting in reception so Mrs Farheem wouldn't have to find the cabin on her own, but she was sure her advisor would understand her need for discretion. Nina had left instructions with the helpful lady at the front desk.

She placed two plastic chairs a few feet from one another in the centre of the room. Then she prayed quietly. A few minutes after the appointed time, she heard footsteps and voices – Mrs Farheem was being shown the way. Nina felt herself shudder. She adjusted her headscarf.

Mrs Farheem looked very like her online photograph, except that she wore glasses – plain, round ones. Her hijab was light blue, with no patterns, and she had no makeup as far as Nina could see. She looked about fifty years old, smaller than Nina had imagined, and with a purposeful, no-nonsense demeanour. She took her gloves off and the two women shook hands, Nina using both of hers.

After they had exchanged greetings, Nina wondered if she should compliment Mrs Farheem on something, but could find nothing physical about the woman that could be convincingly admired.

'You're very punctual,' she said.

Mrs Farheem seemed surprised by the remark, as if being anything else was unthinkable.

'I am so grateful to you for agreeing to meet me,' added Nina.

'That's quite all right,' said Mrs Fahreem, as she unbuttoned her coat.

'Shall I take that?'

Both women looked round for a hook but there were none, so Mrs Farheem hung the coat on the back of her chair.

'Was the journey okay?' asked Nina, nervously, as they sat down.

'I got a little lost, but satnav is wonderful.' Mrs Farheem looked around the room and shivered. 'Why are we in a portacabin?'

'My problem is very private and they are refurbishing the—'

'I understand.' She seemed serious but not unkind: a busy woman who didn't do small-talk. Nina had emailed her saying that she wanted to speak to her in person about a very confidential matter.

'Would you like some tea, Mrs Farheem? There is a machine in the lobby.'

'No, I'm fine. Thank you, Mrs Allam.'

'Nina, please.'

Mrs Farheem dropped her handbag down beside her, and began wiping her glasses with a tissue. Then, without looking up, she began to recite.

'I ask Allah, exalted is he, that the advice I give you is beneficial and leads you to the best decisions.'

Nina nodded, but decided not to speak again until she was asked. Nina felt both frightened and excited about the prospect of letting her story burst forth.

'Why did you choose me?' said Mrs Farheem, donning her glasses.

Nina had found her on the Muslim Women's Council and picked her from a dozen women whose brief biographies were displayed together with contact details.

'You have a degree in Islamic studies,' said Nina, 'and you've said that women have an important role to play in all areas of the community and society.' She did not add that her eyes reminded her of her mother's. 'And you have a kind face – your photograph.'

Mrs Farheem responded with just the hint of a smile. 'I don't imagine most people think I have a kind face. Now, let's get down to it. How can I help?' She put her hands in her lap, as if settling down to hear a story. Nina took a deep breath and began.

'I try to be a good Muslim. We are an observant family. I pray five times every day, I read hadith and Qur'an, and I have brought up my two daughters to do the same.'

Mrs Farheem nodded in way that suggested many women she meets begin with a similar statement.

'But I have committed a haram, a great haram, and I am afraid that Allah may be punishing me for it, in his wisdom.'

Nina paused for a moment, so that her advisor could take time to consider the fact. The fire exhaled its gas like a continuous sigh.

'I just want University educations for my daughters,' said Nina. 'Both are very good students, observant Muslims, top in their class. Aisha is keen to study medicine and Kamila is very good at public speaking and I think would be a great advocate for our community, maybe joining the Muslim Women's Council one day.'

Mrs Farheem tilted her head, but said nothing for a moment. Nina felt herself being X-rayed.

'The council believes that the education of women is a priority, Nina,' said Mrs Farheem, 'presumably that is the reason you contacted us.'

'Yes. My husband is a good man but we don't agree about our daughters. And he certainly wouldn't pay the cost of University, with what little money we have.'

Mrs Farheem nodded knowingly, as if she had expected all this. It gave Nina hope there might be a ready-made solution.

'And he does not believe student loans are mudharabah,' said Nina, 'and therefore he will not allow them. So... I thought of obtaining funds in some other way...' Nina faltered as she was arriving at the dark heart of the issue. 'I gambled.'

Mrs Farheem raised her eyebrows and shuffled in her seat. This part of the story was clearly not so run-of-the-mill. Nina said, 'I hoped that because I was doing this for my daughters, perhaps Allah would be merciful and help me win.'

Mrs Farheem let out an exasperated huff, simultaneously shrugging her shoulders. 'Why would Allah be merciful and *help you win*?'

Nina felt something fall inside her. She had thought it all through days ago, but suddenly she found she couldn't access the reasoning. With rising panic, she felt tricked. The plan that had made so much sense now seemed like a mockery of reason.

'I don't know,' is all she could find to say, and saw an image of men in masks, dancing round her, laughing at her foolish ways.

'Allah does not break laws on a whim, Nina. What kind of gambling did you indulge in? Not the casino, I hope.'

Nina hesitated.

'Lottery tickets. Over a period of time. I bought them from a newsagent, a Bangladeshi lady.'

'It doesn't matter who you bought them from. We at the council are often asked why we don't accept lottery funding for worthy causes, and we have to remind non-Muslims that gambling is haram, and so we must decline any gifts raised by lotteries or raffles, however well intended.'

'May Allah forgive me,' said Nina, and willed herself to feel more remorseful. Mrs Farheem rubbed her arms.

'Are you cold?' asked Nina, and got up to re-angle the fire.

'Do you know *why* gambling is forbidden?'

'It can lead to debt?' Nina remembered that that was at least one of the reasons.

'Nina, when you bought the tickets, you felt excited at the prospect of winning, an adrenaline rush, then a stab of disappointment when you lost, yes?'

Nina nodded.

'Then you felt excitement about your *next* ticket. These feelings drive a compulsion.'

Nina immediately realised just how true that was – the woman could see into her heart.

'But, Nina, these natural feelings are ones most merciful Allah expects us, asks us, to *resist*. The feelings lead us away from Allah and his laws that are there to protect us.'

Nina nodded, of course, *of course.*

'And what does your husband say?'

Nina didn't answer because the question was a formality – of course her husband didn't know.

'You were afraid he would be angry with you?' asked Mrs Farheem, but again, Nina did not need to answer. Instead, she conveyed her shame by making herself as small as possible.

'You didn't think this through, did you?' Mrs Farheem had the slightest of smiles.

Nina felt like saying that she *had* thought it through, even down to explaining to her husband – if she won — how she suddenly had enough money to pay her daughters' fees. She would tell him that she sold some gold trinkets of her late mother's that she'd found in an old box. She would tell Zakir she'd wanted it to be a surprise. It would be a lie, but a good lie.

It was all going to be fine. But now…

She looked Mrs Farheem in the eyes, hoping she would find some of her mother's kindness there.

'It was my mother's great wish,' said Nina, grasping at something that might soften Mrs Farheem, 'that her granddaughters would be educated. Buying lottery tickets seemed like a small sin.'

Mrs Farheem raised her hand for quiet, and the two women sat in silence for a moment.

'Nina, you said that you felt that Allah has already punished you. How?'

'Because one of my tickets… has won. It's such a large sum that I fear he is teaching me a lesson. Am I being shown how foolish I am? Because I cannot possibly accept that amount.'

'No, you can't,' said Mrs Farheem, firmly. She put a hand on each knee, leaning forward in an oddly masculine posture. 'At least you didn't win the billion pounds,' she whispered, with a little laugh in her voice, 'that young coffee fellow beat you to that one.'

Mrs Farheem had a laugh in her voice, and perhaps was beginning to thaw. Nina did not explain that it was the fact that everyone thought Amy's father had won the prize that helped give her the strength to claim it for herself. It seemed to be an extra layer of protection against being discovered. Without that, perhaps she would have let the deadline lapse, and along with it, her daughters' freedom to decide their futures.

'Do you have your own bank account, Nina?'

'I have begun setting one up.'

Mrs Farheem had looked as if she'd found a solution, but she sighed, and whatever answer she had, seemed to melt away. She shook her head and tutted. 'No, I can't think of any way round this.'

Nina felt crushing disappointment. She had dared to believe this woman would help her.

'I am keen for your girls to go to University, Nina, but with money obtained by gambling? And behind your husband's back? No. You have not protected your husband's honour – far from it, you have risked shaming him.'

The clarity of these utterances made Nina wonder how on earth she could have expected any other response. Another long silence ensued, punctuated only by the sound of a door opening and closing in the portacabin next door.

'You can do something, perhaps, to mitigate this sin, apart from praying for forgiveness, of course,' said Mrs Farheem, looking at the fire, then at Nina. Nina nodded, she would do anything.

'Expiation may be accomplished through good deeds,' said Mrs Farheem.

Nina's mind raced.

'How might I achieve this?'

The woman frowned benignly.

'Have you forgotten the five pillars of Islam? Faith, prayer, fasting, pilgrimage and…?'

'Charity.'

'A donation would seem to be the perfect way to repent.'

Nina nodded respectfully before asking her next question.

'How may I donate such a large sum without everyone – especially my husband – finding out? Any charity would be quite overwhelmed.'

Mrs Farheem shrugged, as if this was not a big problem.

'Ask the lottery people if they can help,' she said, and she reached for her gloves. 'But I'm afraid you cannot use the money for your own purposes, however noble. I'm sorry for your daughters and will pray for them.'

It seemed the meeting was over. Hope for Aisha and Kamila had been all but dashed, but Nina held back her tears and thanked her advisor.

As the two women walked across the tarmac to Mrs Farheem's car, they exchanged a few words about the unusually cold spring, and some of the pros and cons of living in Byford. Easy transport routes out of the town were the main pro, said Nina, and litter was the main con. As if on cue, a seagull landed right in front of them, greedily seizing a discarded chicken wing.

As they approached the car, a wall that had been blocking Nina's emotions began to buckle. She tried to distract herself with more inane chatter.

'It's a nice car,' she said, just managing to get the words out before choking up.

Mrs Farheem turned to Nina. 'A Mazda. Air conditioned, nought to sixty in 8.6 seconds.'

'That's pretty fast,' said Nina, not really knowing if it was fast or not.

The women's headscarves fluttered in a sudden waft of air. Nina couldn't help bringing her hand to her face. It would be obvious to Mrs Farheem that she was crying, and the thought made her want to cry more.

'Of course,' said Mrs Farheem, jangling her keys, 'Ulema say that necessity legalises the prohibited.'

She said these words as if they were an inconsequential afterthought. She opened the car door, but then stopped, thinking of something to add.

'Life is like a jigsaw. Allah gives us the pieces, we must discover where to place them.'

When the car drove away Nina pulled her hijab more tightly around herself. She had the feeling that she had been left with a puzzle to solve.

49

I HAVE A WAY OF
KEEPING US SAFE

Helen had heard the term 'hypervigilant' on documentaries about war veterans who, years after leaving the battleground, still scan the environment for threats. Was this her life now? Tony had repeatedly tried to reassure her that danger was not imminent; there would be 'undercover negotiations'. The last thing the bad guys would want to do is harm their two most valuable assets: Amy and her. It would be a last resort, and only if 'talks' failed, and there would be lots of warnings first. They wanted money, not revenge. But still, Helen had shipped off Amy to stay with her parents for a few days, giving work commitments as the reason.

It was only Tony's constant reassurance that he would 'deal with the matter, just give me a little time, I know how to handle this,' that stopped Helen going to the police or discussing the issue with anyone. The worst case scenario, said Tony, was that Leo would have to put some money into an offshore account. 'It would be peanuts for him.' It would not be giving into blackmail, because the bad men (which is what Tony always called them) were simply asking for the amount they believed Tony had deprived them of. Amongst the criminal community, it was not an unreasonable demand. In their twisted world, it was fair.

Helen decided that formally ending her relationship with Tony would have to go on hold until this all blew over. She had no alternative but to believe he could handle things and make them safe, but even so, his visits were rationed, with no more overnights. In fact, the romantic and sexual side of their relationship was over 'for the time being'.

Helen waited for the doorbell to ring four times – the agreed signal – before she opened the door. When he'd phoned earlier he'd sounded optimistic, and she hoped he would have good news.

'I have a way of keeping us safe,' he said. This was all Helen wanted to hear, but even so, the walk from door to the kitchen was full of apprehension.

Once sitting at the table, Tony lifted a plastic shopping bag to head height.

'This is it.' He seemed pleased about something.

'What? What on earth?' said Helen. How could the answer to their problems be in a shopping bag? Tony lowered the bag and it thudded onto the table next to the fruit bowl.

'Guess.'

'It *can't* be a gun,' said Helen, really believing that it *couldn't* be a gun. Tony smiled mischievously, and reached in and pulled out a carton about the size of a lunchbox. He rattled it.

'Enough for a bloodbath,' he said, still smiling.

'No…' said Helen, willing herself to wake up from this dream.

'And this…'

It was an object wrapped in a green velvet cloth. Helen's eyes flicked between the object and Tony. A moment later he was cradling a gun.

The incongruity of seeing such a weapon in her own kitchen switched on a laugh impulse. Helen brought her hand to her open mouth to stifle it, but Tony seemed to welcome the reaction and laughed too. They had rarely laughed together, and now they were, in the least funny situation Helen had ever been in.

'It's not funny,' she said, as she stopped.

'People in my business need protection. So a few of us carry these,' he said, having also stopped laughing. 'Had to talk to a lot of lowlifes, cross a few palms with silver, but that's the trade I'm in.'

'I cannot have that thing in my house. Take it away.'

She would have said more, but there was something about the way Tony slowly brought his finger to his lips that silenced her. And the way he glared. She had never seen eyes like that before. They belonged to something freshly slain.

As she tried to process the scene, Tony held the weapon with one hand, and the fingers of the other ran up and down the barrel. He felt the gun's weight and power. He examined it from all angles, looking along its length, perhaps imaging what damage it could do, what scores it could settle. Then he slipped his finger onto the trigger.

'A Glock 22. Carries 15 rounds. Used by 60 per cent of American cops. It will get between you and trouble.'

Helen's brain searched for a match from her past experiences that might inform her of the likely outcomes, but it was as if red letters flashed on a screen: no match found.

'You must take it away.'

'It's all about confidence.' He placed the gun on the table. 'Your target needs to know you're prepared to use it. Then, chances are you won't have to. I'll teach you how to use it.'

'No, you won't,' said Helen; she just wanted it out of her sight. She tried to grab it and throw it somewhere – in the bin – anywhere, but he beat her to it. He held it in his hand, finger on the trigger. Helen froze. He would surely see the pain on her face and put it down.

Instead, his eyes surveyed the room and found one of Amy's paintings on the fridge door. A red house with yellow flowers, a blue matchstick man – Daddy – waving. He pointed the gun.

'Bang,' he said, and laughed.

50

I'M JUST SAYING IT *FITS*

Having spent an hour at a desktop computer hardly moving a muscle, Donna's neck was beginning to ache, but she wouldn't be fully aware of the pain until she finished. The half dozen journos at the desks around her knew there was no point in trying to engage her in conversation when she wore that frown – no, that *scowl* of concentration. They would just get a shake of the head, a finger pointing at her screen, she'd be too focused even to say, 'I'm busy'.

The Yeovil feeling that Donna had had in the bath days ago had been triggered by memories of the press conference at the Carlton Hotel. It had taken all this time for a nascent doubt, a mote of apprehension, to become uncomfortable enough to warrant further attention.

Such was her concentration that she didn't notice Derek sidle up with two cups of coffee. He placed one next to her keyboard.

'Could you pull up a chair?' said Donna, not taking her eyes off the screen, which was now a frozen image of the two young men in front of the hotel banner.

Derek wheeled over a chair from a vacant desk. 'No word from the mystery caller, then.'

'No,' said Donna. 'I think that's gone away.'

'So update me,' he said. 'You tried to get an exclusive and the Vince guy mentioned a super injunction?'

He had been emailed the basic facts.

'Yup. And he threatened to sue our arses off if we went with the Monica story.'

'Not as dumb as we thought?'

He took a sip of coffee. Donna tried to assess what sort of mood he was in – combative, joshy, serious, world-weary, impatient, flirtatious… she settled on *receptive*.

'Come on, what's new?' he said.

Donna wasn't confident enough of her new hypothesis to present it as such. She decided simply to show him the footage and gently guide him – lure him? – to her own conclusions.

'I've watched this over and over. If you look at it with the supposition that these guys are hoaxers, it fits. I'm not saying they *are* frauds, I'm just saying it *fits*.'

Derek pushed his chair a little further back from the screen, distancing himself from what could be some uncomfortable truth.

'Go on then.'

She rewound a few seconds and clicked play.

'Here we are. Vince is about to explain that the whole thing has been a terrible mistake, and that Leo was drunk.'

Yeah, we've all gone to the pub, got ourselves shit-faced, and started shooting our mouths off, only to wake up the next morning, thinking, what the hell did I say? A pa -ck… oerf… wha.'

She stopped the footage.

'What were those last two words?' asked Donna.

'Dunno. You tell me.'

'I asked techy Paul to get rid of the bass, and make a sound loop, which he did, but only after describing the entire plot of *The Conversation*.'

'Coppola's first film after *The Godfather*.'

'I know that now, and everything else about it, thank you.'

She pressed play. The loop ran the three seconds – Vince's floundering words repeated.

'He's saying *a pack of*…' said Derek. 'Definitely *a pack of*.'

'And what comes in packs?'

'Cards? Oh, no shit. *Lies*. He's definitely about to say *a pack of lies*, don't you think?'

Lure, don't lead.

'What do *you* think?' said Donna.

'Lies. But he might simply be trying to put the genie back in the bottle.'

Donna had considered this, and it was possible. But she had more.

'Look what happens when Poppy enters the room with her parents. The camera isn't on her but you can hear a door open.'

She played from the moment just before the three Lethcos entered the conference room.

'There. Hear the door? Look at Leo's face.'

She hit pause and enlarged the image.

'A look of total terror,' said Derek.

'Their demeanour changes completely,' said Donna, and pressed play again. 'See the alarm in Leo's eyes and a *fuck* glance towards Vince? He's a man wanting the earth to open up. Only after a few laughs from the audience do the boys begin to relax, they realise they can play a game with us.'

'But why would Poppy make them shit the bed?'

'Yeah, that's the billion pound question.'

Derek leaned back, his arms now flopping by his side. Donna felt that something had landed in his brain.

'You know,' he said, 'if *only* this footage were around a week or so ago and you could have done all this *then*. Oh, my mistake, it *was*.'

It was only to be expected that Derek would jokingly throw this back in her face.

'You total tit.'

'Okay,' said Derek, taking the insult in the way it was meant, 'Answer me this: how sure are you, as of *this minute*, that Leo Morphetus is a lottery billionaire?'

She leaned back, so they were level. She would take her time to answer.

'You won't like this, Derek, but if you put it all together…' she rattled off all the evidence that had been churning around in her head like stones in a tumble drier, 'I have no idea.'

Derek threw his head back.

'Great.'

'And it's driving me *mad*. I need to get closer to these guys and the people around them.'

'How will you do that?'

'I don't know, but I won't sleep until I'm certain one way or another.'

Derek nodded, he seemed to believe her.

'Donna, having broken the story that he is a billionaire, I'd like us to be first with the story that he isn't. *If* he isn't. It's the only way we can survive with our heads held high.'

She gave him a wry nod and he responded with a wry smile before picking up his coffee and walking back to his glass domain.

His jibe, that the conference footage had been around for a week, reverberated around Donna's skull. Why had she not clocked these tells before? And she had actually *been there*, in the room. Why had she been so convinced that Leo was the jackpot winner? And why had she had her Yeovil scintilla of doubt only ten minutes after finding enough evidence to persuade Derek to run with the story?

Donna took a sip of coffee and it confirmed her inkling that she was not in a coffee mood. She rubbed her eyes and then closed them, trying to drown out the chatting and keyboard-tapping around her.

A mind trying to comprehend itself is a strange thing. Could it be as simple as this: as soon as she had 'sold' her story to Derek, she no longer needed to believe it herself? Released from the imperative of landing a scoop, the signalmen in her brain relaxed. They no longer needed to direct the facts to a particular point on a map. And then the truth, that wily creature, came out from its hiding place, to roam freely wherever it pleased. Sometimes the numbers only add up because you need them to.

51

I'VE GOT BIG NEWS

Leo had not slept well. Just as dreams had begun to form, something always jostled him awake. This time he was bumped from sleep, not by a throb of anxiety, but by his phone. He opened his eyes and the objects in the room came dancing towards him: an onyx bedside table on which rested a reproduction 1920s phone with a gold and mother-of-pearl theme; beyond that was a coal-effect fireplace, guarded by a pair of life-size bronze lurchers. Not even his own clothes strewn over a white leather armchair felt familiar.

'Frank.'

'Not too early for you?'

It was 8.30. Leo would normally have re-stocked the trike, ridden it two miles at an average gradient of six per cent, and made thirty cappuccinos by now. But it was too early to talk to Frank, and he regretted taking the call.

'I'm a dawn riser,' he said.

'I've got big news. But first, how are we getting on with the paperwork?'

Leo rubbed his eyes. He didn't feel ready to discuss figures, but he would do his best.

'Um… I've had a look through several of the organisations, and I do have a few… um, questions.'

A sigh from Frank.

'Fire away.'

Most of Leo's time had been spent deciding how much to give each of Lethco's families. He'd only spent a few hours on Frank's good causes.

'Let's see. One charity is hiring freelancers, but they're being paid via limited companies, which often means VAT on top of wages and can mean NI on top of that. They save pension contributions, but twenty per cent is a hefty add-on they can't usually reclaim.'

Leo was pretty pleased with how alert he sounded. There was no answer from Frank.

'I have some other questions too.'

'Yeah, look, Leo. I can't go through all these details. Can we just hand it over to an accountant?'

'It really won't take long. Another day or two.'

He could sense Frank's irritation in a small cough.

'Leo, I've organised some photo shoots.'

'I know – your press person called. I've bought a nice suit.'

'Good, good. Okay, now for the big news. Ready for this?'

'I'm all ears, Frank.'

'I managed to get a message to Bernard,' said Frank, 'who passed it on to the PM's press secretary. Are you *sure* you're ready for this?'

Leo sat up a little straighter.

'Hello?'

'Er, yes, I'm listening, Frank.' His heart beat a little faster.

'The PM's PRs are bloody delighted apparently; you're just the sort of young celeb that politicians want to be seen with.'

'Including you, Frank,' said Leo, trying not to sound too knowing.

Frank laughed. 'It won't do me any harm! Now, here's the thing, the PM is going to put aside two minutes for a meet-and-greet and a photo. How's about that? Amazing or what?'

'I'd have to look at my diary.'

'Oh, you kill me,' Frank said, and told him to expect an important call from Number Ten. They then discussed some photo shoots in more detail. Leo avoided making any firm commitments and managed to get off the phone.

He threw the duvet aside and sat on the edge of the bed. His feet touched the carpet, and he wondered if it was the kind of wool favoured by his mother-in-law.

Going to Number Ten. Could that really happen? He had a vision of his mother being so proud, if only for a while. Same with Helen. If he wasn't her husband she would see the funny side of all this. She might even hold that bogus billionaire up as an example. 'You see, Leo? That's what you can do if you have enough balls.'

52

IT'S AN EXTRAORDINARY THING, A GUN

Helen placed the bracelet on the chopping board. It had come to this. Forensic detective work. She gazed at it for a moment, half expecting it to wriggle away like a worm. She hadn't paid much attention to Leo's text saying it wasn't gold – surely that was jealousy talking. And what did he know about gold anyway? She'd also missed the significance of Amy's wide-eyed revelation that the bracelet was magnetic. She'd been too distracted by her own negligence – any responsible parent would have stopped a child from wearing a solid gold bracelet to school. But she'd been stressed, she'd had a lot on her mind that morning.

In the middle of the night, she had turned over in her half-sleep and it was as if there had been a beast lying underneath her that she'd suddenly disturbed. These two events – the magnet and Leo's text – had been dormant facts, knowledge she didn't know she had. Now the facts lurched into her consciousness and were asking questions. She would find the answers – but not in the cold, lonely hours of darkness. She would wait till day.

As she stood over the chopping board, she drew on imaginary conversations with her friends. Positive Sharon would no doubt say, 'It's only a bracelet, what does it matter?' But Sharon was a disaster area, and had been all her life. Rachel, the uber-functioning single mother and solicitor, would give Tony no quarter: 'Who lies to a kid about something like that? I mean, a gem trader, and he pretends a bracelet is solid gold? And it's not like he could be mistaken. Or maybe he's not even a gem trader. Ditch the loser asap.'

Panic must be contained, chaotic thoughts eschewed. Helen gripped the pizza knife and began to scrape. After three strokes, she stopped and held the deformed chinks right up to the window. Beneath the bright yellow, a silvery lustre.

Rather than alarm, Helen felt relief, as if the brightness of the metal had shone a light on a threat lurking in the shadows, and shown it to be a mere hat-stand. Now she *knew* Tony had lied about the bracelet, and she could add that to the lie about owning the rented Mazda. Both small lies, tiny really, but if he lied about things like that then she couldn't believe anything he said. It was just as if his clothes had suddenly fallen from him, and he was standing there shivering, his penis shrivelled. She would no longer quiver and tremble while he went on about 'bad men'.

She felt power surge from her heart right up to her neck.

She kneeled down to the bottom cupboard and reached behind the wok.

She grabbed it, still in its bag. It was heavy, far heavier than she'd imagined. And then something took her by surprise: the urge to hold the gun in her hands.

She took it to the table. It was colder than she'd expected. She ran her fingers across the barrel just as Tony had done. A sleek sheen. So smooth, so lean, so perfect. It's an extraordinary thing, a gun: forbidden, exotic, dangerous, mysterious and cold, phallic and beautiful, capable of both protecting and penetrating – who would not experience a thrill? Only a few seconds passed before she felt that her time was up. This liaison was a one-off, never-to-be-repeated tryst with the devil.

She wrapped the weapon in the Robert Dyas bag, pushed it into a Shreddies packet she had emptied for the purpose and went outside, heart pounding. She looked up both ends of the street; it was empty.

A putrid smell filled her nostrils as she lifted the lid. She slipped the package behind a kitchen bin liner. It would be emptied tomorrow. She would tell Tony that the gun was in a landfill somewhere, gone for good. If he got angry, then so be it. It would be the perfect time to finish with him.

Just as the lid came down, she heard her name being called and she jumped. Tony was striding towards her. She had a few seconds to think as he walked the twenty metres from the corner.

When he was close enough, she said, 'I needed to do this,' and as she spoke, she did not hear the weak, pleading tones of the victim that she had almost grown used to, but those of someone gaining strength.

Tony's eyes flickered between hers and the bin. He nodded.

'We must have it. To protect you.' She felt his firm hand on her arm. 'Be sensible, Helen.'

He opened the bin lid, and the stench returned. He lifted the package out, giving Helen a disgusted look. He inspected it for filth and seemed satisfied that it was clean enough to carry.

'I'll be in touch,' he said, and began walking away.

This must end. And soon it would. As Rachel would say, 'Ditch the loser asap.'

53

VANISHINGLY UNLIKELY

Nina Allam sat waiting in the same portacabin at the community centre where she had met Mrs Farheem. More than anything else, it was the smell of burning dust from the gas fire that gave Nina a sense of déjà vu.

As far she could recall, the cautionary posters on the wall were the same as before, but she didn't remember seeing a whiteboard. On it was written the word, **GOALS.**

The word was underlined twice. Nothing else was written. Perhaps a long list of objectives had been wiped off, or the meeting had been abandoned when it was discovered that no one had any goals.

'Thank you for coming, Mrs Butterworth,' said Nina, after opening the portacabin door.

'It's all part of the service,' said the Winners' Adviser, smiling, 'and congratulations, Mrs Allam – oh, and do call me Susan,' she added, after they had shaken hands.

Nina felt the same anxiety she had when she'd met Mrs Farheem, but less intensely.

Susan Butterworth took the seat nearest the gas fire. Nina noticed that the woman did not seem in any way unsettled, yet how many big winners had worn the hijab? Probably not one. Perhaps Nina's name, Allam, had alerted her. Susan was late forties, maybe fifty, wore a light blue blouse and a black blazer that looked to Nina like it might be part of a uniform, and yet it couldn't be, given the anonymity of her role. She busied herself taking some forms from her aluminium attaché case.

Her boss, the Chief Winners' Advisor, Michael Winterborne, had planned to meet the record-breaking jackpot winner, but when they had spoken on a special number, Nina told him that for 'cultural reasons' she could only see a female. Her request was granted without hesitation, and Mr Winterborne assured her that only two people on the planet knew of her win: himself, and the person who answered her initial call. Soon, a third person would know: a very nice lady called Susan Butterworth, one of seven Winners' Advisors employed by Camelot, each taking a different region of the UK. Contrary to popular assumptions, the winners do not have to make their way to the Watford office. Susan would phone, and she would ask for a password, and then they would arrange for a visit.

Thanks to Mrs Farheem's parting words, 'necessity legalises the prohibited', and 'Life is like a jigsaw', things made sense to Nina now. Days of reading, praying and thinking had delivered clarity of vision. Millions of other people in the world might have won this money, but it was she, Nina Allam, whom God had chosen. Such a vanishingly unlikely event could only occur by his direct command. And not only that, Allah had made sure that an abundant gift to charity would pardon her of sin, and he had provided a simple way that his gift could be donated without bringing dishonour on her husband and family. These were the pieces of the jigsaw. The solutions had been provided, not by her, but by a Higher Power.

She waited patiently for Susan to begin proceedings.

'Right, that's everything,' said Susan, with the friendly professionalism of a nurse who had just come on duty. 'First things first, Nina. I have to check your ticket.'

Nina reached into a compartment in her handbag and brought out a green envelope, which contained the ticket. She gave it to Susan, who held the ticket up to the light. Nina felt a swirling sensation in her stomach.

'If it's damaged in any way there will be a ten day delay in payment.'

The Winners' Advisor examined it on both sides. 'But it's in perfect condition, which is very good news,' she said with a chuckle.

Nina realised she'd been holding her breath, and exhaled.

'It's not over yet,' said Susan. She carefully checked the long row of small numbers just above the barcode and made sure they tallied with those on her form. She made some notes.

'Okay, the ticket is present and correct. I am delighted to reconfirm your win, so congratulations again.'

'Thank you, Susan.' Nina closed her eyes and offered a silent prayer. Susan then asked her to sign the back of the ticket with a black ballpoint pen she provided.

'Once we've finished our meeting, I can authorise the payment from here, over the internet. We now pay by CHAPS, which means it will reach your account straight away. Exciting, isn't it?'

'May we talk about that?' asked Nina.

Susan nodded earnestly, indicating that there was a serious side to this business, and she was here to help. 'Of course,' she said, 'I am here to give any advice you need. I must also ask you about privacy. Now, I may be jumping the gun here, but I… well, I assume you don't want publicity?'

Nina nodded, and with that, Susan clasped her hands together and seemed to feel ever more relaxed.

'Contrary to what people think, it doesn't do us any good if, well, let's say, the *wrong people* get publicity.' Susan said *wrong people* in a way that suggested there were a few stories she could tell. 'So if there are issues that might arise from going public we always suggest the no-publicity option. I can also advise you on keeping your win as discreet as possible, because in a close-knit community people can notice a change in spending patterns very quickly. With this amount, keeping it secret could prove quite a challenge.'

Nina smiled. 'Yes, but thanks be…' she hesitated for a second, 'but thanks be to God, everyone thinks Mr Morphetus is the winner.'

Susan brushed something from her sleeve before answering.

'I can't comment on whether any other individual has won anything or not, even if I knew,' said Susan, deliberately busying herself with forms. Nina was reassured by this lady's discretion but wanted to test it further.

'Don't you think it's quite *bizarre*?'

Susan seemed unfazed.

'As I say, I can't comment.'

Nina was impressed. The woman must know as well as she does that Morphetus is a fake – there couldn't be two billion pound winners. What harm would it do just to nod knowingly? Maybe she could tempt her.

'You must know the whole thing is a sham,' she said, light-heartedly.

Susan stopped fidgeting and looked at her directly.

'My grandfather was a code breaker during the war. I think I must get my discretion from him. Careless talk costs lives, and all that. Now, Nina,' she smiled warmly, 'I have come to see *you*, so let's not talk about anyone else.'

More impressed than ever by this woman, and feeling that she could trust her implicitly, Nina moved the conversation on.

'I need to tell you something very important.'

'Please do,' said Susan, paying full attention. Nina gathered her thoughts.

'By playing the lottery... I have committed a sin in my religion – which I take very seriously.'

Susan did not seem surprised, and she smiled sympathetically. Perhaps Nina's last name and then the hijab and might have led her to expect a religious complication of some kind.

'I understand,' she said, 'and for what it's worth, I respect it.'

Nina appreciated the sentiment.

'I've made a decision to have a relatively small sum paid into my personal account,' she said, 'which I am still setting up, and the rest, which will go to good causes, into another account.'

Susan tilted her head apologetically.

'I respect your wish to donate to charity, of course, but I'm afraid the full amount must be paid into the winner's own account, I'm so sorry. Rules are rules, I'm afraid.'

Nina had been prepared to face a bureaucratic barrier, but still felt heat on her face.

'I have signed a letter saying where I want the money deposited,' she said, as gently as she could, but was afraid that frustration would soon begin to show. She produced a letter from her bag. 'I can sign it again in your presence.'

'I'm so sorry,' sighed Susan, 'but it must go into an account with your name.' She now sounded just a little like a nurse at the *end* of her shift.

'That's simply not possible, it cannot happen!'

Nina had seldom raised her voice in anger, except to quell rowdy schoolchildren, and then only rarely. The default smile that Susan had worn since she came in now dropped.

'But, Nina, once the money is in your account you can pay it to whoever you want.'

'But whoever-it-is would know it was from me,' Nina said, whilst berating herself for talking too loudly.

'Send it to someone you trust. Or a solicitor, who can then pass it on.'

Nina stayed silent for a moment, so that they could both take stock of this situation.

'I had thought of a solicitor,' she said, calmly. 'But I cannot trust someone I've never met, and their assistants. People gossip.'

'I think they are more professional than that.'

'Ha. It only takes an anonymous call. I would be living under the constant threat of discovery.'

There was another silence as both women remained still, heads bowed, deep in thought. As the seconds passed, Nina decided to increase the pressure.

'Susan, my friend, let me tell you what will happen if my husband ever finds out I have won this money. He will shout at me and call me a sinner and an apostate. Then he will insist I give all the money away, or return it to Camelot for all I know. My daughters will never go to University.'

Susan's lips curved into a half-smile, expressing sympathy balanced by steely resolve. Nina continued.

'The money might find its way to terrorist organisations, jihadists.'

By looking at her hands, the way they were so tightly clasped, Nina felt Susan was holding back emotion, but she was not ready to comply. She needed to go a little further.

'He will make a fool of me. He will shame me to my community. Then he will divorce me on the spot, by saying *I divorce you* three times. And his family may take revenge – you have heard of honour killings?' Susan flinched and looked away. 'I could be beheaded, and it could end up on YouTube. How would *that* be for publicity? And—'

Susan put her hand up and asked Nina to stop. Then she pressed her fingers onto her lips, trying not to be sick or burst into tears, or both. Suddenly Nina felt sorry for her. She had taken the story far too far. She had prepared the speech, but the reference to beheading was going to be her absolute last resort. Before she could find a way to ameliorate the situation, Susan spoke, her voice shaking, her eyes watery.

'How am I supposed to know what to do? I've been in this job for seventeen years, and nothing has prepared me for this!'

Nina took a tissue from her bag and handed it to her. She needed to back-pedal.

'Susan, I… I was only talking, um… hypothetically. I mean, my husband's family would never do something like that.' Could a little humour help? 'They're too lazy, for a start. I let my imagination run wild, because I'm so upset. I'm so sorry for alarming you.'

Susan blew her nose and then smiled tearfully.

'I will talk to Mr Winterborne,' she said, with quiet determination. 'He's very sympathetic – the sort of man who wants everyone to be happy. You may need to speak to him again for verification. I will take your letter. I hope there is a way round this, though it may take a little while.'

'Thank you so much, Susan,' said Nina, trying to look as grateful as she felt. 'The bank details are in the letter.'

Now surer than ever that her plan was also God's plan, Nina placed her hand on Susan's, and gently squeezed. How could she have ever thought Allah wanted to punish her? In his mercy, he had provided her with the perfect means of disposing of her money in accordance with the five pillars. No one will even wonder who the winner is.

The pieces of the jigsaw are given to us by God, and it is for us to discover where they must go. Things always make sense if you can see all the pieces.

54

WE'VE REACHED THE TOP

Leo and Vince had put on their best new clothes for the occasion, and Driver Dave had given the limo a once-over with a chamois. The men made a point of not drinking on their way; it wouldn't do to turn up at Number Ten half cut, and Leo made Vince promise to be on his best behaviour. The limo was not permitted on the famous street, but had to park in an allotted space several metres away. Dave wasn't best pleased, but then he hadn't been pleased about anything for quite a while.

Once past security and inside the building, the young men were ushered into a room called 'the study'. It looked like a posh dentist's waiting room, and it smelled like one too. There were five large, grey fabric armchairs placed around a coffee table in front of a fireplace. Leather-bound tomes, locked behind wire mesh, were displayed on two of the walls. On the other walls were portraits of serious men with serious moustaches.

'There's nothing to nick here,' said Vince, after looking round disdainfully.

'I think that's deliberate.'

'You mean this is a special room for people who might nick things?'

After twenty minutes there was a knock on the door and a lady said that the PM was ready, would they all follow her. They were kept waiting in the lobby for a few minutes, flanked by two young assistants, before the PM emerged from a side door.

The PM congratulated Leo on his win and mentioned some of the good causes he was supporting.

'My view is that a billion pounds is far too much for one person, but I am delighted that it has gone to someone so public spirited.'

'It's been a great experience.'

'Nice place you have here,' said Vince.

Leo found himself feeling tongue-tied but was determined to make his point.

'Prime Minister, if I may raise an issue that is of deep concern to me...'

The PM clearly hadn't bargained on hearing an appeal, but she made a reasonable job of looking interested. Leo did his best to put his case that our NHS should not be virtually blackmailed by international drug companies. Could pressure be put on these corporations? Could something be done in international law?

'It's something we're aware of and is of deep concern to me too, Leo. Thanks for raising it.'

'You see, the drug companies are gaming the system. They're supposed to let other companies make generic copies of the drug once their patent and expired but that's not what happens. Plus, how long is the NHS going to develop drugs at the tax payer's expense only for private companies to profit from them?'

Leo hadn't expected even to be able to talk for this long, so he floundered. The PM filled the void.

'The companies do need to make a profit for all the R & D they do.'

'Oh I totally get that. I'm a businessman myself.'

The PM smiled at this.

'But there's turning a profit, and profiteering. It's incredible what they get up to. I think it's getting worse all the time.'

And at that moment, the lady who seemed to be in charge of them said that they were ready to go outside for the photoshoot.

'I'm going to tell the minister of health to look out for an email from you.'

'Okay. I'll write to her.'

'Thanks, PM,' added Vince. 'He knows what he's talking about.'

The press were waiting on the other side of the street. Cameras snapped and a few questions were shouted, but Leo and Vince ignored them. Leo resisted the temptation to shout an off-the-cuff slogan about Big Pharma. They said their goodbyes and hot-footed it to the gates, beyond which their sanctuary was waiting, engine running.

Once the limo had turned into Trafalgar Square, Vince popped open a half bottle of Moët. Driver Dave's screen descended and he asked if the next stop might be Buckingham Palace.

'Instead of Buck House, I'd like a sharpener at the Gong, 52nd floor of The Shard,' said Vince. 'I hear it's a *must* for high altitude drinking,' he said to Leo. 'We've reached the top figuratively, let's go to the top literally.'

The Gong Bar had a Chinese vibe. On one side, the walls were decorated with interlocking wooden brackets and on the other, twelve foot high windows looked out onto the whole of North London.

The two men bought drinks and took them to the massive windows. As clouds parted, a curtain of shadow withdrew over the Thames, providing a moment of brightness. Another curtain of shadow raced across from the East.

Neither men spoke, because the spectacle didn't need words. After a few minutes, Leo broke the silence.

'We've reached the top, and I've done what I set out to do, Vince.'

Vince nodded, and put his arm over Leo's shoulder.

'The riskiest part of any climb is the descent,' he said.

55

WE NEED TO TALK

Helen had called Tony. *We need to talk.* She had used that phrase deliberately, hoping it would do half the work for her. They hadn't spoken since she'd tried to ditch the gun. He'd sent a few texts saying that he'd made contact with his former 'associates', and they were 'willing to negotiate'. Helen had given minimal responses; 'Good, glad to hear it'. She began to doubt these people even existed. Tony could not be trusted and she wanted him out of her life.

Of course, guilt at having let this strange, cold, untrustworthy, man into her life had been ever-present. She should have dumped him the minute he mentioned any kind of threat. How could she have let it carry on? She'd never thought she would ever be a victim of abuse, which in a way this was. She was too clever, too good a judge of character, too strong. And yet here she was.

But she was doing something about it, right now.

After the signal – four short rings – she answered the door wearing her dowdiest grey jumper. She was laden with Amy's clothes – this meant she could politely avoid an embrace or even a peck.

She noticed that he hadn't shaved and his usually ironed shirt looked as if he'd slept in it. After showing him into the sitting room, she fetched the glass of water he'd requested. While at the sink she concluded that he must know what was coming because he was stony-faced, even for him.

'Look, this isn't easy, but… I think we need to stop seeing each other,' she said, once she'd sat down and taken a breath. Tony sipped the water and nodded solemnly, just as she'd expected him to.

'But I'm doing very well with the negotiations. I think we're very close to a deal,' he said.

Helen wanted to say she didn't believe a word, and how dare he talk about *a deal* and *negotiations* when her and her daughter's safety was involved. But she didn't want this to end with an argument, and she certainly didn't want to make an enemy of a man with a gun.

'That's good,' she said, stifling her fury. 'But, as I say, we should go our separate ways. I've sure that's the right thing.'

She had decided not to bring up his lies about the bracelet and the car because it would be too easy for him to dismiss these as trivial – just a silly woman reading too much into things.

'What about the—'

'I don't want to hear any more about bad men. I can look after myself.' She said this as firmly as she'd rehearsed it.

Tony ran a finger along the seam of his trousers.

'Can we be friends?'

The most obvious question in the world, and yet she hadn't prepared for it. She inhaled slowly, just to buy an extra second.

'Yes. That would be nice,' she lied. 'But only when all this blows over, which I'm sure it will.'

He stayed silent. She felt compelled to fill the void.

'I'm sorry it hasn't worked out.' *Throw him a bone?* 'Maybe at another time, you know…'

He nodded. Helen had come to the conclusion that he did the silent nodding just to look in control, showing his contempt for spontaneity, and the weaknesses it might reveal.

She stared at the coffee table, focusing on a mark that she would later clean off. In a few moments it would be gone, along with Tony. She looked up to see him bring the fingertips of each hand together – a spiritual sort of gesture. What's he doing? Does he think he's a Buddhist now? It seemed bewildering that only a fortnight ago this man could make her feel giddy just with a text.

He spoke quietly and with a rasp in his voice.

'He's gone to Downing Street.'

'Yes,' said Helen. 'Who would have thought it?'

She smiled, but hoped that the chat would end there. After a pause, he let out a sigh.

'Okay.'

It was Helen's turn to nod sombrely, but inside she felt the euphoria of an escaping prisoner ascending the outer wall.

He stood up.

'Bye, then.'

She walked him to the door and gave him a perfunctory hug, patting his back as she did so. He didn't try to make it any more than it was – the embrace of a colleague whose name you barely know at the end of a leaving do. A moment later he was gone.

Helen rested her head against the door. She surprised herself by filling up with tears.

56

A PERFECTLY EQUIPPED FAILURE

Several dishes and cups had accumulated on the study desk. Helen had managed to turn Leo into quite a tidy person. She'd told him that unilateral tidiness was a mug's game, so she needed him to raise his standards to match her own, which were a notch below obsessive. Leo could see the logic of this very clearly. But now his standards had dropped to the level of The Manor's most slovenly occupant, Vincent Campbell.

Leo had spent days going through the mound of paperwork from various organisations, so at least Frank could be stalled with some authority. He had reached a decision about the four Lethco families: he was out-of-his depth. He transferred the money to the highly recommended lawyer who – for no fee – would make sure that the money was fairly distributed. Once that had been done, it was time to draw the whole thing to a close, and Leo reckoned that Frank's 'thank you' gala lunch would be a suitable platform. The press would be there, and he would be given the stage.

He was now alone in the house. Various disagreements had culminated in Vince's departure. They'd spent several days holed up, Vince whiling away his time soaking in the hot tub with a book (Henry James's *The Ambassadors*), or playing on the full size snooker table. He was losing interest in his role of press secretary, and had, by his own admission, become brusquer with journalists.

After a particularly heated debate concerning Neil Diamond, and Leo's accusation that Vince was a music snob, Vince started laying into him for his ignorance and general illiteracy. Leo asked him why Vince had been friends with someone so stupid for so long. He then answered his own question: because he was no threat: Vince could quote (or misquote) anything he liked, knowing his ill-read friend could only either be impressed or bored, but could never challenge him. 'Perhaps when you were in London, you met people who were harder to impress than me, and that's why you came back to Byford, a town you hate. You may be the brightest man in the bakery, but that's all you'll ever be.'

This last remark, more than any other, hit home. Vince picked up his book and threw it across the room, saying, 'That's what I am, a perfectly equipped failure,' which was apparently a quote from the novel. Then he sulked for an hour, after which he taunted Leo with long words and literary references, but no amount of erudite posturing seemed to make him feel better.

At dinnertime, Leo looked for him and called his name. He checked the hot tub, the snooker room and then the bedrooms. All his things were gone. Leo suspected that, apart from anything else, he'd left in order to spend more time with his pharmaceuticals.

Meanwhile, food had almost run out because the last time they'd visited Waitrose Leo's card had been declined, something they'd laughed off as a technical glitch. The story appeared on page four of The Sun, but only as a funny anomaly.

Driver Dave remained on duty because he'd had a month's pay in advance and Leo had kept up the pretence of actually liking Neil Diamond. The one or two paps who'd been sniffing around had gone, but somewhat alarmingly, they had re-appeared that morning, long lenses and all. Leo wondered if they were acting on a tipoff.

Leo re-read the statement he'd been working on since dawn. It was a brief admission of mistakes, but with an assertion that he had not intended to do harm. Each time he read that part he balked. He couldn't say, hand on heart, that he hadn't wanted to exact some revenge. On the Sterlings. On Tony. On his teachers for underestimating him, even on

Helen to some extent. He'd fooled the press, the bank, the public and the politicians. No one could say he wasn't smart anymore.

Leo left the study because he found it easier to rehearse his speech while walking around. He'd felt alone in the big house, so he'd switched on the TVs in most of the rooms just for company, a different channel in each room. He hadn't eaten for twenty-four hours, and not just because of the lack of food in the house: he'd lost his appetite. But feeling that he *should* eat, he made his way to the kitchen.

Friends was showing on the TV, and the irony didn't escape him. Ignoring yet another call from Frank, he forced himself to open the tin of Irish stew that Vince had bought as a joke. As it rotated in the wall-mounted electric opener the smell brought back memories of his first home. He heated the contents in a saucepan, but the thought of taking even one bite, especially before noon, threatened to bring up bile.

He read his speech once more. In just a couple of hours, he would read it at the gala lunch. It would mark the end of his adventure and, inevitably, the start of a new one.

57

THIS IS ALL FOR BYFORD

Frank Sterling returned his phone to his jacket pocket. He'd at last made contact with Leo and everything was fine. He surveyed the Great Hall, a room the size and shape of a gymnasium. Built in the 1930s, it retained the original art deco light fittings and panelling. Tall, Georgian-style windows made it bright and airy.

A dozen staff were putting the finishing touches to the preparations: balloons, flowers, long trellis tables for the buffet. Two waiting staff unpacked champagne flutes and laid them on a makeshift bar, while the sound guys set up the mic stands on the two stages: one for the jazz band, and a smaller one for speeches. Gill, the Australian events co-ordinator, had done a first-rate job.

'How's the AV system shaping up, Gill?' asked Frank. AV systems were always the weak link in the chain.

'Got the visuals, still working on the sound,' said Gill. *Very reliable workers, Australians*, thought Frank.

'There have been a few last minute cancellations, but that's not very unusual,' added Gill, before rushing off to get something sorted.

The number of positive RSVPs had been impressive, all wanting to see the Barista Billionaire, Byford's Benefactor, Saint Leo. Everyone loved him and his flamboyant friend – for reasons Frank couldn't quite fathom, but that's the world we live in today. Celebrities who've contributed next to nothing to society get all the attention, while sloggers-and-grafters like him and his wife hardly get a mention, except in local rags no one reads.

Harriet arrived with a special bouquet and Frank rushed over to help her. Together they fussed about where to hide it – on the left of the stage, or behind the blacks? Or maybe that room to the side? They decided on behind the blacks. They would ask Gill to find a suitable receptacle.

'Everything okay?' asked Harriet.

Why the concerned frown? thought Frank. 'Yes, yes, fine. You look wonderful, by the way.'

His wife always wore bright primary colours, and never patterns, just like the Queen.

'Um…'

'What?'

'Have you checked the emails?'

'Not since yesterday,' said Frank. 'Like I say, it will just take him a few more days to go through all the figures then he'll start paying out. I just spoke to him and it's all in hand. He's writing a speech.'

Frank and Harriet had had some tense discussions during the last few days. There had been rumblings; a few malcontents from local organisations not understanding exactly what they would get paid and when. It all seemed very vague. Frank had been dismissive of these 'bellyachers', while Harriet had been pensive, seeing it from their side, understanding their disquiet.

'I've had two more calls this morning,'

'And?' Frank asked casually, refusing to acknowledge his wife's anxiety. His eye was caught by some youngster who was filling the ice buckets far too early in the day.

'Well… I don't want to worry you again…'

'Go on, spit it out,' said Frank, impatiently – let's knock this on the head.

'Can we go somewhere private?'

He reluctantly followed his wife into a utility room, knowing that he was not going to like what he'd hear. The space was not much bigger than a cupboard, containing a large catering dishwasher and an inordinate number of giant rolls of blue paper towelling. A fluorescent tube buzzed overhead.

'We've had a few more cancellations by phone; two people saying they weren't happy about the press release re the pledges, and there were questions about the timing,' said Harriet.

'*Why*?' asked Frank, his defences now fully up. His wife had on her dreaded 'worried mother' expression.

'I think most recipients thought they were special, Frank. Now they realise practically every good cause in Byford has been pledged something. All this just before the election. It seems...'

She shrugged.

'I can't help it if the man won the money just before the poll! The timing is not my choice. And it would have been negligent *not* to have grabbed as much as I could for Byford. This is all for Byford.'

'Okay, calm down,' said Harriet, perhaps wishing she hadn't broached this subject at all.

'I'm perfectly calm. Any more surprises?'

'Yes,' said Harriet apologetically. 'Someone was unhappy about having their picture published on the Council website with a giant prop cheque before getting a *real* cheque.'

'Name?'

'The Child Cancer Trust.'

'Fuck them.'

'I did warn you not to release the pictures until the money had actually been paid, or at least pledged in writing.'

Oh, so it's told-you-so time.

'So wait till *after* the election? Great.'

'You do know Leo has us over a barrel?'

'Do you want me to announce that Mr Billionaire isn't going to pay anyone because he's a mong?'

'Frank, that's—'

'I'm sorry, but I've had it up to here.'

He sat down heavily on the giant kitchen rolls. There was no point in being angry, he told himself. Harriet was his rock, his eternal ally. After a few deep breaths, he would try to sound conciliatory.

'I realise the situation is not ideal, love,' he said, deep breaths, 'but this is where we are. We have four dozen guests coming, and we can't exactly cancel, can we? Leo was hunky dory when I spoke to him just now, there were no problems, he's just a nerd who's a bit OCD when it comes to spreadsheets. There are no problems. No problems.'

'Okay,' said Harriet. She smiled and nodded. Frank had successfully allayed his wife's fears, her remonstrations would now cease.

He rose to open the door. The Byford Dixie Swingers were setting up on the band stage. Somewhere a plate smashed noisily to the floor and a few people cheered.

58

YOU DON'T LOOK PLEASED TO SEE ME

Helen was startled when she opened the door to find him standing there, hands in pockets, with a small rucksack on his back. Tony had not used his usual signal. In her shock she may have let out a little yelp, she wasn't sure. He was more unshaved and unkempt than before, and his eyes were bloodshot.

Her heart pounded.

'You don't look pleased to see me, Helen.'

'It's… just that I'm still nervous, you know… about everything.'

She put her hand to her chest, as if it would slow down the pulse.

'I just wanted to clear something up.'

'Now? Um…'

'Won't take a minute.'

She did not want to provoke Tony. All her friends, after congratulating her for dumping him, cautioned against doing anything that would enrage the man. He seemed like the kind who would not take humiliation lightly.

'Are you going to ask me in?'

'I, er – have to pick up Amy.'

'She's at her grandparents,' he said, and Helen remembered that he kept track of such routines – it was one of the things she'd liked about him. She could bluster something about a change of plan, but she sensed that lying wouldn't work; he had the air of someone who wouldn't be fobbed off. Instead, she mumbled that she'd been confused, and then, ignoring the voice that told her not to, she beckoned him inside.

As she followed him to the kitchen, she smelt alcohol in his wake. It had been several days since they'd split, and there had been no communication since, so what the hell could he want?

Helen had managed to put fears about 'bad men' in a box, and the box had been getting smaller and further away. She had convinced herself that the threats he'd talked of were either exaggerated, or complete fantasies.

He took his usual seat at the kitchen table, gently dropping his rucksack on the floor. Instead of asking what he wanted to drink, Helen handed him a glass of water.

'Thanks for agreeing to have this chat,' he said.

She nodded, although a *chat* wasn't what she was expecting. She began to hope this was a meeting to clear the air, to explain some aspect of his behaviour, apologise for something – or even to tell her that the 'bad men' had gone away. She remained standing, leaning against the sink.

'Let me tell you where I am…' he said. Helen balked. Wasn't this the language of Dragon's Den? (Leo's favourite show).

'You and I went out together, we had a nice time. I thought you liked me and… one day might even… love me.'

The word 'love' seemed incongruous, coming as it did with such an ice-cold delivery.

'And I thought, hey, maybe this is going to last. That's the impression you gave.'

So it's my fault for leading you on? She would let it pass.

'Then, out of the blue, Leo wins a billion quid.'

He threw his arms out wide, like an innocent man proclaiming against some injustice, *how dare that happen?* She would let him finish.

'That changes everything. Suddenly, the bad men' – *fuck him and his bad men*, thought Helen – 'that I helped bring to justice, and their associates, get wind of my access to untold wealth. I am under threat, and through no fault of mine, so are you, and so is Amy. But instead of running away like a coward, I offer you protection, and put myself in great personal danger in order to acquire a piece.'

Piece? He means gun. She tried not to guess where this was leading, but possibilities flooded her mind.

'Getting hold of a Glock is not easy, and as you probably know, there's a mandatory prison sentence for possession.'

Then why did you leave it in my house? was what she wanted to shout. She kept her arms folded. She would not speak until he'd finished.

'I risked that for you,' he said, looking at her for the first time since he sat down. Then he leaned back on the kitchen chair, and put his hands on his hips, arms akimbo. His usual contained and measured movements now had the casual defiance of a scolded teenager.

'And then what? You slam the door in my face. And what thanks do I get? You go back to Mr Moneybags.'

She couldn't stay quiet for that. 'I have *not* gone back to Leo.'

He looked up.

'I don't believe you.'

'I honestly haven't, Tony.'

But it was clear he wouldn't be persuaded. Such was the man's belief in the lure of money, thought Helen, that he assumed every woman would put it above all else.

He slouched further down, so that his body was almost a straight line from head to foot. 'But you see, you've left me high and dry, with bad men after the millions they believe I have access to. *So I am fucked!*' The last few words were shouted, and Helen flinched. 'I'll have to watch my back for years, sleep with the piece under my pillow. That doesn't seem very fair... Well, does it?'

Helen tilted her head and frowned. She wanted to project sympathy and concern, anything to ameliorate this situation, keep a lid on his anger.

'So let's clear the air. Let's draw a line under all this.'

'I'd *so* like to do that, Tony, whatever you say. Let's just move on,' she said, daring to believe this could all be resolved soon. 'Let's talk about something else. Can we talk about something else? What about books?' Inexplicably her mind must have gone to their first ever date. 'Tell me about E. M. Forster. Why do you like him?'

Distract, distract.

'I don't know anything about the guy. I just like to impress.'

Helen couldn't help but be curious.

'Why *Forster*?'

Tony revealed a microsmile.

'Jane Austen would have been too obvious. And also dangerous, as you're the expert and I've never read a word of her.'

'But why—'

'Customers who liked… also liked…'

'Very clever,' she said, only to flatter him. 'I was certainly impressed.' Damn it, she *had* been impressed, what a fool. But her distraction ploy seemed to be working.

'And I also thought you were handsome.'

And she immediately realised she'd gone too far. Tony snapped back to the task in hand.

'I'm glad. So. Right. Here's the deal. You get Coffee Guy to transfer some funds, not a lot, a modest sum, to this offshore account,' he brought out a piece of paper with some numbers on it. 'Then tomorrow I disappear to a destination I will not reveal. Zoom, I'm gonzo. You won't have sight nor sound of me again. I will use that money to square it with the bad guys, and keep some for myself as compensation for the personal stress I've been through. I'll start a new life.'

She tried to quell a surge of guilt for bringing this on herself, and imagined her friend Julia scolding her for thinking that any of this was her fault. The one to blame was right in front of her. She took a deep breath through her nose. Keep calm.

'But why would Leo give you anything? He hates you.'

'I'm aware that the gentleman and I are not besties,' he said, with a smirk. He heaved himself back to an upright position, 'So you might have to tell a few fibs.' Helen sickened at the cod TV talk. 'Tell him that you're being leant on. It might help him concentrate.'

'Are you serious?'

It was a pointless question, nevertheless…

'Oh, very much so.'

'I can't do that. I can't frighten him like that.'

Suddenly he thumped the table with each fist in turn, making Helen recoil. When he stopped, nothing was said and there was no sound but for the odd drip from the tap.

Helen guessed that he had worked out a plan quite rationally, but really he was fuelled by emotion. He'd been dumped, he'd been denied money that for some reason he'd felt entitled to, he'd been bettered by a loser on a trike. Perhaps he'd spent days drinking, seething, planning ways to avenge these assaults on his pride. Having alighted on this theory, Helen felt compelled to voice it.

'Tony, you're angry with me, I get that. But can we step away from the brink? You and I both know there are no *bad men*. You want this money for yourself. And you want to punish me. The bad men stuff is *bullshit*.'

For the second time since he sat down he looked at her straight in the eye, and with something between pain and fury. Dammit, she should have stuck to her policy of compliance.

He reached down into the rucksack by his feet while Helen fought an impulse to open the patio door and run. His hand reappeared holding the Glock. Seeing it again made her want to scream – with anger rather than fear – *how dare he?*

He placed it on the table and twirled it around. He was back to his coldly clinical approach.

'See it from my point of view, Helen. What would you do if you were me? Crawl under a stone, while the two causes of your torment are living it up, leading the life of Riley?'

'I'll do whatever you want,' she said, in her meekest voice.

'Good. Because I haven't come here for a debate. I am angry, but if you do the right thing, I'll be as nice as pie and I'll soon be gone.'

Pacify, be nice, said Helen's logical brain.

'Please, Tony. Can we talk this over without... *that*? I thought we were friends.'

When tears began to flow she didn't try to hide them. Surely seeing her cry might...

'Just do as I say,' he said. There wasn't hatred or anger in his eyes now so much as merciless determination. 'And stop fucking crying.'

The words shocked her into doing just that for a moment. When she recovered her composure, she shut her eyes and told herself to think calmly. Perhaps there were some practical obstacles that she could throw in his way? If she could pick holes in his plan then maybe...

'What if Leo doesn't answer?'

Tony snorted.

'I won't be leaving until he does.'

'What if he refuses?'

He shook his head and smiled, as if amused by these childish ruses to put him off. 'He won't refuse, because you're going to be a very, very persuasive damsel in distress.'

She pictured Leo as she told him what was happening, and could almost feel his heart explode.

'I'm sure you know what you're doing, but... even if he transfers the money, he's bound to call the police right afterwards. Won't that be dangerous for you?'

Christ, she even managed to sound *concerned* for him. Tony seemed amused.

'You will explain that calling the police will be a death sentence for you.' He glanced at her. 'I'm sorry to put it like that. And anyway, I'll be out of here by then.'

'Won't you be stopped at the airport?'

He huffed.

'Airport? Didn't you *ever* listen to me?'

Helen took only a second to realise what he meant. He'd often told her that the gem trade was full of guys who travel in boats, under the radar, and don't bother with passports and certainly don't need airports. She had run out of holes to pick.

Tony leaned back and cradled his head in his hands. Leaving the Glock unguarded seemed to be an act of dark playfulness: grab it if you dare. He spoke softly, 'For me, it's either prison again or…' he picked up the weapon and held it to his temple.

Helen was confused. Did he mean that he might shoot *himself*? And fuck, and what did he mean by—

'Prison *again?*' she said.

'Never you mind.'

He put the gun down and folded his arms. He seemed pleased with the effect of this prison bombshell. Perhaps he'd been saving it up.

So this was a criminal in front of her. Fresh waves of panic, a new flood of thoughts. Everything about this situation needed to be recalibrated.

'The point is, Helen, I have nothing to lose, no one trusts me in the trade. I'm finished. A man who has nothing to lose is a dangerous beast. I made a promise to myself this morning. Tony, I said, by the end of today you will either have a million pounds in the bank, or both you and that woman will be dead.'

Helen felt as if a huge, dark bird had just flapped its wings in her stomach. Tony fished out the box of bullets and began loading. She remembered what he'd said about guns: *your target must believe that you're prepared to use it.* Perhaps everything he'd said and done since he came in was simply to convince her of that fact. Was it all nonsense? Bluff? How could she know?

She must *think for her life, think for her life.*

'What if…' she gulped, 'what if the bank won't transfer such a large amount?'

'What do you think I am, a cunt?' he said, going back to his angry mode. Perhaps the mood shifts were deliberate.

'He'll use CHAPS. And he'll send you a screenshot of the confirmation. Now, let's have a little rehearsal. Whenever you're ready.'

He finished loading and resumed his playing. The clicks and clunks were clean and crisp, like the crisp lines of the gun itself.

With his eyes focused on the weapon, he told Helen to go over what she would say to Leo, sometimes interrupting her, correcting her, and asking the sort of questions a distraught partner might ask. He'd decided that even if Leo wasn't near a computer he could soon get to one. He went through the procedures he must follow. And there was something he insisted that she repeat: Leo had just fifteen minutes to send the screenshot. 'Otherwise I'll know he's playing silly-buggers with the police.'

Even through her panic, Helen continued thinking. She edged herself towards the landline attached to the wall. If she could casually position herself by it, then when the time came it would seem natural enough to reach for it, and Leo would know exactly where she was calling from. When she was right next to the phone she said, 'Look, haven't we gone over it enough?' with deliberate breathlessness. Tony settled into a comfortable position, as if he were a director watching a rehearsal.

'Go for it.'

Helen expected him to add *and don't try anything clever.* She reached for the receiver and pressed speed dial. Help would soon be on its way.

'From your mobile,' said Tony.

59

YOU HAVE 15 MINUTES

He had just finished talking to Frank about the big thank you luncheon at the Great Hall and was emptying the Irish stew into the bin. He heard voices from outside. At first Leo thought they were just curious children, but it was soon clear that some were adults, perhaps angry locals to whom Frank had promised money and who now wanted delivery. To avoid being spotted, he crouched down below the kitchen island. He ran his hands along the cool marble tiles. He could see an ice cream lid, a Haribo, a crisp, a champagne cork. If Vince ever committed a murder, forensics would have a field day.

His phone. Helen. The breathing was both strange and familiar.

'Helen?'

More breaths – a blocked nose. Crying?

Why doesn't she speak?

'Helen? What's the matter? Talk to me.'

'They've got me, Leo.'

He froze.

'What? Who? Tell me.'

Silence. Not even breathing. *Why doesn't she speak?*

'Helen?'

Her voice bled through a wall of fear.

'You need to transfer a million pounds to an offshore account. Take down these details. Use CHAPS, and send a screenshot of the confirmation. Do you understand?'

Leo couldn't think straight. He could only see Helen bound in a chair with grey men standing over her.

'Say that again, Helen,' he managed to say.

'Take a screen shot, or a picture of the screen, whatever. You got that?'

'Yes, yes. But Helen, I'm not sure I can do that. Can I... can I speak to whoever is there?'

'*No, Leo.*' That was adamant. 'Here are the details.'

Leo found a scrap of paper and, hands trembling, scribbled down the numbers. He wanted to seem calm, hoping the pretence at calmness would actually relax him. 'I don't know if transferring such a... a large amount is even possible.'

'How the fuck do Londoners buy houses?' said Helen, so quickly that it sounded prepared. 'Go online and do it *now*. Do not talk to anyone about this, not Vince or anyone, especially not the police. *Do not contact the police.*'

'Helen...'

'You can do this, Leo. Just do this, and I'll be okay.'

The phrase *I'll be okay* gave Leo a fragment of hope.

'There can be no delays, and no fuck-ups. The fifteen minutes starts now.'

She rang off.

Leo tried to focus on his phone, but the keys were a blur. He pressed a button, but hung up when he realised he had no plan. How could he tell her he had no money? Neither she nor her captors would believe it. The lie had become more credible than the truth.

He told himself as firmly as he could: *panic later, panic later.* He called Vince. They had not spoken since he'd left. Leo felt painfully alone. *Come on, answer.* He got voice mail.

'Pay attention. Helen's in trouble. Meet me at the bank as soon as you can. Probably quickest if you ran. I can't say more.'

Leo, phone still in hand, rushed out of the door and stared at where the limo should be. Its absence felt like a punch. *Where was Dave?*

Options flicked through his mind. Running to the bank would take too long – twenty minutes. Ask a neighbour to drive him? But even if they were in, it would entail explanations, and they might insist on calling the police. If only he had his trike... Leo didn't have his trike, but he did have two things: a gradient map of Byford in his head – he knew every hill plus every pedestrian shortcut – and he also had a child's scooter.

A moment later Leo was hurtling down the hill (18 per cent gradient) at 20 mph, calculating that he would jump two traffic lights, carry the scooter across Elm Green, cut through the pedestrian arcade, and be at the bank in eight minutes.

60

JUST THE PLACE

Donna had been waiting in her car in this god-forsaken car park behind Waitrose for half an hour. Bins, deliveries, men urinating and spitting; it was no place for a news reporter. Or maybe it was just the place. Her phone bleeped with a text.

Won't be long.

She felt the same impending elation as when she was on the brink of landing her first job. This could be a proper, old-fashioned mega-scoop, far juicier than a story about a guy who got lucky, or even a guy who got lucky and then paid twenty grand for sex. This would be about two young men who had fooled the press, the world's news stations, and the Prime Minister.

The issue was time. This was a race and Donna needed to be first.

She'd seen rival journalists in the high street, presumably gathering for Frank Sterling's thank you lunch. Thanks for what? If her source came good, the gala would be a car crash. There were already rumours about charitable pledges that Leo had apparently made but hadn't honoured. The fact that he seemed to have taken a political stance just before local elections was rattling the Tweetersphere.

There are a billion reasons not to vote Conservative #billionairebarista

Coffee Guy, why not stand outside the poll booths handing out tenners and cappuccinos? #billionairebarista.

The fledgling celebrity was losing the power of flight and would come tumbling to the ground.

Donna looked across at the Waitrose sign, and thought back to the incident of the other day. It had barely caused a ripple, but had the card been declined because *they were actually broke?* She had gone over it all so many times that her thoughts were becoming stale.

She opened a window to get some air, but was hit with a stench of rotten cabbage so she closed it again.

Her phone buzzed. Derek.

'Still waiting, Derek.'

'Fuck's sake. We need this as soon—'

'I'm not a magician.'

She could hear the frustration in his breath.

'Have you phoned again?'

'Loads of times. I just got a text saying, *won't be long.*'

'Tamar and I are standing by, we'll keep the line clear.'

'Okay.'

She couldn't remember a more agonising wait. Just as she was about to go through all the facts for the umpteenth time, there it was, turning into the car park, spick and span, nine metres long, a more incongruous vehicle would be hard to imagine amongst the industrial bins. Donna waved, and the driver nodded. She opened her door and was hit again by the cabbage smell. The limo pulled up and the engine fell silent.

'No one will bother us here, Donna,' said the driver, as he got out to greet her. 'Park anywhere else and you get gawped at, wankers think there's a celeb inside.'

Dave looked like an overweight darts player from the 80s – the type who drank, smoked, and probably farted their way through tournaments. He held the door open, and Donna climbed in, feeling like a burglar, because this was more like a bachelor pad than a vehicle. Clothes, shopping bags, champagne and beer bottles, brushes and combs, toiletries, it was a scene left by a disorganised groom late for the church.

Dave heaved himself onto the seat opposite.

'Welcome to my world.'

'Yes, the famous limo,' said Donna, trying to make him feel proud. She needed this to be quick, but experience had taught her that punters don't like to be rushed, especially when betrayal is involved.

'Vince is the messy one. Keeps *himself* as shiny as a fire engine, but leaves crap be'ind. I stopped bovering to tidy up.'

He had no inhibitions about looking Donna up and down as he spoke, lingering on her legs and heels, then up at her face, chewing her with his eyes. She made a mental note to keep her knees together.

'What are they really like, the two lads?' she asked. This was a question any Joe could ask, but it's what everyone wants to know about their fellow humans: *what are they really like*?

'Nice enough fellas,' said Dave, then added after a sniff, 'well, Leo is.'

Donna ran her hands along the purple seat and breathed in a smell that matched the sight: leather, alcohol, cologne and beyond that, a hint of stale tobacco.

'Did you sign a contract with them?' She tried to make the question sound casual, its subtext being: did you sign a confidentiality agreement?

He laughed, 'A contract? I figured a billionaire would be good for the money. They chucked some cash at me, all off the books – don't tell Mr Taxman.' He tapped his nose, and Donna chuckled obligingly.

'Dave or David?' she asked.

'Dave.'

'Dave, you rang our news desk a few days ago, but didn't leave a name or number. Why?'

He thought for a moment.

'I rang 'cause the boys did me 'ead in. Especially Vince. He went on about my taste in music. It's offensive to knock people's passions.' He took in Donna's response, which was an emphatic nod. 'What's your view of Neil Diamond?'

Donna smiled. She knew to tread carefully. Could this be a wind-up? This character seemed daft enough to be a hoaxer: perhaps this was a hoax on a hoax. She would indulge him up to a point, hedge her bets.

'I don't see how anyone could *hate* Neil Diamond,' she said, 'but as time is short, mind if we get down to business?'

'I'm also interested in other artistes categorised as Easy Listening.' Dave could adopt a near-as-dammit RP accent when he wanted. 'Andy Williams, Humperdinck, Streisand, Gilberto, The Carpenters, and Sinatra. Yes, that's surprised you: Frank. The net is widening. Simon and Garfunkel, Billy Joel, they're all in.'

She sensed that she had no choice but to engage him on the subject.

'Billy Joel is one of the greats.'

'I'm bringing in Dionne Warwick – yes, controversial, but she belongs in EL.'

He leant forward and rested his elbows on his knees, which made Donna involuntarily lean back to avoid the whiff of cigarette-breath. Donna decided that this was no hoaxer. He pulled a remote control from his pocket.

"ave a listen,' he said, and gentle piano music began.

'Actually, I would *love* to but I'm on a very, very tight deadline. You see—'

He shook his head calmly, as if she had made a wrong guess. A voice began singing, *I remember all my life...* The song was familiar but she couldn't place it.

'Know it?' he asked.

'I'm not sure.'

'Manilow.'

She waited for a few bars before saying, 'The thing is, Dave, I'm being shouted at by my boss to get this story to him in the next few minutes, literally. There are other journalists sniffing around and—'

'He never wanted to be a singer. He didn't fink 'e 'ad the voice. Or the face. But listen to *that*.'

As the music swelled into the chorus he closed his eyes and moved his lips to the words. He began to sing, quietly at first, but he grew in confidence and volume with each line.

'*Oh Mandy, you came and you gave without taking,*
But I sent you away,

Oh Mandy, well you kissed me and stopped me from shaking.'

By the time the chorus finished, he was in full voice. Donna was surer than ever this wasn't a hoax – the performance was too heartfelt. But she had lost Dave and had no idea how to get him back. She could feel the biggest break of her life slipping away.

61

UNAUTHORISED TRANSACTIONS

The one uphill gradient that Leo had to climb at Dover Lane had been harder work than he'd anticipated. He arrived at the bank red and sweaty, after a nine-minute journey. Dropping the scooter, he barged to the front of a small queue.

'I need to see Hughes right away,' he said breathlessly, to the pudding-faced teller.

'Mr Hughes is on leave.'

Leo wanted to strangle the girl for giving such devastating news so casually.

'Valerie Mason is in charge now, and you will need an appointment.'

Her demeanour showed no reverence for the billionaire.

'This is an emergency. I have to see her right now.'

The girl reddened and stiffened. A few customers turned to stare.

On the ride to the bank, Leo reckoned that the only person who would agree to transferring a million pounds would be Hughes – and there was no certainty even about that. Was there really any point in seeing this new person? But what other option did he have? He could be at Helen's in five minutes but he had no idea who he'd be up against or what weapons they might have, or even if she was there – they would surely have taken her away. In any case, she would not appreciate a pathetic attempt to play the hero. *Why the fuck didn't you just do what I asked?* Try as he might to think clearly, a tide of chaos-inducing panic threatened to rise.

Customers' eyes turned to see Vince shoulder open the door and walk in, breathless, dishevelled, with headphones round his neck. Even in his state of distress, Leo felt a ripple of comfort just to have someone on his side. He grabbed Vince by the arm and led him to a corner, where he explained the situation as quickly as he could. He hoped Vince's usual detachment from other people's pain might enable him to have calm, rational thoughts, but instead he seemed to have trouble focusing.

'Are you okay, mate?'

'I'm fine, Leo,' he said, but it seemed like wishful thinking.

It was now eleven minutes since Helen's call. Having consulted Valerie Mason, the pudding face girl told Leo that she was 'very anxious to see him'. Leo didn't stop to consider why that might be before rushing through to the office, Vince trailing behind.

Valerie Mason had her hair up in a severe bun and wore a dark business suit with a blouse buttoned to the neck. She had the air of a new broom that was going to sweep with ruthless precision.

'Belated congratulations on your win, Mr Morphetus,' she said, with a mouth-only smile.

'Look—'

'I have left phone messages. And did you get our letter? As yours is a joint account, it was sent to both your addresses.'

'I've been away,' said Vince. He failed to conceal his underlying insolence.

'It would have gone to my old house,' said Leo, 'but I need to talk to you about something extremely urgent. You see—'

'—I can print a copy of it right now.' It was as if he hadn't spoken. 'It concerns unauthorised transactions.'

A printer began to spew paper. Leo wiped away sweat that was all over his face.

'I appreciate there have been some issues,' he tried to sound reasonable, 'But please can we resolve them another time?'

The last phrase was directed to Valerie Mason's back as she retrieved the letter from the printer.

'We need a million pounds,' blurted Vince. Leo gave him a sharp nudge – it was far too abrupt.

Mason turned around, letter in hand, and placed it on the desk. She made no sign that she had heard Vince speak, and looked only at Leo.

'We are very concerned,' she said, clasping her hands together on the table after sitting down, 'that the sizable deposit we had expected to arrive has still not materialised. Not having heard from you, we have been forced notify our resolution team.'

Leo wondered if the 'resolution team' had been the ones hammering on his front door an hour earlier.

'Ms Mason, please believe me when I say that's not important right now,' said Leo, 'we just need to transfer some money. Um, a... a million. It's a very urgent matter.'

Mason laid her hands flat on the desk.

'You don't have a million pounds, far from it. That letter explains that we are freezing all withdrawals until you are in credit.'

She was determined not to be bamboozled, and any outburst from Leo would surely make cooperation even less likely than it was already.

'You see, Ms Mason, this is a matter of...' he couldn't quite say *life and death*, 'a matter of someone... getting hurt.'

Valerie Mason's cheek twitched, the first tangible proof that she'd been affected by anything he'd said.

'If you suspect criminal activity, then I suggest you contact the police.'

Leo put his hands on each knee and squeezed hard, just to redirect the anger and panic rising in his chest.

'I swear to God we will call the police,' pleaded Leo, 'but first we need you to pay the money to this account,' he indicated the scrap of paper in his hand, 'Right now, *right now*. We have been given a deadline, and we're talking minutes here.'

Valerie Mason looked down at her hands, looking uncomfortable for a microsecond, before restoring complete composure.

'As I said, I cannot authorise any payments whatsoever. The police will surely—'

'—This is ridiculous, we're *billionaires*,' said Vince, making things worse.

Leo checked his watch. He had been at the bank for three minutes and he was no closer to getting the transfer. He felt his phone vibrate. Helen?

Harriet. She might have information.

'Yes?'

'Helen's neighbour called me…' She was crying. 'She says she heard a… a shot. Two gunshots. But that can't be, can it? Please say it can't be.'

He couldn't speak. He was watching a new photo story in his head: men trying to frighten Helen with guns.

'And… Leo? A man ran from the house with a gun. She's not answering her phone. This can't be happening, it can't!'

'But they haven't given me a chance,' said Leo. 'Why would they—'

'The neighbour called the police and so have I. They must want your money, Leo.'

'I'm coming. I'll talk to them.'

He fought down an urge to rage at the banker for her part in the death of a young mother. Instead, he stood for a moment, trying not to fall over while the floor and walls seemed to turn to liquid.

'They have guns,' he mouthed to Vince, shielding his lips from Mason. He handed him the piece of paper with the bank details. 'Stay here. Do your best.'

How exactly he arrived at the estate agent's next door, he couldn't say. But there he was, standing in front of a desk. Behind it was a young man, late twenties, with a pasty face, short shiny hair, and a crisp, fitted shirt.

'Ah, Mr Morphetus,' Leo recognised the voice. 'I trust you're still enjoying your new abode?'

'Drive me to my wife's house, right now.'

Clive Entwhistle put down his mug of coffee, but his other hand retained a biscuit. 'I would love to help, but sadly I'm the only one in the office and – er – are you okay?'

'Take me to your car or I'll break your neck.'

Leo heard the words, but couldn't quite believe he'd said them. Entwhistle opened his mouth to speak, and then simply froze. A second later the biscuit dropped from his hand and he stood to attention as if chosen by God. The two men ran to a white Audi parked on a side road, almost knocking over a father and a child as they went.

62

THUS FAR AND NO FURTHER

After an eternity, 'Mandy' came to an end. Dave had sung along with almost every line, his eyes closed in ecstasy. Donna clapped, and she even proffered a 'bravo'. Of all the indignities and moral compromises of her career, this would one day make her cringe the most.

'*So…*' she said, as pointedly as she could.

'Yeah, you want to see what I've got.'

'That would be *great*.' She reached for her tablet.

'You asked me why I called TrueNewz?'

'It doesn't matter about that now, Dave. I just really need to see your evidence, asap.'

He wasn't listening.

'You see,' he said, 'Vince gave me the 'ump, and in a moment of wrath, I phoned. A girl took a message.'

'Yes, she passed on your information.'

'But den I fought, it's snitching, innit? I mean, the fellas are all right – well Leo is. He's a Diamond fan.' He smiled wistfully. 'And it's not every day you get to drive round the biggest fraudsters since Eve.'

Donna blinked at the theological error.

'So I rang off.'

He leaned back, folded his arms and sucked his teeth like someone about to take a stand on a thorny issue, but instead he looked out the window, lost in thought.

Donna took this moment to check her phone: several texts from Derek, but she didn't want to read them.

'I fink Downing Street decided me. Dat was the last straw. I'm finkin' to meself, *thus far and no further*. 'Cause you know what a be next?'

She shook her head, almost becoming resigned to kissing this whole scoop goodbye.

'Buckingham Palace,' said Dave. 'And dez no way I'm gonna to be a party to doin' a job on the royal family. Lovely people, they do a great job for the country.'

'Absolutely,' said Donna, but she didn't have time for a homage to the monarchy.

'Dat was a few days ago, and I been bidin' me time, wondering who to call. Then, while I'm cleanin' up – for the last time – I find your business card, wedged in the back seat.'

Donna remembered that she handed her card to Leo right after the press conference.

'I finks, at least now, when I'm good and ready, I have someone to speak to, someone who knows the case a bit, a nice-looking lady.' He winked, Donna did not acknowledge the compliment.

'You see, Dave, if we don't break the story *now*.'

He didn't react. *It comes to something*, thought Donna, *when offering a blowjob enters one's mind, however hypothetically*.

Dave gave a snort and nodded his head. 'See that?' He pointed to a top corner of the limo.

'No.'

'I have free eyes in the back of me 'ead.'

Free? He means three.

'Where?'

'Look closer, love.'

She peered at the corner. She couldn't see it, but there must be a camera there. This was excellent news. Nothing is as convincing as actual footage.

'You won't clock it 'cause it's 'idden. Tiny. You get all sorts in a limo. Underage girls, drugs, knives, guns, orgies. But that's not why I had free cameras installed.'

It would be reason enough.

'A hen party a few years ago…'

Donna willed him not to embark on an anecdote.

'Day after the do, the chief hen rings up and says that I touched up the fat one, and four of the others saw it, so could I possibly waive the second half fee, and we'll say no more about it?'

Christ, thought Donna, *the great big darts player's eyes are moistening*. She felt she just had to give him a moment. She watched the clock on her phone and a minute slipped by before he slapped his thighs and snapped out of his reverie. 'So, if it happens again, I'll say: you *show* me where I touched anyone.'

Her heart sank at the word *show*. Had she come all this way to look at some *soundless* footage?

'Do you only record the picture, Dave?'

'Nah, sound too. Poor quality, but I spliced up the best bits for you.'

Audio would be far more important than pictures. Dave reached into his breast pocket and took out a USB stick.

Finally.

He placed it on the table. This was the prize, this was what Donna had come for.

She uploaded a file called *Arseholes*, as instructed. She was so close now, so close. Dave reached over to the minibar and brought out two bottles of Stella, opened them, and handed one to Donna.

'Thanks,' she said. 'I don't suppose you asked permission to film them?'

'Do I look like a mug?'

That was okay. She had discussed it with Tamar, who said he'd sign off a covert recording because hoaxing the Prime Minister was a strong basis on which to build a public interest defence. The boys had 'diminished their right to privacy'. Besides, if they weren't filthy rich, then they'd be in no position to sue. *One rule for the rich…*

'Before we hand over a fee,' said Donna, as the file finished loading, 'I should tell you that this has to be *emphatic*, it's got to be Leo admitting straight out he didn't win. Nothing equivocal.'

Dave shrugged. 'You be the judge.'

'I'd like my editor and lawyer to see the footage at the same time as me. If they sign off we could have this online within minutes.'

'Be my guest.'

Donna used Facetime to call, and Derek answered immediately. Her heart boomed as she lined up the footage and pressed play.

63

THERE MIGHT BE ANOTHER SHOOTING

Clive Entwhistle drove up alongside a police van that had parked sideways, blocking the road. It was one of four emergency vehicles around Helen's house, including one ambulance, blue lights flashing. A small crowd had gathered behind some yellow tape, but no press yet. Leo was out of the car before it came to a stop. The PC on traffic duty recognised him and invited him to step under the barrier. Leo had spent half the journey with his eyes closed, feeling sick, hearing distant sirens, and wanting to be dead rather than hear the news he most feared. But now, as he walked towards the ambulance, police radios crackling, he was enveloped by a cloak of dreamy detachment, the bubble he'd inhabited on and off for years. Perhaps something had told his subconscious that Helen was okay.

'She's in there,' said a PC, pointing to the ambulance. The rear doors were open – surely a good sign. A paramedic appeared from the other side and, as he approached, she nodded a smile.

'Physically fine, but shaken,' was her concise diagnosis.

He had never felt such a rush of happiness before. It had the same intensity as the dread he'd felt minutes earlier. He felt like kissing the world.

And there she was, a blanket round her, a mug in her hand, mascara streaming, hair matted down. There was a second of confusion when she saw him, and then a smile, and then a strange laugh-cry.

She put down her mug and Leo hugged her as hard as he could.

'What happened?' he asked, gently.

'They shot Tony. He's gone to hospital,' she said.

A cascade of possibilities rushed into his mind, and then a question: had Tony been trying to protect her, and been hurt in the process? He felt ashamed that jealousy should visit at this moment, but he couldn't shake off the image of *Tony the hero*. He saw himself having to shake his hand and say 'Well done, mate'. Almost as repellent as that image was the thought that he was thinking of himself at all. He was trapped in an eddy of self-loathing from which he must swim away.

'Do you want to be at his side now? I can take you.'

'Christ, no, never. *Never ever*. I never want to see him again.'

A rush of confused happiness. Had Tony somehow been…?

The paramedic came to say they had a couple of minutes before the ambulance would have to go back to base. Helen told her that a friend was coming to collect her.

For a moment, the pair simply gazed at the mysterious paraphernalia around them: the gadgets and compounds that separate life from death.

'Very different from the trike,' said Leo.

Helen laugh-cried again, exposing her fang-tooth. She explained that someone – or maybe several people – had fired two shots from the back garden. The first one had smashed the glass patio door, the second one had hit Tony. A man, or men, had apparently darted along the side of the house and at least one was seen running away. Neighbours had given descriptions to the detectives. She paused, but rather than bombard her with questions, Leo waited patiently for her to continue.

'Tony says he's mixed up with people he calls *bad men*. Maybe it was them. I don't know who or what to believe. He threatened me. I'll tell you all about it, but not right now.'

'Is Amy at school?' said Leo, standing up. 'I'll go and get her, they might try to—'

'It's okay, the police are onto it. She's going for a play-date with Samira.'

He sat down again. A helicopter pulsed overhead. Helen said her parents were in the lounge helping the police. He replied that he would not rush in to meet them. She told him she felt ashamed and stupid, and he told her she mustn't feel like that, even though he didn't really know what she'd done, or what anyone had done. After another silence, she nudged him with her shoulder.

'What's this about you not being a billionaire?' she asked, quite calmly, as if making conversation.

And suddenly it was all over. It didn't feel so much like a house of cards collapsing as someone telling him kindly to tidy the cards away because it was time for bed. He felt so light, as if he was floating.

He didn't bother to ask how she knew. Had it been on the news? Had Vince decided to cash in and tell all? He'd certainly know who to call. But no, thought Leo, after more thought. Vince was a vain and selfish man, but always loyal – at least to him.

'Mum and Dad say there's a video,' she said. 'You made the whole thing up?' Her matter-of-fact tone matched his own detachment. They say that a brush with death teaches you what's important and what isn't. This didn't seem important.

'That's basically true, Helen.'

She blew her nose. She had always blown her nose in a very loud and unladylike manner and it made Leo smile.

'Let's talk about all that another time. You've been through a lot.'

The words felt like a giant full stop on a sentence that had lasted days. There seemed no point in adding more.

Except:

'I'm sorry.'

She had a right to be furious, and in some ways, Leo wished she would rain down punches all over his body. Instead, she put her head in her hands so her face was completely obscured and let out a muffled wail. Anger, frustration, disbelief. He nodded, as if clocking each emotion in turn. Then, her feelings expelled, she seemed empty and calm.

'Never in my wildest dreams would I think you could… pull off something like that. Fooling all those people. Everyone. *How*? How did you do it?'

Could he detect a little admiration? He couldn't help but feel the aloof pride of the magician. She nudged him again, harder this time.

'It caused a fuck load of trouble for me,' she said. 'But I'm the pot and you're the kettle: I went out with a psycho. I'm an idiot.'

Leo wanted to know more, but he told himself that the dots would join in their own time. The paramedic popped her head round and said that Helen's friend had arrived. A moment later a policeman came to say the detectives would want to interview her again soon, but now they needed to speak to Leo.

'You better stay clear of Dad,' she said, as she got up. 'Or there might be another shooting.'

64

FUCK

Vince sat in one of the blue chairs in the lobby, trying to get his head together. He was in no state to negotiate anything, let alone deal with an actual emergency. He wondered if Leo realised that the reason he'd left The Manor was as much to do with drugs as with anything else. There were simply too many eyes on it to risk a bust.

Vince's comedown had a leitmotif of paranoia, but when there are men with guns threatening your best mate's ex, it's hard to know where the delusion ends and reality begins. He held a plastic cup he'd filled at the water cooler. He'd drunk it all but his tongue still felt like paper.

The girl at the counter kept giving him the evil eye. Had she organised all this? Was it a staged drama? This whole thing had all the hallmarks of some kind of conspiracy. Then Vince remembered that he only thought things like that after a night of excess.

But what was he supposed to do now? He knew that they were meant to put a million pounds into a bank account, and the details were in his hand. Once Leo had left, Vince had huffed and puffed, trying to get the stupid banker woman to make the transfer. In the end, Valerie Mason said she would consult her line manager, provided Vince would kindly wait outside. It was just a ruse to get rid of him. That was ten minutes ago. Or maybe two minutes ago. Or maybe it was half an hour ago. Or maybe it never happened.

Fuck. Paranoia felt like a demon inside him that he needed to fight off before it completely took over.

He looked down at the numbers on the scrap of paper, but they danced around. Numbers, numbers, why was everything about numbers? Lottery numbers, bank numbers, money numbers, millions of numbers, billions of numbers, Number Ten…

'Would you like to step into my office now?' said Valerie Mason.

'Shit,' said Vince, suddenly zoning back into the world, and looking up at the woman, who, unless he was much mistaken, was smiling maniacally. This was sinister. Some kind of trap.

On autopilot, he followed Mason into the office and took a seat. He felt as if he were in a play, a strange surreal thriller, and everyone had been given a role except him. While the banker busied herself with the printer, his phone bleeped. A text from Leo:

emergency over.

Good. Things could get back to normal. He could go home and get some sleep. Goodbye, see you all in the morning.

As he got up, Valerie Mason, still smiling, said, 'I'm satisfied that this is a bono fide joint account.'

Vince was irritated by this bureaucratic non sequitur.

'Yeah, yeah, that Hughes fellow arranged that for us.'

'Without going through all the proper procedures, but still… I can now make the transfer.'

'Too late. Emergency over, mate.'

Mason's smile dropped just a little. Vince was near the door, keen to get out of the bank and never come back.

'I don't know what it was that all about, but I'm pleased it has been resolved. I trust everyone is okay?'

'Yeah, well… no thanks to you.'

Vince wondered if he'd left his headphones somewhere but then felt them round his neck.

'I have called head office,' said Valerie Mason, 'so I can transfer the million pounds, if that's still necessary.'

What? So this surreal dream or play or film wasn't over yet. Vince scratched his head hard, as if to chivvy his brain cells into getting a grip.

'Stop making stuff up,' he whispered, but it was to his head, not to the woman smiling at him.

The printer spewed out a document. Mason handed it to Vince, who stepped forward to take it, but was too confused even to give it a glance.

'Have a look,' she said, grinning.

He gazed at the statement, but the figures jumbled around.

'It's at the end of row two,' said the woman.

Still just mushy blur.

'I don't know about you, Mr Campbell, but I've never seen such a large figure on a bank statement.' This beaming woman was not the same one from earlier. Had she been body-snatched? Was she an actress? A doppelganger?

He finally focused enough to read the numbers on the page, but couldn't understand them.

'I assume that's the amount you were expecting?' said Mason.

'Where did this come from?' asked Vince, as bewildered as he'd ever been in his life. 'What the fuck? What the fucking fuck?'

At last Valerie Mason's smile dropped, and her lips tightened.

'I think you'll find it's from Globomillions. Or were you expecting it to be from someone else?' she said, tersely.

Vince did not respond because he was distracted by the thought of Leo laughing at him. Was this his massive joke? Was everyone out to get him? All his life, he had kept his fellow man at a distance, never trusting, and never asking for trust. And now, in this crystallising moment, his island existence was getting its final, incontrovertible validation. His best mate had fucked him over.

My world view was right. 'Vince the vindicated' is what I am.

He should have realised that when Leo became a 'family man' that it was over between them. He felt the bitter-sweet pain of simultaneously being wronged, and proved right. Twenty grand for a fuck? *Of course Leo was a billionaire!*

'Mr Campbell, are you okay?' asked Mason. 'Can I get you a glass of water?'

He placed the statement on the desk. His whole body chemistry had changed.

'Can I get fifty copies of this?'

Fuelled by righteous fury and a heady dose of post-drug paranoia, Vincent Campbell cast off his walk-on part, and was ready to take on a central role.

65

I'M AS CONFUSED AS ANYONE

The Great Hall was a mess. Chairs had been pushed around and there was little semblance of the neat arrangement of earlier in the day. Dirty plates from the buffet had been left on any available surface. Most of the waiting staff had gone home, having only been booked till five. Journalists, honoured guests – the ones who'd bothered to stay – were tired and fed up. Women had slipped off their heels, men had removed their jackets and loosened their ties. There was a feel of an airport during a strike, boredom mixed with rumours about what would happen next.

This was not how Frank had planned it. His idea of giving Leo a 'thank you' gala, and thereby basking in his reflected glory (and what's wrong with that?) had turned into a damage-limitation exercise – something at which he had had some practice, but even so, this was going to be tough.

He wasn't usually nervous about public speaking, but now his palms sweated. Harriet had tried to persuade him to go home. 'You could say that due to the incident at your daughter's house, you need to be by her side,' she'd suggested – very gently, because her husband didn't take well to advice when he was stressed. He replied that he had never been one to shirk responsibility. Besides, it might make him look culpable, and he'd done nothing to be ashamed of. He was the *casualty* in all this. Just because he was an affluent white male didn't mean he couldn't be a victim; every other bugger in the world was claiming persecution, why not Frank Sterling? He'd been shafted by a duplicitous, feckless conman, and he needed everyone to know it.

Standing in the wing of the stage, he ran through his speech once again, but was distracted by Tina, his Entertainments Officer, who had her eyes closed, whispering.

'Are you *praying*?' asked Frank.

'Just going through my words,' said Tina, startled by the intrusion.

'You're just going to welcome me to the stage,' he said, irritably.

The woman, withered by the admonishment, bowed her head.

'Okay, I'm ready. Let's go,' said Frank.

She looked up at him and said, 'Actually, I *was* praying. For *you.*'

Before he could digest the statement, Tina walked on stage. After managing to get some attention, she asked the assembled to please welcome the Chairman of Byford Council, Frank Sterling. It was said with all the enthusiasm of someone announcing the end of a fire drill. Frank waited for applause, but all he heard was some vigorous clapping from his little team, and not much from anyone else.

Once at the lectern, he looked around the room. He would have words with Gill about the state of disarray.

'Ladies and gentlemen,' he began, 'Thank you for your patience. Many of you have been waiting for hours. I notice it didn't ruin your appetites.' He chuckled and nodded towards the empty platters on the buffet table. No one laughed or even smiled. The lightness of the comment had been inappropriate.

'I am only going to make a short speech, because as you know, earlier today my daughter was involved in a traumatic incident.' There were a few nods, everyone knew the basic gist of what had happened. Frank was a wily enough politician to know exactly what to say next.

'I would like to pay tribute to the police and ambulance services, who responded with consummate professionalism and bravery.'

This round of applause contrasted starkly with the paltry claps of a moment ago.

'My daughter, Helen, a hardworking medic herself, is physically unharmed but she's shaken. It's been hard on us all.' He looked over to Harriet, who had her hands clasped in her lap, head slightly bowed, the perfect pose for a wronged man's wife. He cleared his throat. *Come on, you bastards, have a bit of sympathy.*

'Turning now to what *was* to be the theme of today's lunch – now dinner. It was to be a *thank you* to Leo Morphetus.'

He paused for the inevitable embarrassed smiles and knowing looks.

'We all believed – didn't we? – that he had won nearly a billion pounds on Globomillions. We have *all* been swindled.'

So it's everyone's fault, not just mine, do you hear?

'Now, I know many of you want answers. Well, you aren't the only ones. Many wonderful organisations, charities, individuals, including our own Prime Minister, were duped. I can only say that Morphetus is clever, ingenious, and cunning as hell. And I...' then he remembered his tactic of implicating everyone, not just himself, 'We *all* – didn't we? – credited him with a social conscience. We trusted him when he said he was going to donate to the many charities and worthy organisations just as soon as he'd examined the paperwork. But all that 'due diligence' was a ruse, simply a way of playing for time, delaying the moment when his despicable scam would come to light.'

He looked for nodding heads, but the only ones he could see were on his payroll.

'But, um... I want to pay tribute to the press for their work in helping to uncover this dastardly plot. I gather it was a *lady* who broke the story. I believe she's here?'

Someone called Donna White's name, and Donna, sitting in the middle of the throng, raised herself to a half-standing position, which prompted a few claps and a desultory wolf-whistle.

'I hope and pray that Morphetus and his partner in crime – yes, *crime* – Vincent Campbell, will be brought to justice. Meanwhile, I will do everything I can to make amends.' He paused. It occurred to him that any strong feelings he had publicly expressed before had always been controlled and premeditated, such as when he'd had to say that 'lessons would be learned' after a tragic fire or ruinous flood. Emotion had never just burst forth.

'I am sorry that... I'm just—' His voice faltered, the stress of the day taking this moment to wreak havoc on his body, which began to sway. He tried to pull it back, but he'd had no experience, no precedent for this.

'I need to be with my daughter at this time so I'm afraid I... won't be taking any—' And he stopped, and felt an overwhelming sense that he had stopped for good. This was not a pause but an end. Years at the forefront of local politics had brought him to this point. His eyes glazed and became watery. Swaying as he was, his wife, who had been sitting near the front, leapt up and together with Gill and Tina, guided him down the steps and into a chair to the side of the stage.

Unmoved by seeing an elderly man break down, the press began their salvo. 'Why did you trust Morphetus?', 'Will you resign?', 'What about the timing of all this just before the election?', 'Why did you pose with giant cheques before any money had been paid?'

He wanted to get up and defend himself, to remind these vultures what he had done for the town: the one-way system he'd scrapped, axing the sex shop in the high street, the 'Keep our Fun Bus' campaign, the Donkey Sanctuary he'd championed, but when he tried to stand Harriett pressed him gently back into the chair. The barrage continued: 'Was it all just a way to win votes?', 'Why didn't you wait till the money was actually paid?', 'Aren't you a poor judge of character?' These questions were interspersed with others about his daughter: 'What do you know about the shooting?', 'Was it linked to Leo?', 'Where is Morphetus now?', 'Has he been questioned?'

At the back of the hall, Leo, who had been listening to the speech from behind the door, entered unseen by most of the assembled. He was flanked by the two Community Support Officers who had driven him there because they thought he might need protection. He made his way to the front. Heads turned, followed by questions and flashing cameras. He recognised some faces: the guys from the fledgling boxing gym, Dan from Snappy Snaps, the redheaded man from *Byford News* – or was it *Byford Gazette*? – and there, behind a tripod, was Donna White, busy with her camera. No one looked hostile, just tired and curious.

He didn't meet his in-laws' eyes as he approached the stage, but he did glance over at them. Harriet, now sitting down with her back straight, was resolutely composed. Frank looked like a man who had just seen a vision of his own bloated body washed up on a beach.

Leo looked around for Vince, who had not been answering his phone. He was disappointed that this friend, who had been with him at the beginning, would not be with him at the end.

The Coffee Guy, Saint Leo, the Billionaire Barista, and now the Bogus Billionaire, walked up the three steps of the rostrum, and with each one he felt stronger. Perhaps his power came from the sight of his once-revered father-in-law looking so helpless, or the fact that he had fooled the press all this time, so why should he be in awe of them? He was ready, more than ready, to be held to account.

'Hello, and thank you for staying. It's been a long day,' he said into the mic, and the room fell quiet. It was as if he had been given mastery of time: seconds and minutes would pass as quickly or slowly as he wanted. The anticipation of the assemblage felt like warmth from a fire.

'Regarding the incident earlier today... Helen Sterling, the mother of our child, is being comforted by friends. One person was hurt, but he is recovering well in hospital. The police have asked me to say that if anyone knows anything, or saw anything suspicious, please get in touch. Before going on, I would like to thank the emergency services for their diligence and bravery.' *I'm not such a slow learner*, he thought, during the applause. Despite the constant flashing of cameras and random bumps and knocks of equipment, he found he could concentrate, and words came easily.

'It's been a difficult few hours. You've no doubt all seen the video of me and Vince on your tablets and smart phones.' A few heads nodded, some smiles, some frowns. 'I'm not here to justify or diminish what I've done. But I am going to point out that since starting on this strange adventure, Vince and I managed not to lie. We didn't need to. Some of you guys did our lying for us.' There were a few sideways looks and folding of arms. The redhead from the gazette let out an audible harrumph.

'However, I did mislead. And there are people who have been harmed and upset by what I did. But I did not authorise Frank Sterling to go round talking about pledges, and I did not sanction the release of photographs of giant cheques. I said I would look into the organisations *before* making any promises.'

Many eyes, including Leo's, looked over to Frank, who had been given a glass of water. He made no reaction. Harriet, on the other hand, sent rays of hatred.

'But that said, some worthy organisations have been left very disappointed. My friend Vincent has always told me that *the Universe will provide.* I must say I have always thought, with respect to Vince, that that was a load of cobblers.'

A couple at the front laughed at this, but the general mood was one of quiet attentiveness.

'Since the Universe is unlikely to provide, I intend to do what I can myself. I will try to rebuild bridges – including our own Byford Bridge. If my fame – well, notoriety now – can help in any way, then I will do my best. Some charitable souls have made donations to the foundation that Vince and I are still going to set up; although it doesn't amount to a hill of beans, it's a start.' He paused for a moment. He noticed that Donna White was repositioning her tripod for a closer shot. 'And now I want to tell you some good news. You may remember that at my first – well, my only – other press conference, I told you about Poppy, a young girl with a rare kind of blood disorder. I'd promised to pay for her operation in America. With the help of some nice people at Barclays who... um, forwarded some money... I honoured that promise.' He allowed himself a smile. 'Half an hour ago, I got news that Poppy is on her way to America. It's too soon to know how the treatment will go. I'm helping four other families as well.'

'What did you want to gain from all this?' someone shouted.

Leo saw no reason to answer the question just because it had been asked. Besides, it seemed to open a floodgate, and the audience erupted with questions overlapping so much that he decided to wait until everyone had calmed down. He simply stood still, observing the crowd as if they were on the other side of bars in a zoo. They could not harm him.

Just as the room was beginning to settle down a little, a loud clatter drew his eyes to the doors at the back. There, looking dishevelled and drunk, stood Vince, hugging a wad of papers to his chest. Leo felt warmed by the sight of his friend, but also a little concerned by the state of him.

'There is my old mate Vincent, whom many of you know,' he said above the throng, and a few of the press turned to look at where he was pointing. 'He's been my gatekeeper, telling most of you to get lost. I'm sorry if he was sometimes rude.'

Now all eyes were on Vince and cameras flashed with increased frequency. People fired questions at him, but he was focused on the band stage, and moved through the crowd without looking right or left. When someone touched his arm he shooed them off roughly.

Once on the platform, he stood in front of the mic. He looked angry, bewildered, focused, but also somehow lost. He said something but couldn't be heard. He waved his arms to say that someone had better switch on the PA. He tapped the mic and a low thud went round the hall.

After a moment of stillness, he thrust an arm towards Leo and held it there, pointing. Leo couldn't imagine what was about to come from his friend's mouth.

'Arbuthnot!' he shouted.

If Leo had thought of a thousand possibilities, none of them would have been this. Was he as high as a kite?

Confused mutters filled the hall. *What did he just say?*

'Arbuthnot,' repeated Vince.

'What are you talking about?' said Leo, not really believing that a reasonable conversation would be possible.

'Yeah, what's going on?' said someone in the pack.

'I've looked at our bank account,' said Vince. He then addressed the audience. 'You can see for yourselves.'

He gathered himself, and then with both hands, threw his wad of paper high into the air. The sheets separated, and then floated down like confused birds.

'Sit down, mate, you don't know what you're saying,' said Leo.

Vince didn't answer, he just stared straight ahead, his eyes fixed.

The words *genuine, bogus, hoax, fake, proof, forged, copy,* filled the hall as people read the statement in their hands. Leo tried to project his voice over the mayhem.

'I'm sorry about this. And I'm as confused as anyone,' he said, but he doubted if anyone heard.

Donna White reached for one of the printed statements. She glanced at it and then raised her head slowly. Leo was looking right at her. As the people around them shouted, waved, grabbed at their tablets, and screeched into their phones, she and Leo stood stock still. He shrugged. She mouthed a question, '*How?*' He shrugged again, and shook his head apologetically.

'He told me he wasn't the winner,' said Vince. 'I believed him. But over there,' he thrust his arm towards Leo again, his index finger straight as a knife, 'that there, is the winner of the Globomillions jackpot. Leo Morphetus is a billionaire.'

66

SIX WEEKS LATER

He flopped down on the golden sofa next to Amy and pressed the button that made their feet go up and their heads down.

'It's not a big deal any more, Dad,' said Amy, long-sufferingly. Leo still thought it was quite a big deal.

'I tell you what *is* a big deal,' he said, taking a sheet of headed paper from his jacket, and handing it to her.

'Arbuthnot... Foundation,' she said, reading the letterhead. 'Why *Arbuthnot*?'

'It was a name you made up, remember?'

'At Granny's house?'

'Yes. *King Arbuthnot*, you called me. And it's the name we gave the real winner. It's out of respect to him.'

'Or *her*,' said Amy, reproachfully.

'Or her. Hey, I don't really like staring at the ceiling, do you?'

He pressed the button to bring them back to a sitting position. Amy folded her arms, and looked at her father suspiciously.

'And how will you spend the money? On poor people, like you said you would?'

'Yes. Of course, I have taken some for myself, your mother, and Vince.'

Amy seemed satisfied with this answer, but her interrogation was not over.

'Why did everyone believe you had that money, Dad? Mummy never really explained it.'

He stroked his chin and put on his 'wise man' face.

'If I told you, it would take a long time and you'd have to sit very still.'

She pondered this for a moment.

'Okay,' she said, 'I'll ask you again when I have more time. I want to know why Mummy liked Tony, if he was such a bad person.'

'I don't know if I can answer that.' He struggled for something that would make his daughter feel better without criticising her mother. 'It's to do with hope and belief, and getting the two things muddled. Everyone does it – I do it all the time,' and he nearly added that he had spent a long time hoping and believing that he and her mother would get back together.

'Maybe there should be a word – *hopeaving*?' said Amy.

'That's a great idea!' He slapped his thigh.

'Children *hopeave* in Santa Clause, don't they?'

'Yes, and sometimes what people *hopeave*, is also true,' he said, but heard the lack of conviction in his voice.

'But not Santa. You can tell me, Dad. It's okay.'

He shrugged and stalled, 'Well, you see… um…' and in that instant he knew that, for his daughter, the magic of Santa was over. She nodded sagely, and they shared a moment.

The doorbell rang and Leo's heart quickened.

'This will be the journalist I told you about.'

'Oh!' said Amy, covering her mouth with her hand.

'What is it?'

'Mummy gave me a letter that came to our house. It's for you.'

'Where is it?'

'I forgot it.' She grasped her head in frustration.

'Never mind. Mum can bring it when she comes to collect you.'

***

Donna White was dressed as sharply as ever: heels, pencil skirt, a polo neck under a smart jacket. Leo felt shabby in his t-shirt.

'Sorry it's not a limousine,' she said, as they approached the blue Nissan Micra, which was exactly where the limo used to park. It looked tiny by comparison.

'I guess we'll have to manage, won't we?' said Leo to Amy.

All three climbed into the car, with Amy in the back. Leo was glad there were no onlookers milling around. The public were losing interest in him, and it couldn't have happened soon enough.

'Speaking of limos, I haven't seen Driver Dave for a while,' he said as he fastened his seatbelt. 'Funny, that.'

Donna kept her eyes to the front, but the side of her mouth rose.

'Did you give him thirty pieces of silver?' he asked.

'Trade secret,' she said, as they turned onto the hill that he'd scooted down just a few weeks ago.

Leo gave directions, and after a short drive, they pulled up at their destination, a parking zone on the high street a few doors down from Barclays. In front of them was a shop with five large windows, and a newly painted sign above. Red letters spelled *Bean Roasting*.

'Do you like the name?' he asked, as Donna yanked up the handbrake.

'Want an honest answer?'

'You just gave it,' he said. 'It has sentimental value.'

'I like the name,' said Amy. 'And don't forget the hard hat.'

She had been promised a hard hat. It being a Saturday afternoon, there were no workmen on site, but a helmet would have to be found. Once inside, Leo noticed one lying on a trestle table and placed it on her head. It came down to her nose, but she was content to find her way with her hands for the time being. The hat and her drawing book would keep her busy for at least half an hour.

'So this is the famous barista's coffee,' said Donna, after her first sip of the white Americano that Leo had prepared using a Gaggia machine the size of a bath.

'How is it?' he asked, with more than idle curiosity. She took another sip.

'You want an honest answer?'

He laughed.

'Seriously,' she said, 'I'd say it's smooth. Not at all bitter. Very nice.'

'I'm glad, because I've ordered a tonne of the stuff. Literally, a metric tonne.'

While he'd been making coffee, Donna had been taking photographs. There were ten small tables and a long one at back; room for about fifteen covers. The floor was roughly hewn wood, the walls had a lot of exposed brick and vintage tiles. Small Victorian chandeliers hung from the ceiling.

'It's going to be the most stylish place in all of Byford,' she said.

'You're a very rude woman,' he said, supressing a smile.

She took out her recorder and placed it on the table. 'Do you mind? It's for your protection as well as mine.'

He nodded, not really buying the 'your protection' line, but not caring either. She rubbed her arms.

'It should warm up in ten minutes or so. Assuming they've fixed the heating.'

She took her tablet from her bag and fired it up.

'I'll be taking notes, too. Okay, shall we begin? First off, thanks for agreeing to this, it means a lot because I've been following this story from the start.'

'That's why you're getting the exclusive.'

She looked at him as if she were interpreting hieroglyphics on his face. He'd never felt so observed.

'Was I enemy number one?' she asked, with an inscrutable grin. He shrugged.

'I didn't know what you were up to most of the time, but I know some of it now. The call to my mother-in-law, for example, on day one. Clever. I appreciate the due diligence.'

A nod indicated a tentative 'thank you'.

'And,' Leo said, 'it seemed to me that with your exposure of *The Express* for that bogus newsagent footage, you were one of the few journalists who actually cared about the truth.'

'We're very old-school like that,' said Donna, checking the levels on her recorder.

'Maybe you could work for me.'

'You already have a PR person.'

'Vince is leaving the Foundation.'

'You've fallen out already?'

'Would that make a good story?'

'Only if true.' *She's quick-on-the-draw*, thought Leo.

'No, we're fine.'

'He seemed pretty angry last time I saw him.'

Leo smiled.

'Once he recovered from the paranoid delusion that I was Arbuthnot we had a few drinks together in the hot tub.' He directed his gaze to the window, and enjoyed the memory for a moment before continuing. 'Vince likes to surprise, and he has certainly done that. He's going to take A Levels and apply to Uni. This was after bumping into his old English teacher. Something clicked, and he'll use his share of the money to pay his way. His heart's set on Cambridge. Oh, and he bought this.'

He brought out his phone and showed Donna a photograph.

'It looks like a sheep with a bad hairdo,' she said.

'It's an alpaca. Called Stephen.'

Donna was suitably charmed and asked to be sent the picture.

'It must have been very strange,' she said, while typing, 'to have been mysteriously handed nearly a billion pounds.'

'Vince always said the Universe would provide. I'm now a believer.' He made sure to laugh so that she would not take the statement at face value.

'And the lottery people have said nothing?'

'They said that the winner or winners requested the money be paid to my account, and that's all I can get out of them.'

Donna paused for some more visual scrutiny.

'Can we talk about the real winner?'

'Sure,' said Leo, in a way that he hoped would suggest that there was nothing to say.

'Arbuthnot. It's the name of your daughter's imaginary friend, right?' Donna asked, softly, with a glance towards Amy.

'No, it's just a name she made up.'

Amy was busy drawing, tongue hanging out, on one of the tables a few feet away. She had taken the helmet off.

'You know there's a spoof Twitter account, Facebook page, and a website?' said Donna.

He nodded. He was on the low-media diet, but he had heard that Arbuthnot had become a name people used to fill in gaps in their knowledge. What caused the Big Bang? Arbuthnot. Where's my phone? Arbuthnot must have it.

'You're maintaining your silence as to his or her identity?'

'I'm silent because I have no idea who Arbuthnot is.'

She let this hang, as if the truth could be winkled out through the power of awkward silence.

'And why do you think he or she chose you?'

'My charm and good looks? I don't know. Probably because I said on television that if I had a billion pounds I'd spend it on good causes. And they believed me, and they believed me because it's true.'

Donna nodded; it did appear to be true.

'We know he or she lives in Byford, of course. Could he or she be someone you know?'

'Yes, but *anyone* could have got my bank details – Vince put them on my website.'

Her eyes flicked around his face as if a lie might show itself somewhere on his cheeks or forehead. Uncomfortable, he decided not to wait for the next question.

'Vince and I have a pretty clear image of Arbuthnot,' he said. 'He's old, lonely. He has two kids in Australia who he hates. And I've come to the conclusion that he's dying and has no one to leave his money to. He's not daft enough to bequeath it to a cat sanctuary, but doesn't have the know-how to distribute it himself, so handing it to me seemed like a good option.'

'And this is *pure* conjecture?' she asked, looking steadily into his eyes.

'Totally. And, by the way, he didn't give me the whole win, he trousered some himself. And we have kept some for ourselves too, and no, I won't tell you how much.'

She tapped her fingers on the table and her eyes narrowed. Leo narrowed his own eyes to match.

'Can we go back to the beginning?' she said, not enjoying the staring competition. 'It would be good to have it all in your own words, don't you think?'

Drawing his hands together, Leo's mind went back nearly two weeks. He told her about the red Mazda, his conclusion that Helen was seeing a new man, the cash pouring from his pockets, Hamir getting the wrong idea, setting fire to everything he owned.

'So, it's all down to seeing a red car?' said Donna.

'If it hadn't been for the Mazda, the most important consequence of all this… well…'

He halted for a moment. It was a weird thought.

'The most important consequence?'

'Poppy. I got a message… from her last night,' he said, coughing away a frog in his throat. Why was he suddenly feeling this emotion rush into him? He'd been fine about it last night. 'And a photo. Growing her hair.' He pursed his lips tightly to stop them wobbling. 'Everything is on track for a full recovery.'

He rubbed an eye with a knuckle. He recalled Alan Lethco's excited revelation that some of the winning numbers almost matched Poppy's birthday, and the conversation they'd had about probability and chance.

'I used to think that if things don't add up it's because we can't see all the numbers. Now I think that if we can't see all the numbers, we make them up.'

Donna smiled as if she had only been playing with him.

'Going to go back to the 12th May…'

'Meltdown, a lifetime in one day.'

'Can you take me through it?'

He began with the call from Helen and the demand for money, and ended in the ambulance with her revelations about the shooting.

'When did you discover who had shot Tony?'

Leo stifled a laugh.

'Do you think it's funny?' she asked, reproachfully.

'Well, yes, I do think it's funny. That doesn't mean it's not sad or horrible. Everything has a funny side.'

His eyes went down to his cup, but he was seeing the ambulance parked by Helen's house, blue light flashing.

'You asked a question, what was it?'

'When did you discover who'd shot Tony?'

'The next day. The police called to say they had Donald Hughes with them.'

Donna made a note, then looked up.

'Had Hughes… had he shown any sign of… mental…'

Leo saved her the trouble of finding a politically correct term.

'Actually, yes. He practically had a breakdown in front of us one time. We thought he was just very stressed, and a bit weird, but apparently he had had paranoid episodes before. This has to be off-the-record.'

He glanced down at the recorder then back at Donna.

'It's *sub judice* anyway,' she said. 'I'll be lucky if I can publish half of this until after the trials.'

He smiled and shrugged. 'Hughes was convinced I was trying to destroy him. He'd given us the money without authority and when the billion pounds didn't appear in my account… and then the bank suspended him… it confirmed the story he'd told himself, that I was out to get him. I once called him a name under my breath and he'd heard it. I think it all festered.'

'I heard he used a rifle?'

Leo nodded. 'A hunting rifle of some kind. He hid in the back garden, and aimed through the window – at the man he thought was me.'

He thought of a joke, something about being mistaken for a man with a comb-over, but decided to leave it.

'So how did you feel about dodging a bullet that was meant for you?' she asked, moving some hair from her face.

'I never thought about it. Too much else was going on. But, looking back, something Hughes said made sense.'

'Yes?'

'When we last saw him he said, *I know where the Holy Grail is.* I wasn't really supposed to understand it, but it meant he knew where I lived, or used to live, and so where Helen and Amy lived.'

'Creepy,' said Donna, wincing.

'Look, I'm never going to be best buddies with him, but I hope he gets treatment.'

She nodded thoughtfully, framing her next question.

'And the bank? They still haven't pressed charges.'

He gave a contemptuous huff.

'It would be very hard to prove fraud, and banks hate bad publicity – they have enough of it already. I paid all the money back, and I've gone to the Nat West.'

While Donna tapped on her tablet, Leo looked over at Amy, who still had her tongue hanging out. It was a habit that her father had kept well into his teens.

'What are your thoughts on Tony?'

He heaved a sigh.

'I don't want to know,' he said, leaning back in his chair.

'How much *do* you know?'

He wanted to get this over quickly, partly for Helen's sake. She was still suffering guilt, confusion, and mistrust. She didn't need her private life transmitted to the world.

'I really don't want to think much about a guy who threatened the mother of our child, and anyway I assume legally it's, you know—'

'Also *sub judice.*'

'All I know – *want* to know – is that he had a fake social media profile and used to deal in dodgy jewels. He spent some time in prison and when he came out he wanted to shack up with a… with a woman with a nice house and a proper job. Start afresh. Helen fitted the bill. She sees the good in people – even when it's not there.'

He ran his hands through his hair. He pictured himself at the kitchen table when Helen told him she was seeing someone. He felt the ghost of a wound.

'Then he saw a chance of making an easy million,' he said.

'Too good an opportunity to miss for an old lag?'

He nodded. 'He started hatching his plan, inventing threats. Can we move on?'

Donna ran a finger round the rim of her cup.

'Will you get back with her?'

Leo thought this question might come up, but wasn't expecting it to be thrown in so abruptly, and he felt ambushed. For the last few weeks he had tried to grapple with his anger at Helen for choosing this lowlife conman over him, at the same time knowing that he shouldn't blame the victim.

He wiped his face with his hand.

'I don't want to talk about Helen just now.'

She nodded, accepting the reticence, but he had a feeling that she would return to the theme.

'What about Monica?'

One uncomfortable question after another. At least this had an easy answer.

'We're not in touch.'

'She threw wine over me, you know.'

'*Why*?' he said, surprised to be laughing.

'I *may* have implied that she was a shallow fortune hunter,' she said, almost proudly.

'You deserved it then.'

She shrugged. 'She never tried to stitch you up.'

'I know. She called me a few times, and at first I didn't answer, but one time I did… and she explained her change of heart about selling the story. She used the twenty grand to go back to Holland and go on some media course.'

'And chance of…? She's such a lovely girl.' Leo couldn't help smiling at Donna's shamelessness.

'We discussed going for a drink, a date, but I'm very busy with the coffee shop and the Foundation. We will keep in touch,' he said. 'Which reminds me, can we talk about the Foundation now?'

It was a stipulation for the interview that they would discuss the Foundation. He pointed towards the ceiling.

'Follow me.'

They climbed up the stairs at the back and arrived at a large open space, about the area of a tennis court but longer and narrower. There were eight desks, mostly covered in brick dust, a stack of chairs in one corner, and a few wires dangling from the ceiling.

'We'll save a fortune by basing ourselves in Byford instead of London,' he said, aligning one of the desks in front of half a dozen headshots pinned to the wall.

'The main task has been trying to find these guys,' he said.

'An eclectic bunch,' said Donna. The photographs were evenly balanced between men and women, and about a third were non-white.

'They're from all round the world. We'll be using Skype a lot, I expect. That's Claudia Goldin, a Harvard Professor in economics. I'm trying to get Stephen Pinker and Paul Bloom, and Joy Kiirui from Nairobi. I want real brain boxes, not idealists or soppy do-gooders. People who can make sure the money isn't wasted.'

Donna nodded, but Leo had the feeling she was more interested in the call girl, the mad banker and the conman than an organisation dedicated to the relief of suffering, but as far as he was concerned she was there to help get a message across. He explained that since his meeting with the Prime Minister he was in communication with the Department of Health and some MPs, and they seemed actually to be taking notice of his mission to raise awareness of the skulduggery that goes on in big pharma. He had found a few people who were looking at ways to solve the problem and was being listened to. Donna made notes, even asked a few questions, and after another coffee said she had to head back.

***

As they walked to her car, he remembered seeing Donna outside the Carlton Hotel leaning on the limousine, doing her lipstick. It felt more like a picture on a postcard than a memory.

'Now the part I dread – the drive back to London,' she said, bristling against the wind. 'Sure I can't give you a lift?'

'No, we're fine, aren't we, Amy?'

Amy nodded.

As she stowed her camera and tripod in the boot, he wondered whether they should part with a kiss or a handshake. Before he could make up his mind she leant forward planted a peck on his cheek. She then patted the top of Amy's head. Amy grinned shyly and reached for her father's hand.

'You've done well out of all this, haven't you, Donna?' he said, after opening a door. It was said without resentment.

'I've had some tempting job offers,' she said, sliding onto the seat.

'Oh, one more question,' she added, and Leo sensed she had planned this.

'Does paying for Poppy's treatment and also the other families' justify all the harm and chaos you caused?'

'Leaving the big questions till last?'

She smiled as if she'd been paid a professional compliment.

'A child is alive who certainly would have died,' he said.

'So it *does* justify it?'

'Ask a philosopher – or a priest,' he said, not because he felt attacked, he just couldn't deliver a soundbite on demand.

She weighed something in her mind.

'What were you *after*, Leo? Really?'

She had asked about his motives several times during their interview but he'd always replied with a joke. He didn't have any left. He didn't want to say it was all about saving lives, because he knew that wasn't the whole story.

'Everyone wants to be looked at in the right way,' he said.

She frowned.

'We don't get to choose how people look at us,' said Donna. It was the first time she'd expressed an opinion. He gave the smallest of responses: a little smile, and then he closed the door.

Father and daughter walked a short distance to see the cottage that Clive Entwhistle said had been 'priced to sell'. Leo's cash offer had been accepted. Amy's verdict was that it was much nicer than Mrs Klyne's but not as nice as Mummy's house. Leo gave her a little talk about how minds think comparatively, which is very useful, but can also make people unhappy. They took a cab up the steep hill to The Manor.

He made a meal of waffles with poached egg and baked beans. Soon afterwards Helen arrived for the handover and brought with her the letter that Amy had forgotten. The two parents spent a while chatting at the breakfast counter. There was so much to discuss – two impending trials, Amy, her parents – it was a lot to fit in. After losing the local election and resigning, Frank had dusted himself off and was now considering running as an independent. Leo, feeling guilty about Frank and all the organisations that had been affected by the debacle, honoured all the pledges that Frank had made on his behalf.

The way they talked was different now. Helen repeated a remark she'd made a couple of times of late, 'You don't seem as sleepy these days. You seem to have fallen awake.' She touched on the subject of blame – did he blame her for what had happened, for choosing that man? Leo assured her yet again that she should not think of blaming herself.

Amy wanted to sing a song she had just learnt. Then another. Then another. Perhaps it was a ploy to keep her two parents together for just a little longer.

Once they'd gone, he opened the fridge and grabbed a can of Camden Hells. On his way to the yellow couch, he picked up the green envelope Helen had brought with her. Although a lot of mail came to his last official address – Mrs Klyne's flat – hardly any went to his old family home. The handwriting on the envelope was neat and even – he guessed from a female hand. He opened it. There was a date at the top of the letter, but no address.

Dear Leo,

First, thank you. Without you, I would not have had the strength to claim the prize, such was my need for secrecy. You were the perfect decoy. While you pretended to have won a billion, I had to pretend I had not; a two-piece jigsaw. It all fits together, Leo, as everything does.

By requesting that the money be forwarded to you, I hoped that the existence of the 'real winner' would never be made public, thus averting speculation as to my identity. But that's not how things turned out. (It reminds me of a joke: How do you make God laugh?... Tell him your plans.)

You are honouring your promise to share the treasure with those who need it. Be in no doubt: that is why you have been chosen.

God, or the Universe, has provided.

Leo, you have a great responsibility, which I believe you will discharge with wisdom and compassion. Please use all your ability to help those in greatest pain first, wherever they are in the world, of whatever race or creed and in whatever numbers. I am sure you will use your head as well as your heart.

I appreciate your stated resolve not to attempt to discover who I am or invite conjecture. Should you be able to guess, I implore you not to make any attempt to contact me or reveal your thoughts to anyone, even your friend Vince. This is not just to save myself from embarrassment or prurient interest, it is to protect my family from humiliation and conflict. Please destroy this letter and refrain from discussing it with anyone.

I will always keep an eye on the progress of the Foundation.

May our gift bring peace to ourselves, and many deserving souls.

God bless you.

"Arbuthnot"

Acknowledgments

Erin Kelly and Arzu Tahsin read various drafts and gave me invaluable feedback and a lot of encouragement, for which I'm very grateful. Shortly after I began writing this novel, my friend Sarah Shepherd just happened to land a job in the Camelot press office – what are the chances? Her inside knowledge was extremely handy. I would also like to thank Pete Sinclair for spotting a number of atrocious errors and typos.

I am grateful to Lucy Jagger for the cover design.

Request

If you enjoyed this book, please don't keep it a secret.

Milton Keynes UK
Ingram Content Group UK Ltd.
UKHW012019180923
428919UK00005B/253

9 781913 036744